Persephone's

Children

Persephone's Children is a work of fiction. Names, characters, places, and incidents are the product of the author's imagination or are used fictitiously. Any resemblance to actual events, locales, or persons, living or dead, is coincidental.

Copyright © 2024 PJ Braley

Cover Design by Cherie Fox

Between the Lines Publishing and its imprints support the right to free expression and the value of copyright. The scanning, uploading, and distribution of this book without permission is a theft of the author's intellectual property. If you would like permission to use material from the book (other than for review purposes), please contact info@btwnthelines.com.

Liminal Books
Between the Lines Publishing
1769 Lexington Ave North #286
Roseville MN 55113
btwnthelines.com

First Published: January 2025

Liminal Books is an imprint of Between the Lines Publishing.
The Liminal Books name and logo are trademarks of Between the Lines Publishing.

ISBN: (paperback) 978-1-965059-22-7

ISBN: (eBook) 978-1-965059-23-4

Library of Congress Control Number: 2024951747

The publisher is not responsible for websites (or their content) that are not owned by the publisher.

Persephone's Children

PJ Braley

Other Books in the Fire Slayers series

The Fire Slayers

Finding Persephone

*For Remi,
who taught me that love never dies.*

A Conversation

Gregory walked into the underground dormitory and immediately noticed Grant's empty cot. Smiling to himself, he found Grayson in the conference room.

"So, Grayson, it looks like she decided to keep him. I may lose the bet after all."

"Perhaps, Gregory, but it's not morning yet. He could be, um, just taking his time."

"Do you think it's too late to pay him a surprise visit to see if there is anything left?"

Grayson looked at Gregory long and hard. "I would rather walk a mile in hell than go anywhere near that door tonight."

Gregory pulled out a chair and sat down. "Why would you say that?"

Grayson began counting on his fingers. "One, it has taken him weeks to get her to accept the idea of living here; two, she's still recovering from nearly losing her baby this morning; three, he spent most of the day either trying to keep her alive or devising ways to kill her without destroying us all; and four, right now, she is where we want her—in the colony, still pregnant, and happy to be so. Lastly, I have no doubt that if anything disturbs that delicate balance—such as a 'surprise' visit—Grant is likely to shoot first and sort it out later."

Gregory laughed nervously, "You think he'd really shoot us?"

"No, but we would regret it, one way or another."

After a few moments of silence, Gregory asked, "So, what happens now?"

"Grant and I discussed a few ideas that might be useful in keeping her here without causing too much trouble."

"Such as ...?"

"Nothing too drastic, just doing or saying whatever it takes to keep her content and quiet—within reason, of course."

"Something could still happen. The baby, you know, it's early yet."

"Yes, we discussed that scenario as well."

"And?"

"'Here she is, and here she will stay,' is how he put it."

"And you believed him?"

"You didn't see the look on his face when he said it. She will never leave here alive—regardless of what happens to the baby." Then, shuddering at the memory of his last conversation with Grant, Grayson added, "He will never let her go."

A New Beginning

Grant woke up slowly as his father's words rose through the layers of his consciousness.

"... If you ever find a woman who cares for you, loves you like that, my son, please don't push it away. Try to find a way to protect and hold onto her for as long as you can."

For as long as you can. Now that he had found her, Grant was unsure how much time they would have together. He was ready to die or kill to protect Caroline and the secret she carried, but these acts of devotion were meaningless if her commitment did not equal his. Staying with him for a few months out of kindness or because she believed he was dying was unacceptable. His love was worth more than a temporary sacrifice; it demanded the voluntary surrender of the remainder of her existence. If he could not secure her complete allegiance, she would die. Grant's dream shifted to a nightmare as he imagined her body lying ravaged in the serai, his son's charred remains buried, indistinguishable, and unmarked, in a forgotten ash pit.

Recoiling from the images he dreaded more than a silent death, Grant sought refuge in his visions of Caroline sleeping safely in their nest of infinitesimal light. He had not created such beauty for her to die in but so she might accept him and love his son.

Bowing to his father's wisdom, Grant promised to hold Caroline, not just for as long as he could, but with enough love, patience, and tenderness to last a lifetime ... a human lifetime.

Grant's thoughts swirled with a hundred different ways to love her, each more delicious than the last. Caught up in his hope and desire, the softness beneath his hands felt almost real, and he reveled in the fragrant warmth of her that haunted his dreams.

The slight movement of Caroline's fingers on his chest brought him to full consciousness.

She was not a dream. It *was* her breath on his shoulder, her body pressed against his side, and her leg crossed over his in careless ownership.

The prior evening's memories replayed themselves in Grant's mind. Once again, he felt the relief and pleasure of watching Caroline gracefully and gratefully enter the underground sanctuary he had created for her. Pregnant and perfect, he had found a woman worthy of the myth and legend of Persephone and brought her home.

Hades himself could not have felt more victorious.

He had found Persephone and claimed her for his own.

Acknowledging the acquisition of a compliant mother for his son as the single greatest achievement of his life, Grant placed his hand over hers and opened his eyes.

A Marriage

Something lightly touched my ear, but in the unbroken darkness, I wasn't sure if I was awake or still sleeping. I only knew that never in my life had I felt so perfectly at peace.

If this is a dream, I never want to wake up.

Roused just enough to recognize the scent of honey in the air, my hand moved instinctively to my abdomen.

"He's fine," whispered a singing voice behind me. "You're fine, we're fine."

I remembered where I was. Trusting Grant wouldn't disappear, I turned toward the sound of his voice.

"Grant?"

"Yes, love."

"How long have you been awake?"

"Long enough to kiss your ear a couple of times. Sleep well?"

"Um, hmm."

"Not too angry about the sleeping tea?"

"No, this is all so overwhelming. I would have been too excited to sleep without it."

"So, you like your bower?"

"Oh, Grant, it is the most fantastically romantic room I've ever seen or imagined. I love it. Shall I show you how much?" My fingertips feathered down his bare chest, saying words I was too shy to express.

The intimacy of his soft laughter echoed in my ears.

"Oh, if it were only that easy, Caroline," he said, catching my hands and kissing each in turn. "Nothing, and I mean nothing, on this planet would give me greater pleasure, but that is not possible for me."

"Not possible? It was possible before, as I willingly, beautifully recall."

"Two fundamental things are different now, and there is one slight consideration."

"Yes?"

"The first is during that particular segment in your dream, you were physically aroused, and your body was releasing pheromones into the air. Humans cannot detect them, but the scent is like ambrosia to us, and you ...."

Grant trembled slightly and held me closer.

"Were intoxicating," he said. "I was drowning in the air of you, the loveliness of you, and my desire caused a reaction I didn't believe possible, and I, well, I went with my instincts."

I couldn't miss the undercurrent of sensuality in his voice as his hands moved slowly to my hips and pulled me into the curve of his body. "Caroline, I didn't know what it felt like to want anything or anyone so much. And the second is—"

"Grant, wait a minute. I'm sure, with a little help, I can get those pheromones activated again."

"And the second is," he continued, pressing his finger lightly on my lips, "you are pregnant, and your body will not release pheromones until you are fertile again."

"Oh. And the consideration?"

"I told you the first time took away about a year of my life—something it is impossible for me to regret—but even if I could make love to you without pheromones, I would not do it. I will not risk missing the vision of you holding my ... *our* son in your arms. You have no idea what you have given me, Caroline, first yourself, then the opportunity of an actual child of ... our own. Such things are worth living for, and dying for, aren't they?"

Although I could not see his face, I could feel him looking directly into my eyes.

"Aren't they?" he repeated softly.

"Yes, Grant," I whispered. With the memory of yesterday's heartbreak still fresh, I could not keep the tears from my voice.

"We won't ever make love again?"

"No, not like we did before. But I promise to hold you, tease you, and play with you. I will care for you, feed you toast and honey or strawberries and cream whenever you ask. I will wait on you, talk with you, promise to answer all your questions, and do anything that will make you happy. Caroline, I will *love* you."

This declaration was my first glimpse into *how* Grant loved me. Although I wasn't sure what kind of love we would share—or if it would be enough for either of us—it didn't matter. All I heard was that *he loved me.*

"Hold me, Grant. Hold me so tight there is not one speck of air between us; hold me so our son will feel how we love each other. You have given me so much, but even if we were on a cot in the corner of one of the exercise rooms, I would want only you. Your voice, your warmth, your strength. I just want to melt into you and through you so that we will be together always, no matter what happens."

He was very still for a moment, and although I could not see him move, I was suddenly aware of his warm breath against my neck.

"Do you mean that?"

"Yes, Grant, every word."

"That is my wish as well."

He placed his hands under my back and lifted my shoulders. Starting at the hollow of my neck, he kissed me slowly, moving upward, and then, for the first time, Grant kissed my mouth. Tilting my head back, his lips parted slightly, and something slid from his mouth and pressed the back of my throat. In that instant, everything he was existed in my mind.

Like an old-fashioned flicker book, I saw his carefully crafted exterior change as each mutation from countless generations going back to his original alien ancestors lined up behind him. Seconds later, the images reversed and went back up the chain, culminating in his birth. The pictures sharpened. I saw a newborn baby with little L-shaped antennae, no nose or ears, and his tiny hands and feet were fused and curved. I saw one pair of eyes splinter, and two became four, then eight … each a slightly different shade of blue and green. There were other changes, too. Hands and feet, once wrapped in bandages, became fingers and toes. Then the antennae disappeared, and he had a perfect nose and ears. I watched him grow strong and beautiful, and when my hands reached behind his head, everything stopped until he realized I only wanted him closer.

The pressure on my throat intensified as Grant gave me the only things that were truly his: the memories of his life. Like a wondrously fragrant scrapbook, the pictures seemed unending. His childhood transformed into an adolescence filled with scenes of a ranch and horses in the desert, a lake with palm trees, and a blue and white striped tent. A school with tall sand-colored buildings appeared in the background then, for a moment, everything blurred. When the pictures resumed, Grant was much older, and his eyes had changed from blue and green to amber. He was wearing a lab coat in a hospital, walking down the halls of the spa, and in a flash of radiant light, I saw him seeing me.

At that moment, my own scrapbook opened. At first, they were all family pictures with my son, Brendon; memories of us at graduation, football games, and playing chess together, and as he progressively got younger, I did, too. Within seconds, I was wearing a wedding dress, and Dan was there, looking happy and proud. Then I was graduating from high school, becoming younger and younger, holding Easter baskets, opening Christmas gifts, pictures of me with my mom and later with my grandmother—they looked so *young* my heart twisted—and, finally, my sister Leann and I standing in the front seat of my grandfather's Ford Fairlane 500 with scenes of downtown Savannah flying by. Then, it all inverted. I watched myself get older, but this time, the images went beyond my memories of Brendon. I saw myself on the day of my spa visit, lying on the meditation bed with a headset over my ears, someone bathing me, and then the photos began to shimmer.

A montage of pictures of my face from dozens of angles flashed in my mind, and I knew I was seeing Grant's memories. Yesterday's pain returned as I saw myself lying on an operating table, my eyes awash with tears. However, the sadness left me as quickly as it had come when those images were immediately followed by others of a stuffed bunny and storybooks, me walking out of the bathroom and finding my dragonfly robe, and lastly, my face with the nursery in the background. I realized the pictures were shining because I saw them through Grant's love for me. Love for *me* because in the memories when he believed I was no longer pregnant, the shimmer did not disappear.

The connection faded. The pressure in my throat eased, and my slide show ended. His lips pulled away from mine as he gently lowered my head onto the pillow. Nestled between us, our son gave a little flip as if to say he wanted to see the pictures again.

"Nothing tastes as good as being kissed feels," Grant said.

"Grant, I don't know what to say. What, what was that?"

"I am not sure what you mean, exactly. Three distinctly different things happened, four if you count the baby's approval."

"You were in my mind. Did you see the picture show? You, then me, back and forth? Grant, did you *see* it?"

He touched his forehead to mine. "Yes. You have always been lovely and loved. I did not see much pain in your life, and you were always a good person. Your life was a pleasure to witness."

"And you," I said, "have always been beautiful."

"Even with claws for hands and no nose?"

"Yes, even then. Grant, is that why you showed me those pictures? So, I wouldn't be frightened if our son is born like that?"

He lowered his face very close to my ear. "What I showed you, Carolina, is the truth of my existence. I am the result of a long line of engineered and accidental genetic modifications. Our son's generation will take our species to a new and different level of evolution. But some things will not change. I hope the fact that you did not pull away when you saw my earliest memories means you will accept the temporary vestiges of his ancestry."

"How temporary?"

"Just a few weeks, maybe less." Then he said, in a softer voice, "Will it matter so much?"

"No, I don't think so now that I expect it. The bandages?"

"Most hands and feet de–fuse on their own after a few weeks; mine didn't. They had to be surgically separated. It wasn't a genetic abnormality, just a developmental one. I ... I was born before I was fully developed."

"The scars on your hands?"

"Yes."

"Do I want to ask?"

"No, please, not now. This moment is too perfect for those memories."

"But how did I see your memories?"

"I cannot show you in the dark, and I am too comfortable to move. There is something quite wonderful in knowing that only a few millimeters of skin and muscle separate me from my son and even less separates me from my ..." His voice dropped to a whisper. "Which brings me to the second and third things I did. I know I should have asked your permission first, but I occasionally lose track of sequences when I am around you."

"What did you do?"

"I married you."

I was suddenly awake.

"What? When?"

"About ten minutes ago."

"I don't understand. How is that possible?" Reaching through the darkness, I touched his face. "Please explain it to me, Grant, so I can remember everything."

"While you were showering last night, I searched the collective's archives to learn how my ancestors chose their mates. I discovered it was a common occurrence when we could create our own females. Mutual consent was required, but I cannot determine whether they fell in love or if it was just a chemical attraction. However, a monogamous social contract existed that was respected by all colony members. I couldn't locate any details of a formal ceremony. However, the archives were very specific about the elements that bound them together: the exchange of memories so they could see into each other's hearts; she would bear his children, and, in return, he could give her a new name honoring her place in his life. Then, in time, he would reward her with the most precious thing he possessed."

Although I could not see his face clearly, there was a smile in his voice.

"So, you see, we are a little out of sequence, but the most binding of these elements is the first. I know I should have asked you if marrying me was something you might consider, but since I do not share a human's life span, and it's for such a short period of time, I thought you would think it unnecessary. I'm sorry I married you without your knowledge, but please tell me it was not against your will."

"Grant, please turn on one tiny light where it won't bother you too much."

He reached above me and touched the table. Soft pink light filtered through the netting above the alcove's curtain, and pale bands of color encircled the room. Once again, I was in awe of the beauty of the bedroom, and it occurred to me that Grant had created more than just—as he called it—a bower; he had designed a bridal suite.

"Grant, how much of this room was changed back to its original design last night?"

"No physical changes were ever made to this room, but the lights would have blinded me, so I reprogramed them for complete darkness so that I could stay with you if you wanted me to live here."

"If" I wanted him to live here. What woman wouldn't want to be surrounded by such beauty while loving and having that love returned? I was still unsure if I was dreaming, but I could not disguise the gratefulness in my heart.

"Thank you ... husband."

"Wife."

Whispering the word like a prayer, he kissed me again, but there were no pictures this time, just his mouth and his hands. Naked together for the first time, we touched and explored under our silken covers, laughing and talking until his kisses became more serious. A deft touch here, a little unhurried pressure there, testing and teasing my body until I trembled under his hands as they caressed my skin.

"Oh, Grant, that ... that was ... wonderful," I said shakily.

"Well, now I know what pleases you," he said, his fingers moving lightly on my thigh, "we will go slower next time."

I traced the muscles of his back to his waist. "So, short of causing you cardiac arrest, what can I do for your pleasure?"

"Oh, Carolina," he said, embracing me, "just breathing the same air as you is one of the greatest pleasures of my life."

"You've called me Carolina twice. You know that's a state, don't you?"

"Two states," he said.

"Okay, once for each state. Why?"

"It sounds like music to me. I've wanted to call you 'Carolina' for several days. It was the third element that occurred this morning. Do you like it at all?"

"My favorite grandmother called me Carolina when I was little, but then everyone started calling me Carrie or Carrie Ann, and that was the end of Carolina." I looked up at him. "I would love for you to call me Carolina."

Turning off the light, he kissed my neck and whispered "Carolina" in my ear.

My fingers moved softly over his cheekbones. "It only sounds like music, Grant, because you sing it." Continuing to caress his face and shoulders, I slowly pulled him toward me, and my lips followed the lines of my fingers on his skin.

Grant was entranced. He was completely prepared to assume the role of a suitor in their relationship, hoping she would acquiesce to his advances, but that she would meet those advances halfway, reciprocating with a level of intensity that matched his own, was unexpected. Psychologically, she would only do that if she felt secure in his affections. Had he succeeded in bringing her to that point already? Was it possible that he could now enjoy her without spending every moment worrying that she would take herself and their son out of his life?

He'd promised Grayson she would be under his complete control before noon, but that was only a matter of manipulating the conversation. Grant's heart quaked at the thought that it could be real—*that she* wanted *to belong to him*. Glimpsing the edge of the only immortality he understood, he would risk anything for the chance to live forever in her heart.

Reliving the touch of her lips on his as she drowsed in his arms, he lifted her hair and sought the warmer places on her skin. Enjoying the luxurious taste of her, it occurred to him that she might be hungry, too. As if on cue, her stomach rumbled.

"Breakfast in bed, or would you like to meet me in the kitchen after you shower?"

"But Grant," she said sleepily, "isn't it Tuesday? Don't we have to work today?"

"No, Carolina, I told you. A marriage is respected by the colony, and, well, today is our honeymoon."

"Only one day?"

"One day at a time."

I pressed my lips to his neck and kissed him. At first, I kissed him because I wanted to feel the warmth of his body against my lips. Then I kissed him again for all the times I had wanted to and could not. But more than anything else, I kissed him because he responded with a passion I never expected. It was not Dr. Grant who held me in the dark; it wasn't even the Grant I'd fallen in love with during those late summer days. It was another man, sensuous, intimate, and free from any desire beyond loving me.

"I have just thought of something," he said. "Breakfast will have to wait. Don't move."

I lost him in the darkness until, silhouetted by candlelight emanating from the bathroom, he came toward me with a towel over his arm and carrying a small bottle.

"What is in the bottle?" I asked.

"A surprise. My recent review of your records indicates that you haven't had a massage in nearly a month, and your doctor thinks that is far too long."

I didn't know what to say. I couldn't believe he *really* wanted to give me a massage. Dan had never done that—not even before we were married, and it certainly never occurred to him afterward. It was too much. Already stunned by Grant's generosity, I was embarrassed that he thought I expected more.

"That would be lovely, Grant," I said slowly.

"You didn't like them?"

"They were great."

"I'm pretty good at it, you know."

"I'm quite sure you're wonderful at everything," I whispered.

"What is the matter, Carolina? Something is wrong, and you will have to tell me sooner or later, so it might as well be now."

Placing the bottle on the table, he sat on the edge of the bed and turned toward me, his face in shadow.

I took a deep breath.

"You don't have to do this," I said quietly. "I'm here, Grant, and all this beauty takes my breath away. It's more amazing than I could ever imagine, and I love you. If I knew a stronger word, I would use it. So, you see, it's okay. I know I cannot return your kindnesses or ever give you anything equal to this," my arms took in the entire room, "or, as you said, give you any pleasure at all … physically … so you don't have to be so nice."

I paused and, hearing no argument, faced the truth—he could not possibly want to keep up this level of attention. My heart broke at the thought of the inevitability of losing a little more of it each day. Rather than facing that pain again, I tried to resign myself to another relationship of loving loneliness. Looking down so he would not see the sorrow in my eyes, I hoped he could not hear it in my voice.

"You saved my life and gave me rainbows, Grant, and I … I'm honored to be your wife, but I don't want my, um, needs to be a burden to you. So, it's okay if we're … you know … platonic."

Grant's mind reeled. She didn't want him to touch her? Did that mean she didn't want to touch him? How was he to live with her and not touch her? He couldn't. All at once, everything he thought he had disappeared, and he blessed the darkness so she could not see his face.

Despite his rising emotional instability, he managed to say evenly, "You don't want me to touch you?"

"No, I don't mean that at all. But when most human men can't, um, participate, no one makes love anymore. Cuddling, kissing … everything goes out the bedroom window; even tenderness and affection fade. You know I love you. I love you touching me. I love touching you and kissing you. My goodness, Grant, haven't you noticed that I practically purr after … after … But I can't give you that. You've already given me so much that it seems selfish to expect more from you than I can ever repay."

Grant began breathing again. *It was just her limited frame of reference; she was comparing him to human men. He was tempted to show her all the ways he was different from human men but reconsidered. There would be time enough for that later. He was certain that despite his "picture show," one of the reasons she felt at ease with him was because he had always presented the most human version of himself. That she was willing to deny her own pleasure to spare his "human feelings" confirmed that his disguise worked.*

Watching her face while making a mental note to add these findings to his report, he saw her trying to blink back her tears. There was much

Grant knew he would have to endure living with her, but tears were not part of that equation. A woman who cries is unhappy, an unhappy woman is unpredictable, and an unpredictable woman is too dangerous to live, and Carolina had to live.

Moving from the edge of the bed to gather her in his arms, Grant wiped the tears from her face. Then, using his softest voice, he said, "Please let me love you every way I can. Why would either of us put limits on your pleasure just because I cannot respond as you do? Believe me, Carolina, the pleasure of our intimate relationship is not yours alone. It is not a sacrifice for me to love you. To see, hear, and feel your response to my touch is very ... gratifying.

"Hasn't it occurred to you, Carolina, my own, that perhaps I brought you here to satisfy my desires? That this," he began kissing her throat, "and this," he whispered as the back of his hands slowly slid from her neck to her waist, "are just my ways of saying thank you?"

"Grant—"

"Shh," he said, pulling her toward the towel, "turn over."

His hands slipped slowly over my back and thighs, and I knew that, regardless of what he said, there would be a reckoning one day, and I hoped what I had would be enough. Then, to remind me that I had something worth more to him than the world, I felt his son move. Turning over, I smiled up at Grant.

"I think your son wants a massage, too."

"From the inside or the outside?"

My breath caught. "I'm, I'm not sure," I stammered.

"Well, then, it is a good thing he is so small, and I have two hands."

Grant began making small circles on my skin above and below the little bump. With his face near my stomach, he began singing as the circles grew wider. Soon he was kissing me, and his hands made endless spirals until all the circles in the world, the moon, and the stars collided.

Persephone's Children

Every expression of human love I had ever experienced vanished with the inescapable euphoria of the touch of Grant's lips, the warmth of his skin, and the gentle insistence of his hands. Bringing his face up to mine, I did not care what the price was for his kind of love; I would pay it gladly, even if it cost me my life.

Wrapped in Grant's arms, I was suspended in the cool darkness of a world I wanted to inhabit forever. When my heartbeat returned to normal, he asked, "Better now?"

I nodded.

Stepping out of the bed, he kissed me.

"Where are you going?" I asked.

"To make breakfast while you shower."

Right on cue, my stomach growled.

"Okay, and tomorrow, I'll get breakfast for us."

There was a steady pause before he responded.

"As you wish."

Panic Room

Grant pulled on his robe as I walked toward the candlelit bathroom. Expecting the amenities of an upscale hotel, I was completely unprepared for the sunken hot tub, the shower stall with the now-familiar lines of pale blue tiles, or the gold-streaked mirror that hung above the marble countertop. Baskets on the glass shelves held everything I would ever need for my personal care. Snowy white towels were stacked on the bench next to the shower. On the other side of the wall, where the steam from the hot water would not fog it, a vintage three-panel mirror hung above a matching vanity table where small ornate boxes held a variety of cosmetics. Never before had I seen a room so exquisitely equipped for a woman's comfort.

Again, Grant's attention to detail was unexpected and humbling. Placing my hand on my stomach, I thought, *No, dear. I had no choice about you—you were mine from the beginning. But this generosity and care, even before he knew I loved and wanted you, means that your father must love us very much.*

Impatient to share my appreciation and admiration of my mini spa with Grant, I showered quickly, then realized I had no clean clothes. Wrapped in a towel, I tiptoed out of the bathroom and flitted around to the bottom of the bed to retrieve my dragonfly kimono.

Once dressed, I started toward the door, but there was no door. Pulling back one of the curtains from the wall, I found seamless metal sheeting from ceiling to floor. I circled the room, trying to detect a break or indentation behind the curtains, anything that indicated a doorway, but found nothing.

An edge of panic crept into my consciousness, but I fought it down. I was being silly. *I got in here, didn't I?* Then I remembered that the light switches were next to the door that led into the nursery. Searching for the light panel, I found it on the wall directly across from the bed. I started randomly pressing the buttons. Lights went on and off all over the room, but no door opened. Running back to the bed, I pressed the buttons there. Lights flickered on and off, and I heard a slight hum under the bed, but still no exit. Returning to the light panel, I pounded my fists against the wall where I thought the door should be.

"Grant!" I called as loud as I could, "Grant!"

There was no response.

My slim grasp on reality started to slip, and the hysteria I had been fighting crept into my throat. What if breakfast was just an excuse to leave? I couldn't believe he could not hear me *if* he was still in the apartment. Without a door or window, there was no escape. Thinking there might be a telephone, I frantically moved the pillows away from the table around the bed and ran to the dining alcove but found nothing. I opened the dragonfly bag. My wallet and the few pieces of jewelry I'd brought were there, but my address book was missing. I shook my head. *Who would I call?* No one would believe me.

Alone and heartbroken, I wondered when Grant would come back. Would *he* come back? Or would he send interns to verify I was okay, take my measurements, and bring the sonogram cart into the room occasionally to check on the baby? The thought of anyone else touching me made me ill, and I leaned against the wall for support. Then, passing my hand over my stomach, I froze.

My thoughts spiraled downward in fright. *Oh, dear God, would he? After I had given birth ... Would Grant let them take our son from me?*

I had never felt so powerless. Disowned by Dan and no longer employed outside the clinic, no one would think to look for me. As Grant's wife, I was now part of the colony, and regardless of my feelings, he could do anything he liked with the baby or me, and no one would stop him. My fears consumed me. Had Grant lied to me? Were there more rooms like this where his other mothers waited for their daily checkups? Was I nothing more than the means to an end? And, lastly, was it the baby—not me—he wanted? At the thought of losing our son to a colony orphanage, every apprehension I'd experienced in the last two weeks became real and filled me with terror.

I thought of my sweet golden butterfly; I would never be allowed to keep him. Trapped with no way out and no hope, a moan from the depths of my broken heart escaped my lips as I slid from the wall to the floor.

For how long? I thought dully. I knew the answer to that, too. *Until I gave birth, went crazy, or died ... or maybe all three.*

I glanced around the room. Now fully lit, it was still exquisite, but I realized that my lovely white bridal bower was essentially a carefully constructed cage I had so willingly walked—*no*, skipped, danced, and twirled into, that I never noticed when the door locked behind me.

Crawling to the foot of the bed, I threw my arm over the edge and gripped the corner of a silken wrap. I pulled it to my face. Breathing in Grant's scent, I recalled a thought I often had when Dan ignored my tentative affections.

We could have been so happy.

Once again, that chance had somehow slipped away. All my brave confidence of the morning crumbled in that one memory. Heartsick and alone, I couldn't hold back the tears that stained the soft silk.

Their Reaction

HE MARRIED HER?! Gregory couldn't stop laughing long enough to say the words out loud. *I don't know which of them I feel sorrier for.*

"I know," said Grayson, "but, as Grant pointed out, it solves all kinds of problems. Think about it. By tradition, married human women live with their husbands and, more importantly, obey them. By physically separating and emotionally divorcing her from her human mate, he has eliminated the possibility of divided loyalties and her one legal avenue of escape."

"It's still a little extreme," Gabriel said. "She already wants the child; isn't that enough for him, or for us, to keep her here?"

"Not, according to Grant, if she feels she can leave any time while she's still pregnant—thereby taking the child with her. By marrying her, he said, and I agree, she will feel she belongs here and will stay. He also said it would be easier on him if she believed she was married; that way, he wouldn't have to keep up the pretense of 'courting' her. She will accept less attention in return for what she perceives is the security of a more binding relationship."

"More's the pity for her," said Gabriel. Grant was his brother, but they all knew how merciless he could be.

"It's how married women behave and not our fault they are willing to accept less. It was, however, clever of him to take advantage of their susceptibility. I suspect that, after today, we will see a definite change in her attitude. Less independent, I'm thinking. Compliant is the word he used."

"After today? What is he doing today that is supposed to create that kind of change in her?" Gabriel was only slightly alarmed. He knew Grant wouldn't physically harm her unless she tried to leave.

"Depends on which of them you ask. Grant referred to it as systematic brainwashing. However, he said she would call it a honeymoon."

"She would call it a *honeymoon*?" Gregory's laughter echoed throughout the tunnels.

Gabriel shuddered. He thought he knew all too well what was happening in those rooms above the garage; he had witnessed Grant's methods of persuasion before.

Oblivious to Gabriel's concerns, Grayson smiled. Everything was going as planned.

The Dressing Room

"Carolina, did you fall asleep? I thought you were hungry."

Grant moved the curtain aside. Blinded by the barrage of light, he threw his hand over the control buttons, darkening the room at once. When the eight flashes of fire cutting through his brain cooled, he opened his eyes and quickly scanned the room. Not immediately seeing her, he became alarmed at the scattered pillows and the curtains pulled away from the walls. Fear gripped his heart as Grant searched the room incrementally until he found her huddled and silent on the floor beside the bed.

As he lifted her into his arms, Carolina looked up.

Sorrow etched her face, and tears blurred her eyes. His fear mounting with every moment, Grant cradled her against his shoulder and said as calmly as he could, "What happened, Carolina? Did you fall? Are you in pain?"

Fighting their way from despair to recognition, Carolina's eyes slowly focused on Grant's face. In a voice reminiscent of a young girl, she said, "It's you ... You came back."

"Carolina," he said, holding her tighter, "talk to me, please. Are you in any pain?"

She slowly shook her head.

Bowing to the inevitable but refusing to give up hope, he rocked her and quietly asked her the three sanity test questions. "Where did you go to college?"

"The University of Florida."

"Where is it located?"

"Gainesville, Florida."

"Your major was?"

"English, then art history, then performance art, and then I dropped out because I couldn't make up my mind."

Then he asked in the same tone, "Are you in any pain?"

"No."

His confidence returned with an unexpected feeling of optimism, and he smiled slightly as he lifted her chin.

"My darling, please tell me what happened."

"I came out of the shower to tell you how wonderful my spa bathroom is, but you weren't here, so I put my kimono back on and then—" her voice cracked.

"And then?"

"There wasn't a door," she cried. "I looked everywhere. Then I called and called and beat on the wall, but you didn't come. I thought you had locked me in, and I would never see you again. That, that you had left me and ...." Overcome by sorrow, her words were lost as she dissolved into tears.

"Shh, shh, love."

Grant looked at the delicate tracery of incandescence he had created to surround the mother of his child and realized that despite his loving intentions, it did resemble a spider's web.

"You believed I made all this to trap you?"

She nodded, wiping her tears with the sash of her kimono.

"Did you not hear one thing I said to you this morning?"

"Yes, everything. That's what made it all so terrible, Grant. I believed every word, and all I could think of was how much I'd lost. That we could have been so happy if what you said was true, and I had somehow lost that chance. I was afraid you had left me when I couldn't get out to find you. Oh, Grant, you cannot understand how abandoned I felt or how frightened I was for our son."

He pressed her hands against his heart to calm her.

"Everything I said this morning was true, Carolina, every word. And we will be happy. I cannot promise that I will not leave your side from time to time, but now and forever, I promise you that I will always come back for you. I am so sorry I did not show you where the doors were. That your suffering was so unnecessary and due completely to my negligence will take a long time to make up to you."

Trying to take away the pain, he lifted her bruised hands to his lips and kissed them. "So soft," he whispered.

Feeling her gradually relax against him, Grant realized that isolating her from all outside human connections had successfully destroyed much of her independence. Her resulting emotional dependence on him was earlier than he expected. Soon, she would be entirely under his control, and then, layer by layer, he would reconstruct this bit of human clay into his idealized image of the obedient wife, the perfect mother. He wondered abstractedly how much of her would be left when he finished.

"Underneath the beautiful woman, lover, and mother that you are, Carolina, I am beginning to suspect is a little girl who just wants to feel loved and wanted."

"Grant, underneath every woman, lover, and mother is a little girl who wants to feel loved and wanted. Isn't it the same with men? Isn't there a young boy within you that craves security and love?"

Several moments passed before he admitted grudgingly, "Yes, there is."

Tasting salt on her lips, Grant held her close until her heartbeat steadied and then gently released her. She still looked pale but not as scared as before, and he could again see his Carolina in her face. His earlier resolve wavered. It would be unforgivable to deliberately deprive his son of the loving light that shone from her eyes. Regardless of the consequences, he vowed not to destroy all he revered about this wonderfully complex human woman who loved and wanted them both.

Caressing the fine silk above her breast, he said, "So tell me again why you are wearing this gown. I thought human women liked to change clothes."

***

The haze of desperation clouding my mind slowly receded. It *was* Grant's voice in my ear and his arms around me. Love and reassurance existed in every movement, in the cadence of his voice and soothing touch. I rewarded his patience with my foolish tears by smiling up at him.

"Well, we do if we have something to change into, but as soft as the towels are, I really do prefer this," I said, smoothing the lovely fabric.

"Let's see what else we can find. Can you stand if I help you?"

"Yes."

Grant sat on the firm edge of the bed and pulled me toward him.

"Just a moment."

Untying the sash to my robe, he separated the edges of my kimono and placed his ear against my stomach. He listened for a moment and, turning his face to his son, kissed him. When he stood up, I started to tie the sash.

"Don't," he said, catching my hand in his. "You aren't going to be wearing it much longer."

Walking through the door into the bathroom, he went to the right side of the shower. The paneled wall had the same wainscoting as in the nursery.

"Here," he said.

Operating like the nursery door, pressing a lever under the wainscoting opened an entryway to a walk-in closet. Grant adjusted the rheostat until a faint circle of light appeared in the center of the curved room. Three large, full-length mirrors surrounded half of the circle, and three armoires completed the other half. He pointed to the armoires.

"Work clothes ... play clothes ... my clothes."

"You still want me to be your assistant?"

"Yes," he said, "to keep you with me as much as I can, but if you don't feel well or are tired, you don't have to."

"You mean I can either be with you or stay here and wish I was with you? Hmm, tough decision," I said, my eyes getting a little misty.

"I hope you won't take too long to decide. I hate to think of spending most of my day running down here to check on you." He turned and removed a pair of slacks and a shirt from his area of the closet.

Knowing the mirrors were behind me, I took off the kimono. "So, I'm thinking ...."

"For you? Play clothes, definitely play clothes."

On our way out of the dressing room, Grant turned to me.

"Open the door," he asked.

I quickly demonstrated that I understood how it worked.

Returning to our bedroom, he straightened the curtains while I reassembled the bed. When we finished, he looked around.

"You are right, Carolina; there is no direct exit out of this room into the building. Instead, you must either go through the nursery into the rest of the apartment or out this way."

Pressing a button on the headboard, the alcove curtain moved aside. It only took a moment for me to realize that those walls were also paneled. Standing in the alcove, he took my hand and ran it down the length of the third panel until I touched another lever.

"Press that," he said.

The panel to the right slid behind the one on the left, revealing a small elevator. I stepped inside. There were no floor buttons, just two arrows.

"The up arrow," he said, "goes directly to my office. Then, if you want to leave, you can take the main elevator to the lobby and walk out the front door. The down arrow brings you back here."

He looked down at the floor for a moment and then back at me. I could not mistake the seriousness in his voice.

"This elevator also stops at one other place. Please listen very carefully to me, Carolina, because someday this may be your only option. Pressing the down button twice will take you to the garage level. Hidden behind a partition in the left corner of the garage is a dark grey sedan. In it are the papers and accounts I have arranged for you. With our son or alone, that option is always open to you. Even now, if you want to leave, I will not stop you. But I wish you would wait until after the baby is born so I could see you together just once ...," his voice slowed, "before you leave me."

"I won't leave you, Grant."

He was silent for a few moments.

"I hope you will not leave me, Carolina, but it is unwise to make promises you may not be able to keep. I want you to stay with me so much that I did not plan to tell you about the car until after our son is born, but it is more important to me that you know I never intended to trap you. I kept my promise to take care of you, so if you want to leave *everyone*, you can."

I put my arms around him. "Thank you, Grant."

He watched as I operated the panel several times. When we left the alcove, he pulled the curtains to the edge of the paneling, and I noticed that the way the curtains overlapped looked like a continuation of the wall. Almost, I thought, as though he was hiding the alcove.

I walked over to the light panel.

"Grant, the most important thing I would like to know is how to open the nursery door."

"The light buttons," he said.

"No, they don't work. I pressed and pressed; you would think I was programming my own light show in here."

"That is exactly how it is supposed to look. However, if you do it this way," he said, pressing five of the six buttons to form a C, "it opens quite easily."

At his words, the door sprang open without a sound. He closed it again, and it melted invisibly into the wall.

I couldn't resist hugging him. "Oh, thank you."

The relief flooding through me was followed by a twinge of shame, and I stepped back. "Please forgive me for getting so upset. It was my worst nightmare; I couldn't get to you, and I panicked. I'm sorry, Grant, I should have known better."

"No, no, I understand. It is a terrible thing to feel abandoned and alone. I will never forgive myself for giving you cause to feel that way. You feel better now, don't you?"

"Yes, but Grant, why is this necessary? Why not normal doors? Why a personal elevator? Why must I choose to either be with you in your office or here alone?" Then, remembering my earlier thought, I asked, "Are you hiding me?"

"No, I'm not really hiding you. Everyone knows exactly where you are. I have just made it very difficult for anyone else to have access to you or our son. Except for you and me, no one knows about the elevator, and it cannot be seen by a casual glance in my office or the garage, and no one has any reason to look for it. Not having a designated door to this room makes it harder to enter, but not impossible. The fact you saw where the nursery door was located last night made me realize it needs to be better concealed. I will not change where it is or how to open it, but you will no longer be able to recognize it as a doorway."

He pulled me into his embrace and whispered, "What is important ... *very* important to me, Carolina, is for you to understand that it was never my intention to trap you or leave you without any way out. In fact, there is one more exit—"

"In the dressing room?"

"Yes."

"The right mirror or the one on the left?"

"So smart. The one on the right, under the edge of the mirror frame. Look for it later. Let me know immediately if you cannot find it, and I will show you where it is."

"But you still haven't told me why, Grant. Why all the precautions? I'm not money in a vault."

"You are to me," he said. "Another reason is, well, my brothers are stronger than I am now. We are not quite equal anymore."

"But you said some die sooner."

"Yes, but unless we have suffered an injury, we do not weaken; we die, like blowing out a candle. But I *am* weaker. If they do not sense it now, they will, even if they do not know the cause. If my brothers discover the reason, the collective will want to study our son because he will be considered an anomaly, and ...," his face tightened, "take him away from you, from us."

"The orphanages," I said in horror.

"Yes," he said. "They would, um, test him there." Then, trying to ease the tension, he added, "But it is my way to prepare for the worst and avoid unpleasant surprises, but I do hope for the best, my darling, and the best is that you will have our son without any problems or interference. I know you have already given birth to one child, but it will be much easier this time. There will be minimal discomfort because he will be born still encapsulated and small, only about four pounds." Grant leaned his head against mine. "I can hardly wait to see him."

The hope in his voice that it was all going to be wonderful was reflected on his face, and I promised myself that I would do anything to make wonderful happen.

"What do I need to do to make them think—? Wait a minute, why *do* your brothers think you've married me?"

He hesitated briefly. "Because cohabitation would allow me to study you up close. The books and toy rabbit you brought impressed my brothers, and they wanted to know what I had done to make you so caring. Given the circumstances, I thought it best not to share the real reason with them—and withholding information is a banishable offense—so I told them I did not know and needed to observe you. Gordon and Gabriel also volunteered, especially seeing how brave you were yesterday and that your instincts were correct. However, I told them that you were my client and you trusted me. Now that we are married according to the collective's earliest traditions, I hope my brothers will respect that and leave us alone, at least until the baby is born."

Grant sighed. Even talking was tiring him these days. "Carolina, I know you are hungry, but could we please lie down for a short while? I'm suddenly very tired and would like to hold you for a few minutes."

I nodded. He lifted me into the middle of the bed, and, like the night before, it recessed into a shallow nest. Fully clothed, he got in beside me with his back against the inside curve of the mattress and covered us with one of the quilts. His hand slipped between the folds of my kimono to rest gently on top of my stomach.

"Sweet, soft wife," he murmured.

Moving deep into the warmth of his body, I thought of his carefully conceived escape plans and realized that regardless of what he said, he would not have told me about the car if he intended to come with us.

PJ Braley

Alone then, I thought, but our son had his own plans and moved under his father's hand as though to remind me that I would never be alone again.

The Mind Meld

Feeling her relax against him, Grant closed his eyes. The last twenty-four hours, in addition to the previous three weeks of non-stop planning, ordering, designing, and building, had been exhausting. He could not stop to rest now, but he needed time to think. There was something else he had promised Grayson.

"It will help us with the other mothers," Grayson had said.

Although it was part of their marriage tradition, Grant hesitated because he had already taken so much from her. However, finding an undeniable reason for it—that he would always know if she was in danger—decided him.

Of course, it would also let him know the truth behind her spoken commitment to him, whether she genuinely loved him or if her affection was merely a way of showing her gratitude. He tried to pretend it wasn't crucial to him to know if her feelings were real.

After silently rehearsing the words, he said, "Carolina, earlier I mentioned that the husband gives his wife the dearest thing he has to honor their commitment to each other."

"Yes, but Grant, you don't have to give me anything ever again. Honest. I'm not sure how I will ever repay you for all the loveliness you have given me. It's already too much—"

"Carolina, I am not talking about something you can wear. I am referring to a gift that will keep you from ever being afraid again. Regardless of where you are in the facility, you can call me, and I will hear you. If you are in pain or in any danger, I will know and be able to find you immediately. You will not feel alone or frightened again. I cannot bear that you should suffer one minute that I can prevent."

Drowsy, warm, and very comfortable, I nestled closer to him.

"And what would that be?" I murmured, thinking, *Some kind of alien mind meld?* I smiled at the thought until I realized that was *precisely* what he meant.

"Well, it is like the picture show you saw this morning. But instead of the images being temporary, I can leave them so that you will always have my memories. Whether that will make it easier or more difficult for you ... later ... I am not sure."

I thought about it. Many of the images were already fading, but would I want them forever? Years from now, when it was just our son and me, would I want to remember Grant so clearly? Wouldn't it break my heart? *Perhaps*, but why was he asking me this now?

"Grant, is there more to this, this memory implant? You didn't ask before when you showed me the images; why are you asking now if you can leave them?"

"They are for two different purposes. The first is an informational exchange, so the couple is aware of each other's past actions; you might call it a mental background check—before committing to a shared existence. The second is a more lasting symbol of commitment by solidifying their relationship into a single existence. My memories would become your memories."

"And my memories would be yours?"

"No more than they already are. Your memories do not exist independently in my mind, but implanting my memories would connect our minds, allowing me to share any new memories you make. You have done everything I've asked of you, Carolina, and I will not do this without your permission. But you were so frightened and believed I had left you because I could not hear you. This would prevent that from ever happening again; I will always hear you."

I sat up.

"Wait a minute. Are you saying you will be able to read my mind? All the time? I am not sure I want to do that. What if I have thoughts that I don't want to share with anyone, thoughts that are private? Grant, you're asking me to give up the privacy of my mind."

"Yes and no. For example, when we are talking, and our eyes meet, there is a connection, and we know we are talking to each other. I can hear what you say when I know it is me you are talking to, so it is only when you direct your thoughts to me that I will hear you."

"How will this make a difference?"

"If you are hurt, in pain, or feel trapped, as long as you are in the facility and direct your thoughts to me, I will hear you. If you had thought to me when you were unable to leave our bedroom, 'Where is the door?' or 'Grant, I can't find the door,' I would have come immediately. You would never have experienced all that self-doubt and fear. Oh, Carolina, you will never be alone, and because you can talk to our son or me that way, we will never be alone, either. To us, my darling wife, that assurance of unity is our greatest gift.

"In my culture, losing our connection to each other is the worst fear of our lives, even more than death. Death is not an option, but dying in silence is a choice we would never make. I know humans are quite good at being alone and adapting to smaller and smaller communities. Many people even search out places where there are no other humans at all, but for us, that kind of existence is an unending hell. It is the only punishment worse than death."

Listening to his voice, I knew he was telling me the truth. If abandonment was the worst thing he could imagine, then saving me from ever feeling that again would be sharing his greatest treasure. I also knew that if his brothers threatened him with banishment from the collective, it would make him stronger if he was still connected to us.

"You know, Grant, living in my head may not be the greatest place to be sometimes."

"As long as I live in your heart and in the memories of our son, I will be able to endure, quite literally, anything you can dream up."

"One last question. If I share my thoughts with you, will I also be sharing them with your brothers?"

"Only if I chose to share your thoughts with them. There would have to be a link, and I would be that link."

Seeing her indecision, Grant wondered at the human attachment to their individual minds. It would be ludicrous even if they were not so predictable. They had no idea how susceptible they were to divide–and–conquer techniques. When feeling desperate and isolated, with no one to depend on, their instinct for self-preservation made them easy to manipulate. Looking into her eyes, he saw they were still red from crying and realized that she was already too vulnerable. Leaving her to herself was becoming less and less possible, and he had told her too much to pretend constant surveillance was still optional. Nevertheless, he wanted her to choose.

He sat up and looked directly at her. "The reason this synthesis is given later rather than earlier in marriage is because it is a matter of trust. I know that while love is a gift, trust must be earned, and I have obviously failed to earn that trust if, after all I have said and done," he lifted her hand to his face, "you thought I would abandon you.

"Believe me, Carolina, I know what I am asking of you. Sharing does not come easily for your species, but it would be so much easier for me to care for you and our son, both physically and mentally, if I knew the moment something started to go wrong and could work to save you before ... before it was too late, and I lost you both."

He sighed and added, "Sometimes minutes can make a difference."

He would have to be very careful, he thought, *to pretend he could only hear the thoughts she directed to him and not answer questions or respond to the thoughts she believed she was keeping to herself. He knew that despite her human limitations, she would test him, and his Carolina was no fool.*

"But you said our son could hear me because our minds are already connected, so this isn't about him; this is about you and me—"

She abruptly withdrew her hand from his face. "And your brothers, isn't it? Is this your idea or theirs?"

"There is no 'their,' Carolina; we are one."

She looked up at him, her eyes wide with apprehension. "Grant," she whispered, "will I be *their* wife, too?"

Grant was struck by the full weight of his betrayal. Not only against her—and his guilt for the deceit and manipulation he used to bring her there would be eternal—but he had not thought of how their relationship would affect his standing within the colony. Before her, he disciplined his brothers with his Fire Slayer ability to send lightning thoughts of pain to ensure the facility ran smoothly. However, loving her had cost him the wall between sending pain and feeling it himself. Every lightning thought he sent to control them weakened him further, and Grant knew he could not fight them all. Even armed with his pistol, he knew he would be defeated if he were banished and could not hear their plans.

The repercussions for such disobedience would be horrific.

Visions rushed into his mind of Caroline being ripped from his side; their son autopsied in front of him, while he, Grant Gates—the highest-ranking Lyostian vanguard on the planet—watched alone, powerless, and screaming in silence.

"No!"

The anguish of his protest echoed in her ears, and he clasped her to him as though passion alone could make his denial true for either of them if he failed.

It was several minutes before his breathing slowed, and his arms released me. I leaned back so I could see his face in the shadows.

"Just one more question, Grant. Can you take it out? After our son is born and before you … leave me … is it possible?"

"Yes, but why? If I am gone, what difference will it make?"

Brushing my lips back and forth across his cheek, I whispered, "Do you not understand how much it will hurt me to call out for you, as I will for the rest of my life, and each time face the knowledge that you will not answer? The pain of losing you will never end."

"I will never do anything to cause you more sorrow, Carolina. This decision is yours. Regardless of how difficult it will be for me to live without your voice in my mind, I will remove it whenever you ask."

"Promise me."

"Why?"

"Because I want to promise you something in return."

"What is that?"

"If you do not take it out when I ask you, I will remove it myself."

"But you would have to cut your own throat."

"So be it," I said calmly. Staring into my eyes, he seemed to grasp the enormity of what he was asking me to do.

"That is not loving our son, Carolina," he said, adding softly, "or me."

"Isn't it? If we are truly doing this because it will keep us safe, then I need to be free of it to protect him if we have to leave. What if they threaten you and you cannot fight back? Or if they want you to tell them something you've promised to keep to yourself? Then they will find us ... and if they can find us later, why hide from them now?"

Even in the dimness of the room, I could see a sudden flash of guilt on his face.

"Grant, I've always heard there are two reasons for everything: the rational reason and the real reason. You've told me the rational reason. Now, please tell me the real reason."

Pulling me near, he encircled me with his long arms and legs.

"We are a very selfish species, Carolina," he whispered. "When we love, we love completely: bodies, hearts, and minds. You are a wonderful, giving woman. You have shared your body with me, and I do not doubt that you love our son with all your heart, but in our culture, the highest reward I can give you for all you have given me is to bring us into a single existence. I want your thoughts in my head. I want the constant reassurance that you are near and that our son is well because, Carolina, when I cannot see you, touch you, or hear your voice, you are almost a dream to me. If there comes a time when you want to take yourself away from me, then I will, I promise, do everything I can to protect your thoughts from reaching anyone who can harm you or our son. I will promise you that."

He started kissing my neck, lingering for an extra moment on the place where I had felt the pressure in my throat. "Kimono or no kimono?" he whispered.

"No kimo—"

I had barely said one syllable of the word when I was lifted up and out of my gown. The only light in the room was extinguished, and Grant's glasses hit the table. Moving to the center of the mattress, his hands came up under my hair, and tilting my head back, he kissed me. Relaxing into the moment, I barely noticed the pressure against my throat. It was so sweet and mesmerizing that I could scarcely remember to keep breathing. Something painlessly scratched the inside of my throat, but it was very quick, and by the time I thought I'd imagined it, I was asleep.

The distant hum of hummingbird wings woke me, but it wasn't my son's heartbeat I heard—it was Grant's. Cocooned in a silk coverlet, he held me tightly to his chest as he leaned against the pillows with his head tilted slightly to the side.

"Don't talk," he said, "just wait a few more minutes."

I knew that in the dark he could see me perfectly, so wiggling my hand from under the silk, I began writing L I G H T on his chest, but before I got to the "I," he pulled the white netting around the bed to diffuse the shaded lamp from the alcove. I wanted to thank him, but he interrupted me.

"Shh," he whispered, "or I will be forced, forced do you hear, to do some shockingly wonderful things to your body. There can be an advantage to being married ... oh, Carolina, married!" He embraced me quickly, "To a doctor." Then he laughed out loud. It was a sound so joyous and free that I snuggled down and contented myself by looking up at his face silhouetted against the iridescent fabric.

Grant Gates was a beautiful replica of a human male. His hair was a thick dark brown that shone with coppery shadows beneath fluorescent lights. His skin had the blush of a summer tan, and although I did not know the color of his eyes, I had seen flashes of light in their depths. To the world, Grant's face was an unchangeable mask behind which he hid his thoughts, his emotions, even his desires ... everything except his undeniable power. His chiseled features and angled cheekbones gave nothing unintentional away, and I was just as concerned about sharing his thoughts as sharing mine. My gaze lingered on his lips. The thought of kissing those lips brought me out of my reverie, and as I tried to sit up to get closer to him, he bent down and kissed me. Hard.

He smiled down at me. "Well, it was what you wanted, wasn't it?"

I raised a single eyebrow.

"Yes, you can talk now. Though for a woman—a wife—who likes to be kissed, you didn't think much of my last performance."

"I don't know why I got so sleepy. Did I hurt your feelings?"

"No, you fell asleep with your head in my hands. Such trust, Carolina, makes me very happy."

Feeling warm and slightly sticky, I tried to remove the quilt he had folded tightly around me.

"Do not struggle; I will help you."

Easing me into the middle of the bed, he slowly pulled back the silken edges as if setting a butterfly free. Then, he immediately covered my nakedness with his own as though I were in danger of flying away.

Gently kissing the hollow of my throat, he said, "I have you, Carolina. You are truly mine now."

With his lips against my skin, I heard a sound in my mind that I only recognized because of its cadenced and lilting voice.

Carolina, can you hear me?

"Yes. Oh, Grant, is that you?"

Do not answer out loud. Think to me. Now, Carolina, can you hear me?

Yes. In my head, it sounds like I am singing to you. Does it sound that way to you? Is my mental voice, well, pleasing to you?

You have allowed me entrance into your mind, and you want to know if I like what I hear? Oh, my dear wife, never say again that I have given you too much.

Can you hear the baby?

Not yet, but soon. He can hear us, though.

Oh, sweet baby boy, whatever happens, please remember that we were all together in the beginning with our bodies, hearts, and minds.

Umm, wife of mine? Grant asked as my hands snaked around his neck.

Yes.

Care to direct a few of those loving thoughts this way?

PJ Braley

Only if you plan to feed me afterward, I thought to him, playfully licking his bare shoulder.

Anything you want.

The Edge of Dawn

Getting up was the last thing on my mind, but I wanted to wash my face before breakfast. But, although I tried, I could not find a graceful way to climb out of the bed.

"Grant, is there a trick to this, or do I need to learn how to pole vault?"

Laughing, he pressed a button on the keypad. The center of the bed rose level with the sides.

"You are going to have to show me that sometime."

"As you wish. I'll pencil in 'keypad training' on your calendar for this afternoon."

"Well, I hope it won't take too long …."

"We'll work it in between kissing sessions just to keep you awake."

After rinsing the tear stains from my face, I walked into the front room. I expected it to be brighter than last night because it was still summer. It was only then I realized that even though the sun might rise in the east, it would never rise here. In Grant's underground world, we would never share rainy mornings, picnics on shaded grass at noon, or watch the sunset change from fiery red to dusty amethyst. Without any source of natural light, we were forever suspended on the edge of dawn.

The sound of Grant closing the cabinet doors and the scent of warm honey caught my attention. I sat down at the counter of the small bar as he placed a tray of honeyed toast and apple slices with two cups of tea in front of me. Picking up a triangle of toast, I turned back to the room and continued to survey the perfect balance of beauty and surrealism around me. Again, I sensed an underlying timelessness that would have been disorienting if it hadn't felt so liberating. I turned toward Grant.

Grant, what time is it?

About nine in the morning.

How do you know that? I don't see a clock anywhere.

Do you truly care, Carolina, what time it is? Because if you do, I will tell you the exact position of the sun in relation to the Earth's rotation in any time zone in the world right now. In fact, if it is important to you, I can chart the position of each and every planet and star in your solar system, all testifying to this very moment.

That won't be necessary, I thought, smiling up at him. Realizing that in these rooms of shadows and refracted light, he was my only frame of reference, I added, *Because time, like everything else here, Grant, is whatever you say it is.*

You say that so seriously, Carolina, he answered, laughing. *You should not give up quite so easily.*

Opening the vented cabinet door, he showed me the clock on the microwave.

It doesn't change my statement, but Grant, out of curiosity ... can you really do that? Tell me the time zones of the world or draw a chart of the planets?

Yes.

Would you do me a favor someday when you have nothing to do?

There is no such day, Carolina, but I will make a priority of anything you request.

Then, please, draw a chart of the planets and solar system at exactly the time you married me this morning. It, it could be our wedding picture.

That is very sentimental of you, Carolina, he sang softly in my head.

And below it —
A chart of our son's birthday?
Please.
Of course.
I rubbed my forehead.
What is wrong?

"A headache. Can we talk out loud for a while? I know my spoken voice isn't as pretty, but maybe my head would feel better."

"All of your voices are beautiful. Can I get you something? I think there is a medical bag around here somewhere."

"No ... my brain just needs a telepathic rest. Speaking of medical bags, are you sure you don't have to work today? Keeping you from the clinic for two days seems very selfish and, as your assistant, very inconvenient. Not that I mind having you to myself; I just know that one hundred and ninety-nine other women are wondering where you are."

"I am exactly where I wish to be and where I need to be, Carolina. I have eleven brothers who have been looking out for you these two days, as well as my responsibilities. We take care of each other and see each other's clients as necessary."

"Even each other's prospective mothers?"

"Yes."

No matter how much his answer might hurt me, I had to know the truth.

"How many other mothers have seen your picture show, Grant?" I asked slowly. "How many bowers did you design? Do they live behind the other doors on this floor? Am I going to walk into my kitchen one morning and find other mothers in here eating my strawberries?"

In the same manner, he answered, "No, but if they were here, wouldn't you be generous and share your strawberries with the mothers of your son's brothers?"

"Half–brothers."

"There is no such relationship in our culture. They will all be his brothers, not just the sons of my clients but of all the facility's prospective mothers. He will just be a little, a very little, more human, and he will have our memories and remember what we tell him."

"You gave him our memories, too?"

"Everything you saw in your mind, he saw. In time, he will understand what he has seen and add this knowledge to the collective's archives."

"And what do you tell him?"

"Three things: to survive, never let anything hurt his mother, and to protect his brothers. To give him the confidence to do those things, I tell him he is stronger than he knows."

"Is he?"

"Even more than I can tell you."

"Do I have to worry about him leaping tall buildings in a single bound or kryptonite?"

"He, and all of his generation, will be quicker and more focused than humans because they work together. By stronger, I refer to his integrity and ability to see things through rather than bullets ricocheting off his chest. He will be more resilient than humans because his pain receptors are not as finely tuned as yours. His bones are nearly unbreakable, but he can be killed. As to kryptonite, he will have to decide for himself what to fear."

"What do you fear?"

"I fear losing him, losing you, losing the respect of my brothers, and dying in wretched silence alone—all of the things I have risked since that afternoon when something in you called out and was answered by something in me."

The memory of that afternoon reminded me of my earlier question. "How many bowers did you make, Grant?" I asked softly.

He walked around the counter and took me in his arms. "There is just this one, Carolina. I only have one son ... only one wife."

"Your other mothers, Grant, where are they?"

"Going about their lives with a less strenuous exercise program, and there are fewer all the time. The post–reconception blood tests indicated nearly half of the embryos were female and not sustainable. If these mothers haven't miscarried already, those cells will be expelled during their next cycle. The cells are so small at this stage that they are not harmful, nor will they be noticed.

"As to the remaining five, current statistics indicate I could lose up to ninety-five percent of them in the next couple of weeks due to the human body's tendency to reject offspring with genetic abnormalities. If the mothers are eating honey as we hope they are—and they seem to be consuming it at predicted levels—we are projecting a ten-to-twenty percent success rate."

"How important is the honey to the mothers?"

"Very important. Because it is part of our physiology, it must also be part of our mothers' endocrine system for our new brothers to develop both physically and mentally before birth and to thrive afterward."

"Is that why you make me eat it?"

"Do I *make* you eat it, Carolina?" he asked.

"No," I said, smiling, "you know I love the taste of it. The V4 honey Gordon blended is so delicious you would probably have to take it away to make me stop."

"Yes, love, and that is how all our mothers feel. However, we have not had to tell our prospective mothers why they are getting the newer version because we have not yet told them they are pregnant. You knew you were pregnant because, when the twins were competing for you and moved in their attempt to dislodge each other, you recognized immediately what that movement represented. None of the other prospective mothers have ever been pregnant, and we have no reason to believe any of them are carrying twins."

"But Grant, I was one of the ninety-five percent just yesterday, and I was threatened with a hysterectomy. Is that what they are facing if they miscarry? Because, from a female point of view, that's not acceptable, *you didn't ask them*. You cannot tell me that you and your brothers love these women while endangering not only their lives but possibly their ability to have more children; the very thing you told me your species prizes above all else. It seems to me that someone could have spent a little time in all those centuries of research to find better ways to take care of your mothers."

"Our mothers were already pregnant, Carolina, and that choice always carries an inherent risk to the mother, even in fully human pregnancies. Regrettably, we cannot control how a woman's body will respond to our DNA or the few fetal cells that remain in her bloodstream after pregnancy. And, well, you have so many women here. If we take a few for our purposes, we do not impact your species' ability to survive. If we don't, then we *will* die. And while I understand your skepticism, we are licensed physicians trained in genetics, and obstetrics is our field of expertise. Before re–conceiving the first hybrid, we spent years refining the serum. Then, to be as non-invasive as possible, we simplified the re-conception procedure to just a sonogram, a small incision, and a needle. Finally, we designed a timing sequence specifically tested to save our mothers. So, you see, we do not treat them as callously as you may think. We respect, worship, and adore every woman on this planet—you are our only hope for survival."

"Why not hire surrogates? At least they would be compensated and know what to expect."

"Because a woman who wants to be a mother is more than her biology. She is tender and loving with nurturing thoughts. Our children live in their mother's minds as well as her body; it is important that she *care*. That is something money cannot buy."

"And each one is precious, Grant. You cannot say that you 'worship and adore' women and then hurt them. No. You must do more. Talk to your brothers and find a way so no one else dies or will not be able to have more children."

"Death or sterility is not the worst that can happen," he said quietly. "We care for all of them, Carolina; it is a fundamental part of who we are. We don't want any of them to die, but we don't want them to exist in a living hell, either. If we can remove the embryonic sac without compromising its structure, then we do so, but better to adopt a child, or even die, than spend your life—"

He looked down at his hands and could not finish.

Then, I understood as clearly as if *I* were reading *his* mind. I knew why he had been born early; the embryonic sac in which he was developing ruptured, and the doctors saved him so he would not die inside his mother.

When he raised his head, I could not miss the pain on his face.

"Did she die when you were born?" I asked, gently taking his hands in mine.

"No. At the time, it was important that the child connect with his mother regardless of her state of mind, so they kept me with her to aid in my physical development. One day, just before I was a year old, she left to look for my father. Confused and lost, there was an accident. It's a terrible burden, knowing you killed your own mother."

He pulled his hands away and brushed back my hair. "We do everything we can, but the risk is always there for them and still exists for you, too. I am sorry, Carolina, if what I am distresses you so much. But the truth is our other prospective mothers are in my thoughts as often as you are. I cannot care less for them. You are my main concern, but their importance has not diminished with our relationship, so please do not think that I will neglect them or put them at any additional risk for you."

He looked at the door for a moment, then turned back to me. "You know that I am not human, but I am not a monster, either. That said, I do not now, nor will I ever, share your priorities. This planet is our home, too. You cannot expect me to care more for your species than my own, especially when you consider how prolific and destructive humans are and how hard it is for us to merely survive."

"I just keep thinking about how horrible this is—all those women ...."

"Yes, but if we don't proceed with our plans, we will die. Is that what you wish, Carolina? That I had never been born? That our son would never be born or will have to live without knowing the pleasure or hope of children?"

"No."

"As a species, we are intertwined with yours, just as you and I are caught up in this whirlwind we cannot control. Neither species can return to the beginning. We must move forward together."

Sighing, he picked up my hand and kissed the palm. "I'm sorry I cannot be who you are ... nor do I wish to be. Your species has almost pushed this planet to the point where your future generations are doomed to extinction. And the worst part is that humans know this, and most do nothing. We cannot stand by and let you destroy our future as well as your own. I love you, Carolina, but I love our son, and his children, more. I am sorry if I cannot make you understand." He dropped my hand and looked toward the door.

"You are right about one thing, though, there is always work to be done. I'll just get my coat and return at noon. If you need anything or feel unwell, you can think to me or use the telephone." Pointing to the handset on the wall, he said, "Pressing zero connects you to the front desk, and they will page me."

He kissed me lightly on the forehead and stepped back.

Her mind a turmoil, she stared at him in silence for several moments. "Promise me, Grant," she said.

"Promise you?"

"Yes. Promise me that no woman will die."

"I can only promise you that no woman here will die."

He heard a deep sigh. Hoping it was one of resignation and not regret, he looked into her eyes. "I promise you, Carolina."

Moving slowly to give her time to decide, Grant picked up his lab coat and hesitated before opening the door.

Choose carefully, Carolina, your species or mine? Everything—her life and the life of their son—depended on her accepting who he was and wanting to stay with him. It had to be her decision. Standing there, he didn't pray; he didn't even breathe. He only hoped that she loved them enough.

"Grant," she asked softly, "does this mean our honeymoon is over?"

He heard hurried footsteps behind him, felt her embrace, and saw her perfect hands cross over his heart. She pressed her forehead against his back, and once again, the most beautiful voice he had ever heard resounded in his mind.

Husband, you said we had all day.

Fully knowing the consequences, she'd chosen him and his son above her own life. She would not try to leave him; he would not have to kill her. Grant was exultant. As he had always been hers, she was now irrevocably his.

Before his coat touched the floor, Grant turned and lifted me in his arms. Sitting together in the velvet chair, I rested my head against his shoulder as he sang to our son in words I didn't understand. The baby, however, moved as though he understood everything.

"What are you saying to him?" I asked.

"I am telling him how wonderful you are … how fortunate we are that you love us. I am telling him that your happiness should be his first concern every day of his life. Because I am telling him these things as his father, they can never be disobeyed."

He lifted my chin to kiss me, but as if on cue, my stomach growled, and he laughed.

"Are you going to finish breakfast now or later?"

I traced an imaginary line from his cheekbone to his jaw. "I think we should bring it with us."

Grant carried the tray and held my hand as we turned toward the bedroom. Despite the dreaminess of this new life, I was under no illusions. He was not the man I believed him to be that spring day five short months earlier when I walked into his office; he was far more than I could ever imagine. I knew what I'd accepted and committed to during that long morning of metamorphosis, but I also knew I didn't want anything else. Every fiber in my mind and body hummed not just with love but with loving. No human ceremony could have made me feel more married to Grant or more committed to his happiness. I longed for his thoughts in my mind, his voice in my ear, the touch of his hand, and, most of all, to hold his son in my arms. At the center of my soul, I knew the three of us belonged together. There was no going back. Not anymore.

Leading her through their bedroom door, Grant tilted his head and sent her slightly edited private thoughts throughout the colony. As he'd promised Grayson, it wasn't even noon yet, and now they all knew.

By her own admission, Carrie Taylor was there—and there she would stay.

Persephone's Children

Grant felt the tension of the morning fall away. *He wouldn't have to kill her today,* he thought to himself and smiled as he closed the bedroom door.

A Wager

"Pay up, Gregory."

"I can't believe you all bet against me. That's $80!"

Garrett grinned at him. "No, it's $100."

"How is that possible?"

"Grant's twenty."

"Grant can't bet; he is the bet."

"No, she was the bet. It's $100, Gregory."

"Okay, okay. $20, $40, $60, $80, and here's Grant's $20. How in the hell was he able to do that? I am starting to think that human women are the stup—"

Tell us, Gregory, thought Grant to his brothers. *We would all like to hear what you think about human women.*

"That they are stupendously beautiful, and we are humbly grateful for their kindness, generosity, and grace."

Yes, Gregory, that is exactly how we hope you feel about the only creatures standing between us and total oblivion.

After the others left the room, Gregory looked at Gordon. "Well, that was close. Who knew he was listening?"

"No one ever knows when he is listening. You've got to stop being so reckless. It's going to get you killed."

"Oh, I wouldn't bet on it...."

Breakfast

I woke up to the sounds of CNN news and Grant's voice singing, "Time to get up, lovely wife of mine. Our first day, are you nervous?"

"Should I be? Are you?"

"No, not anymore. Now that you are part of my world, Carolina, I feel quite at ease."

I wished I felt the same way. "Is there anything I should expect from your brothers? Or what they are going to expect from me? I mean, are they going to want me to *hug* them or something now that we're related?"

I imagined nearly any response except Grant's peal of laughter that not even the curtained walls could muffle. He sounded so *happy*. His laughter was infectious, and before I knew it, we were both laughing.

"What, what was so funny, Grant?" I asked once we caught our breath.

"Grayson's face if you hugged him." Sending me a mental picture of what he believed Grayson would look like made me laugh again. *It might actually be worth it to see that in person. What do you think?*

"Let's play it by ear."

After a moment, he stopped smiling and took my hand.

"Seriously, though, Carolina."

"Yes, Grant."

"When we are around other people …"

"No PDA. I understand."

"What is a PDA?"

"Public Displays of Affection."

"Is that okay with you?"

"It makes sense. After everything you've said, it probably isn't good for anyone, including your brothers, to know how much I love you. Don't worry, Grant. We will be as we have always been when we are working. I might sneak a provocative thought to you now and then, however, just to see if you are paying attention. But I warn you, when we are here, you are my husband. I don't care if the entire Seventh Calvary shows up."

I could tell by his face that it was exactly what he needed to hear. *Did I ever tell you, Carolina, how wonderful you are?*

Not in the last five minutes.

Can we shower together while I show you how wonderful you are?

It was then I realized it must be an acquired skill to laugh and do telepathy at the same time. "We tried that yesterday, remember? We simply do not have that much time in the mornings … unless getting to work at noon is okay with you. It's certainly fine with me." I blushed slightly at the memory and changed the subject.

"What's in the news, Grant?"

"Anything specific you are interested in?"

"The war in Iraq."

"The U.S. is still protecting the no-fly zones in the southern region."

"That's good?"

He took me in his arms. *Yes, Carolina, it's good. The war in Iraq is winding down. Your son will be fine. This is just Brendan's first year in college; ROTC programs are very thorough, and it will be at least five years before he's deployed or sees any action.*

Thank you, Grant, I said, kissing him lightly.

Better than that, Carolina, or it is going to be a exceedingly long day.

I started preparing breakfast while Grant was getting dressed. I took out the blender, cut up some fruit, made tea, found some frozen waffles, and opened the jar of honey. Walking into the front room after securely closing both doors behind him, Grant looked surprised to see me in the kitchen.

"Hi! I'm making breakfast like I promised."

"That's right," he said, "I'd forgotten."

"You know, it didn't occur to me until just recently, but I've never seen you eat anything, just drink tea. So, you are going to have to tell me—"

Carolina. Please stop. Now. Grant's disapproval resonated through my mind straight into my heart.

"Okay, Grant. This is me, stopping." I placed my hands on the counter and wondered what I had done. I'd wanted it to be perfect, and yet something was wrong. Tears filled my eyes. *Damn!* I thought, *don't cry, don't cry.*

He smiled in apology. "I'm sorry. I didn't mean to sound so abrupt. We just don't have time to eat breakfast here this morning, Carolina. There is plenty of food in the office for you, so do you mind if we wait and have this for dinner? Then we won't have to hurry."

"Of course. I will be two seconds. You're right. We both need to get in early after being out for two days." I put the fruit in plastic bags as he tossed the waffles back into the freezer.

"All done!" I said, closing the refrigerator door.

Checking his watch, he walked toward the front door.

"Grant, if we are in a hurry, why aren't we taking our elevator to your office?"

"Emergencies only, Carolina, not convenience. We must be seen using the same hallways and elevators we have always used."

"Grant, one more question. Is our relationship a secret from everyone?"

"Do you mind? So far, we've managed to avoid any kind of scandal or whispering. We would appreciate your discretion."

"I would be a scandal?"

He looked at me for what seemed like a solid minute before I remembered I was already married.

"I'm sorry, Grant. I'd totally forgotten."

He held my hand as we walked out the door.

"Thank you for that, Carolina."

Breakfast – Part II

Entering their private dining room for a bite of breakfast, Grant was not surprised to see his brothers file in after him. He knew they would want a report. The lights went from dim to dark as they removed the glasses that protected and focused their eyes so they could watch every part of his face. Grant took his glasses off for the same reason.

"Good morning," he said.

"Good morning, Grant," they said in unison.

"Two nights, Grant," Grayson said.

"Yes."

"More?"

"Yes. It looks like I should have packed after all."

"We discussed other methods. You didn't have to marry her."

"It solved a lot of problems. I thought that was obvious yesterday when her response indicated it was a successful strategy."

"Yes. Will she, um, behave herself?"

"Yes. She has promised no PDA ... public displays of affection. If she would only control her private displays of affection, my life would cease to become a living hell. However, blessed Anya watches over her. Carrie is healthy, the child is healthy, and for me, she will do anything."

"Any additions to yesterday's report?"

"Yes. I find it advantageous to know what she is thinking. And, if not for the fact that every useful thought she has is accompanied by 2.3 million other thoughts that are pure drivel—or worse—I would recommend consciousness implants in all our prospective mothers for monitoring purposes. However, being chained to that is ... difficult."

They nodded sympathetically.

Grant poured a tall glass of juice. Still holding the pitcher, he looked at them.

"Isn't anyone else having breakfast?" he asked.

"No. Haven't you eaten?"

"Not for days."

"Ha! I knew it."

"Knew what, Gregory?" Grayson asked.

"I want my money back. She's never seen you eat, has she? You've got her eating out of your hand because she thinks she's married to a nice, almost human kind of guy ... and that's not who you are, is it, Grant? I bet she hasn't seen you without clothes either, married or not."

Grant turned and looked directly at Gregory. "She knows exactly who—and what—I am. She also knows what kind of child she is carrying and what he is born to do. If I haven't eaten, it is because I spent the last thirty-six hours ensuring that when she has the child, she will accept and nurture him as she now gives every indication of doing. Achieving this level of acquiescence has required, and will continue to require, certain sacrifices on my part. Wouldn't you do the same to bring a fully developed hybrid into the collective?"

"Yes. Yes, I would, Grant."

"I thought so. In the future, Gregory, do not disparage my marital relationship. As humorous as it may seem to you, I take my commitments to the future of the collective very seriously—regardless of personal consequence."

"I'm sorry, Grant."

"Yes."

As his brothers left the room, Gregory looked down and was ashamed to see five $20 bills crumpled at his feet.

62

Breakfast Part III

When I entered the office, fresh flowers were in my crystal vase, and the candle was already lit. On my desk was a square envelope addressed to *Mrs. Grant Gates*, and I was surprised to find a small bottle of champagne in the refrigerator. I decided to wait and open the envelope with Grant. I didn't recognize the handwriting, and although it was addressed to me, I was sure the card, like the champagne, was intended for both of us.

Grant had meetings scheduled all day. It was to be expected. Not only had he missed the last two days, but I also suspected he had spent much of the last two weeks supervising the construction of our apartment. I sorted the accumulation of client applications and began entering data from the questionnaires.

It was about ten when I heard, *Carrie?*

Yes, Grant.

How are you feeling?

Fine.

Busy?

Oh, yes. There was a stack of newly approved applications on my desk.

I'll try to stop by at noon.

I'll be here.

He didn't stop by at noon.

Persephone's Children

At three o'clock, I finished my work and checked my emails. The was an inter-office email from my former student assistant, Suzanne, asking to get together as soon as we could arrange it. I looked at the message and smiled. *If it hadn't been for an end-of-semester lunch with Suzanne, I wouldn't be sitting here; I'd still be at my job at the university.* I blew her email a kiss in gratitude and replied that I would get back to her in a day or two. I was relieved to see there were no new emails from Eric. I had put our brief affair out of my mind, and although he was my son's human father, I no longer thought of him that way and hoped he'd found someone who could make him happy.

I skimmed the news on the internet and, at four o'clock, began to feel tired and went to rest in the chair. Grant had to come for me because unless I used our private elevator, I couldn't get into the apartment without him. He had forgotten to tell me the key code.

When I woke up, the room was so dark I could barely make out Grant's outline at his desk.

Grant?

One minute.

'kay.

I closed my eyes and went back to sleep.

Carolina?

Yes.

Would you like to go home now?

Go home? I never wanted to go home. Leave here, leave him? My heart ached at the thought. *No, please. I want to stay here with you.*

You do stay here with me, my sweet wife. Aloud, he said, "Wake up, Carolina. You're dreaming."

I opened my eyes. Grant was sitting beside me, and memories of the past two days flooded back. It was true. I *was* home. I sat up quickly and hugged him.

Grant kissed my cheek. "From now on, I'll wake you up with my voice instead of thinking to you ... at least until you are accustomed to waking up next to me."

"Will that ever happen?"

"Yes, and soon, very soon."

"It's been nearly all day, you know. I am starting to feel very kiss deprived."

Then we'd better leave right away, or we'll be spending the night here, and our bed is much more comfortable than our chair.

Please say that again.

Say what, exactly?

Our bed.

Not for five minutes.

Getting my things together, I picked up the envelope, took the champagne out of the refrigerator, and put them in my gym bag.

Less than five minutes later, he was whispering in my ear as we tumbled onto the silk and satin of "our bed." After catching up with the kisses I'd missed that day, Grant folded me in his arms.

"How were you today? I'm sorry I didn't see you at noon."

"I'm fine, we're fine, and I didn't really think I'd see you; your calendar was so packed. But thank you for checking on me."

"I wanted you to know that I was thinking of you, Carolina."

My name sounded so beautiful when he said it, but there was something I didn't quite understand.

"Grant, why do you call me Carrie sometimes instead of Caroline or Carolina?"

"When it is for my brothers' benefit, I call you Carrie. You are Caroline when there are clients or staff present, but, most especially, Carolina is just for your ears ... and such nice ears they are, too," he said, nibbling one of my nice ears.

Persephone's Children

After a few moments of mutual nibbling, the playful tone in his voice disappeared.

Sitting up and facing me, he said, "Carolina, I want to ask you two questions. Please don't answer with the first thing that comes into your mind. Think your answer through carefully. Will you do that? Even if you believe you know the answer right away?"

"Yes."

"You have seen, and we have discussed in some detail, my memories. The first question is, do you fully understand *who* I am? The second is—and your response will not change how I feel about you—do you really love *me*? The truth of me that I have shared with you, regardless of my outward appearance?"

It only took a moment to understand that he was asking if I *pretended* he was human to make our relationship easier for me to accept. I knew what pretending was; I had pretended for the last ten years of my twenty-year marriage to Dan was enough, that we were happy, and our relationship was secure when it was all a lie. There was no pretense about my feelings for Grant. I knew he was not human, but it didn't matter. No human male had ever made me feel cherished or had been so kind, loving, or patient. My only response to that kind of devotion was to love him back with all the passion within me that Dan never wanted. No, I was not pretending. With a grateful heart, I thought of our son, curled up inside me with claws for hands and antennae, but he wasn't only Lyostian; he was part of me, too.

I answered him just as seriously. "Yes, Grant, I know who you are. Mutated from insect, alien, and human DNA, you look like this to protect and advance the survival of your species and its collective consciousness. And yes, I love you, all of you, from your four pairs of eyes to the scars on your hands and feet. There is not one square inch of you that is not as dear to me as the rain is to the earth. I love only one thing more than you, and that is my son. Your care and attention have kept us alive, and my gratitude is without limits or conditions."

With some careful editing, Grant sent her thoughts and spoken declaration to his brothers, admonishing them. *There will be no more questions about the validity of our relationship.* The general assent he received closed the subject for any future examination or discussion. In the tunnel room where they slept, Gabriel, after hearing her voice so clearly, breathed a sigh of relief and fell into an untroubled sleep for the first time in two days.

Grant was still not quite at ease with Gregory's accusations. There was one remaining Lyostian attribute he had yet to share with her. If she needed any further proof of how alien he was from her species, this last revelation could destroy everything. It was not accidental that he asked for her feelings before showing her how he implanted his memories in her brain and how and what he ate.

Knowing he could not put it off any longer, he asked, "Still in the mood for waffles?"

"Absolutely. Sometimes, it takes all day to make breakfast."

"Yes," he said quietly, but she was so excited about making their first meal in the apartment that she didn't notice his reluctance.

"Which of these buttons raises the bed again?"

"Second left."

"I thought we were going to write them down."

"We will, Carolina, if you want to." *If you ever want to sleep with me again.* He wondered if he should have brought a hypodermic syringe back to the apartment, but it was too late for that. There was an emergency medical kit in the bedroom, but no sedatives.

He sighed. *At least their rooms were soundproofed.* He wasn't afraid for himself or her—but for his son.

What if this was something she could not accept and somehow managed to escape ... what would she do with the child? Keep him hidden from the world? Destroy him out of fear? What if she got desperate and tried to abort ... No! He would not allow any of this to happen. She loved them and had accepted everything else they were. If he held her, explained it to her slowly, and stayed calm, perhaps she would accept this physical anomaly as well.

It only took a few minutes to take the sliced fruit from the refrigerator and the waffles out of the freezer. Setting the blender on the counter, she smiled brightly at him.

"What is your pleasure?"

"Well, what are you having?" Considering the bathroom was two rooms away, Grant tried to decide whether it would be best if she ate something before their discussion or afterward.

"Waffles with fruit and just a little honey, V3; I ate the V4 for breakfast."

"I know. It makes you smell very sweet, so I can usually judge how long it's been since you've eaten it." Coming up behind her, Grant wrapped his arms around her waist and whispered, "I love you, Carolina. I never knew it was possible to love anyone so much."

He could not prevent his hands from trembling. Carolina grabbed them in hers and twirled to face him.

"Grant, what is it? Are you all right? How can I help you?"

Her gentle concern was very gratifying, and he was going to miss that when she ran screaming from him forever. Walking around the counter, Grant sat in one of the bar chairs. Bowing his head, he pressed his hands to his eyes and prayed for guidance.

When he finished, he looked up to see her as white as the countertop she was gripping with both hands.

"Carolina, are you in pain?" he asked quickly, starting to stand.

I placed one hand on his shoulder. "Grant, if you do not tell me, right now, what is bothering you, you will be picking me up off of the floor."

I had barely finished saying the words when I began to feel lightheaded, and my knees buckled. Grant caught me and carried me to the chair. "Carolina, come back to me, Carolina," he sang softly, touching his head to mine.

After a few moments, I said, "Grant, just tell me what it is. Please. I can't help you if I don't know."

Taking my hand, he kissed my fingers slowly, one by one. "Do you remember asking me yesterday morning how I was able to give you my memories?"

"Yes."

"And how I brought our minds together into one consciousness?"

Yes, Grant, I remember.

Remember that I love you?

Always.

Please do not be afraid.

Okay.

I am going to open my mouth, and you are going to see something quite strange. I will answer all your questions, but please be patient.

When Grant opened his mouth, all I could see were his perfect white teeth, healthy pink gums, and tongue. It looked a lot like mine, but then, as I watched, his throat suddenly turned inside out. Something I could not believe physically possible came up and out of his mouth. Pink and gray with pale blue veins, it lengthened until it extended beyond his lips. Slightly protruding from the center was a narrow hollow tube.

"May I touch it?"

It disappeared at once, and his mouth became a smile. "Carolina, I have been dreading for two days having to show you that, and all you can say is, 'May I touch it?'" Laughing from pure relief, he hugged me. "You have never been what I expected. Thank you."

"Well," I said, laughing from relief as well. "You had me so scared. I thought a slimy killer bug was going to pop out of your chest or something. Compared to that, a throat straw is relatively tame. That's what it is, isn't it? Some kind of feeding tube?"

"Yes, the scientific word is haustellum. It isn't original to either ants or our Lyostian ancestors but was an accidental side effect of a mutation that occurred about twelve hundred years ago. Before we could eliminate it through sequential genetic evolution, we became dependent on it for both sustenance and the occasional intercommunication with humans. We can chew our food but cannot swallow it because the haustellum does not recede deeply enough into our throats."

"But I've seen you drink tea."

"No. You've seen me hold a teacup to my lips and sip tea."

"So, you can't swallow food. Do you chew it up, spit it out, and then suck it up the straw?" I imagined that for a moment. "That's kind of gross."

"Well, it's one way, and I agree with you; it isn't pretty."

"And the other way?"

"Two, really. The easiest is to eat things that are already liquid, like soups and juices. The other is to put everything in a blender, liquefy, and sip."

"Okay, but how did you implant your memories into my brain with your throat straw? How can it do two things at once?"

"Think about it, Carolina, your own throat has two functions," he said, tracing lines on my chest with his finger to diagram what he was saying. "If you breathe through it, the air goes to your lungs; if you swallow, nourishment goes to your stomach, but you cannot do both at once without choking. Mine," he said, touching his throat, "has three functions. Air and food like yours, and the haustellum, which consists of a series of nerves attached directly to my brainstem with the tiniest little bone at the tip that enables us to connect telepathically with humans."

"Bone?"

"You didn't feel a scratch in your throat yesterday?"

"Yes, but it didn't hurt."

"The first time, when we ... married," he said, "it was just a temporary puncture, but when you agreed to share your mind, the synthesis required a small incision to embed the connection into your brainstem."

"Brain surgery?"

"No, more like the reverse of removing a splinter from your finger."

Unsure if her nonchalance was natural or carefully concealed fear or disgust, Grant monitored her thoughts for panic. He took her hand by the wrist and held it lightly against his face to check her pulse. It was normal, but concerned she might go into shock when she thought about it, Grant abruptly changed the subject.

"Speaking of which, we were preparing dinner," he said, setting her on her feet. "Let's go see if we can—"

"Blender something up?" she asked.

"Sure," he said, smiling.

"Where do we start? What do you like to eat?"

"I like fruit, all kinds, whipped with raw, free-range eggs or yogurt, cream, or crushed ice, always with V1 bitter honey. I also like vegetable juices and consommés—room temperature. And tea."

"And you don't like ...?"

"Because we cannot control the chemicals injected into domesticated livestock or dumped into streams or oceans, we do not eat any animal, fish, or fowl, cooked or raw, and all fruits and vegetables must be washed and peeled. Pesticides can accumulate in our bodies, resulting in premature death."

"Milkshakes?"

Grant smiled and answered, "Birthdays only."

"How do you taste anything?"

"There are taste buds on the inside edge, not as many as are on your tongue or on my tongue, but enough to know if something is sweet, bitter, salty, or bad. Let us make breakfast together; you prepare the waffle, and I will blend something."

"Okay."

She dropped a waffle in the toaster, opened the jars of honey, and removed spoons and forks from the drawer.

"Save me a strawberry or two, please," were the last words he heard before she fainted.

That Grant caught me as I fell showed how much he was in my mind. When I regained consciousness, I was stretched out on the counter with cold compresses on my wrists, under my knees, and on my forehead. Sitting on one of the bar stools, Grant pressed my right hand to his face. Praying softly, he looked so worried, so caring, and so dear that he nearly broke my heart. I brushed my hand across his forehead.

"I'm sorry I fainted, Grant," I whispered.

"It is not your fault ... I, I never gave you a chance to say no," he said without looking up.

"It wouldn't have mattered. It would never have occurred to me to say no. Not to you. Not about anything."

"But in the beginning ...."

"Not even then, Grant," I said, starting to sit up.

"Please don't move, Carolina. Just rest there a little longer. You are still too pale, and I want to get my stethoscope if you don't mind."

"I promise to stay right here until you get back. Then, I want to ask you another question or two. If you don't mind."

"Of course, Carolina, best to get it all over with tonight." His words echoed back to me as he walked toward the bedroom.

He returned, rubbing his hands against the bell of the stethoscope to warm it. He lightly brushed the flat of his hand over my stomach until he found what he was looking for. Listening, he smiled. I motioned for the earpieces, and he placed them in my ears. The most beautiful music in the world to me was the sound of our son's heart. Like the trill of a hummingbird in flight, the reassurance of his existence calmed me immediately.

Grant put his fingers on my wrist. "It seems the best thing for you, Carolina, is listening to his heartbeat. Your pulse is normal, and so is your heartbeat. It is like a tonic for you. I may have to record it for the next time you start feeling faint."

"Fine by me," I said. "May I get up now?"

"Let us not push our luck, shall we? Why don't you finish your questions, and then we will see if you can stand."

"Okay, I have only one question. May I touch it ... gently?"

Smiling in amusement, he carried me to the couch. A few seconds later, the haustellum came from between his teeth.

I tilted my head. *Does it hurt when you do that?*

Did it hurt when you were a little girl and stuck out your tongue?

That depended on whether or not my mother caught me doing it.

My finger slid along the outside. It was warmer than I expected and smooth. I could see little taste buds on the inside. Impulsively, I gave it a quick kiss.

Four things happened at once. The haustellum disappeared, Grant turned me on my back, his hand hit the table, and everything went black.

"Oh, there is one other thing I forgot to tell you," he said in a very matter-of-fact voice. "The haustellum's primary function is to puncture, taste, and feed."

With his weight pressing down on me, my breath came in gasps. "Grant, I can't … I can't breathe."

"I know. You will pass out again in about fifteen seconds. Shall I help you count?" His breath was warm in my ear, and something sharp scraped the side of my neck. "I will see you again when we *let* you wake up, *wife*."

The last thing I saw before the spinning darkness entered my mind was Grant's brothers standing in the shadows behind him, waiting for their turn.

Shipwrecked

The dream was all wrong. The afternoon breeze had become an evening squall. Shattered upon unseen rocks, my catamaran dragged its tattered sails beneath the whirl and tumult of the sea. Deafened by crashing waves and blinded by salt spray, I held onto the broken mast as rain fell like tears on my face. Then, echoing between the cracks of thunder and flashes of lightning, I heard a distant voice, urgent and pleading. I turned my head to answer, but the waves were too high, and the rain and the sound of the wind drove the words away.

I drifted alone throughout the wet night without direction. The sea spray grew cold, and I shivered, but my makeshift raft was warm, and I held on. Gradually, the storm calmed, the sky became lighter, and I began to hope. Searching the edge of the shoreline, I heard someone calling my name.

"Carolina, Carolina, come back, come back to me."

Oh, dear God, it's Grant.

Grant had found me, and if he was here, his brothers were not far away. I had to escape. I tried to swim in the opposite direction but couldn't bend my legs. Something sharp bit my shoulder, and suddenly, all the butterflies from the garden at Brendan's college were hovering around me, landing on me ... *tasting* me. I tried to brush them off but found I couldn't move my arms. When they began *feeding* on me, I screamed.

When I stopped screaming, I didn't feel cold anymore.

I didn't feel anything at all.

Lost

"Grant, good news, there's no evidence of formic acid in her blood. The baby's safe."

Garrett glanced at Carrie's pale and motionless body wrapped tightly in a quilt on the couch. She had not made one sound since the ear-piercing screams he'd heard shortly after walking into the apartment. He shuddered, remembering similar screams that echoed in the tunnels a year earlier. Neglecting to silence his thoughts, Garrett speculated on what it would take to keep her alive long enough to harvest the child ... then he caught Grant looking at him.

"Thank you, Garrett. That is good news. Please leave the microscope. I will want to check again later if she remains unconscious."

"Of course, Grant." He looked in her direction again. "I hope she'll be okay."

"As do I, Garrett. Thank you, and goodnight."

When the door closed, Grant extinguished the candles and turned off all the lights in the apartment. Then, picking up the V3 jar from the floor, he found a clean spoon and carried them to the bedroom. He removed his clothes and slipped his mother's dagger between the mattress and the wall. If everything he had waited a lifetime to hold died that night, they would not die alone.

Looking into Carolina's ashen face, Grant knew there was little else he could do for her. Centuries of knowledge in the archives, a decade of laboratory research, and years of surgical experience in the catacombs beneath a dozen hospitals were no help to him now.

Singing softly, Grant removed the quilt and lifted Carolina from the couch. As he carried her into the cool darkness of their room, her teeth began to chatter. Moving into the center of their bed, he pulled the heaviest quilt over them and held her trembling naked body close to his to warm her. Grant closed his eyes and sang prayers to Anya to spare her and, if possible, their son.

"If I could, Carolina, I would cut myself open and tuck you inside so you would be safe. I would be your mother, Carolina," he whispered, "your mother." There was no response to his voice, and her eyes, wide open, stared at nothing.

Guilt consumed him. *I didn't mean to frighten you. Please forgive me. Oh, Carolina, my own, please do not take our son and leave me.*

Grant knew it was his fault. He'd let Gregory provoke him into pushing her, and he would be quietly planning Gregory's murder, but there was no doubt in Grant's mind that the shock that caused Carolina's inward retreat was a direct result of his overconfidence and pride.

Please come back to me, Carolina. I love you so much. Still not sure she could hear him, he pressed his forehead to the back of her neck and begged, *Son, tell her, please tell her, we love her. We ... we cannot live without her.*

A few moments later, the trembling stopped, and her skin began to warm; she breathed easier, and her heart rate slowed.

Thank you, my son, rest now. Our mother loves us. Caressing the small bump under his hand, the answering flutter gave Grant a sense of hope for the first time that evening.

He removed the spoon from the jar and lightly touched her lips with honey. Kissing her, he forced the honey into her mouth. Then, gently pressing the back of her throat, he reminded her that he loved her and that it was safe to return to him. Her lips moved under his. Her hand curved around his neck and held him. He let her embrace him as long as she wanted, not keeping her as close as he would have liked, and let her back away. Something had happened—she had disappeared from him and fought him—and he had to know why. It did not matter what Garrett said or didn't say; if there was the slightest chance her mind was in danger, he would do whatever was necessary to save her.

Without scanning her thoughts, he watched her face and waited.

"Grant?"

"Yes, Carolina."

"Am I awake?"

"Yes."

"Did I faint again?"

"You fainted once, Carolina, while you were making dinner. I caught you and put you on the counter. I thought you had regained consciousness at one point, and we talked, but you were out again when I returned from the bedroom with the stethoscope. So, I am not sure you were ever totally conscious."

"No. I was awake when you came back. You let me hear the baby's heartbeat, and I asked you to show me your throat straw. Then you carried me to the couch, and I kissed it, and then everything was dark, and, and …." He saw fear in her eyes, and she started backing away from him.

He sensed the panic in her mind and watched the color in her face drain away.

"No, Carolina. That is not what happened. Please, my darling, whatever is scaring you must have been a dream. When I came back in, I could not wake you. I tried everything. Hot bath, cold bath, and then you started fighting me. I was afraid you might hurt yourself, so I took you out of the water, wrapped you in a quilt, and brought you into the front room. I was so afraid. I called for someone to bring me a microscope and drew some blood to test it. When Garrett walked in, you screamed horrible screams, and I thought I had lost you. When Garrett said there were no contaminants in your blood, I hoped there might be a chance. But you were so pale and cold, I brought you in here and tried to warm you. When you still didn't respond, I asked our son to tell you we loved you, thinking that if you could not hear me, perhaps you could hear him—and you did. I put honey on your lips and kissed you, hoping you would remember me ... remember us."

Afraid she would slip back into unconsciousness before he could calm her, Grant had never talked so fast in his life. His effort was rewarded as her eyes slowly lost their look of desperation.

Oh, my sweet wife, it was agonizing not being able to hear you. Please never leave my thoughts again.

Had it been a dream? Had I again trusted him so little as to believe he would harm me? Twice in two days, my lack of trust had hurt him. I owed him my life and my son's life. I took a deep breath and remembered where I was and the love that brought—and kept—me there.

I put my hands on the sides of his face and touched my forehead to his. *I'm here.*

Yes. He gently wrapped me in his arms.

"Did the haustellum scare you?"

"Not at first. I thought I had accepted it, as I accept and love all that you are, but I do not know why I fainted. In the part you said I dreamed, you told me that the, the, your throat straw had a bone like a tooth, and it was, you said, 'to puncture, to taste, and to feed,' and you were deliberately forcing me to faint so you could do that, Grant, to *feed* on me."

As she related her dream, Grant scanned her thoughts and saw the images that frightened her. Images that could have so easily been real if he was defenseless and she was anyone other than his beloved wife.

Carolina smiled softly as she remembered. "Then there was nothing until I felt warm and loved, and the taste of honey, the taste of you, was in my mouth, and I knew I was alive and in your arms."

She settled into the curve of his body, and he kissed her, grateful to have both of them back in his life. As she relaxed into sleep, he flooded her mind with love, erasing the dark images that frightened her. Unsure how she'd distilled those few half-truths from their dinner discussion, he vowed never to be so unguarded again. Yes, he loved the taste of her, but human skin was too tough to puncture with the haustellum. It was only effective on the skinless area of her throat or fruit with a thin outer membrane like a ripe peach or plum. Lyostians didn't have to puncture the skin of women to enjoy them; their sweetness lay on top of, not beneath, their skin. He hoped that one day she would feel pleasure when he tasted her.

Like now, he thought as she drowsed in his embrace. With his face on the pillow next to her, the haustellum gently slid along her neck as he sipped the honey–infused nectar from her bare shoulders.

Breakfast – Part IV

The following morning my wonderful alien/human/ant/butterfly husband woke me while holding a tray. "It occurred to me last night, Carolina, your fainting may have had less to do with my slightly unusual—"

I raised my eyebrow.

"All right then, *very* unusual anatomical throat muscles, and more to do with the fact that, despite our previous conversations, you are not eating enough. The baby will take as much nutrition as he needs, so you need to eat for both of you. You remember eating for two, do you not?"

"Yes, I just forgot to stop after Brendan was born."

"For which we are all, in retrospect, very grateful," he said, kissing the top of my head. "So, to help you, it has become my personal quest to see that you eat at least three times a day from the entire human food pyramid, not just fruit, vegetables, bread, and honey. And hopefully, we won't have any more fainting spells. Please."

Stepping into the bed, he added, "You must help me take care of you, Carolina; I don't know how many more times I can stand almost losing you."

"But you always save me."

"Not last night," he answered. "Our son saved you, giving me one more reason to treasure his life far more than my own."

Sitting behind me, he spread one of the quilts over my lap like a napkin and set the tray in front of me. I stared. He had brought enough food for four hungry people.

"Grant, I can't eat all of this."

"It is not all for you," he said, putting a tall glass to his lips. Then, looking at the dishes, I instantly knew his breakfast from the food he'd prepared for me. The tall petal-shaped glasses containing yogurt with pale honey, minced-up pieces of toast soaking in a golden cream, and tomato-based juice was his breakfast; everything in flat flower-shaped plates, a waffle with strawberries and dark honey, and a scrambled egg with toast triangles, were mine. A jade green teapot in the shape of an elephant with two teacups crowded the overloaded tray. It was the best meal I'd eaten in weeks.

I leaned against him with my hand on my stomach. "Oh, Grant, I'm so full. That was delicious. Thank you."

"Good. I want you to continue eating like this; no more fainting." Then his voice became serious, "Did we answer all your questions last night, Carolina?"

"Almost. Grant, is there anything you haven't told me? Anything else about your biology or physiology or any other kind of 'ology' I need to know?"

"Well, you have seen me without clothes, Carolina. That is, um, the only other difference that immediately comes to mind. So to speak."

"I have wondered how I could be pregnant with your child if you don't have any, well ...."

"I believe the English word you are searching for, my dear, is scrotum."

"Ye-es."

"It's fairly simple. Like your ovaries, male Lyostian reproductive organs are located within our bodies to avoid injury and temperature fluctuations." He turned and pointed to the storybooks. "So, not too hot, not too cold, perfect for babies and bears."

He looked back at me and smiled, "And so, having eliminated their descension, we have no need for a pocket of skin within which to store them. As you know, Carolina, our genetics are very tightly controlled. Imagine what humans would look like if features and functions were reevaluated and adjusted every twenty-five years to adapt to changes in the environment, societal roles, or for protection."

I laughed as I imagined all kinds of evolutionary changes. Why, we might have more eyes, too! And definitely more arms or even wings! I was so happy, so relaxed. I looked up at Grant to share my thoughts, but an angry expression crossed his face.

"What's wrong?"

Without a word, he went into the bathroom and returned with one of my robes. After helping me out of bed and into the kimono, he picked up the tray, handed me a quilt, and we walked into the front room. Settling me on the couch, he covered me with the quilt and set the tray on the small table.

He looked at me, and I immediately understood he intended to include me in the conversation. Then, tilting his head, he said, *See, Grayson, she is fine.*

What do you think happened?

The embryo's nutrition requirements are outpacing her food intake. As a result, she has agreed to consume more food to meet his needs. We were eating breakfast when you interrupted us.

Garrett said she was screaming.

She experienced delusions while unconscious. When she came to, she said it was a bad dream, but couldn't remember any details, then slept until twenty minutes ago when I woke her up to eat.

We were concerned.

Thank you. I am also concerned because I do not believe Carrie is an isolated case but an indication that we must increase the caloric intake of all our mothers. Any kind of physical trauma can be dangerous to them and the colony's offspring.

Yes, Grant, I agree. Will we see you in the dining room this morning to discuss this further?

Grayson, I just said we were eating breakfast when you interrupted us. He sent them a glance at the nearly empty dishes. *So, no. I will be in my office in one hour.*

Is she working today?

"Carrie, are you well enough to work today?"

"Yes, Grant. I'm perfectly fine. I feel so much better since I've eaten something. I'm sorry for all the trouble. I'll be more careful."

Any other questions?

No. Thank you for taking the time to talk with us. We apologize for the interruption.

Yes.

Gregory walked into the underground conference room with his hair uncombed and an unknotted tie draped around his neck.

"What's going on?"

Grayson looked at Garrett. "Now that *all* of our brothers are here," he said, glancing at Gregory, "I would like to hear what happened from the beginning."

Garrett nodded. "I was in my lab and heard Grant ask if someone could bring him a microscope. I was the closest, so I brought one to Carrie's habitat. Grant opened the door, and she was lying on the couch like this morning—only she was almost blue, her breathing was shallow, and when I felt her pulse, her skin was cold, and her heart was racing."

"And Grant?"

"Fully dressed. He was drawing a vial of blood as I walked in, and then she started writhing and screaming. Just like, just like last year. Remember?"

"Garrett, no one has forgotten the screams from last year, but back to last night."

"After that, she was just silent and lifeless. I checked the blood sample and told Grant it was clear. He thanked me, asked me to leave the microscope, and I left."

"How did the room look?"

"Food was all over the kitchen area, and a blender was turned over on the counter. The rest of the room was immaculate."

"Any ideas about what happened?"

"Well, it looked like they were preparing dinner, and someone cleared the bar in a hurry. The only things there were a few wet dishcloths."

"So," Grayson said, pacing like a lawyer in front of a jury, "they are fixing dinner, she faints, he clears the bar to lay her down, wets some dishcloths to bring her to consciousness. When that failed, and she started having delusions, he called for help because he thought the embryonic sac was ruptured and affecting her brain. She eventually woke up and was just hungry. She's probably been following her original diet now, as she has for the last five months. It's feasible, especially after seeing her and hearing her voice this morning. Gabriel."

"Yes."

"Satisfied?"

"Yes. Thank you, Grayson."

"You like her, don't you?"

"No. She's too much trouble. But if Grant's observations result in a profile of the specific markers and characteristics that will enable us to identify compliant mothers who will want our offspring, then she merits not only our concern but our diligence and respect as both our mother and our model."

Grayson pressed his hands to his eyes, and the rest of the brothers did the same. "Beloved Anya, mother of us all, please bless and keep our mothers and their children safe."

Especially her, Gabriel prayed alone, *especially her*.

Wedding Gifts

On our way out the door, I grabbed my gym bag and wondered at the extra weight until I remembered the bottle of champagne and the card.

"Grant, thank you for the beautiful flowers yesterday."

"I didn't do that, Carolina. I wanted to, but I was unable to meet the florist's delivery in time. It was one of my brothers ... probably Gabriel."

"Do you think Gabriel left this, too?" I asked, showing him the wine and the card. "I didn't open anything because I thought they were meant for both of us."

"Where did you find these?"

"The card was next to the flowers, and the wine was in the refrigerator."

Grant picked up the bottle with two fingers and tossed it into the trash compactor. Then, taking a knife from the cutlery drawer, he sliced the envelope open over the kitchen sink. I didn't know what he expected, but the only thing that fell into the sink was a notecard with GG embossed on the front. Inside the message read:

Welcome to the family.

Grayson, Gabriel, Garrett, Gordon, **Gregory**

"How nice," I said, reading over his arm. "Look, they all signed it, and the champagne was nice, too. I may owe them a round of hugs after all."

The notecard slowly crumbled in Grant's fist.

"Carolina, I will only say this once because if I have to worry about it every day together with everything else, I will not live out the month, let alone your pregnancy. One, my brothers are not being 'nice.' They are doing what we always do to outsiders; presenting a united front. This line of names," he said, smoothing the card on the counter, "is a wall. If they were being nice, they would have written separate cards. Two, they were in my office making changes without me, underscoring that it is not, in fact, *my* office because, as a member of the colony, I own nothing. Three, I know I laughed at the thought and that it goes against your gentle, warmhearted nature, but never touch them voluntarily. Treat them cordially, but not kindly. And four, do not go anywhere with any of them alone. Ever. If anyone tries to get you alone, call me, and I will be there. Please say you understand these four things, and you must promise me, Carolina, you will do all I ask of you regarding my brothers."

For the first time, I caught a glimpse of what it cost Grant to love me.

"Of course, I understand, and those are easy promises to make and keep," I said, smoothing the worry lines around his eyes.

"I didn't come here to make your life harder, Grant. I love you. Just tell me how I can make my disruption in your life easier, and I will do it. You and our child are my first priority, and I trust you implicitly to protect us, but please don't let that trust become a burden. Wives are supposed to be partners, you know. You must let me help you whenever I can." I pulled his head down and whispered, "You are a good husband to me, Grant. You must let me try to be a good wife to you."

Lifting me onto the counter, he looked at me, eye to eyes. "Carolina, you are not a disruption in my life. I realized last night that you have become my life. I promise to share more of my concerns with you, my intelligent, loving wife, and maybe together, we can create a place of peace, a sanctuary of our own. Would you like to do that? Create within our shared existence a quiet place where we can be together without any outside loyalties or memories? Until our son joins us, could you be only mine, totally committed to me, loving me as if no one and nothing else exists?"

All the choices I'd made since walking into his office and realizing it was where I belonged came together in the simple answer to his request. I smiled and leaned my forehead against his.

"That is why I'm here, Grant. Not why I came here, but why I've stayed. I've always believed that no matter how brilliant and brave you were, you needed me, and now that we are one, our circle, our peaceful, loving circle, is complete."

He crushed me to him and, for a few wondrous minutes, kissed me as I've only seen in movies; his mouth on mine, one hand under my hair, and the other on my back pressing my heart against his. A new world was created in that kiss. A promise was made and irrefutably accepted, and I knew, even then, what I had chosen and how this kiss would haunt me for the rest of my life.

I had given Grant every part of me: my heart, my body–inside and out–and my mind. However, it wasn't until that kiss of total acceptance and singular devotion that I surrendered my soul, separating myself forever from a normal human existence.

Wedding Gifts – Part II

Grant entered the Lyostians' dining room. "Brothers."

"Grant," they answered simultaneously.

"I thought you were not joining us for breakfast this morning," said Grayson.

"I am not here for breakfast. I am here to find out who tried to poison my wife."

Grayson stood up. "That is a serious accusation, Grant. What is your evidence?"

"Yesterday, someone placed a bottle of champagne in the office refrigerator where I keep food for Carrie. There was every possibility that she would assume I put it there for her. Luckily, she showed it to me first. I want to know, right now, which of you thought alcohol was an acceptable wedding present."

Grant's anger radiated from him in waves. Four brothers were very relieved they did not have to answer him.

The room was silent until Gregory confessed. "Grant, what's the big deal about a glass of champagne? Humans celebrate weddings all the time with champagne, and no one gets sick."

Gordon stepped next to Gregory as Grant turned his attention to him. "Did you also leave the flowers and card?"

Gabriel interrupted. "Grant, we signed the card, and I took it and the flowers to your office. No one was there, so rather than leave them at the door, I went in and saw the vase. I had a few minutes, so I put the flowers in the vase and left the card. I was not there when Gregory came in. Um, did Carrie like the flowers?"

Without taking his eyes from Gregory, Grant answered, "Yes, Gabriel, she did. Thank you all, on behalf of my wife, for your kind welcome. Gordon."

"Grant."

"Is it also your understanding that alcohol is an acceptable beverage for our mothers?"

"No, of course not. Alcohol can cause miscarriages in otherwise successful pregnancies. For all Lyostians, our mothers, and offspring, alcohol is poison in any form."

"Perhaps you can give remedial instruction to your brother, Gregory, so that he fully understands the consequences of his behavior. Or I can."

"No, Grant, I know you're busy. I will take the responsibility to provide that information to Gregory for his review and retention."

"Thank you, Gordon. Gregory."

"Grant."

"Never, and I cannot stress the word strongly enough, do anything for Carrie or attempt to harm her or her child again. I won't be nearly so forgiving next time."

"I'm sorry, Grant, I just didn't think it through. I never meant to hurt Carrie."

"Gregory, this isn't just about her. You have never tried to hide your growing disdain toward our mothers. If you do anything that harms any of them, I will break you into small pieces. So, think it through next time, Gregory, think it through."

"Yes, Grant. Thank you."

They all breathed easier when Grant left the room.

Except Gabriel.

"You gave one of our prospective mothers alcohol?" The entire room turned to stare at Gabriel. "You may feel quite relieved that Grant left you unpunished, but I will not allow you that relief, Gregory. This is not the first time your short-sightedness has affected our mothers' well-being, though this time without permanent consequences. Therefore, Grayson, I request sanctions."

"But Gabriel, I didn't mean to hurt her; I just wanted to—"

"To what, Gregory? Pretend that she isn't carrying one of your brothers? Pretend it was a wedding scene in some movie, and champagne was an appropriate prop? We are few enough as it is, and your fantasy life is not worth the life of one of our own." Again, he said, "I request sanctions."

Grayson nodded at Gabriel and said, "Gregory, regardless of your intentions, your actions could have caused the death of our brother and harm to one of our mothers. Grant was correct in asking that you be reminded of alcohol's serious risks. Gabriel is correct in requesting that you be sanctioned. Gregory, you will spend three nights in the serai. Beginning tonight."

He looked at Gordon. "Perhaps you can get your brother all the information regarding the effects of alcohol from the colony's medical library. It may help him sleep."

When Grant heard of Gregory's punishment, he scanned the building and found Gabriel and Garrett in Garrett's office.

Sanctioned for three days? I did not request that.

I did, said Gabriel. *It was extremely reckless behavior, and the consequences could have been tragic ... for everyone.*

I thought it was a bit harsh, Garrett said, *nothing bad happened.*

And what, exactly, do you think would have happened to Gregory if she thought the wine was from me ... from me! And opened it?

Well, hum, yes, muttered Garrett, *there is always that.*

Yes.

Sensing Grant had left the conversation, Garrett turned to Gabriel and asked, "What do you think Grant would have done if Carrie opened the champagne?"

"And the worst happened?"

"Yes."

"I have no doubt Grant would have torn Gregory apart before we could stop him."

"Really?"

Grant, who had not gone as far as Garrett believed, ended the discussion.

Yes.

Birthday

The sense of timelessness that surrounded me the first morning I awoke in Grant's arms continued as the days melted beautifully into one another. The promises I made were easy to keep. Grant's brothers did not seek me out but were always courteous when they saw me alone. I knew Grant gave them progress reports of my pregnancy, but I doubted he shared any other information about me. The only classes I attended now were ballet and yoga, but the exercises were limited to stretching, simple positions, and meditation. Although I could not always hear his thoughts, I sensed Grant was never far away. Many times, I imagined him just behind the mirrors, watching me, loving me, waiting for me to return to him.

Our weekly examinations continued on Friday mornings on the kitchen counter. It was the perfect height for an examination table, and I suspected that, like similar coincidences, he designed it that way.

On the first Friday in October, I walked into the front room still dressed in my robe.

"You're wearing a kimono to work?"

"No, it's Friday, our examination day."

"Yes, it is, but I cannot examine you here anymore, Carolina. I need equipment I do not have, and do not wish to have, in our home. So please wear something simple, and I will examine you in the office."

The memory of that horrible yellow room where he offered to kill his own son came back to me. Even without directing my thoughts to him, it was almost as if he could read my mind.

"Please don't be scared. I need an ultrasound. Don't you want a picture?"

"Grant, sonogram carts have wheels."

Silence.

It was the usual impasse where he stopped arguing, and I decided. My feelings about his examination room had not changed, but I had learned to trust him. Smiling, I crossed the room and kissed him.

Sorry to be so difficult this morning, Grant; it will only take me a minute to change.

He laughed at my impossible promise. *I'll believe that when I see it.*

It's your fault for buying me so many pretty things. But don't worry; I'll find something simple.

I could help.

I thought you wanted to work today.

Good point. I'll wait here. I felt him watching me as I left the room. A moment later, I heard him click on CNN.

Hoping to be ready by the second commercial break, I slipped into a lavender and cream silk shirt dress that buttoned up the front. It was a bit snug, and I was dismayed to realize that two weeks of eating three human meals a day had taken its toll on my previous slimness. Tying the belt to the side, I walked into the kitchen.

"Grant, if I keep gaining weight, I may have to wear kimonos to work because they will be the only thing that fits."

Expecting a smile, I looked up. Only one thing made his face look that sad.

"Oh no, Grant! Not another one." I ran and wrapped my arms around him. "Is she, is she okay?"

"She is currently sedated and in the operating room. Carolina—"

"No, go, go, she'll need you. Only I know how much. I'll get to the office by myself and meet you there ... later."

He kissed me. Stepping back, he smiled. "You are beautiful in this," he said.

I looked down at my now slightly rumpled dress and thought maybe it wasn't too tight after all.

There were fresh flowers on my desk. I was getting used to being surrounded by beautiful flowers, but Grant had never given me anything that equaled the exquisite Japanese arrangement of orchids and bare willow branches in front of me. An envelope leaned against the alabaster vase with only one word on the envelope: **Wife**.

Inside the embossed card was a short poem.

> Anya dances with a butterfly
> as the angels sing.
> It's your birthday,
> and the world has taken wing.
>
> Forever in my thoughts,
> **Grant**

Was it my birthday? I quickly looked at the calendar on my computer. It *was* my birthday. When had I ever forgotten my birthday? When had *any* woman? Grant's world had neither sun nor moon, so we had developed our own circadian rhythm. The lights in Grant's office and our apartment were necessarily subdued, but the classrooms were always brightly lit, and I found them to be a nice antidote to my shaded living spaces. Although I always knew what day of the week it was, other than routinely scheduling his appointments, dates had little relevance to me. Grant had projected our son's due date for November twenty-first. Only six weeks and five days until I would hold our son in my arms. His was the only birthday that meant anything to me anymore.

My thoughts traveled to Grant's prospective mother in the operating room who didn't have six more weeks until she held this child, or possibly any child, of her own. Acknowledging the fear I carried with me every day, I prayed for the three of them—that she may completely recover, that Grant may someday forgive himself, and peace for Grant's tiniest brother.

With a sigh, I began sorting a stack of files and found another card. Suzanne's handwriting was just as recognizable as Grant's. The card was all flowery, as only Suzanne could be, but her last line, *"When are we going to have lunch?"* made me realize that she had asked me to lunch weeks ago. Despite trying several times, our schedules refused to mesh.

An electronic ping caught my attention as a reminder notice appeared on my computer monitor from GatesWay Spa Salon. Opening it, I was surprised to read I had a hair and manicure appointment at two o'clock. I smiled to myself. Grant was doing everything he could to make my birthday special. I wasn't sure where he was at that moment, but I sent a few grateful and loving thoughts in his direction.

He came in at noon carrying something that smelled delicious. Leaving it on the refrigerator, he sat in our chair. I clicked the remote, locked the door, and went to sit with him.

"Was it bad?" I asked softly.

"It was already bad, Carolina. The correct question would be, 'How bad did it become.'"

"How bad did it become, Grant?"

"The fetal sac had not torn, and she didn't die."

"Those are two good things."

"Yes, and following your admonition to research ways of saving our mothers, we've finally perfected removing just the fetus. It improves their chances for survival astronomically but could still leave her ...."

"Barren."

"I hope not, Carolina. We did everything we could."

"Grant, I'm sorry," I said, resting my head on his shoulder. "I know how hard you try to protect them."

"I only have two left."

"Other than me or including me?"

"Other than you."

"So, you have three left."

"Yes."

"And your brothers?"

"The same. I think Gregory has four. The rest have three or fewer."

I nodded and did the math. His despair was understandable. They had lost two-thirds of their unborn brothers. But beyond that shared sorrow, my heart went out to the forty women whose lives may have been forever altered, although they did not know it yet, and the twenty more who, also unknowing, waited to live, die, or go insane. The numbers kept multiplying in my mind, and the thought of this happening across the country filled me with horror, but more than the horror was the realization that neither Grant nor I could stop it. Caught up in this moment of destiny, we only had each other for comfort, and I prayed it would not destroy us, too.

"What are you thinking about, Carolina?"

Don't you know?

No, your thoughts are clouded. You are not thinking to me.

I nodded and, taking one of his hands in both of mine, asked, "Has any mother died, Grant?"

"No, just as I promised you, but it gets harder each time."

"Because there are fewer of them, each one becomes more precious. I understand."

"You have always thought so much better of me than I deserve," he said. "I still wonder when your complete lack of awareness of my innate selfishness is going to kill you. And, if you will remember, it nearly did. Twice."

"They were not your fault."

"Oh yes, Carolina, both times were a direct result of my overreaching arrogance, as Gregory succinctly phrases it."

"I don't hold you responsible."

"But you should. That's my point."

"But I never will. And that," I said, "is my point."

"What you are not understanding, my wonderful, though incredibly obtuse wife, is that while you are correct that as there are fewer mothers, each one becomes more precious, what nearly kills me every time is because I know, *know*, Carolina, that this one could have been you, or the next one could be you, or maybe we will lose them all, and that includes you."

He laughed bitterly. "Do not think I am so noble as to mourn them as I would mourn you or that I will ever see them as I see you, despite whatever I may have said to the contrary." He wrapped his arms around me and whispered urgently, "I would kill them all if I knew it would spare you."

He threw his head back against the chair as if uttering some terrible truth for which he must now be struck down. I took his face in my hands.

"My darling husband, you are such a liar," I said, kissing his mouth. "Thank you for that."

"What?"

"Grant, I am not obtuse. I just have a different perspective. One you made me understand in the beginning. You love all of the colony's mothers, but me, I am the one you love who loves you. It is not so much that you fear something will happen to me; I know, and you know you can save *me*, but you are worried something will happen to our love. That is what you guard so selfishly, the one thing you are unwilling to share with your brothers. My wonderfully obtuse husband, please stop letting the fear of losing *us* hurt you so much. No matter what happens in the next six weeks, I will never stop loving you, never stop wanting to be with you, and," I thought quickly for something, anything, to change the subject, "never want you to stop tasting me when you think I'm sleeping."

Grant sat up. "You knew that?"

"Yes, I figured it out about a week ago," I said, smiling at him. "Nothing else feels quite like it ... and besides, how else can you lick my ear when your head is next to mine on the pillow? I know your tongue isn't that long." I thought for a second. "Unless, of course, it is. Is it?"

"No. If it were, you would know it by now."

Grant laughed out loud when I blushed, and I had to join him. Only his son's heartbeat sounded more beautiful to me than his laughter.

He put his arms around me. "Thank you."

"You're welcome. It was getting a little intense in here, you know."

"Yes."

"And thank you for my flowers and the poem. I've never seen such beautiful orchids, and no one has written me a poem since middle school, and that one, I believe, started 'roses are red ....'"

"You're welcome. I just wanted to show you how special you are to me."

"You show me that every day, sometimes two or three times a day."

"No, Carolina, truly special."

"You wouldn't know anything about a spa appointment this afternoon, would you?" I looked down at my nails. "I guess I do need a little professional grooming."

"Oh, yes, I do seem to remember *something* about that."

"Well, you see, I'm feeling more special by the minute—and hungry. Do I have enough time to eat?"

"Yes, I will get it for you, and I'll turn up the light so you won't spill anything on that lovely silk."

"But look, Grant," I said, "my clothes are too small." I tugged at the bodice, trying to straighten the buttons. "I need to lose a little weight."

"No."

He helped me to my feet and looked me up and down. "Lunch may have to wait. You can take it to the spa with you."

Taking my hand, he led me to the door of the room that I remembered only as an ugly yellow execution chamber. He opened the door, and I gasped. It was beautiful. Unlike most of Grant's interior designs that flowed into each other, this room was complete in itself. The architectural details were delicate without being feminine, and the walls were painted with murals of meadows where kites flew in the distance as though being held aloft by a late summer's breeze. The long mirror above the counter was now covered with white wicker cabinets. It was still a functioning examination room, but everything medical was stored below the white railing.

Grant closed the door, adjusted the rheostat, and suddenly, I was standing in the middle of a gazebo on a summer's evening. Filtered light fell from the crown molding, and a paddle fan stirred lavender-scented air. I turned and put my arms around his neck.

"Oh, Grant," I whispered, "it's my dreaming time."

"Yes, love, it is. I have to examine you in here now, Carolina, and I wanted you to stop hating it, and I, I wanted to stop hating it, too."

"It's beautiful, Grant ... a place for happier memories." I pretended to fumble with the buttons on my dress. "Can you help with these?"

He laughed soundlessly and lifted me onto the table.

"Yes, I can," he said. Between kisses, we managed to get the buttons undone in less than ten minutes. Then, slipping me out of the dress, he lifted me from the table.

"I am going to stand you up so I can measure you," he said, removing the tape measure from the drawer. I lifted my arms as I had done every Friday for six weeks.

"Hmm," he said, "Okay, arms behind my neck ... stand tall." Standing behind me with his hands beneath my bosoms, he whispered into my ear, "This is my favorite part."

I whispered back, "Mine, too."

Making notes in his file, he smiled up at me. "This is good, Carolina, very good. But you are right; you are going to need larger clothes."

I made a face.

"*Slightly* larger, beautiful clothes. You did not think it was possible to stay slim *and* be pregnant, did you?"

"No," I said, "I just wanted to stay beautiful for you."

His doctor's voice returned. "Slim and beautiful are not synonymous, Carolina. I told you that you were beautiful the first day you walked into my office. You will not regain all the weight you lost, probably only about another 7 to 10 pounds, and you will lose most of that when you give birth. But you must keep eating three meals a day until you stop nursing. So, in about a year's time, you can resume eating according to the nutritional guidelines Garrett prepared for you. But not," he said seriously, "before then."

Reclining on the examination table, the warmed bell of the stethoscope gently slid across my skin. Watching his face, I knew the moment he found the baby's heartbeat; his smile gave him away every time.

"May I hear, please?"

"Of course," he said, handing me the earpieces.

Once again, I listened to the rhythmic whisper of our son's beating heart. Grateful tears stung my eyes.

"Thank you, Grant."

"For letting you listen?"

I reached toward him. "No, for giving me something so wonderful to listen to."

His hands were warm on my skin, and I had missed him all morning.

"How much time before my spa appointment?"
"Twenty minutes."
I tugged gently on the lapel of his lab coat.
"It's only three minutes away."

Birthday – Part II

I barely made it to the spa on time.

"Carrie Taylor at two," I said to the receptionist.

"Happy birthday, Carrie," she said, smiling warmly. "Come this way."

She led me to a corner station near the back of the salon where a small porcelain vase held a sprig of willow and a single orchid blossom.

Before closing the privacy screen, she said, "Just slide out of your dress and put this on."

Turning toward her, I expected to see one of GatesWay's teal and white wraps. Instead, she held a stunning silk kimono with a pattern of willow branches and orchid blossoms identical to my birthday flowers.

Seeing my surprise, she explained, "It was delivered by messenger this morning." Then, she handed me a card.

For Caroline at 2:00 from her husband.

"The flowers arrived about an hour later." She eyed the fine silk. "He must love you very much."

I ducked my head so she couldn't see the tears. "Yes, yes, he does."

"You're quite lucky, you know."

"I know."

Slipping into the kimono, I thought to him the bursting feelings of my grateful heart. In all the excitement, I had pretty much lost my appetite until I opened the container and discovered shrimp salad ringed with avocado slices. I hoped there would be enough time to finish it, but the stylist walked in after a few delicious bites.

"Happy birthday, Carrie," he said, adding another orchid to the bouquet. "My name is Evan." He noticed the container in my hands. "Would you like me to return in a few minutes after you've finished your lunch?"

"No, you're busy. I'll just eat when I can."

"That's fine," he said, hesitating for a moment. "Usually, we let our clients tell us how they would like their hair styled; however, your husband requested a very specific hair design. I'm supposed to offer you the option."

"Of ...?"

"Letting me do it his way or asking what you would prefer."

"Evan, my husband is a brilliant designer, and I would never second guess him. Truthfully," I said thoughtfully, "I suggest you do it exactly as he requests, not one hair out of place or one millimeter shorter. He can be ... difficult."

Evan's blue eyes never blinked. "Yes, ma'am. I understand. It's fairly simple; just a matter of angles and the separation of color. No problem."

"And Evan."

"Yes, ma'am?"

"Don't show it to me until you're finished. Please."

"Yes, ma'am. I understand."

"Thank you."

I soon learned that everyone had been given specific instructions; even the manicurist did not ask what color polish I wanted on my fingernails. As each one entered, I was wished a happy birthday, and another orchid or a willow branch was added to the vase.

The facial was followed by the cosmetician with her fishing tackle box of colorful powders, tubes, pencils, and brushes. This was unexpected. I had never worn much makeup, and living indoors for a month had lightened my complexion such that any added color made me look like a clown. Except for a bit of mascara, I had given it up altogether.

"Happy birthday, Carrie," she said, adding a willow sprig to the bouquet. "My name is Melanie, and I am here to accentuate your natural beauty a bit."

"Is that what he told you to say?" I laughed.

"No, it's what he told me to do. I was giving you fair warning in case you thought you would leave here looking like a movie star."

I smiled to myself. *Feeling like a movie star is a thousand times better than looking like one. Thank you, Grant.*

Melanie had just finished when Evan returned to wash out the processed color. "Wow, Mellie, good job!"

"Thanks, but it was easy."

"You always say that."

"It always is."

"Hang around; I want you to see her hair."

"Sure, I'll be in the back."

Evan took great care not to disturb Melanie's work while rinsing out the color. Then he started cutting my hair. I thought Grant liked my hair long, but the strands dropping by my face were inches longer than I expected.

"Um, Evan, my husband didn't ask you to shave my head, did he?"

Evan mimicked me perfectly. "Evan, my husband is a brilliant designer, and I would never second guess him. Truthfully, I suggest that you do it exactly as he requests, not one hair out of place or one millimeter shorter. He can be ... difficult." Then he laughed.

"To answer your question, no, but it is layered. I told you it was all about angles. Don't worry, it's perfect for you. Together with Melanie's artistry, you're going to be a knockout. Trust us."

"I trust him, Evan."

I glanced at the polish on my fingernails. Like my toes, it was opalescent, all colors and no color depending on the light. After a few minutes with the blow dryer and a round brush, Evan turned me toward the mirror.

That woman could not be me. I had to lift my hand to confirm it was my reflection in the mirror.

Parted in the middle, my hair was cut into three distinct planes. The top layer was cut in seemingly random sections at slightly different angles; lightened to ash blonde, it glinted like silver under the light. The second layer, almost golden, was cut identically but with slightly wider angled sections, so they did not blend. The final layer, a shimmering mixture of ash and gold, curved inward slightly above my shoulders.

I stared at the woman in the mirror. My hair resembled nothing so much as sunlight on a waterfall. Beneath it, my face, pale with lightly tinted cheekbones, and my eyes, accented to appear pure green, looked otherworldly.

Is this ... is this the woman he sees when he looks at me? I was suddenly surrounded by him as though he was cloaking me with his confidence and strength by lending me some of his beauty.

I couldn't speak. I could only stare.

"Um, Carrie, do you like it? Are you all right?"

"I'm beautiful."

"Yeah, well, duh."

I touched my reflection on the glass. "He loves me so much."

"That can't be too hard," he laughed.

I smiled. "Thank you. I have to go home. He's waiting for me."

"Just a second. I need to call Melanie, or she will never forgive me."

"You have one second."

Melanie must have been standing near the door because she appeared as soon as she heard her name. She stopped when she saw me.

"I've got to take your picture."

I put my hands in front of my face. "No. This is only for him."

"But I thought it was *your* birthday."

"Yes, but I've had a lot of birthdays. This one is special because he remembered," I said as I stood up. "Thank you. You're both wonderful."

Twirling around, I picked up my vase of orchids and walked to the lobby.

Watching her leave, Melanie asked, "I like the cut; when can you do that to my hair?"

"I can't cut anyone else's hair like that."

"You can't … or you won't?"

"I've already shredded the instructions as requested."

"Why would you do that?"

"How much did he pay you for this gig?"

She was silent.

"Right. So don't ask me any questions, either."

Waving an envelope and holding my dress, the receptionist stopped me on my way out.

"Mrs. Taylor? Your husband sent this note."

I opened it to find an embossed card.

> Carolina – Please go directly home.
> I'll join you at 6:30.
> Yours always, Grant

"Thank you."

"You look enchanting. You know, when you came in, I said you were lucky, but now I think he's the lucky one."

"Thank you, but you were right the first time." I took my dress and walked to the main elevator.

Standing with my back to the hall, I heard a voice behind me.

"A little informal this evening, aren't we?"

Turning, I saw Gregory leaning against the wall with a wolfish grin on his handsome face—a face that became as white as his lab coat when he recognized the woman he was ogling.

"Please forgive my attire, Gregory. I was just on my way to meet Grant."

"Carrie, I'm sorry. I had no idea that was you. You're, you're beautiful."

"Pregnant women are, I'm told … often."

"Yes, but this—"

"Is just plaster and paint, Gregory. GatesWay has an excellent salon."

"They aren't that good."

The elevator chimed. "Apparently, they are," I said, quickly stepping into the lift. "They fooled you."

As the elevator began its descent, I took my first real breath since he'd appeared behind me.

Gregory was still staring at the closed elevator doors when Gordon joined him.

"Who were you talking to?"

"Just another client," he said, then quickly corrected himself. "One of our esteemed female clients to whom we owe our livelihood and the future survival of our species."

"One of these days, you will have to explain why that comes so hard for you."

"I'll tell you now," Gregory said bitterly. "I'm tired of fawning over these women who, at any minute, can expose us and get us captured or killed. Plus, they are not even ours. We can't enjoy them, so there is no upside to the fact that every one of them is a living threat to our colony.

I understand their importance, so I'll act the part, but I see no reason to respect or trust them."

"Well, you better hope you can trust Carrie not to tell Grant you were leering at her."

"You saw that?"

"What you see, I see, brother. It's just that most of the time, I don't look. Gordon paused for a moment, then said, "She probably won't say anything or think about it.

"Oh, damn. I forgot he'd implanted her. If she even thinks—"

"Exactly. I know it was an honest mistake, but for safety's sake, if I were you, I'd stay out of Grant's way for a while."

"Yeah. I know."

Birthday – Part III

I had completely forgotten my encounter with Gregory by the time I got home. I set the vase of flowers on the kitchen counter and rushed into the bedroom. Hanging from the door was a long, zippered black bag with a white ribbon tied to an envelope. I removed the card.

Open after bathing.

Excited, I wrapped my hair in a towel and showered quickly. Then, I brushed my teeth, reapplied my lipstick, smoothed my hair, and returned to the bedroom. I unzipped the bag. Taped to a layer of white tissue paper was another card.

Happy Birthday, Carolina. I adore you.

I put the card with the other ones I'd received from him that day and gently pulled back the tissue paper. My hand froze in midflight. There, suspended on a satin hanger, a black and silver sheath shimmered like a moonlit river. A pocket at the bottom of the bag contained black and silver stiletto heels and black stockings. In the corner of the pocket, I found a small jewelry box encasing a pair of black diamond earrings.

I slipped the dress carefully over my head. Gliding on a stream of air, it settled perfectly over the curves of my body. Open from the waist to the neck in the back, the dress fastened with a single jet button at the top. Taking only a moment to admire them, I put the earrings on and, trying not to wobble in the heels, started toward the door. Something glimmered in the bag as I passed it. Curious, I reached in and removed a long matching cape.

It was beautiful, but why would I need a cape? *Where was he taking me?*

Believing there was a patio or balcony somewhere in the building, I put the cape over my arm and walked through the nursery. The front room was dark except for a dimmed spotlight directly above the door. Although I could not see him, I had no doubt Grant was sitting in the shadows. Feeling his gaze and knowing my hair would shine in the light, I gently shook my head. Smiling, I sent him the most grateful thoughts any wife, any woman, could feel on her birthday.

I heard his footsteps coming toward me and gasped when he walked into the light. I expected him to dress up, but I was totally unprepared for the sight of Grant Gates wearing a tuxedo.

I took a step back.

"Oh, Grant, you ... you look ... magnificent."

He smiled and shook his head. "You, obviously, have not seen a mirror. Have you?"

"No, I thought I was late, so I came right out."

"Let me show you something," he said, taking my hand as he led me into the dressing room.

"Do not move."

The lights came up a moment later. Once again, I felt disembodied and unrecognizable. I couldn't see myself, only a stunning young woman who looked out of a halo of silver water with wide green eyes. A moment later, he was standing beside me.

"Grant, this, this can't be me."

"It is exactly the way I've always seen you. I just needed a little help to share my vision with you."

"But I'm beautiful."

"Yes, love. Just as I have always told you." He took my hand again. "We must go now, or we will be late."

"Late for what?"

"Our dinner reservation."

He fastened the cape at my throat, and we took the elevator down to the garage level. A black limousine waited with windows tinted as black as the car.

The chauffeur opened the door. I was excited, scared, and could not remember ever being happier. This evening surpassed every celebration in my entire life combined. I was as thrilled as I could ever imagine, and the best part was that Grant sat next to me, calmly holding my hand like we did this every night.

The limousine smelled of leather and luxury. Illuminated only by the muted lights of the city flashing beyond the car's windows, it was as though I was being whisked away like a princess in a fairytale. Wanting to share my feelings, I leaned against his shoulder and looked up at his face. My heart caught in my throat. In the flickering streetlights, Grant's face was ashen, and he was breathing in short gasps.

"What's wrong, Grant?"

"We are so far away I can barely hear them, Carolina," he whispered.

"Is it the car or the distance?"

"Both, I think."

"But it didn't bother you when you came to get me in the ambulance."

"I had a driver with me. Between the two of us, we could stay connected. But you are only connected to me, and I ... I cannot hear them."

As much as he tried to conceal it, I could sense the panic in his voice.

Moving to the seat next to the driver's window, I tapped the glass. The chauffeur immediately lowered the window.

"Yes, Mrs. Gates," he said.

"Please turn around and take us back. I'm feeling quite carsick."

"I'm sorry to hear that, Mrs. Gates. Is there anything I can do?"

No, Carolina.

I looked at him and smiled. *Remind me to tell you later how much I truly, dearly love you.* "Just as quickly as you can, safely, please."

"Yes, ma'am."

"Oh, do you have a phone up there?"

"Yes, ma'am."

"Please call the restaurant and cancel our reservation."

"Yes, ma'am."

"You are very kind."

"Thank you." He closed the window, and I moved next to Grant.

We'll be home in a few minutes.

I am so terribly sorry, Carolina; I could feel your excitement about going out.

No, Grant, I was excited about going out with you.

Is this what humans mean when they say, "All dressed up and no place to go?"

My sweet, wonderful husband, we have the best place to go.

Home?

I took his hands in mine. *Yes, Grant. Our home.* I noticed he was breathing more normally. *Can you hear them now?*

Not entirely, but better.

I knew he was counting the minutes as we neared the colony. I couldn't imagine what it would have been like sitting across a table with him in such emotional turmoil. Wanting to give me what he thought I desired while needing to be connected to the colony, trying with every fiber of his being to be in two places at once. And I knew, right then, that struggle was going to kill him.

It was impossible to pretend that I could return him to his brothers, have the baby, and leave. That time had passed. Determined to make our life together easier for him, I decided to love him more, depend on him less, and put his happiness first. Holding his hand in the dark, I counted the minutes with him.

Grant could not believe it had gotten this bad. When he was younger, he could go an entire day or longer without being connected to a colony, and it did not bother him ... too much. He should have chosen a restaurant closer to the facility; there were a least a dozen by the mall, but he didn't want to risk running into anyone she once knew but would no longer recognize, nor did he want to risk being seen by one of his clients, many of whom knew Carolina was his assistant. His reasoning was sound, but he had overestimated his strength. He would not attempt that again.

When the car arrived back at the garage, the worst was over. The chauffeur opened the door, and Grant stepped out. Giving me his arm, he helped me exit the car. I stood up and pushed out my stomach a little bit.

"I am so sorry, darling," I said to Grant, passing my hand over the front of my dress. "Your son is not being very nice to his mother tonight."

"A boy, huh?" The chauffeur nudged Grant, "They can be harder to carry than girls, I've heard."

Without responding, Grant paid the chauffeur and walked toward me. Returning to the driver's side of the car, the chauffeur waved.

"May all your problems be little ones. Little ones, get it?" Then, laughing at his own joke, he closed the car door and drove away.

Grant swept me up in his arms as we walked back into the building.

"Afraid I can't walk in these heels?"

"No, well, maybe, but I can be gracious, too."

He carried me all the way to our door, holding me while I punched in the key code. Without letting me go, he pushed open the door, and we sat on the sofa together.

"You didn't have to be so nice to the driver," he said.

"Yes, I did."

"Why?"

"He called me 'Mrs. Gates.' It was like getting another birthday gift."

"Oh, thank you for reminding me. There is one more gift." He reached into his jacket and handed me a small black bag.

It was an evening bag that matched my dress. "Oh, Grant, it's perfect. Thank you so much. I love it."

He looked at me for several moments.

"I love you with my whole heart, Carolina. Every time you do something like that, it takes me so completely by surprise that I become slightly breathless when I realize how very dear you are to me." He lifted my chin and looked into my eyes. "The gift is not the bag, my love; the gift is in the bag."

"You mean there's more?"

"It *is* still your birthday."

Inside the black silk purse was a small red velvet pouch. Loosening the ribbons, I tilted it, and a square pendant on a silvery chain fell into my palm. Peering at it closely, I noticed that the pendant had writing on it.

"Grant, may I please look at this in more light?"

"Of course," he said, putting on his glasses.

I turned on the light above the counter. Other than 24k stamped on the back, there was no actual writing on the pendant, only concentric circles surrounding a single diamond. When I recognized it as a sky map, I gripped the countertop.

This was not a drawing or a hurried sketch. Engraved in gold was our wedding date. *Grant, catch me.* I tried to hold on, but everything went dark.

"Carolina, Carolina."

I heard Grant singing my name and slowly opened my eyes.

"There you are," he said, smiling at me. "You know, I had that planned a little better in the restaurant."

"Really? Better than that?"

"Oh, yes."

He looked at me steadily. "Tell me, birthday girl, how much of your lunch did you eat today?"

Uh–oh, I was busted. "Most of it, um, it was quite delicious, too."

"Most of it." He looked at me, waiting.

"Well, maybe I didn't eat *most* of it."

"Yes. So, I think, by the distinct look of guilt on your face, that you did not eat much of it at all. Carolina, I thought we were not going to have this conversation again."

"I know, but there was just so much going on today." I traced a heart on the front of his jacket. "Don't scold me tonight, Grant, please," I said, looking up at him through my lashes.

"All right, but I will get you something to eat. Think you can stand up for a few minutes without keeling over?"

Laughing, I said, "I'll try."

"Thank you."

I started walking toward the bedroom.

"Where are you going?"

"To put my cape away and freshen up. I'll be right back."

When I returned, only the softest light from the crystal chandelier brightened the room. My orchids were in the center of the dining table, surrounded by tall and flat dishes. He stood as I approached, pulled out my chair, and then sat down opposite me.

"This is beautiful."

I reached my hand across the table for his. Entwining his long fingers in mine, he brought my hand to his lips and kissed it lightly.

"Please eat, Carolina. I promise you all the romance you can stand, but you must eat first."

"All the romance I can stand with you, Grant? The world won't last that long."

"You aren't eating if you are talking."

This better?

Only if you are chewing.

I couldn't help but smile. He could be so serious sometimes. I ate everything and pledged never to miss lunch again.

I stood to help him remove the dishes, but he gently pushed me back into my chair. A few minutes later, only the flowers, the tea tray, and a single candle remained on the table. Then, standing beside me, he gently took my hand in his. Holding it against his lips, his eyes never left mine as he slowly got down on one knee. My heart began to pound in my chest, and I could not move my eyes from his face.

"Carolina, I told you once that I lose track of sequences when I am around you. I like to think that in a different world, you and I would have conformed to the prevailing social traditions, and it might have been a little easier for us. Not better, for nothing is better than what we have, just a little less difficult. However, I no longer wish our marriage to be a charade. I call it a charade because I gave you no choice." Taking my hand in both of his, he said, "Carolina, will you be my wife and allow me the honor of loving you for the remainder of our existence?"

At that moment, I realized that Grant had been courting me all day with flowers, notes, personal attention, and lovely gifts. Designing the entire day and evening to right a wrong, he believed, according to his code of chivalry, that he had committed. Remembering my decision in the limousine, I answered, "Yes, Grant, I will marry you, and yes, I promise to love, honor, and cherish you for the rest of our existence."

"And our child, Carolina? Do you promise to love our child?"

"I already love him."

Grant bent over my hand and kissed it. "Thank you, Carolina. You've made me very happy."

"You are truly mine, Grant?"

He pressed my hand against his heart.

"As much as I can belong to anyone, Carolina, I am yours."

I touched my forehead to his. *I'm here.*

Yes.

He stood and reached into his pocket. The pendant engraved with the planetary alignment of our wedding day gleamed in his hand. Looking down at it, he said, "I hoped you would like this."

My hand closed over his, and I stood next to him.

"How could I not love it? I'm sorry I fainted. I was just overwhelmed by everything it symbolized to me, and at the same moment, I realized what our son, our relationship, and I mean to you. Those feelings were quite powerful because, Grant," I whispered, "they were the *same*. Seeing how beautifully you transformed those feelings into something real and permanent literally took my breath away."

I turned around so he could fasten the pendant.

"Now and forever, Grant, this will be the happiest birthday of my life."

"I can only share one birthday with you. Didn't you think I would celebrate it the best I could?"

His hands caressed my neck as they moved from the necklace to the button at the back of my dress. Lifting me into his arms, the discarded silk fell to the floor, shimmering and fluid like a forgotten pool of starlight.

Dan

"Verity Investigative Services, how can I help you?"

"I need you to find my wife."

"How long has she been missing?"

"Since September twentieth."

"Sir, that was nearly three weeks ago. When did you realize she was gone?"

"When she didn't come home on the twenty-first."

"Okay," Travis made a note on his yellow pad. "Do you have any idea where she might be?"

"I know exactly where she is."

"Then, sir, she is not missing."

"If she isn't home where she belongs, then she's missing."

"If you know where she is, why are you calling us?"

"Investigate why she won't come home."

Listening on the speakerphone, Tory rolled her eyes and held up a piece of paper: *No more domestic cases!*

"Sir, why haven't *you* asked her why she won't come home?"

"Because she won't talk to me! She won't take my phone calls or answer my emails. So, I need you to talk to her."

Tory shook her head.

"Sir, at this point, you need a lawyer, not an investigator."

"No. If I get a lawyer, she will think I want a divorce. I don't want a divorce. I want her to come home, and I want you to find out why she won't and if she's okay."

"Why wouldn't she be okay?"

"Because she lives where she works. She never even told me she changed jobs! I took flowers to the university, and they told me she didn't work there anymore. Hadn't worked there for weeks! Do you know how stupid I felt? She's my wife, and I don't know where she works. When I asked my son about it, he told me she was living at the spa ... fitness ... whatever center where she works now. Apparently, she has a room there or something, and she never leaves."

Tory's eyes widened, and Travis sat up. "What do you mean? How do you know she never leaves?"

"One, she never came home, not even to get her car, so I know she isn't driving anywhere. Two, I sit in the parking lot after work, watching the door. She never comes in ... she never goes out."

"Maybe there is another entrance."

"Only the service entrance, and from where I park, I can watch both at the same time."

"What is the name of this fitness center?"

"GatesWay. It's by the mall."

Travis entered "GatesWay" into his computer. Then, looking at Tory with alarm, he turned the monitor in her direction. Two of their missing persons had connections to GatesWay Fitness Clinic and Health Spa. Tory nodded.

"Do you know what she does or who she works for?" he asked.

"No."

"We charge $200 an hour plus expenses."

"Whatever. Just find out if she's okay and why she won't come home."

"Again, what makes you think she's not okay? Specifically."

"Yesterday was October fifth, her birthday, and I sent pink roses, her favorite, you know? Then the florist called and said they were refused. Carrie wouldn't do that. It wouldn't even occur to her to do that. Throw them in the garbage, maybe, but refuse them? No, that isn't anything she would do. So, anyway, can you guys check on her?"

Tory put her hand close to her mouth and whispered, "This could be more than another domestic dispute ... maybe there is a connection to our other clients. Request a thousand-dollar retainer and make an appointment for next week. Tell him to bring a picture."

Travis nodded.

"Are you available to stop by our offices on Monday at 3:30 with a recent photograph of your wife?"

"Yeah, I can be there."

Victoria slipped another piece of paper toward him. *Appointment calendar?*

"If your wife had an appointment calendar or planner, bring that as well."

"There's one on the kitchen wall."

"That will be helpful. Our retainer is $1,000."

"Fine. I just need to know, you know?"

"Yes. Your name, sir?"

"Daniel M. Taylor."

Hanging up the phone with one hand, Dan picked up his glass of Jack Black on ice with the other. His eyes scanned the wall opposite the refrigerator. Suspended from the same hook for ten years, the carefree student faces on Carrie's annual university calendar mocked his confusion. She called it the "family" calendar and highlighted the holidays, drew stars on birthdays, and wrote in Brendan's football practices, track competitions, games, parties, and haircuts, but it wasn't a "family" calendar. She never forgot anything. And, because she didn't forget, Brendan never had to remember. The calendar was kept for him. So he would know where she was when she wasn't home.

Dan couldn't remember the last time he looked at it.

Tearing it from the wall, he sat at the bare kitchen table. Unsure of what he was looking for, he ignored the university co-eds grinning up at him from photo montages and slowly flipped the pages. Scanning the last few months, he realized how little he knew of her life. "Last Day" was written in pencil on the 20th of August. Why was August 13th circled and left blank? What was a "spa reward?" Numbers with minus signs and happy faces decorated every other week back to the beginning of May. Finally, it was beginning to make sense. Completely surrounded by stars and asterisks was the notation "GatesWay @ noon."

Remembering how happy she'd been that morning, he turned to stare in the direction of their bedroom.

Slipping into her shoes, Carrie smiled brightly at him.

"Dan, I'm going to visit a gym today. If it's not too expensive, would we be interested in a family membership?"

"Why? Brendan plays football, and I don't need to lose any weight."

"I know, but their website says they have elliptical trainers and weight equipment. It could be fun; there's a sauna and, I think, a whirlpool ... all kinds of things to do."

"Like what? I'm not into hanging around people who like sweating on treadmills. And, besides, I get enough exercise working around here as it is. But you go ahead, Carrie, have fun."

Have fun.

She wasn't having fun the last time he saw her.

Her tear-streaked face rose up before him, and he poured another drink. Tearing the calendar in half, he used it as a coaster for the rest of the day.

Verity Investigations

Victoria contemptuously lifted the bourbon-stained and rippled stack of glossy paper from her desk where Dan had tossed it.

"What is this?"

"You asked for her calendar."

She handed it to the tall, thin man standing next to her. "Travis, please see what you can make of this." Looking back at Dan, she said, "I hope the photograph is in better shape."

Frozen in time, the three smiling faces in the brass frame looked up at her. The handsome young man in the navy–blue graduation gown was flanked on either side by two smiling adults. Dan, she recognized immediately, then Victoria looked carefully at the woman. Although lovely in her yellow dress, it was obvious she was a bit plump. So, yes, joining GatesWay made sense, and she looked happy, not troubled or preoccupied.

"This was what, late May, early June? Do you have anything more recent?"

"My son just sent me this."

Landing face up on her desk, Victoria could not believe it was the same woman.

"When was this taken?"

"Right after Labor Day weekend when my son moved into his college dorm room."

Just before she left, thought Victoria.

A check for $1,000 fluttered downward, obscuring the photograph.

"How soon before she comes home?"

"We will get back to you in two weeks. If she returns in the meantime, please let us know."

"TWO WEEKS?"

Victoria brushed the check to the side. Looking once more at the beautiful woman surrounded by butterflies, she stood up.

"Yes, two weeks. First, Mr. Taylor, you are not our only client. Second, I have to investigate. That means I need to get in there, find her, meet her, and interview people who know her while trying to earn her trust so she will tell me what is going on. Third, I am not saying she will be home in two weeks; I am saying I will have a report for you in two weeks."

Dan stared into Victoria's resolute expression. Finding no help there, he turned toward the door. "I'll be back in two weeks."

Victoria was still standing when the door slammed shut.

Travis walked over to her. "I can't believe you took this case. Why didn't you just tear up his check and tell him to go to hell?"

Victoria picked up the two photographs and handed them to Travis. "That's why."

Bringing the photographs closer to the light, Travis looked from one to the other several times. He reached across the table for a magnifying glass and asked, "How long?"

"Three, maybe four months."

"Is that even possible?"

"That's what I am going to find out."

Victoria's Interview

My living at GatesWay Health Clinic and Spa did not cause a ripple, question, or whisper. No one noticed I never left at the end of the day, just as I had never noticed that the doctors and interns always seemed to be at the facility regardless of the day or time. The exercise classes, salon appointments, and client meetings went on as they always had. The illusion of normalcy Grant had created within the tall granite building was crucial to the survival of everyone—including the staff and clientele—and I did whatever was necessary to protect it.

Grant's eleven-thirty appointment arrived on time. Watching her enter the office, I thought she may have misunderstood that the meeting was for a fitness consultation. Already thin, fit, and perfectly groomed, she belonged in our advertisements, not our exercise rooms.

"Good morning, Ms. Torrance. It's lovely to meet you. I am Carrie Taylor, Dr. Grant's assistant. Please sit down."

She appeared startled and looked at me closely with a sense of recognition, but I was quite sure we had not met before. She was not someone you would easily forget. She was classically beautiful, with soft dark brown hair curling around her shoulders that perfectly framed her porcelain complexion. Her almond-shaped eyes were a stunning French blue, and when she spoke, her voice had a charming Southern inflection.

Her eyes moved quickly to my left hand and then back to my face.

"Pleased to meet you, Ms. Taylor. I've heard so much about GatesWay that I wanted to come in and see it for myself."

"Are you looking for a fitness clinic, Ms. Torrance?"

"Yes, and please call me Tory; everyone does."

"Only if you will call me Carrie."

"Thank you. What I need, Carrie, is somewhere I can de-stress—if you know what I mean. I've recently moved here and need to start working out again. I prefer exercises that aren't too strenuous, and there are classes mentioned in your brochure that seem to mesh with those I'm used to taking."

"Yes, Tory, I understand. I'm sure we can arrange some interesting classes for you, but if you decide to join, please know that GatesWay is a fitness and health clinic. In addition to exercise classes, we also offer instruction in visualization and meditation techniques."

"That all sounds perfectly wonderful to me, Carrie. Where do I sign up?"

I took the green and blue folders from the credenza. "You sign up right here, Tory." I handed her the revised two-page questionnaire. The clinic didn't need as much information on their new clients anymore.

Motioning her to the small desk, I stood to prepare the refreshments for her interview with Grant.

Tory sat down at the desk.

"Carrie?"

"Yes, Tory."

"Do you take classes here? I mean, are there any you especially recommend?"

"Well, yes, I take beginning ballet and yoga, which I think are great. But your program designer, Dr. Garrett, will arrange classes specific to your needs and work schedule."

"Thank you."

"My pleasure, Tory. Dr. Grant will be with you in a few moments to review your application and discuss any concerns you may have."

Smiling triumphantly, Tory sat at the desk, removed a slender gold pen from her purse, and began completing the form.
Like taking candy from a baby, she thought.

Travis was waiting for her when she returned to the office.
"Did you see her?"
"Yes."
"Tell me everything, saving your impressions of her for last."
He closed his eyes and leaned back in his chair as Victoria described the elegance of the waiting room and her interviews with Dr. Grant and the program designer.
"The rooms are all nicely decorated, the staff organized and professional. It felt more like visiting someone's beautiful home than an appointment at a fitness clinic."
"Now, Carrie Taylor."
"That's where we got extraordinarily lucky. She's my program consultant's assistant, and I managed to get into two of her classes."
"Details, please, Tory."
"Even lovelier than the photograph. Her hair is different, blonde and layered, and she seems kind, honest, and intelligent."
"Coerced in any way?"
"No. She was efficient and unconcerned about her surroundings, and her relationship with the doctor she works for is professional but relaxed. I observed her carefully; her eyes were clear, and her hands and voice were steady and calm. I tried throwing her some curveballs, but her responses were genuine and humorous."
"So ...?"
"So, she's happy."

"Then why doesn't she leave?"

"I'm not so sure she doesn't."

"What do you mean?"

"While I was investigating, I 'accidentally' pressed the bottom button on the elevator, and it took me to an underground garage. The attendant would not let me enter because he said it was for doctors and facility residents only."

"Good, we've ascertained that she's okay. One objective down, one to go. Now we need to find out why she won't go home."

"Really, Travis? You've met him. Don't we already know why?"

"No, we don't. She's been married to him for nearly twenty years. So why did she leave now? And why hasn't she called an attorney?"

He thought for a moment. "Wedding ring?"

"No."

He nodded. "So, her husband wasn't the reason."

"The reason for what?"

"This," he said, pointing to the two photographs lying side by side. "You see, Tory, the commitment required to effect this degree of change requires a reason. We need to find out who, or what, inspired it and whether she is being held captive—emotionally, mentally, or physically. Only then will we know why."

The Tunnels

"Gregory."

"Gordon."

"You can come out of hiding now."

"I have not been hiding."

"Right."

"But suppose I was supervising the work in the tunnels for a specific reason; why would you say now is the time to, um, resurface?"

"I just saw Grant, and he didn't ask where you were. So, either he doesn't care or already knows, in which case we wouldn't be having this conversation. I guess she didn't say anything to him."

"Hmm, I wonder why?"

"Well, my guess is she didn't want to make him angry."

"Why would *she* care about his anger?"

"Like *you* have to ask."

"Yes, but he wouldn't kill *her*."

Gordon looked down and moved some pebbles with his shoe. "Perhaps, but who would he hold responsible if he did?"

"Maybe I'll just stay down here another day or so."

"Um, hmm."

Victoria

At the end of her second week of classes, Victoria played the tape of her most recent conversation with Carrie for Travis.

Do you live close by? It was Victoria's voice.

No, I live here.

That's lucky, no commute.

Yes, it is.

If they have apartments, maybe I could rent one. I've been trying to find a bigger place.

Well, this may not work for you. They don't have apartments, more like rooms where they've renovated some space. I can see if any are available if you'd like.

How did you get one?

Carrie's voice became softer. *I was just in the right place at the right time.*

Do you like living here?

Oh, yes, I love it here. I work full–time, take classes .... It's like a dorm you never have to leave.

Don't you want to leave?

No. Not ever.

Why?

Oh, Tory, it's like a dream come true. Haven't you ever just been somewhere and, from the first moment you walked in, thought this is where I'm supposed to be at this point in my life?

Yes, the college I attended. From the first moment I stepped onto UD's campus, I knew it was where I belonged, but don't you miss your family?

Family?

Yes, someone, I think it was Suzanne, told me you had a husband and a son. Wasn't it hard to leave your family?

Tory, I didn't leave them; they left me. I have new responsibilities now. I'm needed here.

"And then she smiled the sweetest smile I've ever seen. I have never smiled like that in my life. It's the kind of smile you see in religious paintings: happy, contented, and fulfilled. And," she said after a short pause, "I feel that someone is not telling us the truth. Why did she say her family left her? Was she abandoned? We need to arrange a meeting with her husband."

"She sounds kind of dazed. Are you sure you didn't see any evidence of brainwashing?"

"No, her eyes are focused and clear. I was also concerned about the responses to the questions regarding her family, but evidently, when she left Dan, she left that life completely."

"Perhaps. This Suzanne, how well does she know her?"

"Suzanne worked with Carrie at the university and has known her very well for about five years."

"And she sees no change in her manner?"

"Only that Carrie seems less stressed and a lot healthier. Living at GatesWay apparently agrees with her."

"But to say she 'never' wants to leave sounds a little too complacent. Who says that? Did you get the impression that she *couldn't* leave?"

"Absolutely not. Travis, this isn't the only conversation I've had with Carrie. She's just a very gentle soul. She works, exercises, and interacts with everyone on a very genuine level. Her mannerisms are not remote or robotic; she's not coerced or fearful. Instead, she's enthusiastic and happy. She seems knowledgeable about the new stores and restaurants at the mall and is up on current events. The reason this conversation is important is that she says she didn't leave her family, her family left her, and I want to ascertain the truth of that statement. If Dan abandoned Carrie, I am not wasting any more time trying to extricate her from a life that makes her happy just because he's having second thoughts. Please call and schedule a fifteen-minute surveillance update."

Travis glanced at his computer monitor. "Already set for Thursday at 4:30."

"Perfect."

Grayson listened to Garrett's report. *It had been a nice day up to now*, he thought as he tilted his head and asked Grant to join him in his office.

Without knocking, Grant entered the office and sat down.

"How can I help you, Grayson?"

"I'm concerned about one of your new clients."

"Who?"

"Victoria Torrance."

"Yes. Beautiful and intelligent. Perhaps a little too old for our purposes."

"Did Garrett talk to you about her?"

"No. Grayson, what is the point?"

"There's no reason for her to be here."

"Grayson, she is a woman. We offer services to women. She is our demographic."

"Look, Garrett became suspicious because she's already at the ultimate weight and BMI ratio, and when he gave her the initial welcome package, she put everything in her purse without asking a single question. Plus, she's been observed spending more time talking with the staff than attending classes. So, Garrett thinks, and I agree, that she's a reporter, investigator, or working undercover for someone."

"And you want me to ...?"

"Get rid of her."

"We cannot resign a client without thirty days' notice. Our assignment here is nearly complete. We cannot risk another investigation; it will delay our evacuation plans."

"Exactly. And we cannot risk any bad publicity either, especially with the European operation beginning in four months."

"What do you want me to do?"

"I want you to do what you've always been so good at—creating solutions to the colony's problems. At least until recently. I think designing nurseries has made you soft." Grayson smiled, but his eyes were hard.

Grant's eyes were just as hard, but he was not smiling. "Of course, Grayson. I will investigate and neutralize the situation."

"Thank you, Grant. I knew you would."

Returning to his office, Grant phoned the front desk. "Monique, please contact me the next time Victoria Torrance visits. No, don't call or page me; use email. Yes. Thank you."

Viewing Victoria's exercise schedule on his computer, Grant quickly cross-referenced the classes she attended with their other clients to find a connection, but the only person whose classes corresponded with her attendance record were those she had with Carolina. Then, searching the city's business license database, he discovered that Victoria Torrance had applied for a business license as a private investigator d/b/a Verity Investigative Services. Navigating through Verity's website, Grant learned they specialized in locating missing persons, cult retrieval methodology, and counter-self-alienation therapy.

Dan.

He was the only person who would initiate this kind of investigation. After twenty years of having her next to him, a fixture in his life, he wanted her back.

Who wouldn't want her? Who wouldn't want to embrace her in the candlelight, taste her sweetness, touch her softness, feel her tremble, and hear her sigh?

Grant didn't realize his left hand had formed a fist until the pain forced him to open it, and four wet red crescents appeared on his palm. He knew Carolina would never go back to Dan. She'd not given him one thought that lingered longer than two seconds. Maybe he wouldn't have to kill *Victoria*; perhaps he could neutralize this particular difficulty by removing the instigator. Permanently.

Sipping the blood from his palm, Grant smiled as he contemplated the many ways he could murder Dan Taylor.

Dan's Interview

Tory and Travis watched Dan's face carefully as he listened to the tape.

"What does she mean, Mr. Taylor, that her family left her?" Victoria asked.

"Brendan left to enroll in the ROTC program at UNI. I guess she might see that as (air quotes) *leaving* her."

"And you? Did you leave her, too?"

"Look, she got pregnant with some guy and had a miscarriage. When I found out, I told her she didn't have a home anymore. But I didn't mean it. I was just really mad because she made me feel like an idiot."

"What did you do? Just kick her out of the house?"

"Um, no, she wasn't in the house when I told her that."

"Where was she?"

"She was at the clinic, you know, where the ambulance took her."

Victoria stood up. "Let me get this straight. You told your wife, who had just suffered a miscarriage, not to bother coming home while she was what? In a hospital bed?"

"Yeah, I still feel bad about that."

"*You* feel bad?"

"Yeah. So, do you think you can convince her to come home?"

"What *home*? Weren't you listening? Carrie thinks she's home *now*. She feels needed, valued, and welcomed. And, as far as I am concerned, she's right. She *is* home. Among people who care for her. *There*."

Victoria believed she completely understood Carrie's gentleness and simple responses. The doctors and staff she worked with at GatesWay had come to her rescue after Dan abandoned her. It was no wonder she felt at home—it was the only one she had—and she didn't want to leave because she felt emotionally secure there.

She looked at Travis. "Please deduct our expenses from Mr. Taylor's retainer and refund the remainder to him. Based on my investigation, Carrie Taylor is not a missing person or being held against her will, nor is GatesWay a cult that she has been brainwashed to accept. She is a resident employee, one of several, who can leave at any time and is not in danger either from them or to herself."

Turning to Dan, she continued, "As far as our agency is concerned, Mr. Taylor, this case has been successfully completed."

Travis knew better than to argue with her, but the reason behind Carrie Taylor's transformation was still unknown. Dan's confession made it obvious that she cared for someone else, but who—and where—was he? There were still too many unanswered questions. Travis uploaded the transcript from the recorder and Dan's verbatim answers to Tory's questions, but he did not close the file.

Although already investigating a new case, Tory attended the next class she had scheduled with Carrie. She picked up her gym bag and followed Carrie into the hallway when it was over.

"Wait a sec, Carrie."

Carolina turned around and smiled. "I just love yoga, don't you?"

"Um, yes, I guess so. Listen, I wanted to tell you this is my last class. I have a new job on the other side of town and won't be able to come here anymore. But I couldn't leave without, well, saying goodbye. You've always been so nice to me."

"Oh, Tory, you are very easy to be nice to. I'm sorry you're leaving. Wow, you haven't even been here a month, have you? Maybe Dr. Grant can talk to the financial consultant so they won't keep charging you, though I have to say you probably didn't need to lose any weight."

"No, it was just for toning and—"

Carrie interrupted her. "Oh, hi, Dr. Grant."

Tory turned around to find Grant Gates standing behind her.

"Caroline. Ms. Torrance, how are you today?"

"Very well, Dr. Grant," she answered, smiling up at him. "Thank you for asking."

"Please excuse me for a moment, Dr. Grant. Tory just told me she has a new job and won't be able to continue attending her classes. Is it possible to cancel her contract? She was only here for a couple of weeks and ... occasionally ... exceptions are made."

Dr. Grant looked at Tory and said graciously, "Is that something you wish?"

"It would be helpful, but I signed a contract. I don't expect special treatment."

"We take Carrie's suggestions quite seriously here. So, in the interest of customer service, why don't I walk with you to the financial consultant's office and see what we can do?"

"That would be wonderful."

Victoria turned to Carolina and hugged her. "Be happy, Carrie."

"You, too, Tory. I'll miss you." Carolina waved as she walked toward Grant's office.

"Why did you say that?" Grant asked, "'Be happy.'"

"Because she deserves it. Don't you think so?"

"More than you know, Ms. Torrance."

A moment later, they were at Eileen's desk. "Please cancel the remainder of Ms. Torrance's contract."

"Yes, Dr. Grant."

"Thank you."

Waiting outside the door as Eileen handed Tory the cancellation receipt, Grant escorted her to the lobby doors.

Hesitating just a moment before opening the door, he turned toward Victoria and gently touched the hair on her shoulder.

"Is there anything else I can do for you?"

Victoria blushed.

"No, um, you didn't have to do this, but thank you," she said, her southern accent becoming more evident with every word.

"You're welcome ... um, Ms. Torrance?"

"Yes, Dr. Grant. Is there anything else I can do for you?"

Seeing how quickly she took the bait, Grant smiled to himself. *She would have been so easy to kill.* Using his most professional voice, he said, "Yes, I would like to have your wristband, please. I must return it to Dr. Garrett."

"Can't I keep it as a souvenir?" she asked with a smile.

"No, I'm afraid not, but we have several lovely things in the gift shop."

Sighing a little, Victoria removed the pale blue wristband and handed it to him. "Thank you, again, Dr. Grant. Take good care of Carrie, okay?"

"To the best of my ability, Ms. Torrance. Thank you for your kind concern."

Victoria walked through the lobby feeling very virtuous. She was certain Dr. Grant cared about Carrie, and there were worse things than working for a handsome doctor who cared about you. *And one of those things*, she thought, remembering her encounters with Dan, *is being chained to someone who didn't care at all.*

She visited the gift shop, but not for a souvenir. Instead, she wanted another jar of bitter honey. She didn't think the membership list was updated instantaneously, and she was right. When the woman behind the counter said former members could purchase the honey if they wished, Victoria smiled all the way to her car.

Locating Grayson in the tunnels, Grant handed him the blue wristband.

"What's this?"

"Victoria Torrance's wristband."

"Is she ...?"

"Ms. Torrance no longer graces GatesWay Fitness Clinic and Health Spa with her presence."

"Yes, Grant, I understand that, but is she—"

"In the serai?"

"Yes."

"No. Point of fact, by now, she's in her car and on her way to her next assignment."

"Did you find out what it was about?"

"Of course. My research indicated that Mr. Taylor hired her to convince Carrie to return home. It is my belief that Victoria concluded that Carrie was better off here, thereby completing her investigation. We refunded her money and took back the wristband."

"And ...?"

"And if she tries to rejoin, then we are oh, so sorry, but are not accepting any new clients."

"So, we got lucky."

"Only in the sense that Carrie convinced Victoria that she was safe and happy here, exactly as she is supposed to behave toward all our clients and staff."

"So, there was no luck involved?"

"Oh, yes, Grayson. So far, no one has died today. Given this situation's many possible outcomes, there *has been* a certain amount of luck involved."

Grayson knew when to stop pushing Grant's buttons. He was never quite sure when his luck would run out and didn't want to be alone with Grant when it did.

"Thank you, Grant. I am, of course, grateful that any threat Ms. Torrance represented was neutralized so quickly and without any possible culpability on the part of the facility."

"As am I, Grayson."

Caroline looked up from the computer screen and smiled when Grant entered the office.

"Your next appointment isn't for thirty minutes. Did you have a nice meeting?"

"Yes. I am relieved it did not take as long as expected."

Sitting in their chair, he held out his hand. *Come here, Carolina, please.*

"One moment," she said, pressing the button on the remote. Then, finding him in the darkness, she sat down and rested her head on his shoulder.

"Carolina, would you do me a favor?"

"Of course, Grant."

"If you hear from Victoria Torrance again, for any reason, will you let me know?"

"Yes," she said quietly, "Tory is very beautiful."

It was with some amusement that Grant realized she thought he was interested in Victoria. He gently pressed her hand against his lips.

"How many hearts and minds do I have?" he asked her softly.

"Only one."

"And with whom do I share my heart and my mind, Carolina?"

"Only me."

"How many hearts and minds do you have?"

"Only one."

"And with whom do you share your heart and mind?"

"Only you, Grant," she whispered.

"Never think, Carolina, that other than our son, there will ever, and I mean ever, be anyone else." As he pressed his lips to hers, her body rose slightly as his left hand moved deliberately down the length of her body like a brand.

When he released her, she touched her forehead to his.

I'm here.

Yes.

Of course, I will tell you, Grant.

Thank you, Carolina.

Dan's Visit

Summer had faded to fall, and before I knew it, it was my last day in the office. I couldn't stop smiling as I put Grant's files back the way he had initially arranged them to make it easy for him to find whatever he needed while I was at home with the baby.

At home with the baby. The words sounded so unreal. Partly because everything would be different from when I had Brendan, but mainly because the day when I could hold Grant's son, touch him, and *look* at him was mere hours away. Even if the possibility of our son resembling Grant was remote, he would always be beautiful to me.

I was shutting down my computer when the telephone rang. It was the extension in the lobby.

"Hello, Monique. How can I help you this afternoon?"

"This isn't Monique ... she hasn't been feeling well the last few days. This is Emily. Is Dr. Grant there?"

"No. Isn't he answering his pager?"

"I don't want to talk to *him*, Carrie; I want to talk to you. I just wanted to know if he was there."

"Still no, Emily. What's up?"

"Your husband is here."

"Oh. Hmm, Emily, what is the extension of the courtesy phone in the lobby? Thank you. Okay, will you tell him it's for him when it rings?

Sorry to do this to you. I'll come down if I have to, but I'd rather not. Thank you."

I dialed the courtesy phone. Dan picked it up on the first ring.

"Carrie, come down here and talk to me face to face, or I'm coming in there."

"Dan, I have a job. I'm working."

"It's five o'clock. I specifically waited until now so you wouldn't have any excuses. I'm not leaving until I see you. The cops will have to drag me out."

Knowing Grant would hate either alternative and thinking I could take care of Dan myself, I stood and smoothed my pale gold and white silk caftan. Less than forty-eight hours from giving birth, I was still thinner than he had seen me in ten years. I took the elevator down to the lobby.

"Thank you, Emily," I said, passing the reception desk. "This shouldn't take long, but if he's still here in five minutes, please page Dr. Grant. Thank you."

Dan stared at me. "Carrie, is that you?"

No, Dan, isn't it obvious that I am not Carrie? Carrie is gone. She drowned one unforgettable afternoon in August. You just never noticed.

"Yes, Dan. How can I help you?"

"You can put your hair back the way it was and come home with me."

"No to both of those requests. One, because I like it, and two, because you told me I didn't have a home with you. Next."

"But Carrie, don't you think I've been punished enough? And it wasn't even *my* fault. Just come home. Thanksgiving is coming up. Brendan will be there. Wouldn't it be nice to do some holiday things?"

"No, it won't be nice. It will be the same as it has always been, and I'm not doing that anymore. So, thank you for your kind invitation, but no."

"What will I tell Brendan?"

"You don't have to tell him anything. He already knows why I won't be there. Did you think he was blind?"

"Carrie," his voice deepened, and I could tell by the way he was reaching toward me that he could hurt me, and I knew Grant would kill him.

"Dan, listen to me. I'm not leaving, and I'm warning you, if you touch me, I will scream, and at least one dozen men will come in here and throw you out on your butt. Hard."

"Carrie, I know I haven't been the perfect husband, but I love you."

The all–purpose emotional band–aid. The three little words people used to cover up the hurt to make everything "all better now." There just wasn't a band–aid big enough anymore.

"Go home, Dan, and don't ever come back. Don't call, don't email, and don't write. I'm here now. This is where you left me, this is where I want to be, and this is where I'm staying. Goodbye."

Turning to leave, I felt his fingers close around my wrist.

"I'm not putting up with this anymore. You're my wife, and you are coming home with me. Now."

I turned around quickly to tell him to let me go and saw his eyes move upward as he released me. I did not have to look behind me to know who stood there.

"Dr. Grant?"

"Yes, Caroline."

Without taking my eyes off Dan's face, I said, "Mr. Taylor is having difficulty finding the door."

"Mr. Taylor, is that something we can help you with?"

Dan looked down at me. "No."

Meeting his gaze, I repeated, "No emails, no phone calls, no cards or letters, and never come back here."

"Whatever," he said, walking toward the door. Stopping for a moment, he looked back at me. "One day, you'll call me, Carrie. One day, you'll come crawling."

Dan's last words reverberated in my ears. I barely had time to reach for Grant before he caught me and carried me out of the lobby.

Saturday, Dawn

Grant.

Grayson.

Problem yesterday?

I think of it as a problem solved yesterday.

That is uncharacteristically optimistic of you.

Perhaps. But a decisive break was made that proves my methods of relationship control are successful, and, as unpleasant as the experience was for Carrie, the confrontation worked to our benefit. The child will be born here and will stay here. It also reinforces one other prerequisite for all future prospective mothers.

Which prerequisite?

They must not be married or involved in any other legally binding relationship. Make it known, Grayson, that we must avoid any possible entanglements in the future, especially in cultures other than the U.S. We must carefully research the social mores of each country before selecting prospective mothers.

Because ...?

Because in some countries, men own *their wives. Dan could have come in with guns blazing or a court order to reclaim her. We could not have legally stopped him, and it could have ended tragically for all concerned. No more wives, Grayson. This is* not *a recommendation.*

Worried about a gunfight in the GatesWay corral, Grant?

Gallows humor so early in the morning, Grayson? But not necessarily inappropriate. If you will recall, three men died that day.

I couldn't resist. Of course, you're right. It could cause needless deaths of our brothers and, depending on the culturally tolerated level of spouse abuse, prospective mothers as well. I'll take care of it today.

Thank you.

Oh, and speaking of today—

No. Carrie is scheduled for noon tomorrow. Garrett's first, and Gregory's second, are due today. Gabriel and I are tomorrow. Congratulations on your two very fine additions to the colony, as were Gregory's first and Gordon's successes. Mothers?

We will know more when they come out of sedation, and then we will see ... when they see.

Good luck, Grayson.

You, too, Grant.

Yes. Thank you.

Saturday

Finishing his conversation with Grayson, Grant looked down at Carolina's hand resting on his chest. Quietly curled at his side, she did not turn away from him even while she slept but waited for him to love and protect her with his body. She was like a flower to him. At first, she was distant and fragile, then blossomed at his touch into the radiance of full bloom that continuously drew him to her. To the rest of the world, she was a treasure he enclosed in tissue paper, always disguised until she was in his arms and the wrappings fell away.

Her complete faith in him had been so unexpected, and, thinking outside himself, he gazed upon the hopeful creature he had become. He wanted nothing more than to deserve and honor that trust, but he could not silence the clock in his heart as it counted down the minutes, bringing him closer to the end of their relationship. Tomorrow, two would be three. Or she could be dead, or worse. Wonderfully good or heartbreakingly bad, everything would change tomorrow. Her trust, together with his hope and skill, was all he had to get him through the next thirty-six hours.

Would it be enough?

He told his brothers he needed a day of preparation and would not be available. Of course, they thought he was indoctrinating Carolina about what she should expect and finding ways to encourage her acceptance. Smiling, he thought of pleasanter ways to keep her busy today—too busy to worry about tomorrow. That was his responsibility. However, he couldn't spend the day dwelling on all the things that could go wrong; she would know and worry even more. Deciding to spend some time that night reviewing the medical archives and his notes, Grant set thoughts of tomorrow aside.

Taking a deep breath, he caught her scent and could no longer resist her. The pregnancy hormones racing through her bloodstream elevated her temperature, causing the honey she was eating to diffuse into the air and settle on her skin, creating a glaze of pure nectar. Nestling behind her, he pulled her close and covered her with a heavy quilt. Within moments, tiny droplets formed where her body touched his. Pressing his lips against her skin, he sipped from her neck and shoulders.

She was wonderfully his in so many ways, but it was this singular attribute that he guarded so carefully. Like a drug he would rather destroy than share, the pleasure of his wife's sweetness belonged only to him. Brushing aside the silvery strands of her hair, he kissed her slowly. Feeling every curve, his hands traveled down her sides and met on the fullness of her abdomen. His mouth never left her as he carefully avoided the more sensitive areas of her body until she was fully awake.

After all, he reasoned, *she needed to rest. Besides, there was no hurry ... no one would bother them, and he could feast on her all day.*

Tomorrow, with all its uncertainties except that of change, would come soon enough.

Treasures of Darkness

21 November: 3:00 a.m.

"Grant!" I gasped, my hand digging into his thigh.

Instantly awake, he searched my face. "What is it?"

"The baby is coming."

His hand slid over my abdomen, pressing slightly. "He has moved down faster than expected. You should have been in the operating room at least two hours ago."

Grant tilted his head. *Yes, now. Be in the operating room in five minutes. That is not an option. I will not lose her... not now, not after everything I have done to keep them alive.*

When he straightened his head, he was no longer my husband. Using his doctor's voice, he looked at me.

"Did you hear what I just said?"

I nodded. "Why the urgency, Grant?"

"We must get him out before anything happens to you. I thought we had at least one more day, or I would have scheduled a cesarean for yesterday."

I tried to bring him back to me.

"Grant, darling, I'm fine. He's fine. We're fine." Worried by his anxiety, I smiled at him, hoping to take that distant look from his face.

"Yes, Carolina," he said, holding my wrist, but his expression did not change.

Within minutes, there was an IV attached to the top of my hand, and I was on a gurney, racing toward a white room I remembered only in my nightmares. As soon as we arrived, Grant joined two of his brothers in the observation room. I did not know who they were. Their masks and gowns made them indistinguishable.

"We can't operate, Grant. The fetal sac is in the birth canal. We had the same problem earlier this morning."

"What happened to her?"

Gregory paused for a moment. "We're filtering her blood. She should be okay. Luckily, her family is out of town until after the holidays."

"Carrie will have to give birth naturally," said Grayson. "Inducing drugs will make the contractions harder and a rupture more probable. However, the longer the baby stays in her, the greater the risk is for both of them. We'll be able to save the child if he goes into distress, but we can't guarantee Carrie's survival. The good news is that it looks like we will have a healthy brother from her. If the worst happens, you know how to make sure it doesn't come back on us."

Grant's eyes narrowed to mere slits. "Are you saying we aren't even going to try?"

"Grant, we're saying there isn't anything to try. We have no choice but to wait."

He knew they were right—he hated that they were right. Trusting his calculations, this situation was not one of the eventualities he had researched and prepared for so thoroughly the night before. He needed time to think and wanted his brothers to leave, but he had called them and knew they were not going anywhere.

Returning to the operating room, he said, "Carrie, I want you to relax, don't push. Let the contractions move the baby. Are you in any pain?"

"A little, not like with Brendan ... just as you promised."

"Good. I'm sorry he didn't wake you sooner. We could have operated, and you would be holding him now."

"It's not your fault, Grant. He just got in a hurry to meet us. I, I can't wait," she said, reaching toward his face, "to see him. I love him so much."

Grant caught her hand and held it. "Squeeze my hand when you have a contraction so I can time them. Do you want anything? I can get you some ice if you'd like."

"Can you sing to us? I don't understand all the words, but I love the sound of it."

Grant held her hand in both of his. Then, moving his chair closer, he rested his forehead on her pillow and sang prayers to Anya for protection and guidance, opening his eyes only to glance at his watch each time she squeezed his hands.

The contractions were not getting any closer together.

Before his brothers could suggest it, Grant attached a fetal heart monitor to the area below her abdomen to measure the baby's heart rate. The sound of hummingbird wings filled the small room, and further examination indicated the baby was moving but far too slowly for Grant's comfort.

After another hour, her contractions were not coming any faster or harder. Grant considered using forceps, but the membrane was stretched thin at this stage.

What if he accidentally ... No! He could not, would not, think that. Looking into her eyes, he still saw the dream of their son, but time and his options were running out.

"Carrie, we need to move the baby along. He cannot stay inside you much longer. It isn't good for either of you. But you know, this is going to hurt."

"That's okay. I will hold him that much sooner. Do what you think is best, Grant."

Her voice was kind, and Grant knew she was trying to reassure him. That trust of hers, he could not escape its power. She could be dead in an hour, and he was her every thought and care. Nothing in the world—or even the world itself—could compete with the way she loved him. He would do *anything* not to lose her love or her trust.

Hanging up an IV bag of the inducing drug, he changed the leader tube in her hand. It was essential to watch the drugs closely. Too much would cause the baby's heart rate to escalate as well as her pain.

She squeezed his hand, and he looked at his watch. Three minutes later, she squeezed it again, then at two and a half minutes.

Good, he thought, *it's working*.

He heard a sharp intake of breath when she squeezed his hand.

"Carrie, how much does it hurt? One to ten?"

"Only a six."

He knew she was lying.

"I'll back it down."

"Grant, please don't; I think he's moving."

Grant glided his hand along the curves of her abdomen. She was right, but the fetal monitor numbers were increasing. A moment later, the monitor emitted a slow beeping sound.

One of the doctors entered the operating room, pulling on his gloves. As soon as she heard his voice, she knew it was Grayson.

"We must operate now, Grant; the baby is in distress."

"No, he is fine. We need a little more time."

"We cannot wait until the last minute to operate."

"No, we do not need to do this now."

"Grant, she's in pain, and the baby could go into acute distress at any moment. I don't understand why you are hesitating."

She could die.

Yes, but if we wait, the child may die. Remember why we are here.

Grant could feel his emotional stability slipping. His son needed a living mother ... a loving and *sane* mother. Staring at Grayson, Grant clenched and unclenched his hands. He knew *precisely* why he was there.

A breathless but determined voice from the bed broke the tension in the room.

"Grayson, the baby is fine. He would tell Grant if he were hurt. Go away now and leave this to Grant. Go away. Now, please."

There was nothing Grayson could do. In the face of Grant's obstinacy, he had no choice but to obey the will of the mother. All his medical training went against leaving the room, but without Grant's support, nothing in his culture would allow him to stay. Unaware that Carolina had just saved his life, Grayson reluctantly returned to the observation room.

The door closed.

"Grant," she whispered, "don't let our baby die because you are worried about me. That is not loving our son ... or me."

Hearing the warning in her voice, Grant wondered who he was: doctor, father, husband, Lyostian, arthropod? All the experiences of a lifetime gathered at the forefront of his mind, yet, even with that combined focus, he did not know how to help her. He only knew that his sole objective was to save her. She could not love them if she died.

I will do anything you ask, Carolina, but how can I help? What do your instincts tell you I should do?

"Sing to *him*, Grant. Encourage him to move forward. Tell him it's okay to leave me, that I'm waiting here to love him. Put your hand here," she took his hand and placed it on the small bump, "and show him the way."

She smiled up at him. "And tell him that you are here, too, waiting for him." Her eyebrows came together sternly. "Do not tell him he can hurt me; don't make him afraid for me."

"As you wish."

Grant began singing to his son, gently stroking her skin and telepathically telling him everything she told him to say. The beeping of the fetal monitor ceased, and the ceaseless trill of hummingbird wings returned. Whether it was the drugs or Grant's voice and gentle caress, the baby began to move. Turning off all the lights except for a small one above her head, Grant sang softly as he moved to the other end of the bed. A few minutes later, his son was born into his hands.

Grayson and Gregory opened the door to intercept the baby so Grant could take care of her, but seeing the fierce look in her eyes, they stepped back through the door and closed it.

"Where is he?"

"Give me five seconds, Carrie," he said. "There are things to do."

"You have two."

To distract her while examining the embryonic sac for ruptures before removing the infant, he asked her a series of questions about her first conscious memory. Not finding any tears, he knew her mind had not been compromised; he just wanted a moment to prepare himself for her reaction—whatever it would be—to seeing a baby who looked so different from her first son. He cringed inwardly at the thought of her possible rejection. Although the nearly pure estrogen she had ingested for the last several weeks was designed to aid in maternal acceptance, Grant knew from tragic experience how little effect it actually had when seeing a child with feelers for the first time.

He wrapped their son in the pale blue quilt she'd taken from their bed that morning. Then, hoping no one could sense his reluctance to share this moment, he pressed a button on the metal bed frame.

"Let me raise your head," he said.

With no expectations, Grant walked around the bed and stood between her face and the window to give them a moment of privacy. To warn her that his brothers were lined up on the other side of the mirror, watching and recording for all time his wife's reaction to her son, he said, "As promised, *Carrie*, one healthy boy."

Settling the infant in her arms, Grant stepped back.

***

The baby was so small that I instinctively pulled him close to my heart. His eyes were closed, and I could hear him breathing through his mouth. Curious, I folded back the quilt and was amazed at the muscle definition he already possessed. I remembered how Brendan looked when he was born, all round and soft. Weighting almost eight pounds, he had been twice as big as his new brother.

I refolded the quilt and snuggled him to me. He looked so much like Grant's baby memories that I could not help but think him beautiful. Touching his small antennae, I was surprised to find that they were delicate, like thin fingers, not hard at all.

I smiled up at Grant. "I guess I will have to wait awhile before I can count his fingers and toes," I said, kissing the little fused claw at the end of his arm. Conscious of his brothers in the observation room, I took Grant's hand.

"Thank you for your patience with me. He is so beautiful."

I looked beyond the mirror where they were standing. "I want to go back to our rooms now, please. Just the three of us."

"As you wish, Carrie," he said. *You are wonderful*, he thought.

Brothers

Alone in their apartment, Grant stood at the nursery door and watched Carolina marvel at her son. Her fingers traced the outline of his eyes and mouth with soft sighs of tenderness. Gently easing the corner of the blanket over his antennae to keep them warm, she smiled up at him.

"Oh, Grant, isn't he glorious?"

She snuggled the infant close to her and brought his little claw-shaped hand to her face. "Oh, beauty," she whispered, so clearly in love with his son that she appeared to be lit from within.

Grant's mind taunted him. *This, this is what you missed.*

Every instinct he possessed urged him to go to her and claim what was his, but he hesitated. Her joy seemed so complete that he was unsure of his importance in her new life. Willing to accept whatever role she chose, he walked slowly to the bed and waited for her to decide how he would spend the rest of his life.

Carolina looked up at him with a face full of loving gratitude. Then, taking his hand, she pulled him into their nest and laid back in his embrace. Suddenly aware that his arms were around *his family*, Grant's heart expanded nearly to the breaking point. Everything he planned and prayed for had happened; life, hope, and love had come together to create this moment in time. Still alive and loving them, she had fulfilled the dreams of his life. In that moment of self-realization, all his roles in her life came together and validated his existence far more than any one of them ever could.

They sat together for a long time. Grant's mouth near her ear, softly singing or telling her how much she was loved. When she slept, he listened to them breathe while quietly allowing himself to be happy. Occasionally, he glanced at the IV feeding an amber liquid into her hand. The diluted V4 honey masked the estrogen used to encourage her continued acceptance of their child. Remembering the rapturous look on her face, he sensed it was wasted in this case, but better to be sure. Until her hormone levels stabilized, the fluid in the IV also helped her body produce the honey-bonded milk the baby needed to complete his development.

Seeing his son's eyes flutter, Grant waited patiently for him to wake up. It was ironic to think that of the ten embryos he re-conceived, this was the only one who survived, the one he missed. The one that—had he followed strict protocol—would have killed her. Yet, this was the child she held so tenderly. Wondering at the tenacity of his son, Grant soon found himself looking into his own eyes as they once were.

I want to see you grow up, he thought to his newborn son. *I want to see what you will do. Know that wherever I am, if there is any consciousness at all, I will be watching you, loving you, and proud of you. Never forget what I tell you.*

Although he did not expect a response, Grant heard a far-away, *Never forget ... Father*, echoing in his mind, and he replied in the same hushed tone, *Thank you ... Son.*

A pact, unlike anything that had existed in nearly one thousand generations, was created for all time. Absolute and unbreakable; not even death could destroy it.

Carolina, who had been drowsing in Grant's arms, heard the baby make little kissing sounds. She looked up at Grant.

"I think he's hungry. Do you want to stay?"

He grinned down at her. "I wouldn't miss this for the world," he said.

She started opening her kimono, then stopped.

"What is it?" he asked.

"Do you think he will nurse with a throat straw or his mouth?"

A woman's scream echoed distantly in Grant's memory. He took a deep breath and turned around to look directly into her eyes. "Does it matter?" he asked quietly.

"No, it's just that I wasn't able to feed Brendan this way, and I was wondering what to expect."

"Oh, love," he said, kissing her, "thank you for that."

Nestling her in front of him, he eased back the edge of her kimono.

"Why don't we find out?"

"Well," she said, glancing down at her swollen breasts, "at least he won't starve, no matter how he eats." Laughing softly, she brought the baby's face close to her and was amazed, just like every new mother, at the sudden rush of pleasure she felt as her son latched onto her to nurse.

"Oh, wow."

"What is it?"

"It feels wonderful." Looking into his eyes, she added, "Just like your lips on my mouth." Kissing him, she sent what she hoped was the physical sensation of their son nursing.

He pulled his head back. *Really?*

Oh yes, even better than that.

Oh, Carolina.

He pulled her closer, and the three of them descended slowly into the soft hollow of their new world.

I cradled our son as Grant fed me strawberries and cream. "You don't have to do this," I said. "Now that the Demerol has worn off, I am quite capable of feeding myself."

"You have already done enough today, so humor me."

I looked at the IV in my hand.

"How much longer for the IV, Grant?"

"A day or so at the most. The levels of V4 have to stabilize before it is safe to remove it. After that, you can resume eating the V4 honey with breakfast."

Just then, the baby opened his eyes and looked at Grant. Grant tilted his head a bit, and a slow wave of happiness washed over me, and for the first time, our son smiled. Settling back in Grant's arms, I began to feed him again. One more time, I caught my breath and sent what I could of the sensation to Grant.

His eyes widened. "You mean you feel that every time?"

"Yes, at least so far. This is only my second time, too."

He started to smile but became suddenly quite still.

"What's wrong?" I asked.

"I will be right back," he said, standing. Then he turned around and reached for my hand. "No, rather than leave you here, you are coming with me. Can you walk?"

"Yes, if I don't have to walk too fast."

"Okay," he said, lifting us out of bed. "We will walk slowly. I will carry the baby and bring the IV stand."

"Where are we going?"

"Just into the nursery."

Settling me into the blue velvet chair, he handed me the baby. After covering us both with a quilt, he closed the door to the bedroom.

"I'll be right back."

"Where are you going?"

"To answer the door." *I will not leave you, Carolina.*

With the nursery door ajar, I saw two men in lab coats standing at the entrance to our apartment. As I watched, Grant's hand tightly gripped the doorframe. Then he nodded and closed the door.

He walked back into the nursery and, as though very tired, leaned against the blue wall. Something was wrong. The quiet joy of our morning had disappeared from his face. Stolen by his brothers, I was determined to find a way to bring it back. No matter what.

"Carolina."

"Yes, Grant."

"One of our mothers is unable to feed her son."

"Because?"

"She didn't want him after seeing ... you know. Called him a monster. She had to be sedated, and when we told her he died, she was relieved." He put his hands over his eyes and repeated, "Relieved, Carolina."

"Oh, Grant, I'm sorry. Where's the baby? I'm sure he's hungry. Can they find me another bassinet?"

Happiness mixed with gratitude brought joy back into his voice.

"You're sure?"

"Absolutely. Grant, Jr. isn't going to need all this," I said, pointing to my bounteous bosom.

Tilting his head, he was silent for a few moments, then gathering us up in his arms, we sat down together.

"I love you, Carolina Gates. I always intended to have you, but your love for me has been an infinitely precious and unexpected gift. How can I show you how much you mean to me?"

"Never stop loving me, Grant. That's all I ask. Tomorrow and forever, please, *never* stop loving me as much as you do today."

"I promise you, Carolina. I will love you as much as I do today, tomorrow, and forever." He lowered his head to kiss me, then pulled away.

"We've got company."

Grant returned to the front room, and I overheard him respond to his brothers' muffled questions, "No, that's all right, I'll take care of it. Yes, she can. I'll let you know."

My arms were outstretched for the baby when Grant brought him in. Smiling, he handed me the other blue blanket, his head slightly tilted as if trying to hear something far away. I wrapped the baby in the blanket, brought him to me, and nearly jumped when he started nursing.

"This one is slightly starving. But you'll be fine, won't you?" I ran my finger along his cheek and where his eyebrows would be someday. Like our son, he only had curved indentations where his ears would form, and a little bump promised a fine nose, but right now, he was just all eyes and a beautifully shaped pink mouth. His skin was paler than Grant's son, but his hair was darker, almost black.

"You'll be very handsome someday, almost as handsome as my son." As he feasted, I looked up at Grant, who had not moved since handing me the baby.

"Yes, I can ... what?" I asked.

"Later," he said, putting the book he was carrying on the nursery shelf with the binding turned away so I could not read the title.

After Grant returned with another blue chair, he picked up his sleeping son and held him while I nursed the other baby. He did not say anything but sang softly as his son's head rested against his heart. When the new baby was finally sated, I put him in the nursery crib, took my son from Grant, and, kissing his forehead, placed him in his bassinet. Carefully disconnecting the IV from my hand, I returned to the nursery to get Grant, but he wasn't there. Walking into the next room, I could barely find him in the darkness. He was so quiet that I thought he was resting, but as my eyes adjusted, I saw him sitting on the sofa with his head in his hands, shaking it back and forth. Thinking he had another headache, I walked to the refrigerator and poured a glass of juice.

Grant?

His hand was a blur in the darkness as he knocked the glass from my fingers, crashing it against the wall. When I looked back, Grant was standing in front of me. He had never seemed so tall and so ... dangerous.

I backed away from him toward the nursery.

"What's wrong, Grant?"

The intensity of his eyes and his mind went through me like shards of glass, and his words were gravel in my ears. "You are wrong. No, more than that, you are impossible. You must stop it."

I was more confused than afraid. "Stop what, Grant?"

He waved his hand at the nursery door behind me. "That ... that ... performance."

Sitting back down, he pressed his fists to his eyes as though wrestling with a demon he feared and hated. "I just cannot stand it, Carolina."

Kneeling in front of him, I gently took his hands. "Grant, what 'performance?' I don't understand. Please, love, tell me what is hurting you so much."

"You," he said in a strangled voice. "I know how they look to you, how repelled you must feel. I know because I have seen it, Carolina, in a hundred ... a thousand ... different mothers' faces, all looking at our new brothers with disgust. Even when, like you, they knew what to expect, they never really expected it. You cannot be *that* different from them. I *know* it's impossible. So, please stop acting like you care about these children when everything I know tells me it is a lie."

"But Grant, why would you believe that? You are in my mind ... I wouldn't know how to begin to deceive you."

"But I am not 'in your mind' all the time, Carolina. Because I no longer live with my brothers, I must constantly listen to their thoughts and conversations because what they think and do directly affects our life together. Only Anya knows how much I want to believe you, but I cannot always hear what you are thinking. I am not, as some of my brothers have suggested, a Svengali. I do not hold your thoughts captive to my will.

"I have promised to love you today, tomorrow, and forever, regardless of whatever you do or wherever you are, so you do not have to keep up these pretenses for me. If you want to feed them for a few days and then leave us, or leave now, I will not stop you. Only please stop torturing me with 'what, in a perfect world, could have been.' I cannot endure it another moment."

"And what would I do with all this, Grant, if I left?"

I took his hands and placed them under my breasts so he could feel how full and heavy they were. "What would I do with all the love and hope I have for our son? And after you tell me what I would do with my love for him, I want you to tell me what to do with all the tenderness and complete love I feel for you. Because if you do not tell me, Grant, I will not know how to live without him or you.

"Look at me, Grant. I am not pretending. I am the mother of your son, and I love him as dearly as I possibly can. That love is real, substantial, and can be depended upon. I am here because here is where I wish to be. You're my family, so please don't say it's okay for me to leave because then I would have to believe that *you* are the one who has been pretending."

The hands I held under my breasts moved around my shoulders and under my knees and crushed me to him.

"I'm so sorry, Carolina. So many things I've always believed have been lies, or not lies exactly, but wrong information. That you would care for me if you fully understood who I was, or that I could respond to you physically, or that loving someone separate and apart from my brothers would be the most terrifyingly wondrous experience of my life. All those things that happened were deemed impossible, but I was too happy to examine them closely. Until this morning—the first time I saw you with our son—and you looked at him with adoration and such care! Such care, Carolina, I did not believe existed in anyone, human or Lyostian, and you made me a part of it.

"And when I brought you the other baby, you reached for him like he was a real brother and not someone else's baby handed to you. As I watched you with him, everything I thought was true crashed down on me. It was so new; how could I trust it? I called it a performance because I thought you might be acting that way if you thought I expected it of you. I *know* you love me, so you would *pretend* to love them ... and I knew that if you could make me believe that, then you could make me believe anything."

"Yes, I can see why you would think that. Out of fear of losing you, I would try to conceal my real thoughts. Of course, you might suspect I was pretending, but you'd never *really* be sure because believing it was true would be less heartbreaking than looking too closely and discovering it all to be a lie."

I pressed one of my hands to each side of his head until they met in the back and brought his face close to mine.

"But the truth is, Grant, I have loved our son since that afternoon in your office when you kissed him for the first time. At that moment, he became indescribably real and precious to me because he was real and precious to you. I loved him when I saw your baby pictures and knew he would probably look like that. I think I would have been disappointed if he didn't ... it makes him more like you. I love him, Grant. First, as our son, but I also love him because he is an extension of you, your next generation, and his brothers ... all part of you. You have been the most loving and kindest of men to me, and I know that had fate been a little kinder to her, your mother would have been proud of you and loved you so much. So, forgive me if I love you a little bit for her, too."

Persephone's Children

At her words, everything within Grant crumbled and was rebuilt, but without the pain and crushing sense of loss he had endured all his life. This day and her love had redefined him as his love had transformed her. There was one last piece of him that he had not shared with her, but he could no longer keep anything from her *today* that would remind her of his love *tomorrow* and protect her beyond his life, *forever*, just as he promised.

My sweet wife, he thought, *never forget how much I love you.* Tilting her head back, he kissed her. She was not surprised when the haustellum slid into her mouth, and she relaxed her throat. He went deeper than ever before. A sudden quick pressure and something warm, sweet, and intoxicating surrounded them.

Grant, she thought, *I'm getting dizzy.* The pressure against her throat eased, but his kisses didn't.

It may take a few minutes. Just lean your head back.

What did you do?

I am not sure. You may have to tell me.

He carried her into their bedroom. Mentally checking on the babies and knowing they would sleep for a while, he stopped kissing her long enough to lay her down on the bed. A moment later, he joined her, and when she turned her face to his, he tasted the honey he had embedded forever in her throat.

Austin and Alexi

I awoke the following morning when Grant walked in with a tray and the book from the nursery.

"A breakfast fit, well, if not for a queen, then for a mother, which is infinitely better."

Kissing my forehead, he set the tray on my lap. I could see in his face that last night's doubts had been replaced with quiet confidence.

"And," he continued, "if I were you, I'd eat quickly because I think any moment now, you're going to be serving breakfast rather than being served."

"Well," I said, cutting into my pancake, "I hope I taste as good to them as this does to me."

"Oh, you do. Better, actually. More like the honeyed cream you're so fond of."

"Lucky boys!" I said, smiling. "What's the book about?"

"We'll get to that after you've eaten. I want to watch you for a few minutes before I have to share your attention."

I was almost finished with my breakfast when I heard our son start to get restless, and seconds later, kissing sounds were coming from the nursery, too.

"Perfect timing," I said, setting down my fork. "Grant, please help me get up to wash my hands."

"Do you need any help in there?"

I smiled up at him. "Well, they will just have to wait that much longer ...."

He helped me to my feet. "Perhaps later," he said, kissing me. "In fact, I can promise you 'later.'"

Washing up the best I could with an IV in my hand, I accomplished quite a lot in just a few minutes. Smoothing some moisturizer on my skin, I touched the area of my neck where I had felt the pressure last night. Suddenly, my throat was filled with the sensation of bitter honey; it was in my mouth and perfumed the air as though Grant were standing beside me, over me, surrounding me. I looked for him, but I was alone.

I slowly walked out of my bathroom. Grant took one look at the stunned look on my face and ran up to me.

"Carolina, what is wrong? I knew I should have helped you. Did you tear the IV out?"

I shook my head and put my arms around his neck. Knowing my spoken voice would be ugly with tears, I thought to him, *Grant, thank you for sharing your essence with me. Now I will have you with me always.*

He smiled and pulled me closer. *It was the only thing I had not shared with you, but after last night, Carolina, I could not keep anything from you that is in my power to give you. All I am is yours, as all you are is mine; today, tomorrow, forever, as I promised.*

Together, we walked to the nursery, where both boys were waiting, humming faintly. "They don't cry?"

"Only in mental pain. Hunger to our babies is not pain. Physical pain of any kind is more like discomfort than pain as you would define it. Unless they are in emotional distress, they won't cry. They will try to talk to you. That is what they are doing now."

I sat in the blue chair, and he turned toward the crib.

"Both at once, or one at a time?" he asked.

"I don't know. They are so small; let's try both and see how far we get."

Our son fit perfectly into the little crook of my left arm, and with some help, I managed to get his brother on the right. Feeding both at once left me a little breathless.

Needing a distraction, I asked, "Can you tell me about the book now?"

"It is a book of baby names. I've heard you refer to our son as Grant Junior, and we need to do better than that."

"What's wrong with Grant, Jr.? It's a perfectly fine, wonderfully acceptable name."

"New mutation, Carolina, new alphabet. All the names in the first year must start with A. Any suggestions?"

"Can I name both of them?"

"Yes, you can. Mothers have that prerogative."

"Anything special you like?"

"I would like them to have strong names, but it does not matter to me as long as you like them."

Remembering Grant's memories and looking into our son's sea-green eyes, I said, "Our son, Austin, for St. Augustine."

He flipped through the book. "It means venerated, honorable."

"Then it's perfect," I said softly, "I wanted to name him after his father."

Grant knelt by my chair. "Thank you for that, Carolina."

"It's the only way I've ever thought of you, you know." I touched my forehead to his. *I'm here.*

Yes.

I looked at the baby held in my right arm. "This one ... oh, Grant, I bet his mother is beautiful ... I want to name him Alexi, for Alexander."

"All our mothers are beautiful, Carolina," he said, turning a page or two in the book.

"Defender," he said. *Just what I would have chosen,* he thought.

Austin stopped nursing and closed his eyes. Entranced, I watched his long, dark lashes curl upward as they met his cheeks. Alexi's eyelids fluttered a moment later.

"Grant, they seem to sleep a lot. Is that okay?"

"Yes. I would be worried if they were not sleeping. They are still developing and will mostly eat and sleep for the next two to three months, gaining strength and looking a little more human every day. You forget that normally, Austin would still be growing inside you, taking in nourishment, and sleeping while he waited to be born. He and his brother still need to complete their development; that is why nursing him for the full nine–month gestation period is so important."

"And the following three months?"

"Will make him stronger, healthier, and more attached to you. And all of those attributes, Carolina, are very important to me."

Kissing his forehead, Grant set Alexi in the crib. His hand was on my arm before I could get out of the chair with Austin.

"Stop," he said. "Please sit down for a minute." He closed the door to our room like he did the night before.

More company?

"Yes. I'm sure they've come to return Alexi to the neonatal nursery to monitor him. They will bring him back later."

"Will they take Austin?" I asked, trying to keep the fear out of my voice and not succeeding.

"Only if they plan to kill us all," he said.

Grant opened the front door. "Yes," he said. "No, I gave her the book, and she is still considering it. She's a little tired. No, I'll get him." He walked into the nursery, carefully removed the blue blanket from Austin's brother, and handed it to me.

"Let me see him for a minute." Cuddling him, I whispered, "Come back to us soon, Alexi."

Grant handed him to the doctors waiting behind the door, and although I could not see them, I could hear Grant's side of the conversation.

"No, I want two more days until she no longer needs the IV, and then I'll be back. ... Yes, I regret that it's difficult, but I can't have her accidentally pulling out the IV and having to start over again. The bonding process is too important to risk. ... We have to give them the best start we can. ... Yes, four hours."

He closed the door, stood there for a minute, then came into the nursery. After helping me to my feet, we went into our room.

"The IV is staying in two more days?"

"No. I am inventing excuses to stay with you. Apparently, despite my best efforts to stop time and hold on to these moments for all eternity, the universe has kept revolving, and I, I have a real function at this facility besides being at your beck and call."

"Is that so bad?"

"What, going back to my office?"

No, being my beck-and-call guy.

Oh, yes, give me a few minutes, and I will show you exactly how much I hate that.

Take all the time you need.

Andre and Aslan

Exactly four hours later, I was seated in the nursery when Grant answered the door. After closing it, he walked in and handed the baby to me. I took one look at his brown hair.

"Wait, this isn't Alexi."

"What?"

"Look, Alexi had black hair and much paler skin. THIS ISN'T ALEXI, Grant! Where is he?"

"Carolina, calm down."

I could not be stopped. Every "mom" gene within me had gone into overdrive.

"No! I will not calm down. Whose baby is this? AND where is Alexi? They didn't send him away, did they? Did they?"

Not waiting for an answer, I set the baby in the crib. Then, dragging the IV stand with me, I went to the door and opened it. Grant quietly followed me. I wasn't sure what I was doing, but these so-called doctors knew absolutely nothing about mothers if they thought they could change babies around on me without some accountability.

Gregory and Gordon were talking together in the hall and looked surprised when I opened the door. "Excuse me, doctors, where is the other baby?" I asked nicely.

"That's the one from this morning," answered Gregory.

"No, this baby has brown hair. The one you took this morning has black hair. Where is he?" I asked again.

"You're mistaken; perhaps you are tired," Gordon said, glancing at Grant.

Grant, I will start screaming if you don't advise them to tell me the truth. I don't mind another baby. I feel like I can feed an army, but if they do not start telling me what is going on, I will take this IV stand and ram it down their lying throats.

I think you should tell them that. I want to watch their faces as you say it. I assure you, they will think twice about lying to any other mother again.

"Gregory, you and Gordon go back to wherever you came from and bring me the other baby before I start looking for him. Go, now."

I moved toward the IV stand and wrapped my fist around the metal rod. "AND if you dare come back here without him, I will shove this down your lying throats. Then you will know what it feels like to lie to your mother! Now, go."

Gordon moved to step into the room.

I pulled the stand in front of me. "Stop right there. Where do you think you're going? Don't you dare come in here without being invited. This is mine."

Forgive me for this.

Okay.

"Carrie, calm down, now."

Grant spoke to me in an angry voice I didn't know he possessed. He picked up my wrist as though he was checking my pulse and looked at his watch. Then, glowering down at me, he said in the same tone, "There is a hungry baby in the nursery, and you need to see to him. If, and I stress *if*, this is not the same baby, I will find out, but in the meantime, you know what your duty is."

Please be compliant, and, by the way, I love you.

I love you, too, but you will have to explain this to me.

Persephone's Children

Later.

I brought my hand to my eyes. "I ... I'm sorry, Grant. I'm just so tired. Forgive me, please. I *thought* there was another baby ...." I whined, throwing in a sniff or two as I walked toward the nursery, dragging the IV stand behind me. Once inside, I smiled at the tiny brown-haired infant in the crib. I picked him up and wrapped him in Alexi's blanket.

As he nursed, I overheard Grant's voice.

"How many? ... Where are the others? ... I don't know; as you can see, she can be very volatile. ... Yes, I will do that. ... Someone had better bring him back. I don't want her thinking she can't trust you—oh, and she's human, not stupid. ... Well, I know that, but we need her cooperation, don't we? How many more like her do we have? ... Yes, and that is my point, exactly. ... Yes, she will do whatever I ask her as long as she trusts me. And this little farce, by the way, did not help. ... I'll let you know." He closed the door, and I waited. And waited.

"Grant, are you there?"

"Yes. I am just working up the nerve to talk to you."

"You might as well come in and tell me."

"I'm trying to remember if there are any small objects near the chair you might consider hurling at my head should it come into view."

"Well, I might ... if that head wasn't quite so handsome and attached to the shoulders of my loving husband. So, come in, tell me whatever your brothers are trying to hide, and we will go from there. Also, please bring Austin to me and place Andre in the crib."

"Andre?"

"It means warrior," I said as he entered the nursery. "Is that strong enough?"

"It suited you more today than him."

"Well, perhaps he will grow into it."

Once Austin was in my arms, I said, "What happened to Alexi, Grant? Whose baby is in the crib? Just tell me everything. I promise I will still be here when you finish."

Instead of sitting in his chair, he went to stand by the door.

"Why so far away?" I asked.

"Carolina, I am sorry," he whispered. "You know why I had to do that, don't you? Please say you are not angry with me."

I looked up at him. "Grant, I'm getting a little cold over here. Could you please sit with us and keep me warm?"

Moments later, we were sitting in his lap. I snuggled in his arms as Austin nested into mine. *This is so much better*, I thought to him. *Now, please, tell me everything.*

So, you forgive me?

Well, I might exact some cruel and unusual punishment later, but I promise not to bruise you too severely.

After hearing what I have to say, you might change your mind.

About bruising you?

No, about forgiving me.

Everything then, Grant.

Holding me tightly as though worried I would jump up and run away, he whispered, "I won't go into all the details, Carolina, but out of the sixty women we re-conceived, we had eight live births, exceeding our expectations. Anything above ten percent is considered highly successful. The first four were born on Thursday and Friday, three as induced miscarriages, and one natural miscarriage."

"The mothers?"

"All survived, no ruptures. Of course ...."

"They may not be able to have any more babies."

His silence spoke more than words.

"You were right. You are a selfish species." I sighed. "Go on. We have four babies. Any mothers who wanted them?"

"No. They all returned home remembering very little of their experience."

"Where are the babies?"

He rested his forehead on mine. *You know where they are, Carolina.*

"Why didn't you tell me?" I turned to face him. "Why?"

"I didn't know until it was too late. Without mothers, we had to relocate them as soon as possible, and, if you will remember, I was distracted by other things that were going on at the time." He took a deep breath. "They were not mine, and it is the only option we have."

"You said eight. Four went to the orphanages," I said, shuddering slightly. "What about the other three?"

"Well, you've seen two. I cannot believe they did that," he said. "They genuinely thought you wouldn't notice, Carolina, which is more evidence that so much of our data is outdated. You are changing everything we believed about human female behavior and setting a new standard for a new generation. Very fitting," he mused, kissing the back of my neck.

"Thank you, but Grant, please don't let the remaining children be sent to the nurturing colonies. Just tell your brothers to stop being stupid and bring them to me here. I'm not going to be a roving milk truck or 'observed' by them like some kind of brood mare in *their* nursery."

Realizing what I was committing us to, I turned and looked at him. "Oh, darling, I'm sorry."

About what?

About not asking you first. You know, if it was all right with you if they came to live with us. This is our sanctuary, and as much as I want them, I want you—I want us—more. So, it is up to you. Tell them to bring the other babies here, but only if that is your wish, too.

Feeling tired, I leaned against his shoulder, turned my head, and kissed him. Austin had stopped nursing, and I started to pull my kimono closed.

"Are you still cold?" he asked.

"No. With you holding us, I am quite warm."

"Then, please don't do that," he said, lifting my hand from the edge of the gown. Kissing it, he placed my fingers gently on his face.

"Before you agree to this, there is something ... something I haven't told you."

"The other mothers?"

"Yes, I told you about Alexi's mother, and the fourth one had the same reaction, perhaps a little more hysterical, but she left this morning without remembering much of it. But this one's mother ...." I felt his face change under my hand.

"A rupture?"

"Yes."

"How bad?"

"Only toward the end. They are cleaning her blood, but it will take a while. It was you, remember, who encouraged us to find ways to save the mothers. Gordon designed a method specifically targeting the electrons in the formic acid. By destabilizing these electrons and filtering her blood through a temporary electromagnetic mesh, they can be caught before accumulating in her brain. It is a slow process, but we hope ... believe ... she will fully recover. She is our first test case, and we are taking very good care of her."

Although it didn't matter, I couldn't help but ask, "Grant, these other babies, are any of them yours?"

"No," he said, kissing the palm of my hand. "You were my only success." *And I almost lost you twice.*

Persephone's Children

Setting Austin next to us, I turned to face him. *You would never have lost me, Grant. I would have stayed with you as long as you wanted me. So, you see, you cannot lose me ... you can only send me away.*

It would be like death without you.

I sat back from him so he could focus on my face.

"'Till death, my husband?'"

"Until death, my wife," he answered.

We looked solemnly into each other's eyes. This was not the standard until–death–do–us–part vow. With these words, we promised to defend the sanctuary we had created with our lives, and without hesitation. He tilted my head back and kissed the hollow of my throat. My senses rang with him, and when he kissed my mouth, I was overcome by the joy in him. At that moment, a marriage that had begun three months earlier was truly consecrated until—and even beyond—death.

"Remind me to thank you properly for that someday when I've fully recovered and can speak coherently."

"I thought the groom was supposed to kiss the bride."

"Well, making her head explode with pleasure is usually saved for the honeymoon rather than the ceremony."

"I told you, I lose track of sequences when we are together."

Austin nudged closer to me. I looked down at his sleeping face and drew an imaginary line from his cheekbone to his chin. *How many, Grant?*

How many?

How many of Austin's new brothers will you let me love?

As many as will make you happy.

Grant, there isn't a woman who is happier than I am right now with just Austin, but—

All of them, Carolina, I know you want all of them.

And you? What do you want?

I wish for them what we all want and need. I wish for them to have the best mother in the world, and that is you. But it will be four times the work.

And four times the love.

Thank you for that.

Grant, please tell your brothers to bring them here. "Tell them," I said smiling, "that I am becoming 'volatile' and ... oh, yes, 'uncooperative.' I could turn over a few chairs in the front room for effect if you think that would help convince them."

He laughed. "Not this time, but we will hold on to that idea when you want something that is *not* in their best interest to give you." He pulled me close. "Are you sure you want me to call them now? We could wait a while ...."

"Yes, but I would rather have them first. I will need a long hot bath afterward and may need someone to help me since it appears the IV is staying where it is."

He smiled. *As you wish.*

He slightly tilted his head. After a few minutes, his smile faded, his lips were pressed together, and the tension in the room changed. Standing up, he took Austin back to our room, carefully closed the door, and sat in the other chair.

"What is it?" I whispered. "They haven't sent them away, have they?"

"No. They are bringing both of them now, even as we speak."

"Then tell me what is wrong. Quite frankly, darling, you are scaring me."

"I told you that you were going against type, Carolina, and—" he hesitated, "and we have company. Stay in here. I will bring them to you. Say nothing."

Okay.

Perfect. I love you.

I love you, too.

Oh, I know, Carolina, I know.

He opened the front door and returned to the nursery with Alexi.

"Oh, A—"

SAY nothing.

I cooed at the baby and nodded. Putting Alexi up to nurse, he attached himself at once, and I could tell he hadn't been given anything since they took him that morning. A few moments later, Grant came in with the one I had not yet seen.

Using his doctor's voice, he said, "Let me help you with this one, Carrie. He hasn't had anything at all."

I gasped at the ferocity of his nursing. Then, looking down at them, neither one mine, I was struck by the aptness of my earlier analogy of a milk truck.

I heard Grant in the front room. "No, twice a day, only. I cannot be responsible for what she might do if she cannot find them. You will have to leave them here. ... I have observed evidence of a new dimension of human maternal attachment that we may have overlooked. An example would be that of a lioness and her cubs. It's primitive, but I believe worthy of further research. ... Probably, but not if she stops trusting you or me. It will be in the report. Yes, she agreed to ten months, so her mental and physical health must not be compromised. She will be compliant here or wherever as long as she has the babies. Yes, very lucky. ... Of course, for everyone, that is what I meant. It is our duty to ensure our brothers have the best nutrition we can provide, and right now, she is that source. Since she is my wife and therefore my responsibility, I am obligated to do what I can to protect that source to assure their survival."

There was a short silence, and then Grant said, "Tomorrow morning."

The door closed, and he waited by the door for a few minutes like last time. Returning to the nursery, he fell into his chair as though exhausted.

"Good news first, please."

"They are yours, or ours, to be more precise. Except when I am working, I will really be your, and their, beck-and-call guy."

"That bothers you?"

"Yes, insofar as it separates me from my brothers longer than I anticipated."

"I know you miss them; you have been together for years."

"Not for years, Carolina, for millennia."

"This is starting to sound like the bad news."

"No, I am saving the bad news for later."

I tried not to cry. *What*, I thought, *could be worse than hearing him say he didn't want to be with me?*

"I'm, I'm not sure what I will do without you, Grant, but I would rather you not stay than wish you were somewhere else. That would hurt so much. I understand that it's just been us for the last several days and that you might want to escape this enforced captivity to be with your brothers, so go. Please, I'll be here whenever you want to—" I swallowed the lump of tears in my throat. "Visit. I'll be busy too, you know."

His words, "my responsibility" and "I'm obligated," rang in my ears. If, after everything we'd said in the last two days, that was all I was to him, no matter how much it hurt to let him go now, the pain would still be easier to bear than if he stayed against his will, making me feel less and less important to him.

He took the babies out of my arms and placed them in the crib next to Andre. "Alexi," he said, laying him to the right of Andre. Taking the newest arrival, he looked at me and raised an eyebrow.

"Aslan."

"Aslan?"

"It means lion."

Smiling, Grant opened the door to our room. *My room now,* I thought gloomily. He pushed the crib through the door and positioned it along the wall across from the bassinet.

Not even my room anymore, I sighed, *my nursery.* Suddenly, I felt very tired and leaned back into the chair.

Escape Plans

Returning a few minutes later, Grant asked softly, "Can you walk, Carolina?"

I nodded, keeping my head down so he could not see my eyes. Following me into our room, he firmly closed the door and, picking up my left hand, carefully removed the IV.

"Don't I need that?"

"Shh, not now. Stand still, close your eyes, and do as I ask."

Slowly pulling the bow from the knotted sash, my kimono fell to the ground with a silken sigh. Walking around me, his hands caressed my back, my legs, and floated along the curves of my body. My knees trembled, and a quiet moan escaped my lips.

"Put your arms around my neck."

He carried me into the sunken bath. My breath caught when he lowered me into the hot water.

"You'll get used to it in a moment," he said as he sat down on one of the submerged mosaic steps. The steam swirled around us, and he gently raised my face until he could see my eyes.

Why are you crying?

I've destroyed it, haven't I?

Destroyed what?

Our sanctuary.

He waited a moment before answering, *No, Carolina. Our sanctuary can only be destroyed if you stop loving me.*

Or if you stop loving me.

Impossible.

Then, don't.

Don't?

Don't leave me.

Say, please.

Please, Grant.

He tilted my head back a little more and began kissing my neck.

So sweet ... Carolina, I want to try something.

Anything, as long as you never stop kissing me.

Anything?

Oh, yes.

Give me your mind, just relax, and share every thought you have, every feeling, and every sensation with me, as you did earlier when you were nursing the babies, remember? Just like that.

Yes. I love you.

Oh, Carolina, I know you do.

Grant kissed the hollow of my throat, and everything he was went through me and became me. The world was infused with the scent I had grown to love because it was the quintessence of us. It was in the air, the steam, and the water. I shared every moment that followed with him; the sensation of the water, his hands, his mouth, and the concluding undulating convulsion rocked through us both.

After a few moments of awed silence, I looked at him and he was staring at me. *Is it like that for you every time?*

Since you, I answered.

Why not before?

I looked away from him. "No one ever really cared, Grant. Human men are usually too preoccupied in the beginning with their own pleasure, and at the end, well, when it is over for them, it's pretty much over for us, too. I don't have a lot of personal experience, but it seems it isn't something most men work at. I mean, some men try to please their partners, but if their efforts don't succeed, they think it's the woman's fault, not theirs. They don't seem to understand that a woman's most sensitive sexual organ is her brain, not the few inches of real estate, which is usually their primary focus."

"Interesting. So, you are saying that this ... or this ... would have no effect on you if your mind was not already engaged?"

I was suddenly quite unable to catch my breath. *Yes.*

"Human men are stupid."

"I already said that and please, stop teasing me."

"Oh, Carolina, I am not teasing you." His mouth came down hard on mine. *Let me in, love. I can do this better if I know what you are feeling.*

Closing my eyes, I embraced him with my mind and, seeing him in my dream on that hot August afternoon, re-experienced the feeling of the crashing waves as they cascaded over me and through me as if we were drowning, dying, and being reborn.

Not wanting the dream to end, I rested my head on his shoulder with my eyes closed, inhaling the scent of him that never changed, knowing I would always treasure the memory of his love. Regardless of whatever happened to him, to me, or to us, it would remain the most cherished moment of my life.

"Even then?" he asked.

"Yes, even then."

"Tired?"

"Yes, and no. Yes, I am so relaxed I could stay in your arms forever, and no, because I never want to go to sleep, never want this moment to end."

"It isn't going to end, Carolina, not this particular moment."

Two tears leaked out between my closed lids. *Please stop trying not to hurt me, Grant; you miss your brothers. I understand your need to be with them. You are only one person, so I am not asking you to choose. I will never do that. I've just gotten spoiled, that's all, having you with me so much. It will just feel that a part of me is missing when you are gone, and when you come back, for however long a time that is, I will be whole again.*

He didn't say anything to me for so long that I thought he had fallen asleep and started to step out of the tub.

"Please don't move, Carolina; I am not asleep."

"The babies?"

"Are fine and still sleeping."

I didn't understand his silence. "Are you angry with me?"

"Not possible."

"Then why so quiet?"

"I am trying to find a way to tell you the bad news. But first, before you upset yourself any further, what I said in the nursery was not for you but for my brothers' benefit. They were still outside the door, and I wanted them to know that I was disappointed I would not be rejoining them as soon as they would like. I needed your genuine reaction, and you were perfect. I am sorry I hurt you, but it absolutely had to be sincere."

"Why, Grant?"

"They can never suspect our real relationship or the promise we made this afternoon. I cannot lose their confidence that I control our relationship. If I ever treat you with anything less than absolute tenderness, it is for their benefit. You must understand that I am walking a very fine line to keep us together for as long as possible. It is my only objective."

"How can I help?"

"Two things. First, forgive me, right now, for anything I may do, say, or how I say it that hurts you. I cannot send you a message every time to warn you, and I will not do that again—it is too risky. Just say you will forgive me and react as if everything I say and do is real without disputing my authority, even if your natural reaction is to shove an IV stand down my throat."

"I really wanted to do that."

"They believed you. It was talked about quite a bit. They aren't afraid of you, but they are afraid of your human unpredictability, and fear, I have learned, is a useful tool." He paused. "Please, Carolina."

"I forgive you, Grant. Anything."

"Second, I want to establish a code in case I think it best for you to leave at once. Understand that I will not set this in motion unless I am sure you and Austin are in extreme danger, but I have been cautious too long to be careless now. So, without trying to scare you, this is what I want ... no, beg ... you to do whenever my brothers visit, and they will. Now that the children are with us, I cannot prevent that. When any of them are here, I want you to stay in the nursery with the door to our room closed. The nursery door will be slightly open, and I will say, unkindly, to close the nursery door and give us some privacy. But listen to me, Carolina, what I am actually telling you is to close the door, take our son and as many of the others as you can manage, and get out. Take the elevator to the car and leave. Drive east as far and as fast as you can. Do not stop until you feel absolutely safe, and then check the glove box for the documents I have prepared for you. Do not hesitate. Do not come back. Never contact NAFTRAM or call the spa number."

"Grant, I don't even know what NAFTRAM is, let alone how to contact them."

Grant hesitated. He could not tell her the truth about NAFTRAM's real meaning—the New Agenda for the Retribution Against Mankind—it would be too cruel. Instead, he thought quickly and said, "It's many things, Carolina. The letters translate best in English as North American Facilities Teaching Recreation and Moderation. In this sense, it's the corporate office that oversees and administers each facility. In another—and far more dangerous—sense, it is the center of our North American operations that controls every communication and movement between the colonies. I cannot hide from them. One phone call would banish me, and Austin would be lost to us forever. There is a telephone in the car, and I know how to contact you. If you do not hear from me within three days, rip the telephone out and abandon the car."

"Because …?"

"I will be dead."

"But can't I help? Why do I have to leave?"

"Yes, you can help by promising to do what I ask. And you have to leave because … because I think my brothers plan to use you, Carolina, to recruit other mothers and prepare them to be like you, accepting, compliant, and nurturing. They do not understand that you love me; they only think I control you."

"But I don't love them, so how can they control me?" Then I knew, and horror strangled my words.

"Yes, Carolina. First through me, and then after my death, through Austin. My love, you will have no choice but to do what they say. That is not the life I envisioned for us and not the life I will have for you or Austin. I will not allow him to be a hostage. A soldier, yes, a leader, absolutely, but not a pawn to control a queen. There is only one way to prevent that, so you must promise me you will go. Say, 'Grant, I love you, but I love our son more, and if you ask me, I will leave you to save him,' and mean it."

I knew how important it was to his state of mind that I agreed, so I repeated those words back to him with as much meaning as my shaking voice would allow.

He took my hands, kissed their palms, and pressed them to his chest. "Thank you, my own sweet wife."

"But Grant, couldn't this just be a worst-case scenario?"

"The colony vacates this facility on February first at the latest, either together or separately. You and I cannot stay here, and they will not let us leave together because you are too valuable to them. I regret that I cannot see any good with us being separated unless it is you and Austin getting safely away, which leads us back to what you call the worst-case scenario. I will not live in a fool's paradise, Carolina, and I will not let you live in one either, but neither am I willing to sadden one minute we have now by regretting all the moments we will miss. There will be more than enough time for that later."

Even though the water was still almost too hot to stand, I shivered. Wrapping me in a blue and white kimono, he carried me into our bedroom—it was *our* bedroom again—and eased me into the middle of the bed. Taking our sleeping son from the blue bassinet, Grant placed him in my arms and stood back.

"Please smile, Carolina. No one is going to die today."

Knowing he wanted to memorize us, I smiled with all the love I had for him in my eyes. *You must remember this*, I sang to him in my beautiful thought voice.

He watched us for a long time, longer than I expected, and I found myself gradually relaxing. My smile became gentler as I remembered so many of his kindnesses, and then the memory of this afternoon tumbled down on me, and my eyes grew misty with longing. Perhaps I was subconsciously directing these soft thoughts to him because it was only a moment later when he lifted Austin from my arms and returned him to the bassinet.

I smiled up at him.

Kimono or no—

Later, surveying what was left of my lovely blue and white gown, I felt slightly ridiculous for even asking.

***

"Gabriel."

"Grayson."

"So, Grant's little experiment proved successful."

"Total success."

"She will nurse all the children for the full ten months?"

"Yes. Grant confirmed her compliance."

"Her health?"

"Excellent."

"We've been discussing other options."

"Yes?"

"When she's finished nursing these offspring, we are proposing that she stay to encourage and prepare other mothers to accept and nurse their babies. We will send the children she has now to a nurturing colony to be raised and trained."

"Why would Carrie cooperate if you take away her son? She won't have any reason to stay and could die in any attempted escape. Then what would we do? She's too valuable to lose, and we would risk total exposure if she escaped. She is not one of us, nor does she share our survival instincts or our mandate."

"No, but Grant does, and we will prevail upon him to ensure her cooperation. However, you have a point. We will let her keep the boys—at first. If she fails to cooperate, we will take one or two away. Eventually, she will do anything to keep the others. Thank you for the suggestion, Gabriel. Sometimes, all you need is a little leverage."

"What if Grant doesn't agree?"

"Then we will send her away sooner. He's been ... ah, too distracted lately."

"Additional leverage, Grayson?"

"Perhaps."

Covet

Gordon found Gregory pacing up and down in the conference room.

"Did you smell her?" He asked, not slowing down.

"Yes."

"She was just one room away ... just what? Ten, twelve feet?" He stopped pacing, "I want her. Just five minutes, Gordon, I'm entitled. After all, she belongs to the colony."

"Are you out of your mind? She is Grant's wife."

"That is irrelevant. We should all have her. Not just Grant."

"No, it's impossible. Her mental stability is Grant's priority. He would never permit what you are suggesting. More than that, we need her. The colony won't risk the well-being of four infant brothers to satisfy your hunger, Gregory."

"We can send them away to a nurturing colony like the others. They'll be okay."

Gordon pushed him against the wall. "You don't realize what you are saying."

"Why should they have what we never had? I want her, and I'll find a way. Trust me."

"No! If you touch her, Grant will kill you. And if he doesn't kill you, putting her or the children at risk will set the entire colony against us. What you are suggesting isn't even allowed—she is our mother! Listen to me; I'm your twin brother and have loved you all my life, and I will fight for you, but I will not die for you. Not for this."

"You're no help."

"I'm only here to keep you alive, Gregory, not make you happy."

The Examination

"Carolina, time to wake up. I've brought you breakfast. You must eat to make up for removing the IV. Also, if you don't eat, you will be too tired to play with them or me, and that is something," he said, kissing me and setting the tray down on the bed, "I simply will not allow."

"How are our boys this morning, husband of mine?" I asked, echoing his cadence.

"All quite well, except Aslan. I think he has only been fed once, and he is very hungry."

"Okay, Austin and Aslan, then Alexi and Andre. You are right. I am going to have to stay healthy to keep up with them ... and you."

After you feed the boys and they are resting, I have something to show you.
Something good or something bad?
I hope you will think it is something good, but you can be quite unpredictable, you know.
Speaking of unpredictable, are we having visitors this morning?
Yes, in about two hours.

Finished with breakfast, I wiped my hands on the napkin and pulled up a coverlet.

"Babies, please."

I nestled Austin on the left, but before I could get Aslan settled on the right, he was nursing for all he was worth. Grant, smiling at me from the end of the bed, started slowly pulling the quilt toward him. Knowing how helpless I was to stop him with babies in both arms, I said, "You are right. You are a selfish species." I tried to be stern, but I couldn't help but laugh.

"Well, if you insist on modesty ...." He dropped the quilt and turned off all the lights. Seconds later, the coverlet resumed its slow slide to the end of the bed.

As my eyes adjusted to the complete blackness of the room, I realized I could see. I looked around and noticed for the first time how my bower shimmered with luminescent threads interwoven among the netting to create an ethereal canopy of light. I thought my bower's design was lovely before, but the softly glowing and intricate webbing was extraordinary. So caught up in surprise and wonder, I forgot that I was not alone.

Carolina?

I looked in his direction, and my breath caught in my throat. That was the first time I *really* saw Grant. Kneeling at the foot of the bed, a creature outlined in a pale golden sheen grasped the edge of my quilt in his hand. As I was barely able to breathe, speaking was impossible.

Grant, please stand up.

He dropped the quilt and slowly got to his feet. In this underground world of bioluminescence without reflected light and shadows—or even darkness to hide behind—nearly everything human about Grant vanished. It was like seeing a superhero without the costume and cape and, instead of finding him less, realizing the disguise was necessary to conceal beauty too fearsome for human eyes.

What is it, Carolina?

You. You are ... are resplendent. Oh, Grant!

You can see me?

Sending the image of him standing at the foot of the bed, I answered, *Yes, Grant, I can see you. I can see ....*

I looked quickly down at my son. Austin and Aslan had fallen asleep in my arms. I set them down in front of me and started to unwrap the blue blanket from Austin's body.

No, Carolina, don't!

Austin opened his eyes and looked into mine. His curved hand caught my fingers. I hesitated for only a moment, but that was long enough for Grant to turn on the alcove light. My black-lit fairyland disappeared. Grant got into the bed and held me as I leaned back into his arms.

"Why, Grant?"

"It's too soon, love. The babies are still developing, and their apodemes are not fully formed. The bioluminescence of Austin's silhouette does not yet include his arms and legs. You might be frightened at what you see—or don't see." He put his lips close to my ear.

"Austin believes he is beautiful because you do, love. If you think he is ugly, or worse, if you were to reject him because he did not look as you expected, he would know. He will always love you, regardless of how you feel about him, but he must be strong, Carolina, and such doubt will weaken his confidence. So please, be a little patient. Whatever beauty you see in me will soon manifest itself in our son and his brothers."

Grant lifted Austin from the bed and held us in his arms. "Even more so because he also shares your loving and generous spirit."

Realizing that Grant's quick action may well have saved my life a third time, I said, "Of course, Grant, I understand. Thank you."

I glanced around the room; its ethereal tracery temporarily dimmed. "And thank you for this," I said, my hand touching the netting. "It is so unexpectedly exquisite. Has it, has it always looked like that? Even from our first night together?"

"Yes, why?"

Persephone's Children

"There is much I don't know about you, Grant, but I do know that no man—of any species—creates this kind of beauty unless he loves a woman to distraction."

The stillness of the room was broken only by the slow movement of Austin's hand across Grant's heart.

"Yes, Carolina," he said hesitantly, as though I had wrung a truth from him that he was reluctant to admit even to himself.

"Thank you for that," I said, turning in his arms and kissing him. *Don't worry, darling. Your secrets are safe with me.*

If my secrets are not safe with you, Carolina, we are all dead.

Aslan began making kissing noises. I picked the boys up and snuggled them against me again. Grant stood up and, returning to the foot of the bed, he picked up the edge of the quilt where he'd dropped it.

"I don't know why you are able to see in the dark. We may have to do some testing later to determine the reason. But I am happy you can see your bower as I designed it for you and that you like it. So happy, in fact, that if you ask nicely, I will give you the quilt back."

"Well, if you think it looks better on me than on the floor, then please cover me back up."

He dropped the coverlet. "I think it looks great on the floor."

"I thought you might say that."

I smiled at the pile of fabric on the carpet. "I think it's time for some diapers and two more boys."

"As you wish." He caught my eyes and lingered there. Just then, Andre—and I knew it was Andre—made a little mewling sound, and I looked over at the crib. *Just a minute, Andre,* I thought. Then Austin tilted his head just a little, and Andre suddenly quieted.

I looked at Grant quickly.

"What is it? Did one of them bite you?"

"No, in my mind, I told Andre to wait a moment, and then Austin tilted his head, and Andre quieted down. Grant, he understands me."

"Yes, but because you only speak English, he understands your intent, if not the exact words. Whenever you mentally talk to any of the other boys, he will tell them what you said."

"Can I hear him?"

"Let's see."

Suddenly, a warm feeling of love and contentment washed over and melted into me.

"Oh, Grant," I whispered, "he loves me."

"As do we all," he said. "Did you hear him say that?"

"Not in words, but in a wave of emotions: admiration, love, and trust. Like someone lit a small flame inside my heart." I thought for a moment. "Does he talk to you in words?"

"Yes."

"Well, that's all right," I said, bringing Austin close to my face. "Thank you, Austin. Your mother loves you right back." I kissed his forehead, his little bump of a nose, and both cheeks.

He sighed, closed his eyes, and was asleep before I could hand him to his father. Rather than put Austin in the bassinet, Grant laid him carefully beside me and wordlessly continued to hand me babies, diapers, and the occasional wipe, all very professional. His face was calm, with a small smile that did not quite reach his eyes, and he did not look at or tease me anymore.

When all the babies were in the crib, I moved to press the button to raise the bed. "Don't do that, please," he said, getting in next to me. "Are you cold?"

"Just a little. I was going to take a shower. If we are having guests, I should be presentable."

"They are not *guests*, Carolina," he said, pulling me into his warmth. "And you are always presentable, especially the way you look and smell right now, but that is something I will not share with them. Wife."

Never in my life had I heard the word spoken that way. The sound echoed in my ears with respect, honor, and, more than love, an underlying sense of belonging and pride.

Knowing I would remember the way he said it for the rest of my life, I touched his cheek.

"Thank you, my darling."

I sighed. There was only one thing I could give someone who loved me that much: his freedom.

"Grant, you are a brilliant doctor and geneticist, and probably a zillion more things that I don't know yet, and if you want to be somewhere else instead of handing me babies and diapers, I will understand. It's selfish of me to want you here. If there is someone else you trust, then we'll do it that way. I don't want you to feel trapped in this apartment with me. You could be doing so much more."

"Do you feel trapped in this apartment?"

"No, this is heaven on earth to me, but I'm not a doctor who is depriving the world of his particular genius. Besides, I want to be here; this is where my son and his brothers are, and my wonderful husband also lives here."

"Carolina, I thought we had this conversation yesterday, so let's finish it now so we can go on to pleasanter things. One, there is enough going on here to keep me interested on a professional level; two, I have worked very hard to convince my brothers that you need *me*. Turning your care over to an intern could be detrimental to the continuation of our relationship, something I am unwilling to risk; and, three, if you think I am not intensely interested in every breath you take, then you, my dear, are not paying attention."

"You looked so bored when you were helping me with the babies. I felt guilty for asking you to do such menial work."

"I wasn't bored, I was listening. And yes, handing you diapers is not intellectually challenging, but it can be physically stimulating when the view is so beautiful."

"Well, this beautiful view needs a shower. There's only an hour or so before the other doctor fathers show up."

"One hour, ten minutes."

He secured the door and lifted me out of the bed. I looked longingly at the tub. *Well, maybe later*, I thought and started the shower. I was setting the spray at normal levels when I shivered from a rush of cold air.

"You are not doing this right."

Gently moving my hands aside, Grant pressed the recessed buttons and started kissing the back of my neck.

Grant, what are you doing?

I've always been intrigued by your initial expectations of a double massage. I cannot tell you how much thinking of you with someone else enjoying one of our 'incentive' showers bothered me. So, I have decided to transcend my imagination to experience and see exactly what that would be like. We will get clean together, saving time and water, but then again, maybe not.

He reached up and blew out the single candle. When he looked back down at me, I saw that his eyes had gathered the last of the extinguished light and shone golden like the eyes of a tiger in the dark. Only the silhouette of my hand interrupted the perfection of the bronze surface of his chest, and when the water began to fall, it glistened like liquid crystals striking the statue of an ancient god.

An edge of hysteria crawled into my throat; I closed my eyes.

"What is it, Carolina?"

Please relight the candle, Grant.

Without comment, he did as I asked. When I inhaled the candle's fragrance, I opened my eyes only to see him looking at me with as much awe as I had felt.

It's the same, isn't it, Grant?

Yes, love, as I have always told you.

We had showered together many times before, but not like this. At first, he left the candle burning, and it was just a normal shower as his soapy hands moved slowly over my body, each curve, each crevice, stroking, caressing. The water rinsed the soap off, but the scent lingered in the shower steam. He pressed his mouth against my neck. Embracing me, he kissed and sipped the moisture from my shoulders and moved my hands to the blue tiles.

Don't move your hands or feet.

Moving his right hand over mine, he started pressing the buttons in sequence. *Let me in, Carolina ... relax into me and I will be there with you.*

Grant doused the candle, and two strong arms embraced me. I leaned back and rested against him as his consciousness melted into my mind. The shower spray began moving up and down, testing my reactions. I started breathing in short gasps, but the shower was relentless, slowly increasing pressure, slowly increasing speed as his mouth moved over my neck and shoulders, never leaving my skin. Caught in the glimmering pulsating darkness, I wanted it to stop ... I never wanted it to stop. I could not take my hands from the wall; my legs seemed frozen to the floor. The intensity grew, and my ears started to ring. Almost slipping into a faint, I heard his voice, *Come back to me, Carolina.* He lightly stroked the hollow of my throat, and two became one as the shower spray changed direction.

Someone screamed, and the world exploded.

I woke up in the dim light of our dressing room, wrapped in a towel and cradled in Grant's arms. I felt him sipping the beads of moisture still clinging to my shoulders, but he stopped as soon as my eyes opened.

"Carolina, are you okay?"

"I thought you said the babies didn't cry."

"The babies are fast asleep."

"Then who was screaming?"

"I'm pretty sure that was us."

"Together?"

"Yes."

I smiled at him. "So, I guess it was good for you, too."

"It was very good."

"It won't kill you, will it?"

"No. While I feel the mental sensation, I do not share your physical response. It's not the same," he said, "as before, but it is still rather intense, which is why you lose consciousness sometimes. When I am in your mind, your experience isn't shared—it is doubled."

He touched his forehead to mine. "All in all, Mrs. Gates, I would say that in your head is a wonderful place to be."

"Any time," I whispered, getting all relaxed and sleepy. Then I remembered. "Oh gosh, Grant, what time is it?"

"We have about thirty minutes, time enough to get dressed and show you your surprise."

"I'm not sure I can take many more surprises today," I said, touching the side of his face.

"Did I frighten you?" he asked.

"I wasn't frightened by you, Grant, but by my reaction to you."

He bent his head for a moment and then looked up at me.

"A kind of exultation?" he asked softly.

"Yes," I breathed, "how did you know?"

"It's how I've felt every time I've looked at you since the morning Austin was born."

I wanted nothing more at that moment than to fall back into his mind, but as I reached for him, he pressed my hand against his cheek and gently shook his head.

Without a word, he stood and pulled out a shirt, slacks, and a lab coat from his section of the closet.

Gathering the towel around me, I walked over to the other side of the room. "Work clothes or play clothes?" I asked.

"Let's see if we can find something in between."

His fingers danced over the padded hangers and stopped.

"This."

Removing a thigh-length caftan with matching slacks, he pulled the pale blue silk over my head. I slipped on the slacks and began walking toward the vanity area.

"No," he said.

"No?"

"Clean and dressed is one thing; radiantly beautiful is another."

"Can I brush my teeth?"

"Yes, but no makeup, and just run your fingers through your hair."

He made no effort to hide the caution in his voice.

"Grant, what is my role in your brothers' eyes? Am I your wife, and this is our home, or am I just a glorified wet nurse for the facility's motherless babies?"

"The two roles are synonymous. Because you are the first, you have agreed to be the second."

"Because I love you?"

"Because you respect me, love your son, and, since you know who I am, you are slightly afraid of me. But your love for him overcomes your fear of me, which is how, in the eyes of my brothers, I control you."

"I don't understand."

"Because I have threatened to send him away, you are very compliant." He looked into my eyes and repeated slowly, "Very compliant, Carolina."

"I wasn't very compliant yesterday."

"I know," he laughed to himself, "they never saw that coming. But I told them it was a reaction due to too much estrogen in the IV, and it has since been corrected. And speaking of the IV, I am going to have to reattach it to your hand."

"Ouch."

"Just while they are here."

"Okay."

"And now for your surprise."

He paused at the bedroom door and listened.

"Good. They have finished and gone."

Leading me into the nursery, I couldn't believe the changes. The wall to the right of the bedroom door now had a window and a door. Looking through the window, I saw a complete medical examination room with four small beds with clear plastic sides lined up next to each other. On all four sides of the room were counters holding scales, medical supplies, and equipment. Above the counters were glass cabinets containing bins of clothing, socks, and diapers.

I noticed that changes were also made to the nursery. Everything was slightly larger: the crib, the changing table, the bathing sink. Our two chairs were now side by side in the corner, a platform curved around them where four reclining baby chairs were securely fastened. Neatly stacked in one corner of the crib were two dozen blue baby blankets.

There were only two things I didn't understand. Why was the window installed? Was I going to be gawked at after all? And the door had a regular handle; it wasn't one of Grant's secret doors.

"Grant, this is amazing ... and perfect for the boys. Thank you for the extra blankets, but, um, why the window? Are you putting me on display? And why is the door a real door?"

"Two very good questions and a short walk through that real door you are so concerned about will answer them," he said.

"Where is the window, Carolina?" he asked as we walked into the examination room.

I turned around to face the wall. There was no window, just a polished industrial-looking metal surface.

"Very clever. Does it reverse?"

"Only if the lights in this room are darker than the lights in the nursery, which is impossible with this rheostat ... whenever the lights are lowered in this room, they dim in the nursery, keeping the correct light-to-dark ratio so it will never reverse. Since I have requested you to remain in the nursery, I didn't want you to worry about the boys. This way, you can keep an eye on them, but no one will be able to see you."

He pulled me close and said very softly in my ear, "Did you think I was going to *share* you, Carolina? If that had been my intention, I would not have married you." He kissed me very gently and held me for a moment, reluctantly letting me go.

"Now," he said, "where is the door?"

I looked behind me. Where the door had been was a shallow recessed shelving unit that mimicked every other shelving unit in the room.

"How?"

"Here," he said, guiding my fingers under the right side of the fourth shelf. "Four boys, four shelves, to the right. Always the right. As you are right-handed, it is your natural direction."

Totally humbled by his genius in caring for us, I whispered, "Thank you, Grant. Thank you so much for this." I kissed him with gratitude and love, sending every tender feeling to him with all my strength so he would feel as surrounded by me as I was with him.

"As much as that?"

"Yes, and so much more." I looked around at the changes that had been made literally overnight. "Please thank your miracle workers for me; this room is wonderful. I am so amazed at them."

"You simply don't understand," he said. "To them, you are the miracle, and they are completely amazed at you. They would build you a cathedral, Carolina, if you asked them." He glanced at his watch. "We'd better get the children."

"I'll get Austin."

"Wait," he said, tilting his head. "We need to give them other names."

"What?"

"We will keep the names you have given them, but for the archive records, we need to assign them different names, so if you must leave, it will be harder to track you. Just pick four more names. Don't worry about the meanings; *we* will never refer to them by anything other than their real names."

Mentally running through the names beginning with A in the baby book, I said, "Austin is Adam, Alexi is Albert, Andre is Antony, and Aslan is Ashley. Close, but no cigar."

"No cigar?"

"Never mind, it's just a human colloquialism."

"Explain it to me later?"

"Of course."

The boys were half asleep as I dressed them in clean shirts and diapers and wrapped each in a new blanket. I kept Austin while Grant put the rest of the children in the examination room. While waiting, I walked into the outer room to survey the other changes to the apartment. The kitchen area was the same, but the living room had been narrowed. Where there had been a sofa and chair in front of the fireplace, there was now a curving sectional sofa with two ottomans in the center and an additional chair by the door. It occurred to me that if the two outer sections were moved to the other side of the ottomans and the chairs were placed at the end, I could make a circle, another nest.

Setting Austin carefully on the section I was not moving, I rolled the sides around. Running back to the bedroom, I grabbed a coverlet and slid over the arm of the chair. I picked up Austin and covered us with the quilt. Holding him close to my heart, I watched him sleep and waited for Grant.

Leaving the examination room, he smiled at the little circle I'd made.

"If the boys are comfortable, would you like to join us?" I asked.

Moments later, Grant was holding us both in his arms. "Do you think it would be okay if I stayed out here?" I asked, looking up at him. "I promise to be compliantly watching them like a mother hawk. And besides, I don't want Austin just waiting for them. Actually, I would prefer that none of them were just waiting in there, but I want you to carry Austin in so he always has one of us. And Grant, just this once, I'd like to be here between the examination room and the door." I looked down at my hand.

"Oh damn, you'd better get the IV. You know, in case I need a weapon."

"Of course," he laughed, then looked at me seriously. "Just this once, Carolina."

Grant connected the IV and rejoined us on the couch. "Kiss me, please," I asked.

"For luck?"

"For courage."

"I will kiss you anytime, anywhere, but you already have enough courage for a battalion. Like your son, you are stronger than you know. And," he said slowly, "I meant it when I said I would kiss you anywhere."

"Here, for instance," he said, kissing the inside of my elbow. "Or here." His lips lingered on my shoulder. "Or …," he looked into my eyes and leaned toward my mouth, then stopped. "I am sorry, my dear, we will have to wait and explore other options later."

Grant stepped out of my nest, straightened his clothes, and answered the door. Expecting only the two brothers who were here yesterday, my confidence faltered when all five of them walked in. Looking like so many peas in a pod, only Grant stood out to me. Perhaps, I thought, that was because I knew him best, but it was more than that. They stood together as a group, with Grant seemingly on the outside, and I wasn't sure if that was good or bad or just my imagination.

They were all smiling when they walked in, but their smiles disappeared when they saw me sitting in my upholstered nest. Just then, Austin moved, and I looked down at him.

"Oh, Adam," I cooed, echoing Grant's cadence. "Are you waking up?" I took one of the still-fused hands he was waving about and kissed it. Stroking his cheek, I drew an imaginary line from his forehead to the tip of what would someday be his nose. "You are the very best little boy in the world," I said, kissing his forehead.

My tone of voice changed completely as I looked up at them. "Gentlemen," I said very formally. "I would like to introduce you to my son, Adam Grant Gates."

Holding him against my chest, I turned Austin toward the door. Grant dimmed the lights, and one by one, they removed their glasses and looked at Austin. He calmly studied them and then yawned and went back to sleep. Only Grant, standing behind them near the door, was smiling.

They were also not expecting the examination room. "She insisted," Grant said, standing in the doorway. "She doesn't trust you after what you two tried to do yesterday."

They walked in together. After weighing the other babies, they checked their hands and feet and pressed stethoscopes to their chests and backs. A few minutes later, Gregory came out and asked for Adam.

"No," I said, eyeing him suspiciously.

"We have to examine him, too."

"I will give him to Grant. Why can't Grant examine him? Why does it have to be like a circus in there anyway? They are just babies."

Gregory tilted his head.

A moment later, Grant was standing above me. "Carrie, is there a problem?" he said impatiently.

"Gregory wanted Adam, and I, well, he took Albert away, remember, Grant? I just wanted to give Adam to you so he would be safe. If he has to go into that room, he should go with you. Shouldn't he, Grant, shouldn't he?"

Answering me but looking at Gregory, he said, "Yes, Carrie, I should take him if that is how you feel."

His voice gentled as he looked down at me. "And I'll bring him right back. Would you like to see any of the other babies now? I think Albert is waking up."

"Yes, of course. Can you see? I've made us a little nest." I reached toward Austin and straightened the blanket. "You won't leave him, will you? You'll stand right there by him all the time, so he won't be scared. He's so little."

"Yes, Carrie," he said wearily. "I'll stand right there."

On the way back to the examination room, I heard Gregory chuckle and say, "Taking one for the team here, huh, Grant?"

"Tell me about it."

Gabriel came out with Albert.

"Thank you, Gabriel," I said. Nuzzling him, I cooed, "Albert, were you a good boy?"

Gabriel did not move.

"I'm sorry," he said.

"Sorry about what, Gabriel?"

"I didn't believe you really cared about them."

I looked at him steadily. "More than you can possibly understand."

"He was the only one of mine who survived."

"His mother?"

"Thought he was a horrible dream."

I nodded. "I'm sorry, too."

I was going to tell him he could visit, but remembering Grant's admonition, "They are not guests," I thought I should ask Grant before offering any surrogate father visiting privileges.

Smiling at Gabriel, I said, "He's very strong." Turning my attention back to the baby, I kissed his little fused fingers. "Aren't you, sweetheart?"

Gabriel sighed and walked away.

Eventually, all the babies were in my makeshift nest, and we were surrounded by Grant and his brothers. I yawned and, bringing them all close to my body, drew the quilt over us. Smiling up at Grant, I closed my eyes.

Gabriel was the last one out. Standing at the door, he turned to Grant and asked, "When does she nurse them?"

"When they wake up hungry."

"I was wondering—"

"No. This is not a zoo."

"It wouldn't be like that."

"I know," Grant's voice softened, "but she is very private about her body, even when we're alone."

"You could share."

"If she was your *wife*, would you?"

"No, probably not." Gabriel paused for a moment, "I don't envy your position in this situation. You must be bored out of your mind most of the time, but she is kind of special, isn't she?"

"Special, maybe; demanding, yes; stubborn, even more so, but she is willing to be their mother, and even though they need her, I consider her more of a specimen than special."

"If you hadn't married her, we could have taken turns caring for her and the boys. It wouldn't have to be all you."

"Considering her state of mind at the time, if I hadn't married her, who knows what she would have done? She could have hurt herself or been hurt. Then there would be three brothers without a mother instead of four who will have what most of us never experienced, a human mother who truly loves them and ten months of complete development. Think of how strong they will be. For that, any personal sacrifice is acceptable. No, more than that, it is welcome."

Grant glanced down at his watch. "Speaking of which, I've got to make her something to eat. The babies will wake up in about forty-five minutes, and if she doesn't eat first, then she'll be too tired to feed them—and irritable. So, unless you want to be here for *that*."

"No, I'm going. Well, thank you for taking this on, Grant. If you want a break, perhaps one of us could, ah, babysit."

He smiled derisively. "At your own risk."

The door closed, and I peeked over the back of the sofa. Grant stood at the door for several seconds with his head bowed. Listening, I thought.

"What is it?" I whispered.

He turned toward me. "I am waiting for one of the sofa pillows to crash into my head."

"Oh, well, I'd miss at this distance. This specimen is waiting for you to get closer to exact her revenge."

How close?

Oh, very, very close.

This close? He asked, taking a step toward me.

Closer.

Thinking I was teasing him, he smiled and took another step. *How about this?*

Ducking back down, I eased the IV line from my hand. Pulling the remote from between the cushions, I pressed the button. In complete darkness and using the sofa back as a springboard, I hurled myself straight at him. All feigned passivity gone, I slammed us both into the thick carpet.

After months of feeling powerless, of being grateful for every smile or worrying over every frown, for living with the fear that any twinge might trigger another miscarriage, the anxiety during Austin's birth and facing Grant's groundless suspicions afterward, the responsibility of motherless babies, and my anger at his lying brothers all collided in my mind at once. All the repressed fears, anxieties, and passions of the last four months came rushing out of me as adrenaline propelled me over the back of the sofa into the arms of a man who was not a man. Like the praying mantis that devours her mate, I fell on him like he was something to eat.

Pinning him to the floor, I said, "If you say one word, I will show you what an irritated specimen is capable of."

"Carolina," he breathed.

"As *you* wish," I said through gritted teeth.

That he responded with the same ferocity did not faze me. Knowing he would not hurt me, my anger truly knew no bounds. Time and again, he allowed me to rage at him. Deftly catching and imprisoning me in his grasp, he pressed his lips against the closest part of my body, leaving a line of slow, passionate kisses. He laughed and released me when I stopped struggling, saying, "So easy, Carolina." My frustration at his coolness only increased my rage.

The floor was soon littered with the shreds of our clothing as I attacked him. Scratches and bite marks covered his shoulders, chest, and neck; welts and bruises from his kisses covered mine. Escalating the tension of our struggle to the breaking point, he allowed me one final lunge before he rolled over and pinned me beneath him.

"If you want to hurt me, Carolina, make me feel it."

His left hand held the back of my head as his right slid down toward my thighs. At that moment, I loved him, hated him, wanted him, and despised my desire, but most of all, I resented the knowledge that, once again, I was submitting to his control. I fought against the mercilessly slow brush of his fingers over my abdomen and his lips warm on my neck. Even as I pounded his shoulder with my fist, my mind repeating, *I hate you, I hate you,* I could not deny the arousal building within me. As the twin pressures of his hand and mouth came together, I, irresistibly and breathlessly, surrendered to him everything I felt at that moment.

I woke up curved against his warm silk-clad body. When I opened my eyes, he was looking at me.

Did you feel it, Grant?

Yes, I felt it, he answered with genuine sorrow in his gaze.

Sitting up quickly, I put my hands on his face. "Grant, did I hurt you?"

"I may bruise, and I may bleed, but I do not break, Carolina. The arthropods' outer exoskeleton morphed to coat our bones. It makes us stronger, more resilient, and increases our stamina, but leaves us just as vulnerable to bullets, hand grenades, and car wrecks. And evidently," he paused, smiling briefly, "teeth. But you did not injure me," he said, his smile disappearing, "at least not the way you intended." He took one of my hands and kissed the palm.

"Carolina, you *hate* me."

"No, I love you, wonderful, dearest man in the world."

"Then what do you hate? Because something, Carolina, caused all this pain—to both of us."

"That you aren't the dearest *man* in the world."

"I've told you everything since the beginning. I have never pretended to be anything other than what I am."

"You didn't let me finish."

"Sorry. Please, finish."

"That you aren't the dearest man in the world, and because of that, I have been so scared."

"I would never hurt you or let anything hurt you that I can prevent."

"Grant, you are not thinking of it from my perspective. First, I spent months afraid of losing the two most precious things in my life, and now that I have it all—and I truly believe I have it all—I am still fighting every day to keep them, even now when it should be easy. We have Austin, and we have each other, but I am still frightened that it will all be taken from me, and you won't be able to prevent it. You will be gone, your brothers will take Austin, and Dan's prophecy will come true; I will have nothing, and I will be nothing because everything I love—and everything I am—will disappear forever." I gripped his shoulders with my shaking hands and looked into his face.

"You have given me a life I don't want to lose, Grant."

"All of this," he said, his eyes surveying the wreckage in the room, "is because you are afraid? After I saw you and our son stare down my brothers this afternoon? When I said you had enough courage to fight a battalion, Carolina, I woefully misjudged you, and for that, I apologize. Because you are human, I have underestimated you since the beginning. Unsure I could trust your instincts ... or even if I wanted to ... there was too much at stake for me to take that risk and be wrong. But you have shown me over and over that you are not only beautiful, kind, and gentle, but intelligent and, oh, my darling, so brave."

He took my hands and looked at me seriously. "Do not be afraid, Carolina. You will never lose me or what I have given you."

"I won't?"

"No."

Tears came to my eyes, and I whispered, "What do we do now?"

"I feed you so the children won't starve."

I looked at him.

Sighing, Grant pulled me into his embrace and pressed his forehead against mine. *We will love each other, Carolina, and we will love our son and his brothers. We won't stop, no matter what happens. If ... when ... we are separated, that love is not going to change, weaken, or disappear. I am yours, and you are mine. We share a consciousness that wherever one of us is, the other is there as well. Every day, you will be my first and last thought, as I know I will be yours. No power in the universe can change that. No power in the universe would want to.*

Unlike our violent lovemaking that afternoon, Grant kissed me with such tenderness and so much love that I recalled the morning he kissed his son. Captured within it was a dimension that transcended our feelings for each other and showed me what we were together.

Our lives changed that afternoon. All the words we'd said to each other since the morning Austin was born converged, and somewhere between my knocking him to the floor and his tender kiss, I understood what "being one" meant to him and knew I would never have a life apart from his.

Dan was wrong. I would never be nothing.

Damages

Waiting until she was asleep, Grant quietly stepped out of their bed and slipped into the bathroom. He walked quickly to the cabinet containing his medical bag and removed a scalpel, a flat round jar of anti–toxicant, a hemostat, and a package of gauze. After tearing the soft mesh into small pieces, he carefully eased the fabric of his robe away from the oozing lesions. He dipped a towel in scalding hot water, placed it over his chest and shoulders, and willed himself to leave it there.

It was his fault. He was so busy listening to what Grayson was saying to him telepathically that he wasn't paying attention to how stressful the afternoon had been for her. The fact that she retaliated so forcefully meant she was beginning to merge with the darker auras of his mind. Soon, she would be ready to embrace and share *all* he was. However, total synthesis would be impossible if she was distracted by Grayson's recent scheme to separate them. It was intolerable. They had to stay together, and that, too, had to be at Grayson's request.

Grant was suddenly grateful for every festering welt.

Adjusting the three–paneled mirror of Carolina's vanity table, Grant tilted his head.

Garrett.

Grant.

Will you take a look at these, please. Grant lifted the towel.

Oh, sweet Anya, what happened to you?

She attacked and bit me ... several times.

Garrett was afraid to ask the next question. He did not want the children sent away. Almost as deeply as Grant, Garrett knew how important it was for them to have a real mother. However, if other arrangements needed to be made, it was best to begin as soon as possible.

Is she still alive?

For now. Do I need you, or will lancing the punctures myself and bathing them in the anti-toxicant be enough?

Lean closer to the mirrors. Looking through Grant's eyes, Garrett examined the bite marks. *Is this all?*

No, there are comparatively minor scratches on my shoulders and arms where she clawed me.

You should be able to bandage those yourself. I'll, um, meet you in your lab if you need help with the deeper wounds.

Thank you, Garrett. I will take care of it. I just wanted your opinion.

Moving from one bite mark to the other, Grant used his scalpel to make an incision a fraction deeper than the punctures. Lifting the blistered skin, he immediately doused the wounds with gauze saturated with the anti-toxicant. He clenched his teeth in pain and listened. So much depended on who contacted him first.

Grant!

Grayson.

Is everything all right?

Yes. Thank you for your concern.

Is she still ...?

Yes, Grayson. She's alive. The children need her.

Are they safe with her?

Grant laughed hoarsely. *Oh yes, they're safe. I thought you were concerned about me.*

Well, I am, of course, Grant, but the children are our highest priority.

If that is true, Grayson, then why did you want me to propose to her that we move her and the children to the colony's nursery?

I didn't intend for her to move there ... just the children. She could visit them every four hours to feed them instead of us coming to her rooms twice a day. Gregory and Gordon tell me she looks at them like they're kidnappers.

From her perspective, they are. I wish they had been here this afternoon. Maybe I would be slicing up their chests. This is their fault as much as yours.

Before we start accusing anyone, Grant, please explain what happened.

Sending them just enough images of the wreckage in the front room to support his story, Grant fabricated a more useful version of that afternoon's events. *After you left, I woke her up to feed her, and she immediately started complaining about everyone being here. To pacify her, I told her what you suggested. I assumed she was considering it because she was quiet and calm when I scanned her thoughts. I helped her put the boys in the nursery crib and went into the kitchen to clean up. A moment later, the IV stand crashed to the floor behind me, and when I turned around, she slammed into me. I thought it best not to hurt her ... we need her ... but each time I pushed her away, she attacked me again. When she got tired of scratching and biting me, she became hysterical and said the children were either hers or they weren't, but she wasn't an animal to be gawked at or a human milk truck—whatever the hell that means—then she cried herself to sleep.*

Can't you ... um, encourage her?

Encourage her to do what? What else is there? At your request, I separated her from her family, persuaded her to stay so she would have the baby here—just two days ago, I might add—and through emotional manipulation, she has willingly, actually joyfully, agreed to nurse three additional children. You saw how she was today ... she wants them with her. Are you willing to sacrifice that level of compliance for the sake of your convenience? Are you, Gabriel? Are you, Garrett?

Garrett answered first. *No, I'm not, Grant. It is not inconvenient for me to come to Carrie's apartment to examine the children. Gabriel?*

At first, there was no response from Gabriel, but a moment later, they were all receiving images of the colony's nursery being dismantled. Interns were pulling the wires out of the walls, and cabinets were being emptied of their contents and packed neatly into boxes. Gabriel's protégé, Hugo, stood in front of the incinerator chute feeding everything into it that would fit and breaking into smaller pieces anything that was too large.

Hearing their thoughts, Grant could not decide who was angrier: Grayson because the colony's nursery was being destroyed or Gabriel for Grayson's secret attempt to separate the children from a loving mother.

Grayson spoke first. *Gabriel.*

Grayson.

I could order sanctions against you for the deliberate destruction of colony property.

And what, Grayson, is the punishment for the deliberate attempt to sabotage the wellbeing of an infant brother? Unilateral actions have never been tolerated in this colony, and we will not begin now. Never, Grayson, make another decision regarding Albert Gabriel Gates without my direct approval again.

Or Ashley Garrett Gates, said Garrett.

Or Antony Gregory Gates, added Gordon and Gregory simultaneously.

Grant was careful to smother his smile. *The only good news, my brothers, is that these marks indicate she has bonded with all of our children. This early sign of attachment gives us the means of continuing to successfully control her.*

Promise me, Grant, said Gabriel, *promise me that you will not retaliate or punish her for defending her relationship with them. I think, and I leave it to your discretion, of course, that there is still too much estrogen in the V4. I* would suggest backing the IV down a little more and propose constant monitoring until she is stable.

With an expression on his face that they all feared, Grant paused and added more anti-toxicant. *I will promise not to hurt her, Gabriel, unless she attacks me again. However, constant monitoring will be difficult as I am scheduled to return to my office tomorrow morning.* Grant heard them talking and waited for it.

The thought of leaving her alone with their infant brothers was bad enough, but the thought of taking them away from her was far worse. If anything happened to undermine their development, Grayson knew Grant would report to the collective that he was following the colony leader's request to separate the children from not only a compliant mother but a loving one.

Grayson had no defense. He was already outnumbered by half the colony, and if Grant stood against him, it would only be a matter of time before he was demoted to excavating tunnels under Gregory's supervision.

Grant.

Grayson.

Well, um, Grant, we would be gratified if you would delay returning to your administrative responsibilities until Carrie is stabilized. We know this may be difficult for you, but we must prevail upon your patience for the sake of the children. Do you think if we reduce our visits to once a day, at noon perhaps, with only two of us in attendance, that we will not put too much of a burden on Carrie's hospitality?

Grant had just gotten everything he wanted from his impromptu performance; there was only one scene missing, and she was right on time.

Roused from sleep by the sound of running water, I knew immediately Grant was not beside me and grew more awake the longer he was absent. Thinking he was waiting for me to join him, I tiptoed into the bathroom. The shower and the bath were empty. I heard the clink of metal on glass to my left and moved toward the sound. Nothing in our relationship prepared me for the sight of Grant with a bloodied towel thrown loosely over his shoulder, standing in front of my mirror dabbing a greenish paste where I had bitten and scratched him. Each time he touched his skin, his jaw clenched, and the paste turned black as blood bubbled from his wounds.

I froze in my footsteps.

Is this how you love me, Carolina?

Overcome with guilt, I rushed up to him.

"Oh, Grant, I am so sorry," I cried, immediately reaching for the jar. "Can I help you?"

Grant slapped my hands away. Hard.

"No, you cannot *help* me. You have already done quite enough damage for one day."

"But, Grant—"

"Get out of here, Carrie. Now!"

Sobbing, I turned and fled the room.

Um, Grant?

It was just a test, Gabriel. I needed to ascertain her level of repentance. Pretty high, wouldn't you say? Her feelings of guilt will increase her submissiveness.

You promised.

I will not punish her. Grant paused for a moment. He knew that was not what Gabriel—or the colony—wanted to hear. *And with the colony's approval and cooperation, I promise I will never do anything to take the joy of our children from her heart.*

He would not destroy their mother.

Thank you, Grant.

The brothers who had feared and isolated him suddenly came together, and the colony reverberated with their heartfelt thoughts of gratitude. If he had not loved Carolina before, he would have cherished her forever for that single moment of complete solidarity.

Lost in my misery and crying quietly against the far side of the bed so I would not wake the children, I didn't hear Grant return to our room. It was not until I felt the soft terrycloth robe at my back as his arms encircled me that I knew I was forgiven.

"Shh, Carolina, my darling, shh. There is nothing to cry about. In fact, I have some very good news."

Despite his soothing words, I could still hear the pain in his voice and once again saw his face reflected in the mirror. I turned in his arms.

"Oh, Grant, I hurt you. I didn't mean to. I'm so, so sorry."

"Minor tears only, toxic, but not fatal ... this time, but you must not bite me ever again, Carolina. Human bacterium injected directly into our bloodstream is poisonous. I would have mentioned it before, but this, well, it was one of the few things I had not foreseen. Your touch has always been so ... gentle."

"I'm poison?"

His lips were warm against my neck. *Much the same as our formic acid is to you. Although incompatible, both are relatively harmless elements unless a barrier is breached. And, if you will remember, my dear, several barriers were breached this afternoon. I had to use an anti–toxicant to eradicate your microbes from the flesh of my wounds so they will heal.*

But why wouldn't you let me help?

Carolina, you are not listening. The medicine dissolves human microbes. Do you know what exists on your wonderfully soft body, most especially your hands?

Microbes?

Persephone's Children

Yes, and I don't want anything to happen to these beautiful, perfect hands of yours. The way they feel against my skin, Carolina, would have been worth protecting, even at the cost of another dozen incisions.

Wanting to erase the memory of pain on his face and the crescents of blackened blood on his chest, my beautiful, perfect hands slid beneath the edges of his robe.

"Like this, Grant?"

Oh, yes, Carolina. Exactly like that.

Another Child

Shortly after midnight, I went into the nursery and gazed at my son's brothers. Grant came up behind me and threaded his fingers around my waist.

I leaned lightly against him. "Grant," I said, keeping my voice low, "couldn't we ... could we have another child?"

Lifting me into his arms, we sat in his blue chair.

"No, Carolina," he said gently, "for so many reasons. The most important is that I will not allow you to risk your life when I may not be around to save you. You cannot want to leave our son an orphan for that, regardless of how many pheromones you try to put in the air, which, by the way, you cannot do while you are nursing."

Unexpected tears filled my eyes.

"I just wish I could have had more of your children."

Kissing my tears away, he touched his forehead to mine. *That is the kindest compliment I have ever had. Thank you for that, Carolina, my dearest wife.*

"*Grant, couldn't we ... could we have another child?*"

She said that? Exactly like that? Gregory asked.

Are you asking if I gave her a script to read? I told you she would be more submissive. This is just evidence of her repentance.

Are you sure it isn't out of context? Give us the entire memory, Grant.

No, Grayson.

Why?

I am not required to share intimate details of our relationship with the collective.

Intimate? How can you have "intimate" details, Grant? Gregory asked skeptically.

Grant laughed. *Gregory, you, of all my brothers, should know how dream sequencing works. In our little melodrama, she thinks Adam is our child. It was part of the experiment ... the marriage, the baby ... all part of the emotional manipulation to encourage offspring acceptance. I am submitting this incident as further evidence of the experiment's success.*

Give us the context without the intimate details, Grant. I just want to know why she said it and what she was doing at the time.

Of course, Grayson. She was looking at the boys in the nursery crib and asked if she could have another child. I told her it wasn't possible while she was nursing, and she accepted my explanation.

Grant kept his voice even but despised every word that trivialized one of the sweetest moments of his life. It was important to submit evidence that his methods were successful, but as much as he resented the brothers who exacted such a high price, there was nothing he would not say or do to keep his little family together for as long as possible.

I will continue to observe her emotional behavior around the children to determine exactly what triggered that particular response. If we can replicate it in other mothers, perhaps we would not need to find new ones for each generation.

Good work. We will, however, expect the details in your final report, Grant. All of them.

Of course.

A Taste of Honey

Grant had surrounded me with beauty and elegance from the first moment of our lives together, but nothing compared to the sumptuousness of the honey he'd implanted in my throat. It infused my life. Drinking hot tea carried the deliciously sweet heat all the way to my toes, and the air I breathed was perfume.

I was reveling in this new delight one evening when, without thinking, I asked, "Why didn't Eric like the smell of the honey, Grant? He practically threw the jar across the room."

Grant slowly lifted his head and looked over the edge of the laptop screen.

Why this sudden memory of Eric? Grant quickly scanned her thoughts. Realizing she only wanted to know why Eric did not like the honey as much as she did, Grant decided to tell her.

"Of course, Eric hated it. He is *supposed* to."

"What do you mean?"

"We originally introduced the scent into our food as a defense mutation. It was just another thing we learned from nature. For instance, the milkweed that caterpillars feast on makes them toxic to predators. It is how they stay alive long enough to become butterflies. Unless threatened, most predators will not kill what they won't eat, and the odor of our honey made us—as well as our homes and food—very unappetizing to many of our natural enemies, including human men. One of the reasons the scent is so prevalent throughout the clinic is that human men find it noxious and cannot endure it for long. By your laws, we cannot exclude them from the public areas of the facility, but we can make them very uncomfortable. On the other hand, human women love the fragrance and taste of our honey. It not only triggers endorphins, but the honey also temporarily alters their internal chemistry, so they become part of the ambient atmosphere of the clinic. To increase its effectiveness, we encourage them to eat it at breakfast so the scent will have time to dissipate before nightfall."

"I remember Garrett mentioning that, but what difference does it make when we eat it?"

"Most of your species mates between dinner and breakfast, and we needed our clients to be pregnant. Since the scent decreases male virility and controls male lust, it works as a kind of olfactory birth control. It was one of the ways we kept our females, when we had them, safe from human men."

"So, this intoxicatingly wonderful taste that will be in my mouth until I die will prevent men from desiring me?"

Grant looked back down at the laptop and closed his eyes. She had no idea how those words affected him. Unbidden images of Austin's first father holding her, of Dan sleeping next to her for nearly twenty years when he only had a few precious months, and, finally, the faceless human men who would want to touch *his wife* when he would not be there to protect her were the demons populating the darker side of Grant's love for her. She did not know that he wanted her every moment of every day. How hard he fought against taking her into the deepest levels underground, carving a chamber big enough for the two of them, and transforming their sanctuary of peace into a cavern of shadows where he would feed her honey from his own lips until she could not live without him and gradually alter her mind until he was her only memory. Only his devotion to Austin saved her from that fate. Still, even he could not prevent Grant's obsessive hunger for complete control of Carolina's heart.

Grant calmed the flashes of fire burning behind his eyes and looked at her.

"Oh, they will still desire you, Carolina, until they get too close to your lips."

I stared at him unbelievingly.

"Why are you surprised? I told you I could not keep any part of me from you. This ... gift ... is just one more way of sharing what I am and protecting you when I can no longer be with you."

"But why, Grant?" It was barely a whisper.

I caught an almost feline smile on his face before he moved swiftly toward me. His hand slid around the back of my head and pulled my face upward. Kissing me hard, his tongue circled my lips.

"So I could taste my love on your mouth and be reminded every time I kiss you that you are mine. And, before you judge me too harshly, *wife*, please consider my motives," he said as his hands inched toward my throat. "If I would not share you with my brothers, why would I leave you alone and defenseless with *the destroyers*?"

Embracing me, his lips moved against my skin. "Let *them* touch *you*, kiss *your* mouth, *hurt you*? I promised I would protect you to the best of my ability, Carolina, and I have."

"Is this how you love me, Grant? I love you better than this."

"No. You love me differently. Someday soon, Carolina, I will bring you into my mind and let you see the truth of how I love you. Until then, do not attempt to define it by your human limitations."

I tried to step back, but his arms were like steel encircling me.

"Who *are* you?"

I knew he wasn't human, but this, this was something else, something unexpected and frightening. My breath became gasps as I remembered how his brothers treated him. I thought it was because of our relationship, but I was beginning to believe it was much more than that.

His breath was hot on my neck. "Think carefully, Carolina. You know who I am, and you know what I am, and despite all that, you also know why you stay. So, if I were you, my love, I would be very careful with your next question because if you even think it, I will tell you, and trust me, you may not really want to know the answer. I will not lie to you, and nothing will change. You will still be—every square inch of you, inside and out—mine. *Only mine.* I was not the first man to love you, Carolina, but I will be the last. No other man will touch you, kiss you, or hold you. You will bear no other man's child. I will be on your lips every morning and in the last breath you take at night. When you made me promise to love you today, tomorrow, and forever, I *meant* it."

He kissed me slowly, stroking the tips of his fingers from my hips to my shoulders, again and again. When I began to tremble, he brought his mouth down hard on the hollow of my throat, and bitter honey ran like wildfire through my senses. Catching me just as my knees folded, he lifted me and placed me on the bed.

Beautiful and dangerous, he towered above me.

"Carolina, my own, now that you know what this gift from me really means, I want you to thank me again for sharing my ... What did you call it? Oh, yes, my *essence* with you. And, wife, demonstrating a certain level of enthusiasm would be appropriate."

Trembling, aching for him, the words of gratitude I spoke the morning I'd first discovered this *gift* echoed in the room.

"Thank you, Grant, for sharing your essence with me. Now ... now I will have you with me always."

"You are welcome, Carolina," he said, untying the sash to his robe. "Now make me believe you *mean* it."

Later, after my enthusiasm had worn down Grant's resentment and he rested with his head in my lap, my fingers gently smoothed lines on his face that had not been there a few weeks before. He was right. I didn't understand the ambitions and fears that motivated him, but despite my human limitations, I understood that the taste of him would haunt me for the rest of my life.

Tears filled my eyes when I realized that this last part of him would imprison me in a living hell of endless anticipation and disappointment. Every time I looked around, expecting him to be there, I would be reminded he was gone. Waking up every morning anticipating his touch, there would be nothing but the emptiness of scented air.

Swallowing the tears of self–pity of my imagined life without him, I remembered I'd promised to love and accept all that he was and, if sentencing me to a lifetime of delicious torture was just one more facet of the way he loved me, I accepted it as being the only way he could.

Anya

Surrounded by four pairs of sleepy eyes, I read aloud from one of Brendan's storybooks. I wasn't sure they understood my language, so I added images to the words. Not hearing Grant come in, I lost my place when I heard his voice.

"You needn't try so hard, my love; they understand you. In reality, it translates more like a movie than a written book."

"How?"

"Austin sees the story through your eyes and shares it with his brothers. He ignores the words and feels the story through your thoughts and emotions."

"So, I'm reading out loud to myself?"

"No. Although their ears are still forming, they love the sound vibrations of your voice … it is music to them."

"Then I'm a movie producer?"

"Yes," he said, "worthy of an Academy Award—at least from this audience. Gregory would be so jealous."

"Speaking of which, I think I'm losing my audience." Laughing softly, I put the sleepy babies in their crib.

Grant began singing, and, one by one, smiles illuminated the boys' faces. The song was so lovely. I asked him what it was.

"Anya's prayer of children."

"Grant, shouldn't I know who she is and how she figures into your religion?"

"Anya is our goddess mother, our guide to what you would call heaven. And it is not a religion, Carolina. Our love for Anya is at the core of who we are. As Lyostians, we seek the gateway to heaven. The gateway is Atjaro, and Anya is our guide. Without her, we would be lost for eternity."

"Does Anya escort every Lyostian to Atjaro?"

"Not all. Lyostians can be forgiven for actions or thoughts that lead to banishment. Our mother knows we are not perfect, but there is one thing for which we cannot be forgiven."

I looked at him expectantly.

"We cannot be forgiven for taking ourselves out of the collective without permission."

"You mean suicide?"

"Yes, but it is a much harsher word in our language. You see, each colony rests upon the building blocks of its members. As the older generations age, younger brothers are trained to take their elders' places when they die. Those who choose to leave their colony prematurely weaken the colony structure and, depending on their function within the colony, such selfishness can lead to the destruction of the whole. There is no forgiveness for that level of betrayal, only a dark, formless silence for eternity."

"That sounds like hell."

"No, it's worse than a Christian hell. From what I have read, your hell is full of damned or unrepentant souls. We are alone in ours forever. Unable to bear banishment alive for a day, such colony traitors beg for forgiveness or permission to die."

"How can you give someone who is banished permission?"

"It depends on the collective's view of the crime. There are a few ways, none of them pleasant, but sometimes a colony will have a leader or disciplinarian who dispenses punishments and will, um, grant the brother's wish to end his life by assisting him."

"Has that happened in this colony?"

He smiled slightly. "No. Anya has watched over us. All our original brothers are intact."

"How will I explain to our son about the gateway and the guide? I'm not sure I understand it very well myself. Or is that something he already knows?"

"We are born knowing; it is part of the collective consciousness."

"And the songs? Who taught you the songs?"

"They are there also."

"So that's why they respond to your singing. They already understand the words. They know who they are."

"Yes."

"What will happen to him when he grows up?"

"The elders of the collective will call him, and he will have to answer. They will decide how he spends the rest of his life. For the first twenty-five years, however, he will be yours."

"Grant, when the collective calls our son, will it be difficult for him to choose between who he is and who I am?"

"No. You will let him go," he said, bringing my hand to his lips. "Promise me you will let him go."

A sob caught in my throat. I was suddenly overwhelmed with the pain of losing Grant all over again. My eyes pleading for mercy did not find it in his. I tried to move my hand away, but he would not release it.

"Promise me," he insisted, "that you will make it *easy* for him to leave you."

This, I thought, *is the price for his love, the price I vowed to gladly pay.* Not my death, but our son's life. To do later what Grant was unwilling to do now: return our son to the collective, freely and without ties. My eyes filled with tears, but I could not go back, and there was only one way of going forward. I nodded my head, and to emphasize that he was not holding my hand against my will, I gently pressed it against his face.

"I promise he will not have to choose. On his twenty-fifth birthday, I will make it easy for him to leave me." Turning my head into his shoulder, I whispered, "I promise, my love, I will make it easy for *all of them* to leave me."

His lips moved against my skin.

"Thank you."

Later that night, I wondered how I was supposed to make it easy for a son who would love me his entire life to leave me alone. Once again, tears stung my eyes, and I assumed it would be like when Brendan left. Brave faces, shopping, and packing. I knew it wouldn't be easy, but if I could say goodbye to one much-loved son, I was confident I could find a way to do it again.

Changes

With four boys to care for, the late autumn days blurred together. Every morning, Grant went to his office for a few hours, returning just before noon to help prepare the children for their daily examination. One morning, about two weeks after they were born, I lifted Austin out of the bassinet.

"Grant! Look at this."

He quickly crossed the room. Austin's hands and feet had defused overnight. He had actual fingers and toes, still slightly curved but separate and perfect. Grant cradled him, looking at his hands, front and back, carefully examining each finger. He picked up his feet and tested them against his hand to see how much curve was left. Austin's feet went flat against his hand. Handing Austin to me, he went to Alexi and looked at his hands. Two of the five fingers had separated, and his toes were almost completely disconnected. His feet were not quite flat when pressed. Moving to Andre and Aslan, a quick check showed that they, too, had begun forming real fingers and toes.

"This is soon," he said.

"Is that bad?"

"No, it's all good, but I need another minute."

Taking Austin from me, he blew his hair back from the base of his antennae. Instead of the healthy pink color he was born with, it was almost white.

"What does this mean?" I whispered.

Grant didn't answer. Instead, he pointed toward the crib. "Go look at Alexi's feelers and let me know if they look the same. If you can't tell, please bring him to me."

Deciding to do both, I picked up Alexi and took him to Grant, checking on my way. While his antennae were not as pale as Austin's, they were lighter than when he was born.

My love, if you don't say something soon, I may start screaming.

"Well, if you must scream, scream for joy. This rate of development is unprecedented."

Turning Austin's head, Grant looked at his ears and tested the bridge of his nose, nodding in acknowledgment that development had also been made in those areas. He held Austin up and looked into his eyes.

"Austin, your mother is taking very good care of you, and you are growing stronger. I am proud of you, son."

A sudden flush of pleasure warmed my heart. I looked at Grant. *Was that you?*

No, your son just said thank you.

"You're welcome, my darling," I said, kissing his new fingers.

I saw images of Alexi, Andre, and Aslan.

"Yes, of course."

I kissed his forehead. *I should have thought of that myself.*

Walking to the crib, I kissed the hands of each of his brothers, telling them all how proud I was that they were getting so big and strong. Again, Austin thanked me in his unique way.

Watching me, Grant placed Austin in the crib with his brothers and, taking my hand, led me into the nursery. Sitting down, I said, "Okay, tell me everything."

"Just a couple of things. The most important one is that Austin will never let you treat him differently than the others, and you mustn't attempt to single him out ... for anything. I know you will want to, but you must never show him any favoritism. That he can hear your thoughts will make him different enough in their eyes; sharing your thoughts with them is his only way of keeping that particular ability balanced, but he will circumvent any effort you make to show more love to him. Know now that whatever you do for one, you must do for all four ... or as many as you have with you. You cannot treat Austin as your son and his brothers as stepchildren. You must treat them all as your sons. Because," he said, pulling me into his lap and stroking my breast with the back of his fingers, "they are."

He saw the doubt on my face. "Carolina, *he* will always know he has more of your heart, but the others must not see it. It will divide them because they love you just as fiercely as he does. Remember, he will need them someday and must be able to trust them completely. Only you can forge that alliance, and only you can break it. You must embrace them all; it will make them strong and united. It is what is best for him."

"You're right. Of course, I'm not just raising children, I'm raising soldiers. I can do that, Grant. I do love them all, it's just ...."

"I know."

"But they aren't clones. Aren't they going to be just like any other brothers, with different likes, dislikes, and interests? One will be good in math, one will hate it, one will like soccer, and the others will think that the offsides rule is the most confusing thing they've ever heard."

He laughed. "Yes and no. Yes, they are not clones. No, they will always do things together. Whatever it is, if one likes it, they will all be in it. If one wants a skateboard, buy four. They will share, but they will want to do it together. They truly will be all for one and one for all. And," he said, "all for you."

"They will do whatever you ask without hesitation, with love and total trust, and will take every wish as a command. Your happiness is their happiness, and I tell you this to warn you. Be very careful what you ask of them because they will burst their hearts to please you. They will love you unconditionally until you die, and then you will live in their collective memory for all time."

"I've just seen the rest of my life flash before my eyes, and they are still in diapers."

"And how did it look to you?"

"Wonderful, happy, full ... almost," I answered wistfully.

Not now, Carolina, later. There will be plenty of time later.

I snuggled against him while I still could.

"Wonderful, happy, full, and very busy! Now, please tell me what impresses you so much about their fingers and toes ... other than they are perfect," I said, holding his imperfect hands in mine.

"Two very important things, one directly connected to the other. They are developing so rapidly that the predicted effect of the V4 bonding was underestimated by at least fifty percent, maybe more. If they continue at this rate, their antennae will detach, and they will form functioning ears and noses within a week or ten days, allowing them to hear and breathe as humans do. That is more than two weeks ahead of the original estimates."

"That's great, Grant, but why is it affecting you like this? You're practically walking on air."

"Because of the second reason. Soon they will look exactly like human babies, only smaller."

"And?"

"And you could leave without having to explain to anyone why your babies have feelers and no noses."

I got very still. "And my leaving ... taking our children and leaving, makes you happy?"

"No, Carolina, I've told you, it will be like death without you. What makes me happy, if you want to use that word, relieved is more accurate, is that if you *had* to, for your safety or Austin's, you *could* leave. And knowing that you and the children would be safe, I would be strong enough to let you go."

"But what about their strength, Grant? You could barely stay away from the colony for thirty minutes. How will they endure being without you?"

"Because, love, you are their colony. Until they are called, you will be their leader and life force. Since their signature echoes are too weak at this stage to reach the collective consciousness, they have not yet been recorded. Therefore, they cannot be recognized, sought, or tracked. And do not worry; they will not be silent. They can hear each other, and Austin can hear you."

"Can't you leave with us?"

"No, because they will find me, and when they find me, they will find you and Austin. Someone will get hurt. I am quite willing for it to be me, but after using me to find you, I would be expendable, and with me either banished or relocated, you and our son will be powerless."

"But they are your brothers. They love you."

"Oh, my darling wife, only humans believe love and family are synonymous. Loyalty to the collective mandate overrides individual commitment. It has to, or we could all find ourselves in the position I have been in since approximately 3:07 p.m., August 13th. If you remove *choice* from the equation, you will find that it is a fairly simple, and usually rational, way to live."

"But you ...."

"Chose."

I nodded, smiling as bravely as I could. "I will always honor your choice to love me, Grant. I will not disappoint you. If you are willing to die for us, then I can live for them."

"Promise me again."

"I promise you."

With my head on his shoulder, he sang songs until, sighing, he said, "My brothers will be here in fifteen minutes."

"Who's coming?"

"Gabriel and Grayson."

"Good," I said, "Gabriel will be so happy to see Alexi's fingers."

Grant searched her thoughts. No deviousness lurked in her mind. She willingly and lovingly belonged to them. That afternoon, after his brothers left, he began the final alteration to the synapses in her brain. Like a scientist creating a predetermined path for a mouse in a maze, Grant gently closed most of the doors to Carolina's memory. Confident that she would never need them, he had already shaded over secondary relationships such as former work associates, acquaintances, and distant relatives. Now, memories of other entanglements and relationships would slowly fade until each avenue of her mind funneled her thoughts back to her family—her Lyostian family. It was the only way to keep her alive.

Those were not the only changes Grant made over the next few weeks. To eclipse distracting memories, he gave her new ones, impossible but irrefutable. Lastly, testing the triggers of her autonomic nervous system, he delayed her human freeze, fight, or flight response to allow for calm analysis before each reaction.

He could not predict all the obstacles that would come her way, but he would not leave her defenseless.

Grant's Report

Grayson began the meeting. "Before starting, I want to know if all of you have read Grant's report."

"Yes," Gordon, Gabriel, and Garrett responded simultaneously.

"Most of it," Gregory said.

Grayson sighed. "For those who have not finished it, I will recap the central points. According to Grant's model, Persephone is in her 30s, intelligent, and wants to have a child with someone she loves. His research into this field indicates that some women will pay or do anything to have the children they believe will complete their lives. He suggests that NAFTRAM realign its U.S. corporate model to meet those maternal aspirations by reopening under a new name as fertility clinics in two years. As with the fitness clinics, women will seek us out. Based on his recent experience, we don't need women who want to look better—we need women who want to be mothers. To maintain our credibility, we will help married women have human babies. However, healthy divorced or single women listening to their biological clocks tick away their fertility are women who will do whatever we say to conceive successfully, even to the point of living in our facility during that 'crucial' first trimester. Also, most of these women have experienced multiple miscarriages, and if they have another will not be surprised or litigious and will likely be willing to attempt yet another pregnancy. Therefore, if they successfully carry one of our offspring to term, they should be able to do it again. Grant estimates that a prospective mother will make up to three attempts before looking for another fertility clinic."

Gregory interrupted, "If we are spending our time helping married women have human babies, how is this any better than what we are already doing?"

Garrett threw a copy of the report in Gregory's direction. "If you had read this, you would know the most important information is that these women don't have to be pregnant when they come to us. With human technology catching up with our genetic engineering, it can all be done in vitro. We control everything from inception to birth. Not only that, *we* control how many fertilized eggs we implant. Since our offspring are so small, we can say we are implanting one or two when we could implant three or four embryos."

"Yes, but the best part is about the mothers," Gabriel added. "Following Grant's experimental methods, we will establish incrementally escalating relationships with all our unmarried prospective mothers. The successful ones most receptive to their doctor's advances will 'marry' him and become part of that colony. One or two per facility would be all we need."

Gregory smiled. "Yes, I get the percentage estimates, Gabriel, but what if no one is receptive?"

"That shouldn't be an issue. Grant's report indicates that following his methods, there will be at least one mother willing to do anything. We will maintain some of the reward innovations in place here and revert to the psychologically, rather than physically, addictive honey. It's less expensive to produce."

"And less incriminating," said Gordon.

"Wait a minute, he said they will do anything? For us? Why? We can't all be Grant Gates," Gregory said snidely.

"Not for us," Grayson laughed, "they will do anything for love."

Love! Love meant kissing them, and kissing meant tasting them. Gregory sat up eagerly, then shook his head. "But how can we 'marry' them if we are already engaged? Or is that scenario being scrapped as well?"

Gordon looked at his brother in frustration.

"Didn't you read any of this at all?"

"Not much. I've been busy."

"To answer your question, we are still engaged, but the difference is we now know what kind of woman we need. Once we decide who best fits the profile, we escalate the relationship."

"But if she knows we are engaged …?"

Gordon laughed. "Come on, Gregory. You, more than anyone else, should know the fleeting allure of the 'forbidden' relationship, the shipboard romance, the 'we'll always have Paris' plot device."

Gregory's eyes gleamed at his brother, and his smile returned. Rubbing his hands together, he looked at Grayson, "When do we start?"

Before Grayson could answer, Grant's voice cut through the room.

"We already have."

His brothers looked at him standing in the doorway. They knew he had just returned from the fifth room, in the fifth tunnel, on the fifth level that did not exist.

"And?" asked Grayson.

Grant glanced at the copy of his report on the table and echoed the words of the collective.

"We are pleased."

As he turned to leave the room, no one missed the bulge of the gun holster under his lab coat. Turning to look into the faces around the table, Grayson hoped he did not look as shaken as his brothers.

A Matter of Genetics

I was dreaming ... Someone was being hurt. Fear and helplessness washed over me, but it wasn't me. It was a child. A child was being hurt. Love tinged with terror touched my heart.

Oh, my dear God, it was Austin.

My heart pounded. I reached out for Grant, but there was no one beside me. Clutching at Austin's bassinet, it rocked emptily. I ran to the crib. My children were gone.

"Oh, please, God," I prayed, "let this be a nightmare, please, please," I begged as I opened the door and sped into the nursery.

Finding Andre and Aslan sleeping in the nursery crib lessened only part of my anxiety. Where was Alexi, and *where was Austin*? Ready to scream for Grant, I caught a flash of white through the nursery window and saw Grant and the other children in the examination room. As I watched, Grant pulled a needle out of one of the babies' feet. I flew through the door.

"Stop, Grant! What are you doing? Austin, Austin."

Catching Grant by surprise, I pushed him aside and grabbed Austin out of the examination crib. Backing toward the nursery door, I sheltered him with my shoulder and tried to cover him with my hands.

"Carolina," Grant said, holding up his hands—one empty, one holding a blood-filled syringe. "It's all right."

Checking Austin's feet, I found a smear of blood and accused, condemned, and executed Grant with a single glance.

"What kind of father are you," I hissed, "to steal our son in the dead of night and stick needles in him without talking to me first?" I stared at him with outraged disbelief. "How can that *ever* be all right, Grant?"

"Shh, Caro—"

My maternal instincts were in overdrive. I cut him off.

"How can you hurt our son? He woke me, Grant, he called me. You were hurting him!"

The thought of anyone, especially Grant, hurting this tiny baby crushed me. My voice broke, but not my resolve.

Grant looked at Austin, and Austin steadily gazed back at him over my shoulder. After a few seconds, Grant lowered his hands. "I cannot fight you both."

Picking up Alexi, Grant entered the kitchen and placed the syringe in the refrigerator. I followed him one doorway at a time as he walked into the nursery, kissed Alexi, and put him in the crib with his brothers. Still protecting Austin, I backed into the front room.

Grant looked at us from the nursery doorway. "It isn't what you think, Carolina."

"How do I know what to think, Grant? You didn't discuss it with me, remember?"

"Carolina, before we 'discuss' this further, I want you to understand that I have the drugs, the training, and, regrettably, the expertise to convince you that this has all been a dream. Please consider that before you condemn me for what I've done—or was attempting to do—which would be more accurate."

"Why don't you just talk to me instead of threatening me?"

"As you wish."

He turned toward the bedroom. Unconvinced and unwilling to follow him, I sat in the chair nearest the front door.

Grant stood at the foot of their bed, his head bent forward. *It is a matter of trust,* he thought. He picked up the quilt and walked to where she sat with Austin. Not on the sofa where he could join her, but alone and far away from him. Her mind was still in a defensive panic, but Austin, Austin's mind was quite clear.

He brought the quilt to cover them, but she held out her hand.

"Just toss it. It's not necessary for you to come any closer."

He did as she asked and sat at the far end of the sofa.

"Is it all right to sit here, or am I too close?"

Measuring the distance with my eyes, I knew, and he knew, that I would never reach the front door before he could stop me. Mentally surrendering the field of battle, I held on to the prize.

"Isn't that irrelevant, Grant?"

"Yes. But you are right. I'll never make you understand as long as you feel threatened, so I will sit wherever you like until you are rational."

"On the moon, perhaps?"

"Only if I can sit on the dark side."

"Of course." I looked down at Austin. "How do you feel, sweetheart? Better now that Mommy is holding you?"

Austin's love settled over my mind like a warm cloak, and I realized he was no longer frightened. I glanced in Grant's direction.

"And your father, Austin, how do you feel now?"

The strength of the emotion he transmitted to my mind was completely unexpected. It was not the gentle, almost adoring love he felt for me but fiercer with a sense of loyalty that bewildered me. Feelings that intense couldn't possibly be coming from a three-week-old baby. I sent the sensation to Grant.

Okay, explain.

"Will you come over here?"

I kissed Austin and whispered, "Let me know if we need to move."

Austin answered me with a mixture of his feelings for both of us tangled together and indistinguishable. His lack of fear calmed me down completely.

"Yes, Austin, my son, we all love each other very much and should try to understand and," I looked up at Grant, "trust each other." Austin smiled at me and, knowing everything was right again in his world, fell asleep.

I moved to get up, but before I could push against the cushions, Grant had us in his arms, and we were all sitting on the sofa.

"I'm sorry, Carolina," he said, kissing my ear through my hair.

"Not so fast. You have a lot of explaining to do," I said, trying to sound stern. "Start with why there is a syringe full of Austin's blood in the refrigerator."

"But that is the end of our discussion, shouldn't we ... couldn't we ... begin at the beginning?"

"Oh, you mean the beginning you neglected to tell me about before you stuck a needle in my son's foot?"

"Yes."

"Is it going to make a difference?"

"It already has."

"All right then," I said, leaning back into his arms, "from the beginning."

"But you already know the beginning, Carolina. You were there."

After placing Austin carefully in the chair, Grant took his wife in his arms. Pressing her deep into the cushions so she could sense nothing but him, he kissed her passionately and shared every memory he possessed of that summer afternoon four months earlier.

Remember, love? Remember?

"Yes, Grant. I remember. I'll always remember. My life stopped and began again that day."

"As did mine, Carolina," he whispered.

"But what is the connection between that and the syringe ...?" She stopped talking and sat up. "It's the genetics, right? He isn't the same as the others?"

Realizing that she understood his reasoning—if not his methods—he reached for her hand and tried to calm her apprehensions.

"That has yet to be determined. I was in the process of ascertaining Austin's genetic properties when he understood what I was doing and called you to stop me."

"You mean he didn't wake me to stop you because he was scared or hurt? He woke me because ... because he didn't want you to change him?"

Grant guided the thoughts racing through her mind until she understood.

"That explains all the intense feelings of loyalty and love. He doesn't want you to take yourself out of him."

"Evidently."

"Did you tell him what you were doing to him? Or did you think he wouldn't guess or wouldn't care?"

He sighed at her onslaught of questions.

"I told him what I was doing. I didn't tell him why. But he knew, Carolina, he *knew*, and he wasn't scared or hurt; he was angry."

He looked down at his hands. "I didn't expect his anger."

"Or mine?"

"Or yours. I was so focused on rationalizing to our son *why* I couldn't let my physiology undermine his future that I didn't hear your thoughts until you came in and snatched him away from me."

"And you didn't bother telling me any of this because?"

He covered his eyes with his hand. "It was nearly impossible for me to explain to him why I needed to do it, and he understands *everything*. He just won't agree. So how, Carolina, could I tell you? When you know how much having a child with you means to me. You would never willingly let me re-sequence his DNA without mine. But I can't wait any longer. The children are developing so fast that the window is closing for me to make any substantial changes to his genetic structure if there are abnormalities. It was to protect him, but as I said, I can't, I won't fight you both. Anya, help us all."

I knew the consequences if Austin's unique parentage was discovered. If anyone had the slightest suspicion that Grant's DNA might exist in our son—regardless of how it got there—he would be considered an anomaly; they would take him, test him, and very possibly kill him as all the other Fire Slayers except Grant had been killed. I also knew that Grant would never let him be taken from us, and I could lose them both if there was a confrontation.

"Did you get Alexi's blood?" I asked softly.

"Yes."

"And Austin's is in the refrigerator?"

"Yes."

"Can you compare them here?"

"Yes."

"Then let's see."

His head came up. "What?"

"Grant, let's see what the fuss is all about. If, for some reason, your brothers do their own test, we can't let them surprise us. We have to know so we can have an explanation ready." I raised an eyebrow. "I hear you are a gifted geneticist. I'm sure you will think of some brilliant reason to justify it."

He was silent.

"You were going to do that, anyway, weren't you?"

"Yes, and soon. As I said, any re-sequencing must be done while he is still developing."

He smiled as I leaned against him. "And you are right, Carolina, I couldn't risk being taken by surprise."

"How long will the comparison take?"

"Twenty minutes to run Austin's sample through the hemo-spectrometer and another ten to print out the analysis with the DNA markers of both samples."

"Can I help?"

"Can you put Austin in his bassinet and make tea while I set everything up?"

"Of course."

Grant and I sipped our tea and tried to think of things to say, but our thoughts were centered on the machine whirring and clicking in the next room. As soon as the printer stopped, our eyes met. He took my hand, and we walked into the silent examination room together.

Grant unrolled the printout and, using various jars, books, and instruments, we pressed the paper flat on the counter. Checking one line at a time, he compared and analyzed the markers, making notes with a blue pencil in his left hand and a red pencil in his right. Looking over his shoulder, I noticed the graph indicated the comparative analysis of three samples. I knew without asking, but I said, "The third sample, Grant?"

"Mine."

I nodded and unsuccessfully tried to stifle a yawn.

He turned around. "You look tired, Carolina, and this is going to take a while; why don't you go to sleep, and I will tell you everything in the morning?"

"No. If it is bad, you will tell me it was all a dream because 'you have the drugs, training, and expertise' to make me believe it. I'll just go into the front room and do an exercise video or two to stay awake."

He took me into his arms and kissed my forehead.

"I promise I won't do that, Carolina. Please rest. The boys are going to need you in a few hours."

Backing away from him, I smiled and started doing jumping jacks.

"I don't believe you, Grant."

His laughter followed me as I did jumping jacks all the way into the front room.

Grant walked in as I was working my way through the third exercise video.

"Now I know where our son gets his tenaciousness," he said, sitting on the sofa as I was doing crunches on the floor.

I grinned up at him.

"What's the verdict?"

"Carolina, I am a doctor, not a lawyer. The correct question is, 'What is the diagnosis?'"

"You're stalling," I said. "You always get very picky about semantics when you're stalling."

"I do?"

"Yes. Now, what did you find out?" I stopped exercising and looked up at him. "Please."

"Good news or the bad news first?"

"Still stalling, Grant. Please, love, just tell me." Taking his hand, I let him pull me up beside him.

"The analysis would have been more complete if we had your and Eric's DNA to add to the data pool, but we wouldn't have that information on any of the children, so I didn't ask for yours."

"Is something missing, Grant?"

"It isn't what's missing, Carolina, it's what he has in addition to Alexi's markers."

"Like what?"

"Me."

"How much of you?"

"More than I can re-sequence ... if I had to."

"You don't have to?"

"No."

"Why?"

"The DNA markers for the Lyostian strain are all there, as are the markers for the arthropod mutation."

"That's good, but isn't your DNA detectable?"

"Only if my DNA is analyzed against Austin's, and there is no reason for anyone to do that. As it is, his and Alexi's species markers are identical, which makes him the one hundred percent human-hybrid he is supposed to be, which is very good. The additional Lyostian DNA is evident only when comparing our spectrum analyses, as well as other similar specific-to-me anomalies. So many that it is impossible to remove them without damaging the strand, but, as I said, they are only noticeable when seen side by side. However," he shook his head, wonderingly, "there are more similarities than I would have ever believed possible as his second father."

Resting his head against the sofa, he looked at the ceiling as though the answer was written in the colors refracted there. I waited patiently as he reviewed the re-conception protocols in his mind. Suddenly, he lifted his head and looked at me.

"It was you."

"Me?"

He stood and began pacing. "Of course! The specific timing, the precise environment, all of the known quantities and controls we set in place to exact a predetermined DNA sequence were altered because we were inside *you* at the same time."

Hesitating, he sat back down.

"But it still feels as though I am missing something because it doesn't explain the lack of ... and what would cause ...?"

He caught his breath. "Dear, blessed Anya, is that even possible?"

Grant slipped from the sofa to the floor in front of me and, pressing his hands against his eyes, prayed aloud. He seemed to be arguing with someone. Back and forth, their one-sided discourse ran until, as though finally allowing himself to be convinced of something too wonderful to be true, Grant's voice filled the room with joyous praise.

I recognized the words immediately. When he stopped singing, I whispered, "That's my song."

"What?"

"The music I hear before I fall asleep, the words I told you about ... it's that song."

"Then you've always known."

Grant dropped his head into his hands. As still as stone, he shared a continuous stream of Lyostian prayers with me. I waited until he removed his hands from his eyes.

"Grant, my love, what is it I have always known?"

There was a touch of wonderment in his voice when he said, "I forgot about the pheromones."

"What about them? Was there something wrong with me?"

"No, Carolina, there was something incredibly right about you. You were emitting pheromones because nature wasn't finished. The reason we found only one embryo was because there was just one ... but you were still fertile, and the promise of Austin was right here," his finger lightly touched my abdomen, "waiting for me to love you so together we could create a new life—*his* life. My darling, the music you hear hasn't been sung for hundreds and hundreds of years."

With shaking hands, he reached up and eased me beside him. His long arms and legs completely encircled me, and he buried his face in my neck.

"Carolina," he said, his voice ragged and strained, "my sweet, wonderful wife, it was you. You gave me a son, a real son, *mine*."

His fingers dug into my shoulders while tears hot as acid fell upon my breast.

After a few moments, he stood up. Without looking back at me, he wiped his face with his hands. I followed him quietly as he went into our room and picked up his son. Leaving the blue blanket in the bassinet, he touched his forehead to Austin's and stepped into our bed. Layers of iridescent netting closed around them, and the room became completely black. The bioluminescence of my bower glowed softly as I quietly backed out and closed the door.

Returning to the examination room, I put the books and other items we used to flatten the paper back into the cabinets. Covered in Grant's handwriting, blue pencil circled line after line with GG noted at the top. I wanted to keep it like every mother wants a copy of her child's birth certificate or genealogical record, but it was too risky; I knew they would hunt Austin to the ends of the earth if his true parentage was ever discovered.

I took the paper into the kitchen. Lighting a candle, I burned strip after strip in the sink. Watching the last edge blacken and curl, a twinge of sadness touched my heart for the twin I lost. Eric's baby, the little one whose valiant efforts never had a chance against the survival instincts and relentless determination of the Lyostian–conceived son of Grant Gates.

Reluctant to disturb any of the men in my life, I made myself comfortable on the sofa. I was just beginning to hear the voices that would forever sing me to sleep when Grant's arms lifted me to his chest.

Persephone's Children

"Not without me, Carolina," he said, carrying me to our room. "You are never going to sleep or wake up without me again."

It wasn't until much later that I discovered Grant had only cried twice in his life. The first time was when he lost his mother; the second, when he found his son.

Secrets

As he did every evening since the boys arrived, Grant checked on them telepathically before bringing Carolina into the curve of his body so he could sleep. Starting with Aslan, he went from mind to mind, always ending with Austin. As on most nights, he found them wrapped in the reassuring sounds of each other's heartbeats until he touched Austin's mind.

That night, Austin was waiting for him.

Austin.

Father.

You should be sleeping; you need your rest to grow.

I will. I waited so you could sing Anya's song of forgiveness with me.

My son, why do you need Anya's forgiveness?

Because I killed him.

Any lingering reservations about Austin's parentage disappeared with that single confession. Grant knew that possessing almost pure Fire Slayer DNA meant Austin would instinctively destroy any perceived threat.

I know, my son. We are Tuzurias; it is who we are.

Yes, Father, that is why I waited. I know who you are.

Grant was shaken. The horror of his life spent as an assassin rose up and filled him with regret.

You know, then, it was never my choice.

Yes. I promise it will never be mine.

Austin, in my life, I never wanted to burden anyone with those memories — least of all you. I am sorry, my son, more than I can say.

Be sorry for nothing, Father. We are one.

Yes, my son, we are one.

Grant stared into the darkness as Austin slipped into sleep.

We are one, the little voice had said to him, *we are one.*

Hearing those whispered words echo in his mind, Grant had never been more thrilled, or felt more terrified, in his life.

Andre and Suzanne

I was right about Gabriel being happy to see Alexi's new fingers and toes. In the two weeks since the babies' hands and feet began to change, other developmental progress had been made as well. They could breathe through their noses; their little feelers had fallen off, and although their ears were still shell-shaped buds, they could hear. All the doctors were pleased.

Early one afternoon in mid-December, while Grant was in his office, I was feeding the boys one at a time before their nap. I set Alexi in the crib, and as I picked up Andre, he smiled at me.

I froze. It was Suzanne's smile. I would know it anywhere.

I didn't know why I hadn't seen the resemblance before. Andre had Suzanne's complexion, her hair and eye color, as well as her smile. Then I remembered Grant saying the mother who had been affected was able to stay here because her parents were out of town until after the first of the year.

My breath caught in my throat. Suzanne's parents were in England until mid-January. I tried to stay calm until Andre and Aslan finished nursing. Once they were settled back in the crib, I showered and dressed so that when Grant returned, he could take me to her. All I could think was how hurt and scared she might be, and the longer I thought about it, the angrier I became. I was pacing up and down the front room when Grant walked through the door.

"Carolina, are you … are the babies all right?"

"The babies are just fine."

"Then what is it?"

"Grant, do you know what deception is?"

"Yes."

"Do you know what lying by omission is?"

"In some instances, I believe both terms can be synonymous. Please tell me why you are asking these questions."

I was furious. Once before, he had confronted my anger for reasons for which he was not directly responsible, but not today. Today, I blamed him because they were all to blame for hurting Suzanne. I ran toward him with my fists raised. He caught my hands easily and turned me around. Crossing my arms in front of me, he imprisoned me tightly against his body.

"Carolina, may we please start this conversation over?" he said calmly in my ear. "Let's pretend I've just come in the door, and you say …."

But I wasn't having any of his gentle cordiality.

"And I say, where in the hell have you hidden Suzanne? *My* Suzanne, Grant. Where is she?"

"What?" he said, slightly stunned.

He let go of my hands. I turned to face him, and my anger went out of me. He looked so confused that I was instantly ashamed. *Is this how you honor him, Carolina?*

"Andre is Suzanne's son. I know that as well as if I had been there when he was born. You said his mother was infected and that her parents were out of town. Grant, Suzanne's parents are in England until after the holidays." I grabbed the lapels of his lab coat. "Please tell me you didn't know … Even if it's a lie, I will believe you."

The despair I'd held back all morning broke through, and I cried in his arms.

He carried me to the sofa. "I knew Suzanne was one of Gregory's prospective mothers. And, before you say anything, please know that selecting her was entirely against the colony's rules, and he was punished. But Grayson decided we had already lost too many pregnancies to stop hers. That was the last I heard of Suzanne specifically until one minute ago. I did not know she was Andre's mother, and that is the truth."

Bowing his head, he pressed my hand against his forehead. "Carolina, I wouldn't have it any other way, but being here with you has kept me out of several conversations regarding important issues and decisions. I was second only to Grayson, appointed by the collective and not, as he was, elected by the colony. But since I've been with you, he has assumed many of my duties to the collective, and my standing in the colony has diminished. I have a certain reputation that still earns me a great deal of respect but doesn't inspire easy camaraderie or inclusion."

"They don't invite you to join in their reindeer games?"

"No, my darling, they do not," he said, bringing my hand to his lips.

"I'm sorry, Grant."

"I am not sorry, Carolina. Except I am uncertain whom I can trust within the colony, and so, with your safety on the line, I trust no one and must act alone."

You're not alone, my love. I'm here. I'll always be here.

Thank you for that.

And if Austin wasn't fast asleep, he would be here, too. And Grant....

Yes.

You can trust us.

Can I trust you not to fly at my head like that again? Please?

Yes. I'm sorry. I just had too long to think about it. It won't happen again unless I run into Gregory.

Okay. For that, you have my permission.

Grant.

Yes, Carolina, I will find her for you. But do you mind if I rest for a few minutes? My head really hurts.

I dimmed the lights and brought him some juice. When he finished sipping the juice, he stretched out with his head in my lap. I brushed his hair away from his face and rubbed his temples. After a few moments, I began humming one of his prayers.

His eyes flew open. "I may not know the words," I said, "but I can hum."

I continued humming as I prayed for him and Suzanne.

Smiling, he closed his eyes and tilted his head.

Gregory, where is Suzanne?

Suzanne?

Yes. Antony's mother, Suzanne Bradford. Where is she?

Why do you think Antony's mother is Suzanne?

Gregory, if you ask one more question before answering mine, I might regret the outcome, but I know you will.

Okay, okay ... she's fine. Gordon and Garrett were able to filter out the toxins, and Gabriel sent her home with a nice severance check.

Do not be lying to me, Gregory.

Grant stood up and kissed me. "I'll be right back."

Following him into our bedroom, I watched him get into the alcove elevator. A few moments later, he returned with my laptop. Opening it on the kitchen counter, he picked up the telephone.

"Ms. Bradford, this is Dr. Grant Gates from GatesWay, and I am following up on a personnel matter. Yes, I know, but Dr. Gabriel is in a meeting, and I agreed to make a few calls for him. As you may know, we are closing our facility on January first, and we are contacting all our former employees to ascertain that their tax information is correct. Have there been any recent changes to your mailing address or tax status? No? Good. Thank you for your time, Ms. Bradford. Excuse me? Why yes, she is right here. One moment, please."

Well, Carolina, it appears neither of us will have to kill Gregory after all ... and Suzanne would like to talk to you.

My hero, I thought, kissing him before taking the phone.

Suzanne was happy to talk and gushed over the amount of money GatesWay had given her after tripping on a floor mat.

"I'm fine now, but I was unconscious for, like, two weeks. But, you know, Caroline, I don't even remember seeing a floor mat."

"If you'd seen it, you probably wouldn't have tripped on it. Are you sure you're okay?"

"Absolutely! And you'll never guess who I ran into at a club downtown. Give up? Eric Harmon. Wow! You won't believe how great he looks these days. Did you know he's going to law school? Anyway, we've been dating. Who knew?"

"Well, it is amazing how some things work out. Suzanne, are you still going to England in January?"

"Yes, but is there any chance we can get together before then? Lunch or something? I could stop by."

Looking into Grant's face, I knew every moment spent with her was time I would not have with him.

"We can try, but I have so much to do. I have to close Dr. Grant's files and help our clients make other fitness arrangements. Maybe we can get together after the holidays."

"Why are they closing?"

Thinking fast, I said. "They aren't closing, exactly, just relocating to a larger city, um, Chicago, I think. I'll call or email you, though, if I can get away. I ... I love you, Suzanne."

"Love you, too, Caroline. Merry Christmas."

"Merry Christmas, Suzanne," I said, managing to get the words out before my voice cracked.

Gently taking the phone from my hand, Grant was ready for anything except seeing me burst into tears and run into the bathroom. I poured out my guilt in the wet rain of the shower so no one would hear me cry. I was taking Suzanne's son, maybe the only child she would ever have, away from her forever. My sense of betrayal knew no bounds. Only the thought that I would always love and protect him as my own kept me from falling into complete hysteria.

When my sobs subsided, I turned the water off and walked into Grant's arms. Wrapping me in the towel he had been patiently holding, Grant carried me into the nursery. Sitting down, he kissed my eyes and asked, "Feeling better?"

"If I don't think about it."

"You should think about it, Carolina. You saved her mind and her life, and because you love him, you saved Andre as well. Without you, she would have lost both—and she refused her son. I can share that particular memory with you if you want evidence, but it is not pleasant."

No, darling, I don't want to see it. Can we stay here for a few moments, like this? For just a little while, Grant, can I be your child?

Grant looked into her swollen, reddened eyes and felt the pain in her mind. He put his forehead to hers and, remembering her last words to Suzanne, softly sang *Silent Night*. It was the only Christmas carol he knew.

Although Grant didn't say anything, I knew I had treated him badly and that the afternoon had been exhausting for him. After settling the boys in their crib for the night, I left him for a few minutes and filled the hot tub. Turning off all the lights, I walked back to the nursery. Kneeling between his knees, I loosened his tie and began unbuttoning his shirt.

"Carolina, I—"

"Shh, no talking, Grant. I need you to be *very* compliant this evening."

I am yours. Do with me as you will.

I took his hand and led him through the nursery and softly closed the door. Standing next to him in the middle of our room, I tilted my head.

Please don't move.

Yes.

I slowly undressed him, not provocatively, but each brush with his skin became a caress. Each caress was followed by a kiss, and with each kiss, another piece of the day fell from him and lay like skim on the puddled cotton and silk of our clothes.

I bathed him in the shower and programmed the spray to massage his neck, shoulders, and back. Well rinsed, I led him into the hot tub and gathered him up in my arms.

When the water cooled, I picked up the bottle of oil and spread a large towel on the bed. I poured some of the oil into my hands. With long, firm strokes, I tried, with each touch, to send my love through his skin and into his heart and mind.

Easing him into the center of the bed, I covered us with a light quilt. As the bed slowly recessed, I wrapped my arms around his chest and, molding my body to his, kissed the back of his neck.

My husband.

He covered my hands with his left hand and, with his right, reached behind me and pulled my thighs closer to his.

My wife.

The Plan

I've got good news, Grant.

Explain, please, Gregory.

Grayson said that now that the final report regarding your experiment has been submitted, your term as Carrie's nanny is almost finished. I know how much you are looking forward to coming back to the tunnels.

Actually, Gregory, it's much more than you know. What else did Grayson say?

One, that he has confirmed arrangements to send Carrie and the boys to the nearest nurturing colony to care for other orphans; two, he wants you and me to work out the implosion details; and three, as soon as Garrett schedules the transports, we're off to inspect the European facilities. I have to tell you, I cannot wait to see this place fall like the rotten pile of bricks it is. Paris, here we come!

Yes. Excuse me, please.

Hey, Grant, where are you going? We're not finished. I told Grayson we would design the demolition sequence today. Grant?

Grant knew he was being rude. Most Lyostians could not stop listening to a particular voice when it was directed at them, and Grant rarely used that ability, but he lacked the necessary patience to continue their conversation. He had to find Grayson to verify Gregory's message while casually gathering as many details as possible. He also needed to focus, but he could feel the onset of another headache that made concentrating so difficult lately.

The pain was too centrally located to be anything other than one of the transient ischemic episodes that were increasing in both frequency and severity. So far, the small strokes had not caused any visible damage, but he was not only a human specialist—he was a Lyostian physician as well. He knew he had only four, perhaps six, weeks left to live. Less if the tightrope upon which he had been walking for the past five months started swaying the least bit. Even less than that if he dwelled on the worst possible outcome, the one he didn't tell her about, the one where he *doesn't* die.

Focusing on breathing through the pain and clearing his mind, he mentally searched the facility until he found Grayson.

Grayson.

Grant.

I would like to think you would talk to me first before making disposition plans for my wife.

Wife? Please, Grant, you have been too cavalier in your attitude toward Carrie for us to believe you take your relationship seriously. I have no doubt she does, but you have repeatedly said it is nothing but an inconvenience. Using marriage as a tool to bind her to you so she would accept and nurture her son was a brilliant idea that worked exactly as you predicted. It's a little extreme for every case. However, as you indicated, one or two per facility will be very beneficial to future colonies. Carrie is the perfect Persephone: a compliant mother who not only accepts her child but, when introduced to them gradually, accepts others as well. It was an ingenious strategy. Not everyone could do it, but kudos to you, Grant. From start to finish, we have set the standard for every North American colony.

Thank you, Grayson. However, her well-being is still my responsibility, and her mental stability is paramount. She will not understand what is happening to her or why she is being relocated. Perhaps I should accompany her to make the transition easier to accept.

That won't do, Grant. The collective has plans for you in Europe. There are lots of loose ends to tie up before we move into Asia. I know most of us won't transition into the Asian operation, but we can help plan it, and you are, among your many talents, an accomplished designer. We need you there. Our achievements here have made the experiences of our colony very valuable to the success of future generations. Well done!

Thank you, Grayson. That is high praise coming from you. My duty, as it has always been, is to the collective. I have missed my brothers. How long before I can cut Carrie loose?

Not too soon. We don't want to ... ah, spook her, as they say. She's still legally married, and we don't want her calling her husband now that her son resembles a human baby. Garrett tells me we couldn't stop him, and the child would be legally his, too.

I need to be kept informed as to the timeline, Grayson, as well as what my role is to be in securing her continued compliance as they are relocated to ... where exactly?

Probably the Montana or Wyoming orphan colony; it depends on who needs her most.

Good. Thank you again for the kind words. I look forward to assisting you in Europe.

Grayson could barely hear him. *Hey, Grant, are you okay?*

Yes, just a lightning headache. She keeps every damned lamp in that place blazing except the nursery and the examination room. I have been very adamant about that, but it is like talking to a wall sometimes. Let me know when I can come home, Grayson.

Will do, Grant, will do.

Grant's Labyrinth—Endgame

Grant hesitated at the door of his consulting office. He had not been coming here every morning as he had told Carolina but worked from the anteroom of his research lab. Being in his office without her was something he could barely endure, but today, he needed to be alone.

The room was as she left it. Her jacket was on the chair they would never share again, and her last bouquet of flowers stood dead in the vase, black water staining the crystal. The office he'd redesigned especially for her comfort did not belong to either of them anymore.

Sitting at his desk, his finger caressed the rim of her teacup, and he stared at his reflection in the glass. There was no reason to look beyond it; Carolina's gentle presence was gone from these rooms forever. Pressing her cup to his lips, he thought of the months she had spent with him encased within the dark paneled walls, and he was gratified that no one else would sit at her desk or touch the things that were once part of their life together.

Their life together ....

She had exceeded every expectation. Her work was flawlessly done. She was gracious to their clients, careful of the lights, lit the candles, and the tea was always perfectly made. In every aspect of her life, in whatever he asked her to do, she had unstintingly shared the generosity of her patient and loving spirit. And, to reward her for her kindness, love, loyalty, and, most of all, her unwavering faith in him, he was expected to turn *his wife* over to some subterranean colony to be used as a wet nurse.

His beautiful Carolina living in the ground? Memories of Leia Sutton's tormented insanity filled him with foreboding. Carolina's mind was clear; she would know she was trapped—and alone. How long would it take before she, like Leia, became desperate enough to believe suicide was her only escape?

As though conceptualizing that horror wasn't enough, Grant saw the pain of his own mother's death reflected in Austin's eyes a hundredfold, and something broke loose in Grant's heart. He had not kept Carolina alive to abandon her now. Finally acknowledging that the relationship that began as an experiment had evolved into the central force of his life, the struggle between the man he was born to be and the man he had become because of everything she had given him, was over.

Closing his eyes, Grant leaned his head back against the chair and watched his life unwind. Hundreds of memories returned to him as he tracked his journey along a twisting path of blood and fire toward the center of his labyrinth, where screams faded into the music of three hearts beating as one. From the beauty of that moment to this, Carolina gracefully glided over every stone placed in her path. Despite everything that she had endured, she had never let go of his hand and trusted him now, as she had in the beginning, to guide her safely through the intricate curves that remained.

Regardless of the cost to himself, the colony, or the collective, he would not betray that trust.

Turning to look behind him, Grant stared at the paintings that were once only a dream. He closed his eyes, and the candle's fragrance became the scent of wood smoke drifting on the desert air. Years collapsed as the assassin Grant Gates slowly disappeared. Once again, he was Timaeus, the beloved son of Venzel and Destani, listening to the slow crackle and hiss of the campfire as his father told stories of Alazar, the brave Arabian stallion who died valiantly trying to save the colts trapped in a stable fire. It was so long ago, yet as Venzel's last words echoed in his memory, Grant lowered his head and pressed his fists against his eyes, whispering, "Yes, Father. I remember Alazar."

The collective had taken his parents, his beloved horses, and his youth. Without mercy or remorse, it destroyed all that was good and beautiful in his life, and then the collective made its only mistake: it left him alive.

When he lowered his hands, Grant's mind was calm and focused. With a tight smile, he opened his file drawer. Fastened in her folder were all of his official notes and the documentary evidence upon which he had based his archived report. Flipping the pages to the back, Grant found Dan's phone number and wrote it down. Slipping it into his pocket, Grant thought if his plans failed, maybe she could convince Dan to come to the facility and get her ... and perhaps Austin, too.

He had to try.

He would kill them all before he would allow Grayson to bury her alive.

Carolina's Path

Grant spent that evening and most of the next day finalizing the arrangements for Carolina so that, with Anya's grace, she and their child would be safe. There was still much to do before the end of the year regarding the logistics and setting up the accounting nightmare that would never be untangled. By the end of the second day, however, he was satisfied with the life he had built for his small family.

There were other things he hoped would happen, but so much was out of his control. Grant, however, trained by experience and possessing the ability to see where each course of action would take them, carefully traveled over each one, discerning the ways he could influence those actions so they would result in Carolina's escape—if she lived. But he knew that however successful his plans would be, the possibility of his joining her was becoming more tenuous with each passing day.

It was not possible for him to leave the collective, nor would it let him. Regardless of which path kept her safe, he could not find a way that brought them out of his labyrinth together.

Unless the elders believed he was dead, all his plans inevitably led to him submitting, either willingly or by force, to the will of the collective.

The Plan – Part II

The days were tense, and I couldn't escape the feeling that we were living on borrowed time. Grant was distracted and listening practically every waking moment. The boys were getting bigger, but no changes were made to accommodate them. Knowing we would be leaving soon, I said nothing.

Grant worked nearly all day, every day, as the facility began closing down. Looking forward to sharing what little time we had, I rushed to meet him whenever I heard the door. One evening in late December, he embraced me as soon as I entered the front room.

"I'm sorry, Carolina, I've got to run to a planning meeting. Are you and the boys all right?" His eyes searched every inch of my face.

I was instantly concerned. Always in control, Grant seemed anxious and a little shaken. Remembering all the times he'd lent me some of his courage, I smiled at him.

"I'm fine, they're fine, and whatever happens, Grant, we will be fine. Don't let your brothers see you like this, darling. Remember who you are, and, as you tell Austin, you are stronger than you know."

Pressing my body to his, Grant kissed me and calmly walked out the door.

Grant noted with satisfaction that he was not the last to arrive. Taking his seat at the conference table, he waited as Garrett and Gregory came in a couple of minutes later. Garrett sat at his right, and Gregory sat across from him next to Gordon.

Following a grateful prayer to Anya for the success of the colony's mission, Grayson began the meeting.

"Greetings, my brothers. The final details and permits are in place to implode the building on the twelfth of January. With the exception of two interns needed to complete the demolition, we should be exiting this facility no later than the tenth." Realizing that every eye in the room was focused on him, he smiled and continued, "After four successful years together, I'm gratified to report that we've been awarded the privilege of progressing to the European colonization together as one of the advance teams. Using our experiences in the roles we have shared here, we will assess each location in turn, make suggestions, and direct changes."

Listening to Grayson review their evacuation plans, Grant waited for him to address the settlement of the colony's children. However, as concluding remarks were being made, Grant began to think Grayson had forgotten Carolina and the boys, but Gabriel had not.

"I assume we are not bringing Carrie and the children to Europe with us."

The silence in the room was broken by Gregory's short, contemptuous laugh. "I should hope not."

Grant was unstoppable. Rather than go around, he swiftly crossed the table, grabbed Gregory out of his chair, and pinned him to the wall by his throat before anyone else could move. Gordon stood but made no effort to rescue his brother.

"I have asked you repeatedly not to make disparaging remarks about our mothers, Gregory. Do I have to ask you again?"

Barely able to breathe beneath the pressure of Grant's hand, Gregory's eyes were wide as he shook his head.

No, Grant, sorry.

Grant held Gregory against the wall until his eyes closed. When Grant released his hand, Gregory slumped to the floor.

Gordon sat back down. That Gregory was still breathing was rescue enough.

Grant returned to his seat at the table.

"It is regrettable that Gregory's attitude has not improved sufficiently to allow him any further care or concern regarding our mothers. Perhaps his future within the collective might be adjusted to permit him more time to supervise tunnel excavation and repair," Grant said.

"But … but he's a doctor," sputtered Gordon.

"A doctor who does not respect his patients, especially when those patients are essential to the survival of his species, is not a doctor but merely a drone with a lab coat. And a Lyostian who does not respect his mother isn't even that." Grant tapped his finger on the table to punctuate his statement. "I would like a decision made on this right away."

Grant did not join the discussion that followed. He let his brothers decide, and when Gregory came to, he found his entire world had shifted, and not even Gordon would meet his eyes.

"Ahem," Grayson said, "we were discussing Carrie and the children."

Grayson immediately felt Grant's eyes on him. Testing the weight of his gaze, Grayson found it to be curiously indifferent but with an underlying tension.

Believing the tension to be Grant's anxiety to be back with his brothers, Grayson said, "I am pleased to tell you, Grant, we have confirmed arrangements to relocate Carrie and the children to the Wyoming colony on January first by special transport."

"And there her duties will be …?"

"What her duties are here, with the addition of one or two more children, as her comfort and ability permit."

"For how long?"

"For as long as her comfort and ability permit."

"Her 'abilities' are not limited to nursing the collective's orphans. Sooner or later, she is going to want to leave."

"She can leave anytime she wishes."

Although Grant knew Carolina would never be allowed to leave alive, he did not challenge Grayson. He needed more information. "The caveat, Grayson?"

"Without her son."

"Emotional blackmail. A very effective tool when manipulating human mothers."

"You said it yourself. All you need is a little leverage."

Gabriel spoke up. "Wait a minute. Grant has a point. She could be useful in ways other than putting her in a tunnel nursery feeding babies. Regardless of how comfortable she is at first, she could become unhappy enough to harm the children or herself. I don't think that is the best way to care for her. There was some discussion about her usefulness in preparing new mothers to nurture our offspring." He paused for a moment, "The same leverage could be applied in this situation, if necessary, but only as a last resort."

"Meaning what?" Gordon asked. "That she and the boys would accompany us to Europe so she could train mothers there? Logistically, that may be more difficult than you think."

Grant, with an eye on everyone in the room, saw Grayson tilt his head. As if on cue, Garrett snapped his fingers. "Perhaps we should continue to observe her. Create another setting like the one she has now where she could be observed, and her behavior researched as Grant has done. We could make a film or virtual reality segment to show to new mothers around the world. Once they see that our offspring eventually look like human children, they will accept and nurture them. This solution gives us the best of both worlds. Carrie will nurture the four babies she has now while providing a training model for future mothers. In that way, Gabriel, we would be caring for her and future generations."

"Will we be able to do that in Wyoming?"

"As a former member of the collective's property acquisition team, I, um, I have made inquiries," Garrett replied, "and we can move her to our new North American headquarters in Vancouver. It's more modern, and they have plenty of room to build a habitation environment."

Grant briefly lowered his eyelids so his brothers could not see the flames behind his eyes. *A cage. They had decided to put his wife and children in a cage.* Only a lifetime spent controlling his emotions prevented Grant from taking the gun from the pocket of his lab coat and killing them all.

Grant looked calmly at Garrett. "Same timeline?"

"If we agree tonight, it can be finished by the end of the year."

"Grant."

"Yes, Grayson."

"Anything to add?"

"Only what we discussed earlier. One, how much longer, and two, outlining my role in preparing her for this transition."

Grayson nodded. "Brothers, we are voting on a motion to advise our Vancouver facility to prepare an observable habitation for the care of Carrie Tay..., er, Gates, and our colony's remaining children for the following purposes: one, continued surveillance for the archives, two, the nurturing of our offspring and, three, the production of a training video for prospective mothers. All those in favor, please raise your hand."

Grayson counted hands. "Four votes plus mine are five. Opposed? Zero. Abstentions? One, thank you, Grant. Motion carried." He looked around with a sense of satisfaction. "There being no further business, this meeting is adjourned."

Gordon and Gabriel helped Gregory stand, and they left together. Only Garrett and Grant remained in the conference room with Grayson.

Grayson turned to Grant. "January first, Grant, and keep her as calm and happy as you have for the last three months."

"Yes. Thank you, my brothers." He stood to leave. "Just one more question. Is she to know they are being relocated, or would you like me to arrange for her to fall asleep here and wake up there?"

"We expect you to ensure that she will *want* to go, Grant. As she relies on you absolutely, she will trust your judgment as to what is best for her and the children. You have been able to convince her of everything else, and, of course, if your considerable, um, charm, won't persuade her, then it's just—"

"Right. A matter of leverage. I will speak to Carrie immediately. Thank you again, my brothers."

Grayson counted to five after the door closed.

"Thank you, Garrett," he said softly, "that was very well played."

"Well, it is the best place for her, isn't it?"

"Oh, yes," answered Grayson, "for now."

Grant, standing quietly on the other side of the door, slid his hand into his pocket and smiled grimly to himself.

She met him at the nursery room door. "Carolina," he began.

"Shh, is anyone going to die tonight, Grant?"

"No."

"Then shh, love."

Helping him out of his clothes, she pushed him gently toward the bed. Leaving for a moment, she returned with a tray of tea, strawberries, a tall glass of strawberry puree, and three small bowls of whipped cream.

"Carolina, why so much cream?"

"I couldn't get the balance of honey to cream right the first two times, but they were too delicious to throw away, so I thought we might find some use for them," she said, sitting next to him. "Besides, I am so clumsy. I figured I would spill some ... oops, see? Just like that."

Grant sipped the deliciousness from her skin. *We need to discuss some things, Carolina. Diversion tactics won't work.*

Let them work tonight, Grant, please. We can talk tomorrow, but I've missed you so much today. In addition to her thoughts, she sent feelings of love and happiness of being with him, and when she caressed her throat, everything he was became her, too. Bombarded by the passion of her thoughts and emotions, Grant took her in his arms.

"Oh, my sweet wife," he sighed, his mouth moving on her lips, her throat, and shoulders. As helplessly caught up in her as she had always been in him, not an unsynchronized movement or thought divided them.

Much later, when she started to sit up, he took her hand. "Where are you going, love?"

"I should wash off. I'm all sticky."

"Oh, Carolina," he said, pulling her back down into the bed, "that is what I call dessert."

The Plan – Part III

After helping me feed and bathe the boys for their noon examination, Grant said, "I must go to my office, but I won't stay long. And please, Carolina, refrain from staging any more seduction scenes, at least until after we talk." He held me close and whispered, "You have to help me, love. I cannot resist you anymore."

"I've never been able to resist you."

Lifting my chin with his fingers, he kissed me.

"I'll be back before my brothers arrive."

Grant returned shortly before noon. We placed the children on the small examination tables, except Austin. I still held him in the nursery until Grant came to get him for his exam.

As punctual as ever, Gabriel and Garrett stood at the door at noon. Gabriel went to Alexi first, testing the curvature of his feet and hands, listening to his chest, looking at his eyes, the base of his former antennae, and down his throat. The boys had only one pair of eyes, and the doctors were unsure at what stage of development they would separate and watched them closely for any signs of division. Only two small quarter-inch circular scars remained of their antennae, but the marks were hidden now because their hair was longer. There was no evidence of the haustella yet, and this was their most serious concern. Though the children would have baby teeth soon and eventually be able to chew solid food and swallow it, the haustella were more important to their culture than just taking in nourishment.

Walking with his brothers out of the examination room, Grant said, "But we don't want them to develop a haustellum now. They would use it for nursing. That could interfere with their ability to swallow food properly as they grow older, and they must have that ability to blend with humans."

"True," Gabriel added. "Delaying the appearance of the haustella until they can eat and swallow as humans—and learn to control it—should be considered a measure of success."

Garrett agreed. "Absolutely. If they used it while nursing, the muscles would be too developed, and they would instinctively consider it their primary way of feeding. I see this delay as a positive marker in their maturation arc, and I will add it to their charts and the colony's records as such."

Gabriel paused for a moment and looked back at the examination room. He tilted his head and smiled, and I knew, by the look in his eyes, that he was smiling at Alexi. Then he turned to me.

"Thank you, Carrie, for taking such good care of them. You've been quite exemplary, you know, more than we ever hoped." He glanced back at Alexi one more time before leaving.

Returning the babies to the nursery crib, I looked into Alexi's eyes. "Grant, was there a relationship between Gabriel and Monique? He seems to take a more paternal interest in the boys than the other doctor fathers."

"I think there was a kind of sympathy between them, but not affection, and I'm not sure what he said to Grayson to convince him to make an exception for her as a prospective mother." He paused for a moment, then continued, "If I were to contemplate my brother's motives further, which I do not wish to do, I would say that yes, Gabriel cares for her and desires a connection to her, and Alexi is that connection. However, I think most of what you see as paternal interest is guilt for what he took from her as a result of that desire."

"Well, your species *is* part human, and Monique *is* a beautiful woman. She would be easy to care for."

"Yes, and easy to make a mistake. He thought she would be like you and tried to prepare her, but she was still horrified and rejected her son. I think he tries to make that up to Alexi, too."

"At least he tries. You've never told me who Aslan's doctor father is."

"It is Garrett, who is here, I am sure you've noticed, as often as Gabriel."

"Yes, you're right."

"And you don't know this unless you are watching through the window, but he is as careful and tender with Aslan as I am with Austin, or Gabriel is with Alexi, or Gregory and Gordon are with Andre. We love these children, Carolina. They are our brothers, the future of our species, and an extension of who we are. You are not able to hear us, but we talk to them, sing to them, and tell them they are getting stronger every day. I sing songs to them of you, your beauty and gentleness, and your love for them."

In my ignorance, I had slighted these surrogate fathers. Since I did not hear them say anything, I assumed they *didn't* say anything. I was wrong, and the knowledge that they genuinely cared about these children, knowing they would never live long enough to see them grow up, brought tears to my eyes.

"Thank you, Grant," I whispered. "I didn't know they were so kind to the babies. I am happy to know that."

A shadow of pain crossed Grant's face. I immediately turned off the lights and put my arms around him. He kissed the top of my head.

"Carolina, we must talk about the kindness of my brothers." Taking my hand, Grant led me to our bedroom, firmly closing both doors.

My bower glowed softly around us as Grant held me in the darkness.

"Carolina, I have done you a grave injustice. I have taken your gentleness, kindness, and generosity and trivialized them to my brothers. Through my own selfishness, I have belittled your affectionate nature and made light of your accomplishments and talents. I have persuaded them to believe that I do not care for you, and it is only my duty to the children, the colony, and the collective that keeps me here with you instead of living in the tunnels with them. And, Anya forgive me, I have done this so well, Carolina, my sweet wife, that they believe it is acceptable to make disposition plans for you in my presence like you were a pet no one wanted."

"Grant—"

"No, let me finish. Perhaps there was another way," he said. "They might have treated you differently if I loved you less or was willing to share you, but *you are mine*, Carolina, *forever and only mine.* So, regardless of how selfish my reasons were, they were also irrelevant. My brothers do not see you as a member of the colony or as my wife. They only see someone that the collective can use, like they see me as a weapon they can aim and control."

He took a deep breath. "My talents, Carolina, are not limited to designing architectural structures, furniture, clothes, or even," he caressed the gold and silver strands of my hair, "ways to make you appear more beautiful to me. I also have a certain aptitude for devising severe punishments and ruthlessly implementing them. But none of the punishments I have ever designed could compare to the ones I have inflicted upon myself ... and you."

Ashamed, he covered his eyes with his hand.

"And Austin?" I asked calmly.

"Yes."

"And his brothers."

"Yes."

"I forgive you, and they forgive you. Now, what do we need to do to outwit whatever your brothers have planned?"

Looking up, he stared as if he did not hear me correctly. I placed my hand on his chest.

"I know that's what you did, Grant. You once said you had to walk a very fine line to keep us together, so I don't care what you told them to keep me to yourself. I never wanted to belong to the colony. I only wanted to care for you—and wanted you to care for me. We knew it wasn't going to be perfect when we started. That we found perfection along the way just meant we were going in the right direction. Remember, when you asked me, I promised I would forgive anything you had to do to keep us together?"

"Yes."

"I do, I have, and I will. Anything."

"Even this?"

He reached into the pocket of his lab coat and handed me a small syringe case. When I opened it, I saw six syringes neatly lined up and immediately knew what he was asking me to forgive him for now.

If you feel it necessary, Grant, I forgive you, even for this.

I am hoping it won't—

I know.

Grant stood up slowly and put the case in the bureau drawer next to his pistol. *She didn't blame him or hate him. She didn't yell, or scream, or threaten to leave him. To Grant's amazement, she didn't even cry. She accepted everything he had done without a moment's regret. Suddenly he realized that all he ever wanted, he had. They were one. Like Austin, she understood everything and still loved him.*

Grateful words caught in his throat. Humbled at finding this unexpected interlude of understanding and peace so close to the end of his journey was worth every step he'd taken to keep her and would ease his transition into the nightmare to come.

Grant returned and gathered me into his arms.

"Carolina, how can I love you more?"

"Only by promising to do what you just offered to do."

"As you wish."

Cradling my head on his shoulder and wrapping his arms protectively around me, Grant sang Anya's song of praise, her song of protection, and, at the end, a song whose words were new to me. The melody was so loving and sweet that I didn't have to ask; I knew a requiem when I heard one.

When he was quiet, I whispered, "Grant?"

"Yes, my love."

"Are the babies awake?"

"Yes."

"Could we feed them, and then all of us get into our bed together?"

"I would like that very much."

"We will talk more after dinner?"

"Yes."

I wasn't hungry at dinner, but Grant was adamant. Now, more than ever, I could not weaken. Without appetite, I ate the scrambled eggs and toast with honey and made him eat as well. We had to stay strong together.

He came up behind me as I was putting the dishes away and, dipping his finger in the honey, dotted my lips and kissed me.

"It is important that you have an abundance of kisses now," he said. "If you start feeling the least bit kiss deprived, you must tell me right away so I may correct any deficit...."

The words "while I can" hung unsaid in the air.

Sipping tea later that evening in the dining room, I looked at the paper in my hand and said, "So, my husband, please tell me what you and your brothers decided at the planning meeting last night."

Grant took a deep breath. "Well, Carrie, we want to give you and the children an apartment like this in our headquarters in Vancouver. You, we, have to relocate when this building is demolished, and our office building in Canada is new, larger than this one, and not a health spa."

"Can I leave the Vancouver facility after you … after you leave us?"

"Yes."

"What is the downside, Grant?"

He was silent.

"I won't be allowed to take my son away from the colony, will I?"

"No."

"Oh."

"But we are hoping you won't want to leave. There will be much work to do, first with the boys, and then we would like you to help new mothers accept their children. We believe that they will relate to you and listen as you share your experiences—you would be a kind of teacher. And there will always be babies who will need you and love you. You would be treated like a queen for the rest of your life."

"Is this what you want for us, Grant?" I asked softly.

"Yes, Carrie. It is the safest place for all of you."

"If I stay, will they let me keep my son and his brothers with me past the ten months? I would very much like to see them grow up."

"Yes. My brothers there will do anything to make you happy."

"When do we leave?"

"The first day of January."

I glanced down at the script I was holding, then back up at him. "New year, new life."

"Yes."

"Tell them I accept."

Persephone's Children

"I will."

Grant tilted his head, then said, "Carrie, on behalf of my brothers, we appreciate your kindness and patience during the inconvenience of this transition."

I nodded. "I will do whatever you think is best for us, Grant."

Confirmation

Grant stood up and kissed the top of her head. "I'm just going to get out of these clothes. I'll be right back."

"Need any help with that?" she said, smiling mischievously.

"Well, I might later …," he answered.

"Definitely later," she said, getting up to put the dishes in the sink.

When he was sure she wasn't following him, he walked into the dressing room and closed the door.

Grayson.

Grant.

Did you catch that?

Yes. Do you have a plan to avoid leaving with her?

Of course. I am going to tell her that I must go to Vancouver early to make sure her "apartment" is ready. She will trust me to do that because only I know what she needs. Then, instead of leaving, I can return to the tunnels. They depart on the first, and we board transports to Europe on the fifth. Everybody is happy, and it is too late for her because she will already be in Canada, where she will discover a heartfelt letter explaining why I am not there, plus a gift or two to ease her disappointment. Since she knows it will hurt them, she will not leave the boys before the tenth month, and if there are other babies and she feels needed, she won't ever leave. After all, where is she going to go?

Thanks to you, apparently anywhere we want her to go. Excellent work, Grant. Total compliance was, of course, our plan all along.

Yes, and speaking of that, Grayson, I would like to see the final plans for her habitat. There are some modifications that should be considered to accommodate four growing boys.

Ever the designer. Good idea, Grant.

Thank you, Grayson.

If you could go to Vancouver with her or Europe with us, which would you choose?

Now, as always, I choose the collective and will abide by its decisions in all things. We are one.

We are one.

Ant Farm

28 December

"Verity Investigative Services."

"Travis?"

"Yes."

"This is Dan Taylor. Remember investigating GatesWay for me a couple of months ago? My wife was working there?"

"We closed that file, Mr. Taylor."

"Yes, well, it was one thing when she didn't come home for her birthday. That's when I called you the first time, and then Thanksgiving ... sure, no reason to call or come home, I suppose. But Brendan, *her only child*, has been home for nearly two weeks with no call, no Christmas card, not even an email. I tell you, she is either dead in there or so drugged out she doesn't know what day it is. Carrie loves Christmas, Travis. She wouldn't have missed sharing it with Brendan, even if it was just over the phone. Me, maybe ... probably ... but not Brendan. You've got to check this out for me again. Find out if she's still there—and if she's still alive."

"Have you tried contacting her?"

"Yes, the middle of November. I tried to get her to come home."

"How?"

"How what?"

"How did you try to get her to come home? Did you see her? Call her? Did you get down on your knees and beg? Precisely, what method did you use to convince her that she would be better off living with you?"

"Why would I beg her to come home? That's where she belongs. She is still married to me."

"I see. So, despite your powers of persuasion, she did not leave with you?"

"No. And she said never to contact her again."

"And you wonder why she hasn't wished you a Merry Christmas?"

"No, Travis, haven't you been listening? I'm not wondering why she hasn't called *me*. I want to know why she hasn't contacted Brendan. She's broken his heart, well, almost."

"Send Brendan to see her. Alone."

"I tried. He won't go. He said he doesn't want to be rejected by his mother in public. Private is bad enough."

"Mr. Taylor, I'll tell Tory about this. I agree with you. It is unusual for a loving mother not to acknowledge her child, especially at Christmas, unless there has been a psychological breakdown in the relationship. I'll call you after I talk with Tory, probably later today or tomorrow morning."

"Thanks, Travis. I'll be waiting."

Instead of hanging up the telephone, Travis called a friend at the City Planner's office and invited her to lunch. He was examining a set of building plans he'd picked up while he was there when Tory returned from her morning's surveillance assignment.

"I'm glad that's over," she said, setting down her camera. "What are you looking at?"

"Schematics for the NAFTRAM building."

"Why?"

"I received an interesting telephone call this morning from Dan Taylor."

"Oh? Throw another wife away, did he?"

"No. He said Carrie didn't contact her son at Christmas. No phone call, card, gift, not even an email, and he wants us to determine if she's still alive. Tory, you said you talked to her several times while you were there. Did she strike you as a woman, a mother, who would either forget it was Christmas or forget her son at Christmas?"

"No. Carrie wouldn't forget anyone, especially her own son. Not at Christmas, not anytime."

"So, something might be wrong?"

"Only that she might be ill. It's flu season, after all. That's the only reason I can think of."

Suddenly, Travis sat up. "Well, something's wrong here. Look at these room dimensions. Even allowing for soundproofing, they still don't add up to the width of the building. There is nearly a four-foot difference." He looked up from his calculator.

"Tory, we need to get in there."

"How would that help Carrie?"

"There's more to my interest in this case than just the building or her lack of holiday spirit. I've never been able to get her recorded conversation out of my head. Look, Tory, you're a fine investigator, but I'm the psychologist and profiler, and I tell you, every time I listen to that tape, it gives me the creeps. It sounds like she's reciting, not talking. There's no hesitation in her voice and little inflection. Regardless of how 'natural' you said she was, it just sounds wrong. And remember, two of our still missing persons had connections to this facility. It wouldn't hurt to take a closer look."

He opened their calendar. "You're going to have to take a few more classes."

"I, I can't."

Persephone's Children

"I don't understand; you said you had to sign a six-month contract. It hasn't been six months."

"I know, but when I told Carrie I wasn't going to be able to attend classes, she suggested to Dr. Grant that I be let out of my contract. Then he asked me if that was something I wanted, and I said yes. I didn't think I would have to go back, and we wouldn't be on the hook for five more months of membership fees."

"Carrie suggested it?" he asked slowly.

"Yes, why? What are you getting at?"

"She knows, then."

"No, I don't think so. She was just being sweet. I told you, she is a very nice person."

"Tori, if one of our employees deliberately suggested a way for us to lose money *in front of a client,* would you consider them a nice person?"

"Well ...."

"And where was Dr. Grant through all of this?"

"Standing next to me, but Travis, you don't understand. She suggested to him that I be let out of my contract, and *he* asked *me* if that was something I wanted to do, and I said yes. So, you see, it was practically my idea."

"No, Tori, you were played. Somebody noticed something you said or did and wanted you out of there. No company gives back ... How much?"

"Almost a thousand dollars."

"To be nice."

"What do we do?"

"We check into it—one way or another. I'll call Dan Taylor and ask him to come in tomorrow morning."

She nodded. Looking up, her eyes met his.

"I was played?"

"Absolutely."

"It didn't feel that way."

"It never does."

29 December: 09:15 a.m.

Wishing she was talking to almost anyone else, Tory stood next to Travis's desk and asked, "Mr. Taylor, I understand you called to inform us that Carrie hasn't returned home. When was the last time you had direct contact with her?"

"After talking with Travis yesterday, I looked it up. I went over there after work on the nineteenth of November."

"Did you talk to her then?"

"Yes."

"How did she look?"

"Great, I didn't like her hair, but she looked great."

"Was she happy to see you?"

"Um, no. She wasn't really happy to see me."

"What did you say to her?"

"I told her it was time to come home."

"I see. Had she given you any, and I mean *any*, indication that she wanted to come home? Did she call or email you to pick her up? Or did you just show up unannounced and expect her to get in the car?"

"No, she didn't ask me to come get her. She hasn't called, emailed, or even acknowledged that we're married for months. I mean, doesn't a husband have any legal rights to his wife anymore?"

Tory looked at Travis for a response.

"No, Mr. Taylor, not for decades," he said.

Victoria continued, "So, what happened after your attempted coercion failed?"

"She said never to contact her again."

"And?"

"The only thing I did after that was email her the dates Brendan would be home for Christmas. That's it. No response. Nothing. Nada."

Tory turned to stare at Travis. It was unbelievable that she was being dragged back into Dan's chauvinistic nightmare. Every instinct screamed at her to throw him out. However, even if Travis was wrong, Carrie might be ill, and it would not necessarily be a bad thing to check on her.

Dan looked down at the schematics and drawings on Travis's desk. "What kind of corporation is ANTFARM?"

"What? That says NAFTRAM."

"Maybe to you, it does, but I am slightly dyslexic, and at this angle, it spells ANTFARM."

Tory looked down at the letters. "It also spells FRATMAN, but who cares?"

Travis stared at Tory. "The extra space," he said, snapping his fingers. "Tory, are the walls in the exercise rooms mirrors?"

"Of course. All exercise rooms have mirrors."

"Where are they located?"

"On three sides."

"All the walls except the mall side?" he asked.

"Yes. Travis, what are you getting at? You aren't taking this, this ...," she pointed at Dan, "seriously."

Travis turned to Dan. "Mr. Taylor, we're going to look into this further. We'll contact GatesWay, and since Tory is a former client and friend of Carrie's, we should be able to check on her. We will get back to you as soon as we contact her."

"When?"

"Monday at the latest."

"Okay, thanks. Brendan is only going to be home another week or so. It would mean a lot if he could see his mom, if only for a few minutes before he goes back to college."

Travis waited until the door closed. "Tory, it *is* an ant farm."

"You're wrong. It's a beautiful fitness clinic and spa, and the staff associates would do anything for you. They have every level of care available: image consultants, nutrition seminars, classes, representatives who will talk with you any time, and the most delicious vitamin–infused honey you've ever tasted."

"Of course."

"Of course, what?"

"If it wasn't like that, would you go?"

"Well, it isn't the only fitness center in town, if that's what you mean, but it is the only place you can buy their honey."

"Right. Where is it?"

"Where is what?"

"The honey."

"I ate it, of course. I need to get more, though. It's all I can think of since I ran out."

"When did you run out?"

"Two days ago."

"Where's the jar?"

"It went out with yesterday's trash."

"Close your eyes for a moment," he said. "I want you to visualize your life without another drop of that honey. It has ceased to exist. You cannot find it anywhere. It has disappeared forever from the face of the earth."

Tory's eyes flew open. "What do you mean it doesn't exist?"

Travis had seen that look in too many faces over the last twenty years, and now he was seeing it in the eyes of his best friend. Recognizing the panic in her voice, he said calmly, "You understand, of course, Tory, that you're addicted to it."

"No, I'm not," she said defensively, realizing that she may not be telling the truth.

"Think about it. How much of it do you eat?"

"Well, they said to eat only one teaspoon a day. But I sometimes eat more. They keep track, though, and won't sell you more than one jar a month."

"It keeps you coming back, doesn't it?"

"Yes."

"Are you addicted? Think about it."

At the thought of never tasting another drop of the golden elixir, her throat grew parched, and tears came to her eyes.

He misread her tears. "It will be okay, Tory. I'll help you."

Her eyes flashed at him. "I don't need any help. I quit smoking; I can stop eating honey." With renewed determination, she said, "How do we get in and expose those bastards, Travis? Because if I'm addicted, every woman there, including Carrie, is addicted as well."

"First, we're going to buy some honey and have it analyzed for addictive ingredients. Then we'll get a search warrant. Can you buy more without eating it yourself?"

"Yes, I can," she retorted, looking at her watch. *There was still plenty of time to get to the gift shop before it closed.* "Don't go anywhere. I'll be right back."

She looked at the jars of honey under the gift shop counter.

"I would like one jar, please."

"Yes, ma'am, your name?"

"Victoria Torrance."

The clerk typed her name into the computer and nodded to herself. "Yes, ma'am," she said. "Here you are."

Victoria paid for the honey and left. As she pulled into Verity's parking lot, she saw Travis waiting in his car.

"Let's go."

"Where?"

"Forensics lab at M–Tech."

After a short wait, the technician handed Travis back the sample. "Just vitamin–infused honey. Too sweet for my taste but healthy if you can get past the smell. It contains no physically addictive agents or compounds."

"Thanks, Jim," Travis said. Turning to Tory, he added, "We'll need more evidence to get a search warrant if this is only vitamins and honey."

"I'm going to taste it to see if it is the same because, well, it may be the lighting in here, but this doesn't look as dark as before."

"Okay, but I'm keeping the jar."

Dipping a pipette into the honey, Victoria let it drop on her tongue and savored it for a moment. "It's as delicious as ever but lighter somehow, as though something is missing. If it doesn't have any addictive ingredients, can I have it back?"

Travis handed the jar to Jim. "Please dispose of this," he said, watching Tory's eyes follow the jar from his hand to Jim's and from Jim's hand to the waste bin.

Walking to the car, Travis said, "It makes sense. They *would be* stepping their clients down from it. When did you buy the jar you just threw away?"

"My last day at the facility in October."

"Right. November's formula was probably half the strength of October's, and December's would be devoid of whatever addicting agent they used, weaning their clients off the honey because they don't need them anymore."

"What do you mean?"

"I checked their website while I was waiting for you, and they're closing on the last day of December. So, if they aren't selling it, do you have any idea where we can get the full-strength stuff?"

Tory thought for a moment. "I'm sure Carrie has some in her office. We just need to get in there and look."

"We're going to have to do it soon. Why don't you pretend you don't know they are closing and try to arrange an appointment with Dr. Grant?"

When they returned to the office, Victoria called GatesWay.

"I'm sorry, Ms. Torrance," said Monique, "NAFTRAM is closing this facility and has canceled all client contracts. No, I regret that Dr. Grant does not have any appointments available before the end of the year. I'm afraid that is not possible, Carrie Taylor no longer works in his office, but I can get a message to her if you would like. Yes, I'll let her know. Thank you, Ms. Torrance, for your continued interest in GatesWay Fitness Clinic and Health Spa."

Monique's Email

To: GrantGates@GatesWay.net
Subject: Victoria Torrance – Inquiry

Dr. Grant:

Just a note to say that Victoria Torrance called at 10:37 am today to arrange an appointment to discuss a prospective client. When I told her NAFTRAM was closing the GatesWay facility, she asked if she could speak to Carrie Taylor to schedule a meeting with you. I told her that you did not have any appointment times available and that Carrie no longer worked in your office. When she inquired as to whether I could get a message to Carrie, I told her I would try.

Ms. Torrance's telephone number is: 515-555-0166.

Please let me know if I can be of any further assistance.

Monique

Monique Robichaud
GatesWay Fitness Clinic and Health Spa

Grant stared at Monique's email. Determined to find a way to turn this major complication into a means to aid Carolina's escape, several scenarios ran through his mind. After a quick look at the mall's online holiday schedule, he shook his head. *Humans*, he thought, *are so predictable.* A contemptuous sneer slowly stole over his face. *Thank you, Dan, for making this so easy. I'll try not to kill you, but accidents happen.*

Grant pressed the numbers on his phone.

"I knew he liked me," Victoria said triumphantly.

Travis looked at her in surprise. "You have an appointment with Dr. Grant? When?"

"New Year's Eve at ten in the morning."

"You're not going alone."

"But—"

"We don't need another missing person, Tory. I'll stay in the car, but I'm going."

"If you must," she said, smiling innocently. She knew there was more than one jar of honey in that office, and she intended to find them all.

The Plan – Part IV

31 December: 7:00 a.m.

Grant had nearly forgotten what it was like to be in their underground rooms so early in the morning. The familiar fragments of his brothers' conversations and thoughts echoing in his mind were almost comforting. He sat at the conference table alone. Hearing Grayson's voice in the hallway, he slipped his hand into the pocket of his lab coat and released the safety on his pistol. Moments later, Grayson walked into the room.

"Grant."

"Grayson."

"I'm sorry I'm late. Is everything in place?"

"Yes. Tomorrow morning, after a tearful farewell scene, I'll move from the apartment back to the dormitory. Howard has Carrie's passport and the children's papers. They are scheduled to board the Vancouver transport at noon on the second of January."

"Speaking of which, Vancouver was very impressed with the alterations you suggested for their habitat. They wouldn't mind having you there for a few weeks to make sure they met your specifications."

"As ever, Grayson, my life, talents, and abilities are at the disposal of the collective. I will be wherever I am needed for as long as necessary."

"I'll get back to you on that. You'll want to pack, regardless."

"Yes. Two more items before then, Grayson. Carrie would like you and the children's doctor fathers to visit today. Garrett and Gabriel are coming at noon for their last examination. Could you and Gregory come at one o'clock? And Gordon, of course, if he would like to see Antony."

"Of course, we appreciate the invitation."

"You are welcome. Last item, Grayson, I want to confirm the demolition sequence with Howard. When are the charges being set?"

"We went with your original design, and they are already in place. We just have to wait for the twelfth to detonate as the permits allow."

"Perfect. Thank you, Grayson."

Without looking back, Grant left his underground home forever. He started climbing the catwalks and did not reset the safety until he could hear her thoughts. Grayson's report had settled everything. Her voice was the only one that mattered now.

31 December: 08:00 a.m.

Grant walked up behind my chair as I nursed Andre and Aslan.

"We will have company this afternoon," he said.

"All of them?"

"Yes, as you requested, Gabriel and Garrett will be here at noon, Grayson and Gregory at one o'clock."

"Thank you, Grant. I know it is inconvenient, but I think they should have a few minutes together before the boys and I leave. You know, they may never see them again."

"No, Carolina, they *will* never see them again."

"Even more reason, then."

"Yes."

His hands gently massaged my shoulders. "Hmm ... that feels wonderful."

"More?"

"Am I in any position to stop you?"

"Not at all."

Leaning my head back, I shared my mind with him. His fingers eased the edge of the robe away from my skin, and, walking to the side of the chair, he kissed my shoulders where the kimono had fallen back. His hand came around and slyly stroked the hollow of my throat.

"Not fair," I whispered, remembering the babies in my arms. For the first time, I said, "No, Grant."

"No, what, Carolina? No this? Or no this? Because it all feels very good to me. But, if you really want me to stop, all you have to do is say please."

"Please, Grant."

"As you wish."

With a secret smile, Grant stood up immediately and began walking toward the bedroom. Just when she thought he didn't hear her running up behind him, he turned and caught her in a full embrace that tumbled them onto the bed.

"You could stop? Just like that?" she demanded.

"Carolina, you gave me your mind. I knew what you were planning the moment you thought it. Walking away was easy when I knew it was just for a few seconds. Haven't I taught you anything about delayed gratification—or do you need another lesson?"

"How much time do we have?"

She grinned in anticipation when she heard his answering laughter echo throughout the apartment—even the boys smiled. No one suspected the underlying pain that particular question caused him.

Victoria's Appointment

31 December: 10:00 a.m.

Howard escorted Victoria into Grant's office. Entering the reception area, her eyes darted to the side wall. The refrigerator was still there.

The office felt vacant and unused. No one sat at Carrie's desk, and some of the furniture was missing. Blessing her unexpected good luck, she decided to find the honey now and save them a trip that evening. Suspecting that the jars were being kept in the refrigerator, she could not keep her hands from reaching forward as she stepped quietly toward the wall.

Grant sat still as stone on the other side of the partition as he watched Victoria stealthily move in the direction of Carolina's refrigerator. Smiling slowly, he soundlessly arose from his chair and briskly stepped into the office.

"Sorry to keep you waiting, Ms. Torrance. I was catching up on some paperwork."

Totally focused on her objective, Victoria instantly put her hand to her throat. "You almost gave me a heart attack, Dr. Grant. I had no idea you were back there."

"We have a scheduled meeting in my office, Ms. Torrance. Where else would I be?" Motioning her into the chair, he said, "Please, sit down while I prepare some refreshments."

Turning to the refrigerator, he removed a jar of honey and a small package of crackers. Watching her reactions carefully, he handed her a teacup and two crackers with honey.

Victoria, unable to resist, devoured one of the crackers immediately. She could not keep the smile from her face.

"Is everything all right, Ms. Torrance?"

"Yes, this honey tastes so much better than the last jar I bought here."

"When was that?"

Too delighted to lie, she said, "A few days ago."

"Ah, yes. We changed manufacturers, and they still aren't blending the formula correctly. We have had several complaints this month. I regret that you were dissatisfied with your purchase. I will be happy to refund your money if you have it with you."

"Um, no, I don't have it with me."

"I'm sorry. Was that why you requested an appointment, Ms. Torrance? To discuss your recent food purchase?"

"Uh, no. I didn't realize until I called that the facility was closing so soon. I wanted to ask if you would recommend another fitness center where I could attend similar classes."

"As regularly as you attended your classes here?"

She was momentarily taken aback; his response almost sounded like sarcasm. She looked at him closely but saw nothing malicious in the quietly handsome face.

"Perhaps I will be more diligent in the future."

"Yes," he said, handing her a photocopied list. "This directory has two columns, one for fitness and one for spa services, with the membership fees listed in parentheses. Regrettably, no one facility offers all our services to our standards."

She barely glanced at the list.

"Was there anything else?"

"Carrie," she said softly, "where is she today?"

An expression of genuine regret came over his face. He looked so sad that she half expected to hear Carrie had died.

"Carrie has been gravely ill and hasn't felt well enough to work for several weeks. She is better and will be leaving soon, but it has been difficult without her."

"May I see her?"

"No, I'm sorry. Visitors are not permitted on the residence floors."

"But you could make an exception. You did before."

"The residency rules are agreed to by all and kept by all for the mutual benefit of the facility's members, Ms. Torrance. Some exceptions are never made."

"Do you know where she is planning to go?"

"No. Carrie has not disclosed her future residence to me."

"In that case, will you please share my telephone number with her? Perhaps if she hasn't decided, I can help her find another apartment." Taking the last cracker and placing it in her mouth, she smiled and added, "Dr. Grant, I genuinely care about her. Please tell her what I said."

"Of course, Ms. Torrance. Thank you for visiting and your kind concern regarding Mrs. Taylor." Setting the tea tray aside, he watched her eyes follow his hands as he placed the jar in the refrigerator.

"You know, Dr. Grant," she said lightly, "You could let me have that jar to replace the one I just bought."

"Regrettably, I cannot give you anything that has been opened. I can share it with you, of course, but as a doctor, I cannot legally or ethically allow you to leave my office with an opened container."

She stood to leave. "Never hurts to ask," she said.

"Of course not," he said, walking her to the door. "Happy New Year, Ms. Torrance."

"Same to you, Dr. Grant."

He watched her follow Howard to the elevators.

She wanted Carolina's honey, but why?

He looked up Verity's website again, clicking on "Specialization Services." Among those listed were substance dependency detection and psychological evaluation. He reviewed the cash register receipts over the last few days and found that she had missed buying the transition honey in November, calling for an appointment within hours of having bought her last jar of honey. Not trusting her, Grant emptied the refrigerator. He checked his cabinets, drawers, Carolina's desk, and credenza, tossing every jar and spoonful into the contamination chute in his examination room.

He knew Victoria would be back, one way or another, and he could not stand guard over his office—there was too much to do. He considered warning his brothers but decided it would be more interesting to see how far she got before he killed her. *Pity about her*, he thought, *beautiful and intelligent; she would have made a good mother.* But despite her southern charm, there was an arrogant edge to Victoria that he found presumptuous and all too human.

Carolina's soft loveliness flashed into his mind, and his heart quickened. He checked his watch. One or two errands more, and he would be holding her. Grant couldn't move fast enough. He didn't know the day or hour when the sweetness of her had become the very air to him, but he could not deny that over the last few days he was finding it difficult to breathe without her.

The Other Plan

31 December: 10:25 a.m.

Victoria smiled as she walked through the GatesWay parking lot and slipped into Travis's car.

"What did you find out?"

"Everything. Yes, there is a darker version of the honey in Dr. Grant's refrigerator, and although she has been very ill, Carrie is still living on the residence floor."

"Did you see her?"

"No, but the way he talked about her, I believe him."

"What time do they close tonight?"

"Nine, but the staff will probably be here until ten packing up."

"Then we'll come back at half past ten. You'll say you left your purse in a locker or exercise room, and we will make our way to Dr. Grant's office and look in that refrigerator. Who knows what else we might find?"

Sensing their conversation was sufficiently distracting her, Travis grabbed her bag and quickly stepped out of the car. Opening it, he found the jar of honey she had just purchased.

"You had to lie to get this, didn't you?"

When she didn't answer, he looked at the jar in his hand and pulled back his arm.

"No, Travis!" she shouted as he threw it into the dumpster. Any plans of retrieving it later vanished when she heard a metallic thud and the sound of shattering glass.

Timaeus

31 December: 10:40 a.m.

When he returned to the apartment, Grant found Carolina getting dressed for their afternoon visitors. Removing the red velvet pouch from his pocket, he loosened the ribbon ties, and the platinum wedding pendant slid into her hand. The concentric diagram of a moment frozen in time gleamed on her palm. When the new diamond caught the candlelight, it shone like the bright star it represented. Grant turned it over. On the other side, engraved in gold, was Austin's birth chart with its own speck of fire in the center. A new chain, made from interlocking links of platinum and gold, was long enough for the pendant to nestle between her breasts.

"This was made for your eyes only, Carolina, and it would make me very happy if you never took it off."

"Say, 'please,'" she said teasingly.

"Please, Carolina, wear this always ... for me," he said, lowering the chain over her head. He looked so solemn that she set her teasing aside.

"As you wish, Grant," she said softly, loving him with her eyes and placing her hands gently on his face.

"Thank you."

Grant took her hands and held them over his heart. He could not postpone the truth any longer. Lowering his forehead to hers, Grant showed her how he loved her.

Fire changes everything, he thought, *even love.* Without daring to hope, he opened the caverns of his heart and pulled Carolina into the whirlwind of his past, present, and future.

Grant's lips touched my forehead. I closed my eyes and waited for him to fall into my mind, but Grant's loving presence vanished. I felt suddenly weightless. I could no longer sense the crisp texture of his shirt beneath my fingers; my feet did not touch the floor. I heard voices and words in languages I did not understand. Curious but unafraid, I opened my eyes to see images flying past me like leaves in the wind, but they were not the glowing scenes in Grant's picture book. Instead, I saw faded sketches of men writhing in pain, women eviscerated and covered in blood, the body of a man lying on bloodied sand with only half a face, and visions worse … so much worse, swirled around me. Only then did I understand that Grant was not in my mind but that I was falling through the caves and shadows of the past he concealed from the world.

It was not a silent descent. Half-heard conversations became cries of resonating agony. Most were men's voices, but as I plunged deeper into the core of Grant's tortured heart, a woman's scream, terrified and long, lingered unanswered and unforgotten even as the others faded.

Guarded against the blazing heat by a shield of transparent mist, I wondered how anyone could live with such pain. Tears of love and pity stung my eyes but evaporated before touching my cheeks. Moments later, the mist hardened into glass by the relentless heat, and I could only stare helplessly at the pulsation of fire that constantly created and destroyed itself with flames so red they looked like blood.

Persephone's Children

I stopped falling. Embraced by this unquenchable fire, I was trapped behind walls too hot to touch. A shudder of fear went through me, and my clothes, scorched and fragile, disintegrated and fell in ashes at my feet.

Unable to escape, the air burned my throat as I waited for Grant to rescue me. Choking on every incinerating breath, I struggled until breathing became impossible.

I was drowning. Not like the first time, lovely and safe in his arms, but naked and alone, held fast by an unending nightmare of agony and sorrow. I could not survive here.

Grant, oh, my beloved, please do not let me die so far away from you.

If he answered me, I could not hear him.

My skin blistered and cracked; drops of blood sizzled and dried in long crimson trails. I knew I was dying. Still, he did not save me, and I fell to my knees.

Suddenly, Grant's voice screamed in my head, loud and taunting, *Hate me! Please, can't you see what I am? Hate me, Carolina, so I can kill you. Please.*

I cannot, Grant. Kill me if you must, but I will die loving you ... loving both of you, so much.

Amid this torment, a woman's voice, soft and pure as sweet water, drifted through the fire and pain. Like a ray of light, it pierced the rising flames, splintering the glass and sending a thousand prismatic fragments painlessly through me. Irreparably shattered and fluid, I was no longer flesh but a luminous spirit encircling, protecting, and, yes, loving the raging inferno that was the heart, mind, and madness of Grant Gates.

I do not know how long Grant held me there. I only remember that the images gradually dimmed, and the sensations of weightlessness and incandescence faded as I returned to my body. The air I breathed into my lungs did not scorch them. I could sense the texture of silk against my skin—skin that just moments before had disintegrated with my bones—and finally, beneath the crisp cotton of his shirt in my hands, I felt Grant's beating heart. When I was quite sure we were both still alive, I opened my eyes and recognized the fire that consumed me and the love that would not let me die reflected in Grant's face. Never before had I seen anything so terrifying or so beautiful. I moved my hands around his chest to his back and pressed my forehead against his heart.

I'm here.

His head rested lightly on mine. *Yes.*

After a moment, he asked, "Carolina, will you express your feelings about what I showed you in one word of my language?"

"Yes," I whispered, desperately wanting to stand there and hold him forever. "What would you like me to say?"

"Timaeus."

It was not a word I understood. I could not recall hearing it in any of Anya's songs or prayers, but I knew whatever it meant, he did not want me to parrot it back to him. I unbuttoned his shirt so there would be nothing between his warmth and my lips.

Closing my eyes, I relived it all: the grandeur and terror of the inescapable fire, the freedom of changing from flesh to luminescence, and, finally, the love I felt coming out of it alive and still in his arms.

"Timaeus," I whispered.

Although it was comparing match light to a volcanic eruption, pressing my lips against the skin above his heart, I sent him all the passion I felt for him and repeated, "Timaeus," as though the word itself meant love.

The last of Grant's fears fell away. Sharing the force of her emotions and hearing the love in her voice gave him all the strength he needed. He had surrendered his health, his standing in the colony, and abandoned the collective's mandate by putting her survival above his own. Inevitably, each consecutive step brought him to this day, when he had to risk everything by letting her know how he truly loved her. Once again, she not only accepted the truth, understanding what it meant and loving him more, but she illuminated the caverns he believed would be eternally dark and banished the ghosts of brothers long dead. That she had saved him from his own hell validated every decision he had made.

He wished ... then sighed. It was irrelevant what he wished. Their journey was nearly over. Just a few steps more, and she and Austin would be safe and free of his labyrinth of shadows and death.

Reluctantly, he pulled away from her embrace and buttoned his shirt.

As though she was still in his mind and knew his thoughts, she lifted her pendant and looked from the wedding side to his face.

"Did I love you enough to make up for everything you lost because of me? I cannot rain fire down upon you to show you how much I love you, but do you know? Have I left anything unsaid, any gift unappreciated, any part of your love unacknowledged or unreturned with all I am? Oh, Grant," she cried, her voice becoming an urgent whisper, "do you know?"

Releasing the pendant, she pressed her fist to her chest as if willing to rip out her heart and hand it to him.

Memories of the last three months came rushing back to Grant. He bowed his head. Without a single backward glance, she left her career, her family, and her friends. She generously gave him her body, heart, mind, and perhaps even her soul—and nearly died twice—to be with him and protect their child. She had no life or secure future except one defined by her relationship to him, his wife and mother of his son. Knowingly and willingly, she allowed herself to be possessed by a living firestorm and, belonging to him for all time, still asked if he wanted more proof that she loved him. He was humbled. In his mind, there was no comparison between his sacrifice and hers.

Taking her hands, Grant guided her to their bed and knelt in front of her.

"Carolina, you love our son. If you did not care for me at all, I would still say that you have given me more than I deserve. But I have seen into your heart and mind, my darling, and I know you love me, even the horror of me that I kept hidden from you. For a few moments today, you lived in that horror and were not destroyed by the fires that burn within me but transcended flesh to crystalline spirit. Because your love sheltered my heart, I shone through you, and together, we created our own light. Oh, Carolina, I have spent the last ten years of my life surrounding myself with beauty because none existed within me, but nothing I've ever imagined alone compares to the magnificence we create together."

He kissed her hands and pressed them to his forehead.

"So, yes, my dearest wife, I know—because I live in it—how much you love me."

Carolina silently drew Grant into her embrace. The center of their bed recessed as he caressed her and sang to her. Closing his eyes, Grant saw again the dancing flame that would grace his dark world after she left him. Stroking the pendant that lay between her breasts, he took a deep breath. If everything went as planned, it was going to be a brutal day for them both. He prayed to Anya to survive it. He couldn't help her escape if he died that day. Tomorrow would be soon enough.

Hearing the thoughts of his brothers in the hallway, he pressed his lips to her cheek.

"They are here," he said and helped her from the bed.

31 December: Noon

Grant opened the door for Garrett and Gabriel as I sat on the sofa holding Austin. Since the doctor fathers were there at my invitation, Grant allowed me to be in the front room when they arrived.

Gabriel handed me a beautiful bouquet of flowers. "Thank you, Carrie, for being so patient with us these last several weeks. I know our visits were an imposition, but your kindness has not gone unnoticed or unappreciated."

"You're welcome, Gabriel. They are all wonderful boys, and I am sure they will make you very proud."

I handed Austin to Grant and kept an eye on the examination room as I busied myself arranging the flowers. After setting the vase in the center of the dining room table, I waited in the nursery. Grant called me as they were getting ready to leave. After I said goodbye to Gabriel, Garrett thanked me as well and followed Gabriel down the hall.

Grant brought Austin to me and held us like he did on the day Austin was born. When it was time to start the pantomime again, he sighed and opened the door for Grayson and Gregory. Together they walked into the examination room while I kept Austin with me in the nursery. Again, Grant called me as they were getting ready to leave. I set Austin in the nursery crib and went out to say goodbye.

Grayson was as formidable as ever. "Thank you, Carrie, for taking such good care of the children."

"I love them very much, Grayson. We've been very happy here."

Gregory stood silently next to Grayson, but as they were walking out, he turned toward me. "Oh, by the way, Carrie, you're going to be happy in Vancouver, too."

"I hope so, Gregory, but I will miss Grant while he is setting everything up for us."

Gregory laughed. "Grant won't be in Vancouver, Carrie. He'll be in France. Perhaps, *if* he thinks about you at all, he will send you a postcard of the Eiffel Tower. Pity you will never have Paris, but he won't be too busy to send a postcard, will you, Grant? After all, she's your *wife*."

I stared at Grant. "What does he mean? You're not going? Wait, you're sending us there alone?" I tried to fight back the tears and failed. "Grant, you said you were going to meet us in Vancouver. Did you lie to me? To *me*?"

My voice was strained and so high-pitched it hurt my throat. Putting my hand over the pendant he had placed around my neck, I could barely get out the words, "Alone? After everything you've said?"

Staring at Grayson, Grant did not even acknowledge me. Grasping the collar of Gregory's lab coat, Grayson threw him into the hall. Unmoving, Grant did not take his eyes from Grayson's face until he closed the door.

As they waited for the elevator, Grayson and Gregory heard the turmoil in Grant's mind and the even louder sound of something large and breakable hitting the apartment door. Gregory smiled. He didn't care what they did to him. The stunned look of betrayal on Grant's face was worth it.

Betrayed

31 December: 1:30 p.m.

Following the crash of Gabriel's flowers against the apartment door, Grant stood back as Carolina took a knife from the kitchen drawer and told him to leave or she would cut her throat … or his. Slowly opening his collar, Grant fell to his knees in front of her. Crying uncontrollably, she threw the knife into the sink and lunged at him. Afraid she would try to bite him again, Grant pushed her against the sofa and, believing she would stay with the children, left the apartment to find the proper medication to deal with her hysteria.

Widely broadcasting the scene he had just experienced due to Gregory's indiscretion, Grant asked Gabriel to immediately go to the apartment and watch her. When Gabriel arrived, he stepped through an open door. The shattered pieces of the crystal vase cast broken rainbows on the walls. His flowers were crushed and scattered across a carpet darkened with water stains. It was deadly quiet, and he sensed immediately that Carrie and her son were missing. Recalling what she was capable of when angry, Gabriel ran into the examination room and only started to breathe again when he saw the other three infants sleeping.

Gabriel sent the message that Carrie had kidnapped her son, and the entire colony got involved. She was the only one who could nurse the other children. She must be found and, considering her mental state, not permitted to leave the facility. Garrett emailed all the staff terminals in the building, asking to be notified immediately if a woman and child were seen in any corridor or room.

Alone in the apartment for the first, and what would probably be the last, time, Gabriel cradled Alexi in his arms. He caressed Alexi's fine dark hair and looked into the pale blue eyes of his mother. With Monique's image in his mind, Gabriel gently kissed the baby's forehead. Only withholding his endless sorrow at her rejection, Gabriel sent all the love he felt for Monique to her son.

Minutes later, Garrett's telephone rang. It was Emily. Carrie Taylor, holding a baby wrapped in a blue blanket, was in the lobby, pacing in front of the door as if waiting for someone. On Grayson's instructions, Grant met Gabriel at the apartment, and they took the elevator to the lobby level. Grayson and Garrett met them outside the elevator door, and together, they grimly walked toward the lobby. They all knew it was going to be painful. It was early afternoon on New Year's Eve, and practically every salon client had scheduled a last-minute appointment. They dreaded the chatter of women rushing noisily in and out, and although they were shaded, they knew all the lamps would be blazing.

Grant walked into the lobby just as Dan rushed in through the front door.

Running up to me, Dan said, "Carrie, are you okay? You sounded terrible on the phone. Brendan's outside in the car, so let's go."

"Brendan's outside? Really?"

"Yes, really. If you read an email once in a while, you would know he's been home for two weeks."

I turned toward the doors with Austin in my arms and said, "Okay, Dan, I'm ready."

"Uh, Carrie, whose baby is that?"

"Mine, he's mine. Isn't he beautiful?"

Using his doctor's voice, Grant interrupted us.

"Mrs. Taylor, we need to take the baby back now," he said, taking my arm and moving me away from the front doors.

I turned and saw in Grant's face the remote and stern expression that every employee in the facility feared. "No, no. Please don't do this, Dr. Grant. Please, don't."

Ignoring my pleading, Grant reached for the baby.

"Wait a minute. What in the freakin' hell is going on?" asked Dan, a little too loudly. "First, she has a miscarriage, and I don't hear from her for four months, then, all of a sudden, today she calls me to come get her, only to find out she has a baby. A baby that may or may not be hers." Dan took his mobile phone out of its holster. "I'm about two seconds away from calling the cops and letting them sort it out."

Grant's voice was like oil on water. "Mr. Taylor, that is not necessary. Carrie has been extremely ill," he said quietly. "Shortly after you left in November—"

"I didn't leave. You kicked me out."

Grant continued as if Dan had not spoken, "She fainted, and before I could catch her, she hit her head, causing a small subdural hematoma."

"A what?"

"A small bruise formed on her brain. The drugs necessary to dissolve it have made her forgetful. We've been keeping her here at our expense to work in the nursery, where she is wonderful with the children. Sometimes, she likes to believe that one of them, and this is her favorite, is hers and tries to leave with him. Usually, she calls Suzanne, who then calls us, but this time she called you. This is a definite sign that her memory is improving. If you would like to take her home, we will be sorry to lose her, but since we are closing the facility, it would probably be for the best."

"Will she get well?"

"Yes, she just needs continued neurological care and rest. It is my belief that everything will be back to normal in a few months. I would have encouraged her to go home with you last month, but you were becoming angry, and she was getting so upset that, quite truthfully, I am not surprised she collapsed."

Grant turned toward me. "Carrie, don't you want to go home with Dan? He cares about you very much. Just give the baby to me, and you can go. His mom is going to wonder where he is, and we don't want to make her unhappy, do we?"

"Grant," I whispered, "*please* don't do this. Let me take him, please, please, you know he's mine. You were there."

"Mrs. Taylor, this child is no more yours than those children over there," he said, pointing to the inner doors where Gabriel, Grayson, and Garrett stood, each holding one of the babies.

I didn't want to make a scene, but after all our plans and promises, I couldn't believe he was trying to take Austin from me now when I was so close. Then I remembered he'd once said to me, "*Carolina, I'm a very good liar.*"

"Why are you doing this? I thought you cared about me ... about us." I tried to wipe the tears out of my eyes, but they were falling too fast.

"I do care about you. That is why I believe you should leave with your husband." He put his hand on my shoulder. "Look at me, Carrie," he said, "so much of what you believe to be real is actually a bad dream."

Was it a dream? I had given him my mind, but could he make me believe *anything*? *Wasn't any of it real?* Suddenly disconnected from everything I thought was mine, I was too dazed to resist when Grant took Austin from me, but seeing him turn away hurt me too much to be a dream. I looked down at my hands. I had nothing.

Persephone's Children

The agony in my heart would be never-ending even if it were a dream. How could I stop loving them? *I couldn't.* Then Dan said something about Brendan. Brendan was waiting in the car. *My* Brendan. I knew *he* was my son, but he was another dream lost to me. It was just a matter of time before he left me, too. How could I go back to my life without the four boys who loved me? Return to my family ... my friends ... my students? How could I look them in the face, knowing how their lives would change? And I knew if I tried to warn them, they would look at me like that poor Greek oracle who was doomed to tell the truth and be forever disbelieved. Reduced to a hollow shell, I would be a ghost rattling around in a life that was irrelevant and didn't fit anymore.

But Grant was clear there was no future for me with him, either.

Deceived, deserted, and without any other place to go, I turned to follow Dan. Just as I reached the door, an unfamiliar sound cut through the cacophony of women's voices.

Austin was crying.

Not as a human baby cries but a mournful sound that went directly to the center of my heart. I instinctively turned around. Grant stopped walking the moment Austin started crying and looked back at me.

Carrie, don't ... go.

You made him cry. What a cruel father you are!

I did not. You did the moment you decided to leave him. He knows, Carrie, and don't speak of cruelty to me; he is your son, and you are breaking his heart.

You are breaking mine. Grant, you lied to me!

Yes. But beyond that, you must stay.

No. Beyond that, there is nothing.

At those words, Austin began crying like a human baby, a baby who was suddenly all alone. Seconds later, Andre was crying, followed by Alexi and Aslan. The doctors, at a loss with crying babies who were attracting too much attention, ducked inside the clinic. Grant hesitated a moment longer.

As you wish. Goodbye, Carrie. Grant moved toward the clinic's lobby doors. I saw Austin grasp the edge of his lab coat as though to turn him around.

"Aren't you coming, Carrie? That's like the eighteenth time Brendan has driven around the parking lot."

A rush of love, as only Austin could send, came over me. I suspected Grant was behind it, as he had encouraged Austin to save me once before, but it did not matter. I bowed my head in defeat. It would never be Austin's choice to leave me, and I could not choose to leave him. He was more than my child. Unlike Dan, Grant, or even Brendan, Austin lived in my mind as well as my heart and would always be a part of everything I loved. Every instinct I possessed screamed I had to go to him, be with him, *love him*. The desire to hold him safe in my arms blotted out every other emotion flashing through me. No one else mattered—it was only Austin I wanted.

"No, Dan, I'm sorry," I said, smiling at him so he could not doubt my words. "I can't go with you, after all. That is my baby. They are all my babies. I got to name them. I can't leave ... They need me. Go home, Dan, go home forever. Don't you understand? I can't leave as long as they need me. Don't worry. I'll be fine. Kiss Brendan for me, tell him I love him, and I'll always love him. But the other babies, I love them, too."

"What are you saying, Carrie? Aren't you coming?"

"No, Dan, goodbye. I'm sorry I bothered you." As I stood on my toes to kiss his cheek, he moved away. Still. Without regret, I repeated, "I have to go back."

"Carrie, dammit! This is your last chance! Come with me now, or I swear I will let you rot here."

I barely heard him as I ran to Grant. I lifted Austin out of his arms and, pressing his hand to my lips, whispered, "Never again, Austin, my love, never again."

Persephone's Children

Twirling with him through the lobby doors, my eyes caught a glimpse of the look of incredulity on Dan's face.

Grant turned around.

"Don't worry, Mr. Taylor. We will continue to take good care of her."

Grayson

31 December: 2:00 p.m.

As soon as I left the lobby with Austin in my arms, the other babies stopped crying, but Gabriel was the only brother who smiled. With Grayson leading the way, Gabriel and Garrett on either side and Grant behind me, I was escorted back into the elevator. Completely ignoring Grant, I focused all my attention on Austin and his brothers.

Returning to my apartment, I carefully stepped over the broken vase and pushed the chairs around the sofa to make my nest. Before anyone could stop me, I settled down with Austin, unbuttoned the top of my caftan, and, caressing his cheek, began to nurse him.

I looked up at Gabriel, and using the collective's names for our children, I said, "If you would be so kind as to put Albert next to me, I would appreciate it. They are used to being fed in order." I smiled as he did as I asked. "Then Antony and Ashley, on this side, please."

Carrie, please don't do this.

You're so selfish, Grant. Why shouldn't they see me like this? This is the only way they've ever really seen me. Here, you can share this with them, too, if you dare.

I sent him the quiet pleasure of being a mother. I knew the moment he shared that sensation because all at once, they smiled and drew closer. I looked down at Austin so they wouldn't see the contempt in my eyes.

You are killing me, Carrie.

You are leaving us, Grant. Alone. You are already dead.

When Austin finished, I gently set him next to me. I cradled Alexi and lovingly caressed his eyebrows. As he began to nurse, I thought Gabriel was going to kneel.

Oh, Monique, I thought, *you have no idea what you've missed.*

Alexi was nearly sated when Grayson broke the spell. His head had been slightly tilted since I began nursing the boys, and I wondered what was going on.

"Carrie," he said, clearing his throat. "I apologize for Gregory's earlier unfortunate choice of words, which precipitated your desire to leave us. He was unaware of recent changes to the arrangements for your Vancouver relocation."

He turned to Grant.

"Grant, pursuant to the alternatives we previously discussed, the collective has reassigned you to Vancouver to assist in the comfort of ... your wife until she no longer requires your constant attention. After which, you will be free to join us in Europe."

I sat Alexi in my lap and, unbuttoning the next button, picked up Andre and looked at Grayson.

"Grayson," I said in my sweetest spoken voice, "it wasn't Grant's choice to leave us alone in Vancouver? It was yours?"

"It was my recommendation, but it was the decision of the collective."

"Hmm, but if you'd recommended that he come with us to Vancouver in the first place, none of this confusion would have happened?" I blew honeyed kisses to Andre as he nursed.

"Possibly."

"I thought the colony respected a marriage, Grayson."

"It … it does."

"But you don't."

I brought Andre to my lips and kissed his forehead.

"It's not a real marriage."

"Really, Grayson, what's missing? We have a home, I have a child, and my throat drips with the same honey as yours."

Grayson looked quickly at Grant, who was leaning against the wall, his arms crossed in front of him, glaring at me.

"I … I didn't know."

"Humans have a phrase in our wedding ceremony, which you may have heard given Gregory's fondness for dramatic cinema, 'what the Lord hath joined together, let no man put asunder.' Have you ever heard that phrase?"

"Yes."

"Do you know what asunder means, Grayson?" I asked softly. Setting Andre down beside me, I leaned back into the cushions. My eyes never wavered from Grayson's face.

"Yes."

"Then what, exactly, were you thinking?" Before anyone could stop me, I pulled a knife from between the cushions and threw it directly at Grayson's heart.

The Other Plan – Part II

31 December: 2:30 p.m.

"Travis? Dan Taylor here. I got a message you called."

"Yes, good news! We visited GatesWay this morning. Tory met with Dr. Grant, and it seems Carrie has been ill, but she's fine now and will be moving out soon. Tory is going to find out where she's going."

"Well, I saw her about an hour ago, and she *wasn't* fine. She was supposed to leave with me but changed her mind."

"What? Wait ... you *saw* her? Let me put you on speaker."

Putting his hand over the receiver, he repeated what Dan said, then pressed the speaker button.

"Dan, did I understand you to say that Carrie is leaving with you today?"

"Well, she was. She called and asked me to pick her up at that gym, spa, whatever, because she wanted to come home. Then her doctor shows up, takes someone's baby away from her, and tells me she's been sick and, since they were closing the facility, told her she should leave with me. And I thought she was, too, but when the baby started crying, it was like turning on a switch. She got all moony and said she was needed there. Then she had the audacity to thank me for coming and told me to leave. She grabbed up the baby from the doctor and ran back inside."

"Baby?"

"Yes, the doctor said she works in the nursery."

"Nursery?" said Tory. "GatesWay doesn't have a nursery. It was the only thing that kept them from having a five–star rating."

"Well, there were babies."

Forgetting she was on speaker, Tory looked at Travis. "We are going back to GatesWay tonight. This time, we're going to find out what the hell is going on, and I'm not leaving without her."

Travis motioned to Tory that the speaker button was pushed.

"Ah, Dan, listen, we're going to contact GatesWay again and try to make sense of Carrie's behavior. I learned this morning that she has been ill, but I want to, you know, investigate the truth of the nursery. Perhaps it's a recent addition for, er, … the holidays. We'll get back to you as soon as we know something."

"You do that."

Dan hung up the phone. He picked up the bottle of bourbon he had been self–medicating with that afternoon and returned it to the liquor cabinet. If *they* were going back, *he* was going back—and he was going to need a clear head.

Caught

31 December: 2:30 p.m

Grant deflected the knife with his hand, and everyone watched it careen harmlessly away from Grayson's chest, clattering against the tiles in the kitchen. I picked Aslan up to feed him.

Grayson lunged at me, but Grant, Gabriel, and Garrett moved quickly between us, blocking him. Ignoring all of them, I started humming *As Time Goes By*. Always their favorite, the boys smiled and waved their arms.

"Hate you, Grayson," I said lightly, "you too, Grant." I resumed humming and traced the outline of a star on Aslan's forehead.

Running footsteps echoed in the hall. Gordon, Gregory, and all the interns walked into the apartment. They smelled the honeyed milk, and as Grant and Gabriel separated, every eye stared at me as I nursed Aslan. He was the lion cub standing between me and certain death because, while they might attack Grant and Gabriel to get to me, they would not harm one of the babies.

I hoped he was hungry.

Humming to my children, I kissed Aslan's hand when he waved it at me. The tension in the room slowly changed from anger to fascination. I was what they all wanted for themselves and their future generations. When I felt Grant begin to relax, I knew the danger of being ripped to shreds in front of our children had passed.

Grayson tilted his head. With the exception of Grant, every adult in the room turned as one to stand behind Grayson, forming a barrier between us and the door. I put Aslan next to his brothers and climbed out of my nest to stand behind Grant.

Grayson was seething. "An outrageous act has been committed against the colony leadership. Both of you will remain here until we decide what action to take."

I looked into the face of each of his brothers, but they did not acknowledge me at all.

"Yes," said Grant, bowing his head slightly in acquiescence. "I cannot apologize enough for the attempt on your life or her escape. Although I do not feel her actions were within my control, I take full responsibility. Do what you must do."

"We will post two interns in here with you. Do not try to leave."

"If you feel that is necessary, Grayson. But you have requested I stay here, and so I will."

"Your *wife*?" he said, spitting out the word.

"Our mother," Grant said softly, taking my hand and pulling me close behind him, "will stay with me." His head still bowed. "As you have *seen* … the children need her."

I felt suddenly lightheaded. I knew we were dead—all of us. I had gone too far and acted stupidly. Grayson would not forgive me, and Grant would never allow us to be "punished." Overcome with regret, I covered my face with my other hand and bowed my head against his back.

Gabriel disagreed. "I think we should allow them a measure of privacy." He picked the knife from the floor and hefted it in his hand. Smiling, he shook his head. "Other than a hysterical reaction which we, ourselves," he said, looking at Gregory, "may have provoked, we haven't determined there was an intentional act of rebellion committed, especially by our brother. They are not prisoners. We can leave interns in the hall. They will call us if anyone," he looked back at us, "tries to leave."

I felt Grant's quick intake of breath. *Was it possible they would really leave us alone, together? Could I still trust him to keep his promise?* A flicker of hope flashed through my mind. If not a life together, then the luxury of dying in his embrace, his head resting close to mine, was the only consolation I had now.

Grant raised his head. "Thank you, Gabriel, but it is not necessary." He stepped away from me and looked at Grayson.

"Do what you will, Grayson. For myself, I am glad all the pretense and deception are over. It has been exhausting, you know, tearing myself in half. Obeying the collective's, the colony's, and your demands while, at the same time, trying to be whatever the hell she needed—at the precise moment she needed it—was hard work."

He dropped my hand. "Thankless, too, apparently."

His words echoed in my mind.

"What?" The hand over my eyes became a fist pressed to my mouth. The hand he had dropped reached for him, grasping only air as he walked away from me.

"Regardless of anything you may have witnessed today that appears to negate some of the findings in my official report, my experiment is a success. Despite her unpredictability, which can be managed with medication, she will not allow our youngest brothers to suffer no matter what you decide. I guarantee it. She could have left today but chose our brothers over her human son. So, leave your guards, excuse me, interns, take them, or post them in the deepest reaches of hell. It is of little consequence to me, and *Carrie*," he snarled the word, "isn't going anywhere. Not now."

I couldn't prevent a small cry from escaping my lips, "Experiment?"

Grant turned around and looked at me. "Oh, please," he said scathingly, "I don't *ever* have to answer to *you* again."

I stumbled backward. I didn't recognize him. His eyes, flat and cold in total contempt, were narrowed to slits; his skin was pulled taut over the bones of his face; his mouth a gash. Stripped of its softness, I wondered how I ever believed this ... this caricature of a man was human. Or that he loved me.

It all came together in that single moment. I knew Grant wore a mask for everyone else, but it was only then that I realized he also wore a mask for me. I had glimpsed the edges of his cruelty, but for the first time, I saw the full force of it and understood why his brothers treated him differently.

His role, what did he say? "I have a certain aptitude for devising severe punishments and ruthlessly implementing them." *Was it possible?* His role in the colony ... *that he was ...* I was having difficulty wrapping my mind around the word. *That he was their ... executioner?* This was what I loved and gave up my life for? To raise the son of a ... a ....

Murderer? His voice echoed tauntingly in my mind.

I looked at him in horror.

Careful, Carrie. Remember? I warned you that if you asked, I would tell you.

No ... no ... please.

My ears began ringing. The edges of my vision darkened.

"Mercy," I whispered as I fell.

No one caught me.

***

Only Gabriel looked with pity at the woman lying crumpled on the floor. Everyone else stared as Grant, brushing his hands together like a puppet master who had just tossed the discarded marionette's strings over its inert body, walked toward Grayson.

"Why don't you let me come with you so we can discuss this together? The children are safe, and if it's all the same to you, I'd rather not be here when she wakes up."

Grayson's eyes traveled from Carrie's body to the sleeping boys and back to Grant.

"But it's not all the same to me. I think you may have been a little precipitous in your declaration, Grant. We still need to use her trust in you until specific controls are in place. There are others, besides those in this room, who are interested in her."

"Sorry. I thought we were finished here."

"Almost. But there are certain matters under discussion that concern you which do not, at this time, require your input." Grayson's eyes flickered in Carrie's direction. "So, I'm going to leave you here to clean up this mess, stabilize, *and control* the situation. We'll be back in the morning with the collective's final relocation plans for her, the offspring, and you."

Grayson led the way as the rest of the men in the room filed out behind him.

Before leaving, Gabriel felt along the inside of the cushions and found four more knives. Putting them in the pocket of his lab coat, he went into the kitchen and removed everything with a single point or a serrated blade.

"She'll be all right, won't she, Grant? She wouldn't harm herself or the—"

"Babies? No, Gabriel, she loves them too much. I am not, however, as optimistic about my well-being. Care to change places now?"

Grant was surprised to see that, for a moment, Gabriel seriously considered the offer.

"Ah, um, no. That is, I don't think Grayson will let you leave, and, um, I think one of us in here will be enough."

"You are probably right, but it was worth a try. This may not be a safe place for any *adult* Lyostian tonight." He glanced down at the utensils in Gabriel's hands. "Thanks for taking everything ... I think."

A hiccupping moan was heard from the floor.

"Well, look who's finally waking up."

Gabriel watched as Grant pulled a hypodermic syringe from his lab coat and uncapped it.

"I am considering offering an introductory seminar. We will call it Combating Human Hysteria 101. Think any of the interns would care to attend? They might find a use for it someday."

Gabriel tried to smile. "Speaking of which, Grant, Grayson is posting interns in the hall."

"Of course, he is. Until tomorrow, Gabriel."

"Until tomorrow, Grant." Glancing in Carrie's direction, he added, "Good luck."

"Thank you, I will need it," he said, closing the door.

Hearing Grant quietly engage the deadbolt, I raised my head from the floor. Holding up one finger, he tilted his head toward the hallway. Nodding to himself, he pressed a small lever I'd never noticed on the outside of the door frame. There was a slight whirring sound and the faint click of a lock.

I ran to him and kissed him. *You saved us, Grant. Thank you, thank you.*

I suddenly noticed he was not responding, and my heart fell. Had he really meant it this time? Afraid the look of contempt had returned to his eyes, I backed away from him.

"Grant?" I said softly.

"Carolina, I, I need to sit down. Right now," he whispered. Even in the dim light, I could see that his skin was ashen. As I helped him to the couch, I realized that his shirt was damp, and the fingers of his hands were slightly curled.

As soon as he sat down, Grant's head fell back against the cushions. I blew out the last candle and ran to the refrigerator. Putting the tall glass of juice in his left hand, I held the other next to my face as he drank. Fear escalated with each passing second as my mind went in a million different directions at once. Without a word, he closed his eyes, and I barely had time to catch the glass before it slipped from his fingers.

Placing my head on his chest, I listened to his heart. It was racing, and his chest moved as though he was gasping for breath. As he had held me so many times, I pulled him into my arms and cradled him.

"Shh, shh," I whispered, brushing the hair away from his face. "My darling, we're fine. You saved us." I kissed his damp forehead and held him until his breathing slowed and his heartbeat became normal.

Better? I thought to him.

Yes. Can we stay like this forever?

Yes. If that is your wish.

Perhaps there will be some time for us later. I have to stop them, and you must leave.

I know. Can you come with us?

Maybe.

What can I do?

We need to start talking. I am no longer sure what thoughts they can or cannot hear.

Can you hear them?

I am still connected to the colony and the collective—if that is what you mean. My head hurts too much to scan their thoughts right now, but I know they are going to the tunnel rooms in the main corridor.

"Why there?" I said aloud.

"To discuss what to do with me, you, and the children, and discuss it far enough away so that I cannot hear them unless they specifically decide to include me. Other than that, all I can hear is a general buzzing. They will return in the morning to tell us what they have decided."

"Will you know their decision before they come?"

"That depends on whether they allow me to stay within the colony's communication or if they decide to punish me for not keeping you under control."

Even the slight possibility of banishment caused the hand I held to tremble.

"That was my job, you know," he added.

"But after what you said and the way you said it," I said, choking back a sob. "They should know my desertion wasn't your idea."

"My darling, I am so sorry I hurt you. I was undeniably cruel, but I had to create a level of doubt. We were about an hour away from dying—all of us—because if the interns had remained here, I would have killed them, and then no escape would have been possible for any of us."

"I know."

The dampness was evaporating from his face, and I felt hopeful but still shaky. "Grant, what just happened to you?"

"I think you would call it cerebral ischemia."

"What is that?"

"A small cerebral hemorrhage. This afternoon's little performance was very ... difficult for me. Trying, as I was, not to lose either of my families. But mostly, I was trying to keep you alive long enough to escape and to stay alive long enough to help you."

"Well, you convinced me. That wasn't a fake faint. I didn't think you could look or talk like that. You were quite heartless, you know."

"Yes."

"But they weren't surprised?"

"No."

"Don't tell me, Grant," I said, knowing I really didn't want an answer.

"Think about everything I've shared with you, Carolina ... you already know."

Grant had not lied. I knew who—and what—he was, and a calmness came over me as I realized that I had known it for some time. More than that, I also understood that it was through his position within the colony that he was able to keep us safe and together. He *was* their executioner, the monster in their midst. As I accepted this final truth of his identity, I gently stroked his forehead, and my hand did not waver.

"What do we do now?"

"Please feed the boys again as soon as you can and then yet again. There may not be a safe place to stop tomorrow, so it is important they have as much nourishment as possible today. Between feedings, pack one bag you can carry with whatever you will need for a two-day car trip. Your other suitcases are already in the car."

"What are you going to do?"

"Reset the charges."

"Can you get to them?"

"Yes. The secret door in the dressing room goes into the tunnels. I thought it might come to this, and I wanted to be prepared to stop them."

"Stop them or kill them?"

"At midnight, when they are asleep, I will collapse the tunnels between the rooms. It will take them a few days to get out, and we will leave while they are digging."

"Won't they follow us when they get out?"

"No, because of the other explosion."

"What other explosion?"

"The one that implodes the building, of course."

"The whole building?"

"Yes, it has been set for days. That is the final act. The colony leaves, the building implodes and falls in on itself, thereby obliterating all the tunnels directly under the building."

"Is this happening in every city?"

"Yes."

"Won't someone investigate?"

"Why would they? The permits are in place, and everything is legal. NAFTRAM only owns the buildings; we lease the land. Clean–up crews have been hired, and in less than a month, all this will be just another construction site."

"All your beautiful designs, architecture, and furnishings? Everything ... gone?" Tears filled my eyes when I thought of Grant's artistry and skill turned to rubble and dust.

"It was only a trap, Carolina, and a temporary one at that." He kissed my palm and looked up at me. "Just like everything else."

"Even this?" I said, indicating our apartment.

"Until your love made it our home, yes."

"Our love."

"Yes, Carolina, our love changed everything."

Saving Suzanne

He dropped my hand, and I knew by the way he clenched his jaw that the pain had returned. I brought more juice and a damp towel, trying everything to make him feel better. Then, just as he was beginning to sit up, his eyes flew open, and he looked in my direction.

"Oh, hell."

"What is it? Did they change their minds? Are they coming back?"

He closed his eyes again. "No, better. And worse."

"What is it, Grant?"

"Suzanne."

"What? Where?"

"Here. Luckily, the interns were not instructed to keep their thoughts to themselves."

"Right here? Like outside?"

"No. She was in the salon with some friends earlier today and stayed to see you. When she kept asking for you and refused to leave, Gregory and Harris took her upstairs, sedated her, and locked her in Gregory's office."

"What are they going to do with her?"

"Nothing good. Carolina, please, I cannot think about one more thing right now."

"Suzanne is not a thing, Grant. She's my friend and Andre's mother. I'm not leaving her here to be imploded or whatever else they have in mind."

"They probably plan to keep her drugged and take her down into the tunnels tonight."

"For the building to fall on?"

His face full of pain and regret, he said, "Eventually, yes."

"Are there other women in the tunnels for the building to fall on, Grant?"

"Not ... alive."

I felt suddenly lightheaded. Afraid I was going to faint again, I sat down. When the ringing sound in my ears faded, I said, "How ... how many women died here, Grant?"

He looked at me steadily, "Almost four."

"Almost?"

"After your miscarriage and before we realized you were carrying twins, Grayson said you knew too much to live. But I could not kill you, Carolina. I would have hidden you away and protected you. They would have had to kill both of us. I, I was not going to live without you." He passed his hand over his face. "So, you see, Austin saved us all."

"But the other three?"

"My primary assignment is to neutralize all threats against the colony and collective, both external and internal."

"Internal?"

"Yes. You have not asked me how many of my brothers died here."

"Oh, Grant, was it very difficult for you?"

"No. I told you, when you have no choice, you have no conscience; no conscience—no remorse. And, although that premise has rarely been true, I have accepted it as being part of who I am." He took my hand and pressed it against his face. "I regret it now because I realize that if you had met Eric a year ago, and the same chain of events had occurred, one of those bodies could easily, oh, so easily, Carolina, be yours."

"Why?"

"The timing for the serum wasn't perfected. We tried aborting the embryos, but some women had to have hysterectomies to survive … and one was injured outside the facility, rupturing the embryo."

"Like Suzanne."

He made a hoarse sound in his throat. "No, Carolina, not like Suzanne. Suzanne's case was mild from the beginning, and we caught it. A year ago, there was nothing in place to clean Leia's blood and the toxins accumulated in her brain. We had to keep her here." Shuddering at the memory, he said, "We tried to keep her sedated but were not always successful. Her screams were terrifying."

"Until?"

"Until she committed suicide by chewing her own wrist."

Knowing it would not help anyone to fly into the rage I was feeling, I tried to remain calm, but I was adamant. Suzanne was *not* staying here. I mentally reviewed the facility's floor plan.

"When does the spa close?" I asked.

"Because it's New Year's Eve and our last day, we are open until nine tonight."

"How long after that can employees leave before the doors are locked?"

"An hour, maybe less. Most of them have already cleaned out their stations."

I nodded. "Tonight, after closing, I'll take the elevator to your office and call someone to pick her up. Do you think that will be okay?"

"Yes."

"Can she be picked up at the garage level?"

"No. Vehicles cannot enter the garage without an access code, and we cannot use mine."

Then, I recalled one of our midnight tours. "The catwalks, Grant. I'll take her through the employee's exit to the catwalks and down to the service entrance."

"No, you will set off the alarm because you don't have access, and I am sure Garrett will be looking for mine."

"Are there any secret passages from the offices to the catwalks?"

"You have been paying attention. Yes, but not through mine. You will have to access the catwalks through Gregory's office. Luckily, the office entries to the catwalks are not connected to the security alarms, but you will need my access card to move between my office and Gregory's. The doors between the officers were never connected to the alarms but used to keep our clients from letting their curiosity overcome their good sense."

"Someone tried to sneak into Gregory's office?"

"Yes, and not just Gregory's office. That's why we need an access card to unlock them."

"I've never seen you carry an access card."

Grant smiled grimly as he walked into the examination room and brought a scalpel to the kitchen. Holding his arm over the sink, he cut a thin line on top of his wrist. Blood dripped from the wound as he took the blunt edge of the scalpel and dragged it over the skin of his forearm. A white piece of plastic streaked with blood slowly emerged from the slit.

"This is how we can be any place at any time. Do not go through my office door with it; Garrett will be looking for that. You must use our elevator to get to my office and then go through the connecting door into Gregory's office to get to Suzanne and from there to the catwalks. Do not use this to open any of the main doors, or they will know I am out of this room. And that, Carolina, will be the end of all our plans. Except the one to die together."

I placed a dampened towel over his arm and picked up the bloodied chip.

"Remember," he added, "the delivery exit door works with a bar lock from the inside. Pressing it to get out will not alert anyone as several of our staff leave that way. However, using the access card to come back in will alert the colony. Do not let the door close on you, Carolina."

"What time should I take her out?"

"No later than ten–thirty, that's when the telephone service will be disconnected. I am setting the tunnel explosives to detonate at midnight. Anyone outside the facility hearing or feeling anything will assume it is part of the mall's New Year's celebration." He smiled slightly. "New Year. Any resolutions, my dear?" he asked, lifting my hand to his lips.

"To be the woman you love. You?"

"To love you more every day."

He kissed my forehead and held me close. "Who are you going to call for Suzanne?"

"I'm not sure. It depends on who I can get a hold of, or maybe just a cab, anything that will take her home."

He took my face in his hands. I could not miss the sound of desperation in his voice.

"There is so much that could go wrong, Carolina. Please don't come back for me. I beg you, with every ounce of love I have for you, just take Austin and go. You, Suzanne, and Austin. Get in whatever vehicle you can procure and leave." He closed his eyes for a moment. "Forget our plans. Don't risk returning here. Even ... even if you have to call Dan again, please, my darling, just save yourself and our son."

I pulled his hands from my face, kissed each palm, and placed them on my heart. "Is that how I love you, Grant? Honor and cherish you? By abandoning you? Taking your son and leaving you alone with three hungry boys? No, please don't ask me to do that. We have a plan where we all might be together, and you have taken such good care of us. I won't risk losing four to save one."

"Not even if that one is your own son?"

"Not if I throw away the only chance I have to save his father."

"Even when his father is a—"

I interrupted him.

"Grant, there are people who, if they were aware of everything I've done in the last six months, would have some pretty sharp words to describe me, but you know who I am and what I mean to you, so it becomes irrelevant. Please, love, let me treat you with the same kindness. The only thing that matters is what we are to each other."

Wife.

Husband.

In slow motion and defying what little time they had, Grant kissed her and gently pressed the back of her throat.

Remember me, Carolina.

She pressed her lips to his until the taste of him infused her senses, her thoughts, and her memories.

Forever, Grant.

Forgiveness

When he felt stronger, Grant went to the kitchen to make tea.

"Grant, who is with Suzanne now?"

He tilted his head. "No one. Howard is monitoring the upstairs hall where the offices are located, and Hugo is monitoring this one. The rest have returned to the tunnels."

"Why would they go down there so early in the afternoon?"

"Did you not notice the rush in the lobby? With no specific tasks to keep them in the building, they all prefer the tunnels. It's so dark and peaceful down there," he said slowly.

"You've missed that, haven't you, in the last few months?"

"Yes. But I would have regretted missing this more. My world, Carolina, is where you are. Our home is my sanctuary. I could have taken you down to the tunnels and kept you there, but you would not have been happy."

"But—"

"Shh, you would not have been happy there, Carolina, my love, even with me. It would have been harder to focus on my humanness in the tunnels. You might have become frightened and wanted to leave, and I am not quite sure I would have allowed that ... not after I had tasted your sweetness and shared the wonder of your mind. In fact, I am quite sure I would have killed you and died gratefully beside you before I would have let you go."

That is still an option, my darling.

Yes, but it is the last one—not the only one, my soft, sweet wife.

He handed me a cup of tea and sat beside me. I leaned my head against his shoulder. Life without him or death with him, only the boys made the difference. If they did not need me, or I them, I would have considered using one of the syringes on myself and sparing Grant all this pain.

A fingertip of thought touched my heart and my mind. I looked at Grant and smiled.

"What is it?"

"Your son is hungry," I said. "He just told me, not quite in words, more a feeling, unless, of course, I'm hungry, too. Care to help with that?" I looked up at him, hopefully.

"Always my favorite part of the day," he said, the smile almost making it to his eyes.

"Favorite?" I teased him with a raised eyebrow.

"I said it was my favorite part of the day, not the best part." The smile shone from his eyes, and I started to stand.

"I'll get Austin," he said, settling me back down.

While I was nursing the babies, he packed the boys' suitcase for me. Sets of four diapers, shirts, pajamas, and blue blankets. Knowing it might be cold in the car, I asked for one of the quilted coverlets, and he packed the blue one I had with me when Austin was born. He set the suitcase behind the alcove curtain.

He was so efficient. He knew exactly what to do for them, and, at that moment, I knew how much I needed his help to raise these boys into the men he expected them to become. He understood them so well. How crushingly difficult was it going to be for me to be everything to them: mother, father, and ant/alien/human interpreter? I knew he trusted me, but would I ever be enough for them? The tears I had held back all day threatened to spill over.

After setting Aslan in the nursery crib, Grant turned toward the front room.

"Where are you going?" I asked.

"Dinner for two as requested."

Following him, I wondered if we would be able to eat any of it.

We made brave attempts to eat but gave it up completely after a few bites. He took my hand, and we sat together on the sofa. With my head on his shoulder, he stroked the silver and gold strands of my hair. He bent his head down, thinking.

"What is it, Grant?"

"With your hair like this, you might as well be wearing a sign that says, 'Here I am, Carolina Gates, come and get me.' So, let's go."

"Go? Go where?"

"Your mini–spa."

"You can cut hair?" Answering my own question, I said, "Of course, you can cut hair. I suspect that with the exception of driving, you can do anything."

"I can drive, Carolina. It is just that daylight is too bright, and at night, the oncoming headlights are like fire arrows in my eyes. However, even if I couldn't do a good job of it, I would still attempt anything that would make you safer."

A few minutes later, I was sitting on the vanity bench.

"Do you want to face the mirror or face me?"

"Always you."

"Any preference?"

"Would it matter?"

He laughed. "No, my dear, it probably would not."

"Besides, Grant," I said, looking up at him. "You always make me lovelier than anything I could imagine, so have at it."

"Let's see," he said. He gazed at me for a few minutes, each eye taking in a different part of my face. I watched his expression change as ideas were quickly visualized and discarded until a look of calm resignation came over him, and he relaxed.

"We are going to need some color."

He opened the cabinet doors, setting shades of cinnamon and dark brown on the vanity counter.

"But, Grant," I protested, "the boys won't know me if I look too different."

"Carolina, my love, you give them too much credit. Your voice will sound the same, and these lovely breasts will smell the same, and that is pretty much all they care about right now."

His words reminded me of my earlier behavior, and my eyes filled with tears. "I'm so sorry, Grant," I whispered.

About what?

You know, this afternoon, letting your brothers and the interns see, um, me. It wasn't part of our plan, but I needed to get their attention and respect. It was the only thing I could think of. Thank you for not still being angry with me.

I was never angry with you, Carolina, because I always trust your instincts. Nothing would have bound Gabriel and Garrett to you more than seeing you nurse the boys. If you had not done that, it might have been just me standing between you and Grayson, and someone would have gotten hurt. Besides, I do not consider that abbreviated display of motherhood 'sharing you with them,' my dear. It was just reinforcing evidence of my choice of wife.

He kissed the top of my head. *My beautiful,* kiss ... *intelligent,* kiss ... *courageous and* kiss, kiss ... *wonderful wife. They will never be as happy in their entire lives—collectively—as I have been these few months with you.*

He took the scissors in his left hand and, with a light touch on either side of my jaw, leveled my head.

Don't move.

Silver and gold strands glinting with candlelight floated past my eyes, and their feathery weight brushed my shoulders. He opened packages of hair color, mixed them up, then sectioned and painted my hair.

While we waited, he walked away and returned with a small bag in which he had tossed some cosmetics. He knew exactly which ones would look best.

"How will I get along without you?" I tried to say lightly and failed.

"I think you will find that I have left very little to chance, and you may get angry at me for leaving you so little space to make your own decisions. I knew you would be busy with our children and wanted to make it easier for you. Or, you could say that I was selfish and unwilling to let you have a life without me."

"I think," I said, touching the hollow of my throat, "you made it abundantly clear how much you wanted to be the only man in my life—for the rest of my life."

"Yes."

"Protecting me or the boys?"

"Whichever makes you resent it less."

"I'll probably thank you for it more than I will resent it, Grant."

"I hope so, my darling. I hope so."

He looked at his watch. "Shall we see if the reality matches the vision?"

Grant rinsed her hair until the red and brown water swirling in the sink became clear. There was only one other face he wanted to see that day. He lightly combed her hair with his fingers and, using the hairdryer, let the dark copper curls fall around her face. Opening the bag of cosmetics he'd gathered for her, he brushed a little apricot color on her cheeks, lined her eyes in green, and accented them with black mascara. He backed away.

Yes, he thought. *She will look so different to them, yet still so completely mine.*

"Ready, Carolina?"

"Yes."

He turned her around.

The woman in the mirror was not Carrie Taylor; she wasn't even Carolina Gates. The delicate, elfin creature looking back at them was someone else entirely. He knelt beside her so their faces were almost level in the mirror's reflection.

Unbelievingly, Carolina touched her face and whispered, "I love her, Grant. Who is she?"

Mother of my generations.

She thought for a moment. *Your mother?*

Yes. Forgive me, Carolina. I just wanted to see her one more time.

I've never been more beautiful. Thank you, Grant.

He looked at their reflection for several minutes. She thought he was memorizing her, but as she watched, his expression of loving admiration gradually turned to one of sorrow.

Lifting her as though she were the fragile ghost of his memory, Grant carried her with trembling hands into their room. He gently lowered her into the bed and wrapped them both in a single quilt. With his face close to her heart, Grant poured out grieving words of longing, love, and repentance in the language of his ancestors. Carolina listened, as Anya might, to the anguished confession of just one more child who needed her. Humming Anya's prayer of forgiveness, she cradled him with all the love, compassion, and understanding of his goddess mother.

A Single Existence

Grant was calm and breathing softly, and the boys were asleep in their crib. I yearned to rest as well but could not stop thinking and didn't know what to do or say. For the first time, there was an awkward silence between us.

What now? I thought. *How do I keep from going crazy for the next few hours when all I want to do is hold him and cry?*

"By realizing, my love, that is all I want to do as well, but it would be a waste of our time together."

I looked at him, puzzled.

"I don't remember directing those particular thoughts to you."

"You didn't."

"You lied to me," I said, sitting up.

"In this instance, yes," he said, sitting opposite me.

"For them?"

"There is no *them*, Carolina. We are one."

"There is never an IV stand around when you need one," I muttered. "Did you find out anything you didn't already know?"

"No new information," he said, smiling softly to himself.

"Why are you smiling?"

"Because you continually surprised me. I wasn't snooping inside your mind to trap you in a lie, Carolina. I just wanted to know if you were as happy as you seemed. And you were, and because there was no deception in your thoughts, I knew I could trust you, not only with our sons but with everything I am. You never lied to me. So many times, when you said, 'I love you,' I could only answer, 'I know,' because I do know, Carolina, and because I have never had any doubts, I could love you completely."

"A single existence."

"Yes. So, please forgive me. It was only because I knew I had all of you, that I was able to give you all of me."

"So, what am I thinking now?"

"Ahh, an excellent choice," he said, disappearing into the bathroom.

A few minutes later, he wrapped my hair in a small towel and took my hand. The hot tub was full, but the shower was steaming. I looked at him.

"I thought you would like to bathe first."

Despite my earlier feeling that I would be spending the next few hours crying, my laughter bounced off the tile walls, and our sorrow disappeared with the soap bubbles that ran down the drain.

Contented, I leaned against him as he delicately sipped droplets of steam from my skin.

Feeling better now, Carolina?

"Umm hum, you?"

Only by reminding myself that every moment we share today is one we will have forever.

"But maybe never again."

He pulled away and looked at me. "Yes," he sighed. "Everything that lives, dies, Carolina."

"And today?"

"We will not die today."

Believing him because the alternative was too painful, I let him hold me as though it were still summer and we were sharing my dreaming time again. When his lips touched the base of my throat, I fell into him and could not separate his thoughts, his caresses, or his mouth from my own.

Afterward, exhausted and lying in our nest and too blissful to consider the answer to my question, I asked him about the sound I heard when he closed the front door.

"The locking bolts," he said.

"What bolts?"

"There are ten bolts that are embedded twelve inches deep into the door all around the frame and run three feet into the walls, two feet to the ceiling, and about four feet into the ground. Making our sanctuary more than a home—"

"You made it into a fortress."

"Yes."

"Why?"

"I don't like surprises."

"How could they sur ... Oh."

"Yes."

"For me?"

"For us. What happens to you happens to me. *Would you like me to demonstrate that again?*"

Brushing the tips of his fingers along the skin of my back, I not only felt the pressure of his hand but the sensation in my fingers as well.

"Grant," I whispered, "we *are* one."

"Yes."

Austin moved in the crib. "Are the boys hungry again?"

"Soon," he said, pulling me very close. "Lie still, please. I want to feel the joy of you ... just a little longer."

With one hand under my breasts and the other on my abdomen, Grant pulled me into the curve of his body. I reached up with one arm, brought his head close to mine, and wrapped my other arm around the back of his thigh. His manhood curved behind me, and its tulip-shaped head peeked between my thighs as though it were my own. The flickering candlelight surrounding us cast the shadow of a single entity, complete and indivisible.

I relaxed against him and shared his mind, memorizing the cadences of his thoughts, the rhythm of his breathing, and the smell of his skin. Everything that was masculine about him folded around me, and everything that was feminine in me melted into him. Our minds merged, and we swam connected, swirling around each other in a sea of endless indigo. Breaking for the surface, we saw a multicolored sky, and I knew it was just a glimpse of our future, a promise of eons to come.

Then, just like that, time ran out.

Reluctantly, Grant went to the crib and brought me the babies two at a time. They weren't very hungry, but I fed them, and they went back to sleep immediately.

Returning from putting Andre and Aslan back in the crib, he looked at me as I sat against the pillows, a quilt pulled up over my lap. Saying more with his eyes than he trusted either of his voices to say, his lips brushed the top of my head as he leaned over and pressed the button so our bed would rise.

Taking my hand, we went into the nearly empty dressing room. After handing me a pair of jeans, a green turtleneck sweater, and a brown leather jacket, he opened a small drawer in the bureau and took out a set of car keys. Pressing a section of the paneling, a hidden door sprung open, and he removed a leather sheath embroidered with silk thread. A thin gold dagger with a jeweled handle slipped into his hand.

He looked at me wordlessly and then slid the weapon back into the case.

"Take these now," he said, handing me the keys and the weapon, "you never know."

"Yes. Thank you, Grant."

Persephone's Children

The small door became invisible again. Walking to the opposite side of the room, he pressed his hand against the left edge of the frame, and the panel slipped behind the one next to it. Before descending the ladder, he turned and kissed me quickly.

"I'll be back as soon as I can. I love you," he said.

"I know."

I watched the panel close and looked at the items in my hand. I knew which one to use first.

Saving Suzanne

31 December: 10:00 p.m.

Walking into the kitchen, I picked up the piece of plastic that had been in Grant's arm and felt a moment of honest hatred for his brothers. I hoped the tunnels would collapse and destroy them all, but then it occurred to me that if Grant intended to kill them, he would reset the charges over their rooms instead of the connecting tunnels. If he did not plan to kill them with the first implosion, why would he bury them alive with the second?

Unsure of Grant's actual plan regarding his brothers, I was overcome with a sense of urgency. Nothing was more important to either of us than the boys' safety, and I knew getting them to the car was best for all of us. Despite twelve-inch bolts and secret escape panels, I would not leave them in the apartment alone for all the Suzannes in the world.

There was still one thing to do before I could leave. Grant had left something else for me besides his access card. I looked at the clean scalpel, small bandage, and tube of antiseptic on the counter. Grant knew the smell of blood would slow his brothers down, and minutes could make a difference to our escape. Making a fist, I took a deep breath and pressed the point of Grant's scalpel into my hand just below my left thumb. Blood bubbled into my palm. Grateful it was my blood and not his, I walked through the front room, dragging my bloodied hand over the cushions. Opening and tightening my fist, a fresh supply slid down my wrist, and I held my arm out and watched as the dark red drops fell onto the carpet. Before rinsing the wound and applying the medicine and bandage, I moved my hand over the door, leaving a red smear on the doorframe and handle.

Slipping the access card into my pocket, I set the small suitcase inside the elevator and took Austin and Alexi out of the crib. At the garage level, I nudged the suitcase against the door, worried that if the elevator closed, it might not reopen. As Grant promised, I found a partition disguised to look like part of the wall. On the other side, a sleek charcoal grey Lexus blended into the shadows. Opening the door, I saw two twin car seats secured to the backseat. After strapping Austin and Alexi in on the passenger's side, I started the car to get it warmed up. Once all four boys were safely tucked in and the car was toasty, I turned the engine off but left the seat warmers on, so the car would stay as cozy as possible without making any noise. Taking their little hands in mine, I promised I would be back soon. Trusting my love for them, their eyelids fluttered, and they went back to sleep. I moved the suitcase inside the elevator and rode it up to Grant's office.

I stared at the telephone on Grant's desk. *Who would I call?* Suddenly Eric's phone number came into my mind as clearly as though I were reading it from a scrap of paper.

I pressed the numbers quickly. I knew that regardless of his New Year's Eve plans, he would take her wherever she wanted to go.

"Talk."

"Eric, this is—"

"Carrie! Where *are* you?"

"I'm still at work, and um, Suzanne's here. If you're not busy, could you please come to the service entrance at GatesWay Health Spa next to the mall and pick her up?"

"So that's where she is. I've been calling her all afternoon. Is anything wrong?"

"Well, yes and no. She stopped by to visit me this afternoon and fainted. I can't leave right now, and she wants to go home. Please."

"Of course. How, how are you, Carrie?" he asked quietly.

"Fine, I'm fine, Eric, thank you."

"Carrie, um, I've thought about this a lot, the baby, is it still ...?"

"I'm sorry, Eric. I miscarried about three months ago."

"You didn't call me."

"No. It was ... complicated ... and I didn't know what to say." There was no response, only silence. "But about Suzanne, how soon can you get here?"

"I'm on my way. I'll be there in twenty minutes."

"Perfect. She'll meet you outside. Thank you, Eric, for everything."

"Will you be there?"

"Yes, but don't forget; I'll meet you at the *service* entrance. The front doors will be locked."

I pressed the lever next to the narrow panel behind Grant's desk that connected his and Gregory's offices. It slid back soundlessly. The room was dimly lit by a row of marquee lights along the baseboard. As I cautiously glanced around the partition, I saw the outline of someone lying on Gregory's vintage casting couch on the opposite wall.

"Suzanne?" I whispered.

A man's voice answered mine. "Mrs. Grant?"

I froze. I couldn't breathe. I didn't think the situation could get any more desperate. *Had they already killed her? Was I too late? How was I going to get back to the boys?* I heard a roaring sound in my ears.

"I, I just need a moment," I said, reaching for the partition to keep my balance.

The figure on the couch moved.

"Caroline, is that you?" Suzanne asked faintly. "Where have you been? I've been calling and calling you."

A glass of water was handed to me as I sat down.

I fought the impulse to telepathically scream for Grant. If he was in the tunnels, he probably couldn't hear me, and if he did, what would he be running back to? No. Better he got away with the boys than risk both of us dying here.

"Mrs. Grant? How did you get into the office? Where is Dr. Grant?" I raised my head to see Howard's worried expression.

Show no fear; remember who you are.

I smiled brightly at him. "Dr. Grant brought me in through the panel one evening to show me the mural. When he told me that Suzanne was here, I said I wouldn't feed the children until I saw her, so he said I could have fifteen minutes to say goodbye. If I am not back, he will alert the others to come get me. Speaking of which, Howard, why are you here? Isn't there a big life-or-death meeting in the tunnels tonight?"

"There is, but the interns were not invited to take part in the discussion, only in any …."

"Disciplinary action?" I prompted him.

"Yes. If needed."

"So, they assigned you to check on Suzanne?"

"I, I brought her some dinner."

"Suzanne, have you eaten any of the dinner Howard brought you?" I asked softly.

"No, not hungry, just thirsty."

I glanced at the pale amber liquid at the bottom of the cup. "And you're sleepy, aren't you, sweetheart?"

"Um, hum."

I looked at Howard, and he looked down at the carpet.

Recalling some of the horrifying images I'd seen in Grant's mind, I took Suzanne's hand in both of mine. Repressing the terrifying thoughts of Suzanne's life being destroyed, I asked calmly, "When are they taking her into the tunnels, Howard, tonight or tomorrow morning?"

He looked up at me in surprise and then down again. "I'm supposed to keep her, um, sleeping until tomorrow morning."

"No choice, no conscience. Isn't that right, Howard?"

"Not always. She's Antony's *mother*," he said quietly.

"Yes, she is," I said, leaning over to wipe the dampness from her face.

At my touch, Suzanne's eyes fluttered open. She smiled at me and barely had time to say, "Did you see my toes, Caroline?" before her eyes closed again.

I glanced down at her feet. Suzanne was wearing the salon's pedicure sandals. *Where were her shoes?* I saw the edge of her spa bag where someone ... *Gregory?* had stashed it under the end table. It was not in Howard's line of sight. I took the chance he didn't know it was there.

"Where are her shoes, Howard? Oh, my gosh, we have to find her shoes." I pretended to look under the table and shoved her bag behind the sofa as he searched the rest of the room.

"I don't know," he said slowly. "Maybe they are still in a locker downstairs."

I nodded. "You're probably right. You must find her shoes." I looked at him seriously. "Dr. Grant would never leave such incriminating evidence unaccounted for, would he?"

Grant's attention to every detail was one of his more inflexible attributes. Howard was suddenly aware of how irresponsible he would appear if her shoes were not found and destroyed before someone came looking for her. He knew as well as anyone how Grant punished such carelessness.

Seeing the worried look on his face, I smiled.

"Don't worry, Howard, I will make sure Suzanne stays here. When you bring her shoes, bring her a little more tea and some nice toast with honey."

He looked uncertain. Playing the only ace I had, I tilted my head.

"I can always ask Dr. Grant what to do."

"No, Mrs. Grant. That's all right. I'll check the lockers and be right back."

"You are very wise, Howard," I said, straightening my head.

Howard didn't feel very wise and wished there was someone else to send, but each intern had a specific assignment. His had been to neutralize Suzanne, but with her shoes missing, she was a bigger threat dead than alive. He had to find her shoes.

"You will wait here?"

"Of course, Howard, where could I go that Dr. Grant could not find me? But hurry, please. I must get back to the children."

Howard nodded to her as he left the room. Smiling slightly at the memory of her tenderness toward his youngest brothers, he put his hand over his heart. She was a blessing to them.

As soon as the door closed, I bent over Suzanne and started shaking her.

"Wake up, Suzanne. We've got to get out of here now. Please wake up, sweetheart. It's time to go home."

Reaching behind the sofa, I pulled her bag from its hiding place and put her shoes on.

"Home? You mean I'm not home?"

I handed her the bag. "No, dear, you are still at the spa. Let's go home. Your ride will be here in a few minutes."

"My ride?"

"Yes. Eric's coming to take you home."

"Really?" she said. Her sleepy eyes opened a little, and she smiled.

"Yes, he's on his way. Can you stand up?"

"I think so."

Despite her words, I knew from the way her knees buckled when she tried to stand that I would have to practically carry her to the exit. Pressing the latch on the hidden door, I helped her through the opening to the catwalks, steadying her so she would not trip. It was not easy. With one arm wrapped around Suzanne and the other shoulder weighted down by her spa bag, it was all I could do to remain upright.

I paused at the top of the catwalks, listening. There was no one on the ladders, and remembering how Grant led me down the metal scaffolding, I kept Suzanne against the wall as I guided her through the darkness one floor at a time. It was a long and difficult descent. Every moment, I expected to hear footsteps signaling that Howard had returned to find us gone. My mind shuddered when I thought about what they would do to us if they found Suzanne with me—or worse—found me alone.

Despite the stumbling gait, we got to the service entrance quicker than I thought we would. I looked through the window and smiled in grateful relief. Eric was leaning against his car in the parking lot, staring at the building with his arms crossed as though ready to do battle.

"Eric is here, Suzanne. You're almost home."

I eased her down on the bottom stair step, pressed the lock bar, and opened the door. Seeing me standing on the threshold, Eric broke into a short run and gave me a hug.

When he glanced down and saw Suzanne's face pale in the blinking exit light, he knelt immediately beside her.

"Oh, my God, Suzanne! Are you okay?" He looked up at me angrily.

"Eric," I said calmly, "I told you on the phone. She stopped by with some friends for a pedicure, stayed to visit me, and then she fainted. She feels better now, but I can't leave until we close, and she needs a ride home." I let that sink in for a moment and added softly, "Isn't that why you're here?"

Eric gently lifted Suzanne from the steps, and I remembered how it felt being in his arms, but it seemed so long ago … almost as though I'd seen it in a late–night movie in flickering black and white. A few seconds later, the images were gone, forgotten.

I handed him her bag and stood aside to let him walk past me, but I didn't want to let her go. Clasping her to me, I hugged her for the last time.

"Oh, Suzanne, I will love you forever."

"Me, too, Caroline. Bye now. Oh look, Eric, it's snowing … So pretty." Her voice drifted off as her head fell on Eric's shoulder.

Eric looked at me. "Are you sure I can't give you a ride? It's New Year's Eve, Carrie, I'm sure there is someone waiting for you."

"Yes, yes, there is, Eric, but I can't leave until I am finished here." I smiled into his eyes, "Thank you for everything."

He nodded and carried Suzanne to his car, setting her gently into the passenger seat and helping her with the seatbelt. He waved to me from the driver's seat and then wrapped his arm around her shoulders. I knew her head would hurt a little in the morning, but she was alive. I stood in the doorway longer than I should have, waving back at them until the car's taillights disappeared.

Snowflakes melted with the tears on my face as I pulled the door closed and started climbing the steel scaffolding to Gregory's office.

The Other Plan – Part III

31 December: 10:45 p.m.

When Tory and Travis arrived, the facility's parking lot was empty except for one car waiting near the service entrance and one in the visitor's parking area. Tory instantly recognized Dan's car and pointed to the mall side of the visitor's lot.

"Damn," she said, "that's Dan. Park over there and tell him to leave."

Before they could exit Travis's car, Dan walked up to them.

"I've been waiting for you."

"Listen, Dan, I can give you fifty good reasons why you should leave, but I only need one. You can't help us," said Travis.

"I heard you say you were coming back tonight, and I *will* help you get her out of there. I may not have any legal rights, but I'm taking her home to her son tonight, if only for a few minutes. I'll bring her back here if I have to. I just can't stand the look in Brendan's eyes anymore."

"He blames you?"

"A little, mostly he blames himself for leaving her."

"Dan, no matter how tonight turns out, bring Brendan to see me early next week. As a psychologist, cult methodology is one of my specialties. I can explain to him how brainwashing works and the way cults indoctrinate new members. Once he understands that, he won't blame himself—or you."

"Thanks, I'll do that," he said. Then, looking from Travis to the building, he added, "Well, what's the plan? I'm in."

Travis shook his head. "This is not good," he said to Tory. "Maybe we should try to get a search warrant and come back on Monday."

But Tory would not be dissuaded. There were two things she wanted, and she was not giving up either one without a fight. Besides, they had a plan. If it failed, they would leave, but if it worked, well, having another guy along might not be a bad idea.

"Look, Travis, let's try and see how far we get."

She looked at Dan and said in a sharper tone, "Do not get in my way."

"Yes, ma'am," Dan said, backing up with his hands raised in mock surrender.

Surprised to find the front doors unlocked, the three humans entered the lobby. Tory tried to open one of the lobby doors, but it wouldn't budge. At Travis's signal, she began banging on the door as Travis and Dan stepped to the side so they could not be seen through the windows. Travis pulled a small blackjack from his pocket. Tory's fist hammered on the door again. A few moments later, Howard opened the door a few inches.

"What is it?" he asked. "The facility is closed."

"I know! I am so sorry," Tory spoke fast, her hands flying around as she talked. "But I left my gym bag in the locker room."

"Where is your wristband?" he asked suspiciously.

"The receptionist made me give it back when I left."

"Which locker?"

"I don't remember the number; I only know where it is."

Howard was becoming anxious. He hadn't found Suzanne's shoes in the spa lockers and was running out of time. He needed to get back before Dr. Grant alerted the building that Carrie wasn't in the apartment. Howard knew that somehow, despite his best intentions, this delay was going to be all his fault.

He looked at Tory and knew he should not let her inside the facility. However, since he wanted to search the gym lockers again for Suzanne's shoes, and knowing his brothers would resent being disturbed—resent it a lot—Howard decided against calling anyone to help him. Taking a deep breath and believing he was killing two birds with one stone, Howard let Tory walk through the door. As soon as Howard turned to follow her, Travis caught the door and hit him on the back of the head. Howard dropped to the floor.

"Which way?" Travis asked. "We don't have a lot of time."

"Here, let me help you with that," Dan said. Plucking the weapon from Travis's hand, he hit Howard just above his temple. "Now we don't have to hurry so much."

Tory and Travis looked at him.

"What?" Dan asked innocently.

Travis held out his hand. Dan shrugged and returned the blackjack to him as they walked toward the elevator.

When they turned the corner, Travis paused at the sight of the twin glass stairways coiling around the elevator like transparent ribbons. The staircases were different from the ones illustrated on the plans he'd examined so carefully, and he wondered what else had been altered.

Without the slightest hesitation, Tory brushed past him. Following her, he turned the lights on and off in every exercise room. *Yes,* he thought, *every room on the fitness side has a mirrored wall that faces the left side of the building.* He wasn't sure how he would get into the space behind the mirrors, but if there was a way, he was going to find it.

When they arrived at Grant's office, Dan was poised to break down the door, but Tory turned the knob.

"Why would they lock the offices? With the lobby doors locked, they aren't expecting any visitors."

Dan shivered as he entered the room. "Carrie works here?" he asked Tory.

"You didn't know that?"

"No."

"Yes, this is her desk. Usually, there is a laptop on it, but this is where she sits."

Almost at the same time, Dan and Travis said, "What is that awful smell?"

"What awful smell?"

"The smell in the room, like something sickeningly sweet just died."

Tory looked at them as if they had lost their minds. "Why, that's the honey-scented candles; it's wonderful. You mean you don't like it?"

Dan answered her question by lighting a cigarette and waving it around.

Travis pointed to the wall. "Is that the refrigerator?"

"Yes," she said, thinking, *Damn, I wanted to get there first.* Then she remembered Carrie's desk. "I'll check her desk."

Dan interrupted their search. "I thought we were looking for Carrie. She's not here, so let's go find her."

"Uh, do you want to explain this, Travis, while I search the desk?"

Travis looked at Dan. "Did Carrie have a jar of honey that she ate when she took classes here?"

"Yes, disgusting stuff. Sticky and, yeah," he said, looking at Tory, "you're right. This office does smell like the crap in that jar."

"Well, we are looking for more of that because it may contain addictive ingredients."

"Okay, since I know what it looks like, I'll check the fridge. You look somewhere else."

"We are going to need more light in here. Tory, you're closest. Can you turn up the light?" Travis asked, pointing to the rheostat.

When the lights came up in the front room, Grant's office stayed dark.

"Whoa!" said Travis. "Look at this."

Dan and Tory walked behind the partition and looked through the dark window. Tory walked back to Carrie's desk.

"This is a mirror," she said.

"Yeah," said Travis, "a two–way mirror." He whistled low. "He watched every move she made, everything she typed, and heard every word she said."

"But why?" Tory wondered out loud.

Travis began trying to hack into Grant's computer, but the screen remained dark. As Dan turned around to open the refrigerator, he saw a door handle on the paneling.

"What's this?" he asked, opening the door to the examination room. Turning on the light, the three of them looked in.

"This is the most beautiful examination room I've ever seen," Tory said.

Dan and Travis looked at her, dumbfounded.

"He is a doctor, you know; he's allowed to have an examination room."

Travis opened the cabinets, read labels, and examined the medical equipment. "Is he an obstetrician?" he asked Tory.

"I ... I don't know."

"Well, this might help explain the babies because this is an obstetrician's office."

Dan asked, "Could it be an abortionist's office?"

"Yes, same equipment, different objectives." He looked up at Dan. "Why?"

"I don't know how it's connected, but I came here when she had the miscarriage—"

Tory stopped him. "Wait a minute," she said, "Carrie had her miscarriage here?"

"This is where the ambulance brought her. When I got here, she and the doctor said she'd had a miscarriage."

Tory looked at Travis. "You are right. There is more going on here than we ever suspected." Momentarily forgetting the honey, she said, "Let's look for files."

Searching Carrie's credenza, Tory found only new client forms and several honey–scented candles.

Dan searched the examination room but found only medical supplies. Travis, rifling through Grant's desk, stumbled upon the only file Grant had not yet sent to the colony's documentary archives and, inside, a copy of his written report.

Human Experiment of Actualizing Relationships Through Bonding and Encouraging Acceptance Through Submission – Synopsis

Subject: Caroline A. Taylor

Goal: Full maternal acceptance of colony offspring.

Methodology: Slow alienation from family, friends, and previous employment; indoctrination of new cultural norms; consistent psychological and emotional manipulation of subject by controller.

Outcome: Subject acquiesced willingly and compliantly to nurse own and the colony's motherless offspring for the full ten–month development phase in colony habitat provided for observation and recording with the objective of cultivating and indoctrinating mothers of future generations.

Achievement Level: Total Success.

"Dan," said Travis, "according to this file, Carrie didn't have a miscarriage; she had a baby—" He gasped, "Oh, my God, I can't believe what I'm seeing."

All of them stared at the collection of drawings in the file. The first was a sketch of a cluster of eight small pulsating white ovals. They could not understand the words written beneath the pictures, but they didn't have to. The rest of the drawings were a self–explanatory pictorial record of the infants as they emerged from the embryonic sacs with antennae and faces without noses or ears. When he saw the last picture, Dan turned and ran into the examination room to retch into the sink. Travis and Tory couldn't move as they gaped at the drawing of Carrie, luminous and smiling softly like a Renaissance Madonna, cradling a small baby with antennae as it nursed at her breast.

Tory fell into Grant's chair and bowed her head over her folded arms. All her desire for anything in this office had disappeared. She wished she had never come, wished she had never met Carrie, wished Dan had died before he'd called their office. She did not want to believe this level of betrayal existed in the world. She was sickened at the thought that handsome, urbane Dr. Grant was, in reality, a brutal and cruel creature who abused Carrie's gentle nature so atrociously while pretending to sincerely care for her. Everything about GatesWay was a monstrous lie. Lingering beneath her feelings of the nearly unbearable horror of witnessing it was a layer of guilt for having abandoned Carrie to live it.

Travis also wished he had never come but for a much different reason. "You know if they find us, we will never leave here alive."

"I would be more worried about them than us," said Dan, bristling. "Just let one of them come in here, and I will rip him to pieces."

Travis looked at Dan, evaluating his threat. He was thin and broad-shouldered, but you could tell he'd had a desk job for most of his adult life. Travis was in better shape but not as tall. He shook his head.

"There won't be just one—it will be all of them. And they will have only one thought: to destroy us. These are aliens. We don't even know if they have to come in here to kill us, but if they do, it will only be a matter of minutes before we are overrun, overpowered, and dead."

Travis thought for a moment. "Dan, does anyone know you're here?"

"No."

"And no one knows we're here either."

"But our cars ...."

Travis looked at Tory. "Didn't you tell me there's an underground parking garage?"

"So, our cars may not even be in the parking lot anymore?" asked Dan.

Tory looked at them, her calm confidence gone. "Oh, yes, I guess it's possible they've been moved. ... I don't know, don't ask me any more questions. I thought they were human. All of us thought they were human. You saw the guy downstairs. Did he look like an alien to you?"

"We only see what they want us to see," said Travis. He looked at Dan. "We didn't pass any windows, and the way these corridors and stairways are arranged, there's only one way in and one way out. We can only stay here, hope they don't search the offices, and try to leave tomorrow as soon as the sun comes up."

"We should at least kill the lights."

Travis glanced around the room. Seeing no mirrors on the left wall, he believed they were safe from detection. "No, according to this file, they see better in the dark. We need the lights on—all of them—as bright as possible. It is our only defense."

After turning up the rheostat and clicking on the little task lamp, Dan snapped his fingers.

"The phones," he said.

Dan grabbed his mobile phone from his holster, pressed the buttons, and held it to his ear. Nothing. Travis picked up the receiver on the desk phone, looked at them, and shook his head.

There would be no rescue.

In his mind, Travis saw the members of the colony beginning at the elevator and thoroughly searching one room after another, moving in formation until they made their way here. He knew they would be armed. Standing behind Tory, he placed one hand on her shoulder as he read the details of Grant's psychological experiment and waited to die.

Dan slumped to the floor, put his head in his hands, and tried to erase the happiness on Carrie's face from his mind.

Escape

Securely closing the service entrance door, I turned toward the catwalks and froze against the wall. Lights were going on and off in the exercise rooms as though someone was searching for something—or someone. I knew Lyostians didn't need lights, but there was an exit on each floor to the catwalks. If they didn't expect to see me, I wouldn't help them by moving. I was suddenly grateful to Grant for darkening my hair. He had been right; the shimmering silver strands would have caught and reflected even the faintest light. Hugging the wall, I waited as soundlessly as possible and watched the rising trail of flashing lights.

To find Gregory's office, I'd left the rheostat turned to the weakest setting possible so the panel opening would be a shadowy beacon in the tall vertical darkness. Edging my way slowly upwards, a long horizontal shape of bright light suddenly appeared on the same level.

It was Grant's office. My heart nearly stopped as I tried to melt into the wall.

When I didn't see anyone or any new lights for several minutes, I began breathing again. Step by step, I climbed each set of stairs toward the platform outside the brightly lit window, pausing at each landing to listen but only hearing the beating of my heart. Finally, I stood on the platform. The colors of my dreaming time mural were barely visible through the small holes in the woven wicker cabinet doors.

Was Grant in his office? Had he gone back to the apartment and, not finding me or the babies, started searching for me? It was possible. But he would never have turned on the lights. Afraid someone would hear him if he thought to me, it could be a signal, but what? My mind ranged over several alternatives that were not nearly so optimistic. Remembering my recent experience with Howard, I did not want to stumble unawares into another confrontation. I was going to be careful this time. Very careful.

Easing into Gregory's empty office, I turned off the light and listened at the connecting wall. Instead of the Lyostians' cadenced speech, I heard American accents. One of them sounded a lot like Dan, and I could swear I smelled cigarette smoke. Regardless of who they were, they were human and stood between me and the only way I had back to Grant and our children. The sheath of Grant's dagger pressed against the small of my back. My family needed me, and I was willing to kill anyone who tried to keep me from them. Moving the dagger to my side, I soundlessly slid the panel into the wall and crept through the narrow opening.

Stepping into the darkest corner of Grant's office, I stared incredulously at the scene before me. Standing at Grant's desk and flipping through one of his files was a man I didn't know. Tory was sitting in Grant's chair with her head on his desk, and Dan sat on the floor next to the refrigerator.

Reaching behind me, I turned the light off in the examination room and closed the door.

They all turned and stared at me.

I looked at them without fear. They were trespassers here, and I knew I could kill them all just by tilting my head. I took a deep breath. "Tory, Dan, why are you here? And who is this? Why is he going through Grant's files?"

"Carrie, is that you?" Tory asked.

I'd forgotten she had never seen me as a brunette. "Yes, it's me. Who were you expecting? Father Time?" No one laughed at my joke. Still looking at Tory, I pointed to the man holding Grant's file.

"Who?"

"Carrie, this is my business partner, Travis Lau, and we are here investigating a missing person."

"What missing person?"

"You."

"Who said I was missing?"

Dan's surprise at seeing me quickly turned to anger as he stood up.

"I did. You never came home! And as far as I am concerned, if you aren't home, you're missing."

"You just saw me this afternoon. You know I'm not missing! What is this all about?" I looked at Tory. "Tory, I thought you were my friend. Who are you, and why are you here?"

"I am an investigator Dan hired in October to determine your whereabouts. When he told me how he'd treated you, I thought you were well out of it and closed the case."

I turned back to Dan, "You called investigators to find me after you left me lying in a hospital bed without a penny to my name? Just where did you think I was going?"

"I thought that, eventually, you would come home. First, your birthday came and went, then Thanksgiving, but when you didn't come home for Christmas, with Brendan there and everything, I thought, well, that you might be dead. It was the only reason I could think of that would keep you from coming home to see him."

"Other than the fact that you told me it wasn't my home anymore."

He ignored me. "And then you acted so weird this afternoon, with the baby and all; I just wanted to find out what was going on. Brendan misses you. I couldn't let him go back to college without seeing you. So, I came here to hijack you."

"I see." I turned toward Travis. "And you are here because …?"

"I am investigating your disappearance."

"I have not disappeared. I am, and have always been, here of my own free will. Why hasn't that gotten through to any of you?"

"Oh, Carrie," Tory said, "we know better than that now. It's okay. You don't have to pretend anymore."

The look of genuine pity in her eyes unnerved me.

"What? What are you talking about?"

"She's talking about this file, Mrs. Taylor," Travis said, holding out the file to me. "Have you seen this?" he asked.

I shook my head. It had never occurred to me to look through Grant's desk.

"You should know that everything you've ever said was recorded and analyzed. Every wish, every opinion, every memory you've shared with anyone here has been examined and cataloged."

I looked down at the pages of transcripts, graphs, and progress arcs. I saw notes written in Grant's angular handwriting in the margins of my application form, adding details to the questions I had not answered fully.

"This entire dossier is built around methods tested by Dr. Grant Gates to isolate you, alienate you from your family and friends, and to … well, bind you to him with the goal of total obedience. I don't want to scare you, but no matter how he appears to you, Mrs. Taylor, he is not human."

"He's a doctor."

"No, these so-called men posing as doctors are actually aliens. I don't know where they are from or how long they've been here, but this file is very specific about *why* they are here."

"Aliens? Why do you think that?"

He thrust Grant's file in my direction. "Everything is right here."

I looked at the file speechlessly.

Mistaking my silence for ignorance, he continued, "Are you aware you were the object of an experiment to determine the prototype of the women they need to cultivate for their survival? Discovering successful techniques to destroy your natural instinct for self-preservation through neoculturation and brainwashing was his plan all along. Don't you see it? Once you became addicted to the honey, you were hooked to this place like everyone else, but he wasn't satisfied with that. According to this file, sometime in July, he began an incremental program of manipulation to dominate you emotionally. He hired you specifically to design ways to control you, and he couldn't test those controls until he had you here every day. One of his degrees is in psychology, so he knew every button to push, and the ones he didn't know, he analyzed your reactions to certain stimuli until he discovered what they were."

Pointing to the partition, he asked, "Oh, by the way, did you know this is a two-way mirror? He watched every move you made."

I hadn't noticed until then that I could see my desk through the beautiful bamboo filigree. I remembered the morning I came in after he had made the changes to the room.

Even then, I thought. *He loved me even then.* I smiled at the memory.

Dan, who had been quietly seething during Travis's explanation, turned and began ranting at me.

"But you totally 'drank the Kool-Aid,' didn't you? I've looked at some of these papers myself, Carrie. Don't kid yourself that he cares about you. He says over and over that you were a means to an end, a professional challenge, and a burden. I mean, don't you understand? To him, you were just a freakin' human lab rat!"

Looking over Travis' shoulder, he quoted, "Through these methods, the subject became compliant, willing, (air quotes) *enthusiastic*. Really, Carrie?" he paused, "Enthusiastic?"

I dropped my eyes.

He continued reading accusingly. "Loves the babies." He looked at me in disgust. "Have you seen these drawings? These are not 'babies,' they're maggots."

There was nothing I could say.

His voice reverberated in the soundproofed room. "Why did you do this? Why? I gave you everything!" Grabbing the file from Travis, he threw it to the floor. All the notes with Grant's beautiful handwriting flew around, settling in the corners of the room.

I couldn't move. My mind would not accept that our relationship was premeditated. That everything I thought we were to each other was deliberately planned, plotted, and analyzed. Grant's voice echoed in my mind, *"You are so easy, Carolina."* I had believed everything he told me, forgetting that there is always "the reason ... and the *real* reason." I wanted him to love me so much that I never questioned his motives.

"I'm not human," he'd said, *"but I'm not a monster either."*

He'd lied about that, too.

Remembering I had promised Grant to forgive him for anything he said or did that hurt me, I looked up at Dan.

"Yes, and when I needed you, you took it all back."

"Look, for Brendan's sake, and because I know a little bit of what it's like to struggle with an addiction, I'll take you home, Carrie. We'll work something out."

"How are we going to 'work something out,' Dan? You've just accused me of, of what? Cavorting with aliens? How do we get past that?" I turned toward Travis and, hoping to plant a seed of doubt, said, "And you! You've never even met him. All you've seen is one file and some sketches. For all you know, Dr. Grant is a writer. But I do know one thing is certain; if anything in that file is true, and they find out who you are, you are not only dead, but everyone who knows you is dead, too."

Taking a deep breath, I thought of the four boys who loved me, the man who trusted me, and looked at the man in front of me who would never love me, never trust me, and, despite whatever promises he made tonight, would never forgive me—and he would never let Brendan forgive me. It would always be there, a failing that Dan could point to whenever he wished for the rest of my life. There was no decision to make. The thought of leaving with him now was even more unbearable than it was this afternoon. I would not abandon Grant or our sons. Who or what Grant was and the real reasons he cared for me were all irrelevant. We were one.

I was suddenly aware that time was passing too quickly—they had to leave the building. If Grant thought I had already left, he might decide to implode the building before midnight, and then Austin and his brothers could die. I swallowed my disdain for Dan's offer.

"Thank you, Dan, it would be nice to go home. I still have a few rooms to clear before I can leave, but you all must go now. I'll get a cab and meet you back at the house."

"We can't leave, Mrs. Taylor," Travis said. "We knocked one of them unconscious so we could get in, and I think they might be searching for us."

"What? You broke in? How could you have made this any worse?" I turned to Tory. "Who was it?"

"I don't know. One of the interns," she said. "Carrie, please come with us. You can't possibly stay here; we *can* help you."

"AND," Dan roared, "I'm not leaving you here with *them* one minute longer."

Being unconscious would explain why Howard had not yet returned. Believing I had a little more time, I said, "All right, then, I'll come with you. I know another way out."

I turned off the office lights, led them through the panel doors to the catwalks, and once again started the downward trek to the service entrance.

In The Tunnels

31 December: 11:15 p.m.

The Lyostians had spent hours discussing the events of the day. Each moment, from the time Gabriel and Garrett entered the apartment at noon to the abrupt departure of the entire colony from the apartment following Carrie's alleged attempt on Grayson's life, had been carefully examined.

"So, we are all agreed," Grayson said, "Grant will relocate to Vancouver with Carrie to monitor her and initiate a pharmaceutical regimen that will keep her calm yet will allow her to be actively engaged in the boys' welfare. Of course, as the health of our brothers is paramount, drug levels will be kept low so as not to affect their development. Restraints will be installed in the habitat for use as necessary."

Gabriel groaned internally. The vision of Carrie strapped down and forced to feed her sons was a nightmare to him. This would never have happened if Grayson had initially arranged for Grant to go to Vancouver. Despite Grant's nonchalance, Gabriel knew he cared for her—how could he not? After seeing how much she loved their brothers and how tender she was with them, it was impossible not to adore her. He looked at Gregory. They wouldn't still be sitting here if Gregory had not betrayed their plans in such a deliberately provoking way. Thinking of his beautiful flowers, crushed and scattered across the floor, Gabriel got *angry*.

"Any last comments?"

"Yes."

"Gabriel, you've been very quiet this evening. I thought we were boring you."

"Not bored, Grayson. Thinking."

"About?"

"Many things. First, Carrie has been a gift to half our colony's offspring, but she has been treated with suspicion and disrespect and denied her status as a sister and as our mother. We have allowed derogatory remarks and jokes to be made at her expense. We have been poor sons."

Gregory snorted.

Gabriel stood up. "Gregory, I am not Grant, nor do I bear the burden of his reputation, but if you think I will not rip out your throat if you so much as blink an eyelid before I'm finished speaking, you are wrong."

Everyone stared at Gabriel. Usually the quietest brother and the most devout, idle threats were not part of his nature. Gregory did not doubt that Gabriel meant exactly what he said and looked to Gordon for support. Gordon shook his head slightly and looked down.

"This brings me to item number two. I know human psychology is an interest of his, but Grant managed to succeed where each of us failed. He brought a mother into our colony and kept her here. More than that, he made her want to stay here. And, despite everything she has gone through, she is still here taking care of our children, and she isn't doing it for us; she is doing it for him. I don't know if she loves him or just loves the children, but he established a connection that we were unable to achieve. His outstanding report will assist in retaining mothers for future generations, something for which we have afforded him very little gratitude or respect."

He looked at Gregory. "Then there is item number three. Gregory, what were you thinking when you told Carrie that Grant wasn't going to Vancouver? Did you deliberately stage that scene to betray Grant, or were *you* just bored? Isn't Antony yours? Doesn't his well-being mean anything to you? Where is your loyalty?"

Everyone sitting at the table watched Gregory's eyes reluctantly move to Grayson's face.

"Really, Grayson? Et tu?"

Grayson became immediately defensive. "I wanted to separate them. She is too dependent on him. He isn't well and is growing weaker every day. I can feel it. Who is going to control her if ... when he dies? Especially if, as you say, he is her connection to the children. I wanted her to distrust him, dismiss him, and then, hopefully, the children would be enough to control her."

"But you had already separated them. He was going to Europe."

"Yes, but not emotionally separated. I thought she might hurt herself or the children if she got desperate because he wasn't in Vancouver. And it worked, right up to the point—"

"The point where she wanted to kill you?"

"Well, yes."

"You know what I find most interesting about that, Grayson? She had the knife. She didn't try to kill Grant or the baby she was holding ...."

The mental image of his infant brother being killed caused Garrett to gasp and clutch the table.

"Or herself. Only you. Why do you suppose that is?"

"She was irrational ... and upset by what Gregory said."

"Yes. Irrational and upset by what *you* told Gregory to say."

"Yes. He just took it a little further than originally agreed."

"So, basically, we are discussing how to discipline two valuable members, *very* valuable members, of this colony because you instigated an incident for which you were justly held accountable."

"Yes, but with a knife, Gabriel."

At that moment, Carolina's knife landed deep in the center of the table. No one noticed Gabriel remove it from his pocket or saw the blur of rotating steel that followed.

"That knife, Grayson?"

"Um, yes."

"Look at it. It's a small paring knife. The only reason it is buried in the table is that I am very strong and fast and, well, accuracy is one of my interests. But thrown by a woman, sitting down, it would not have cut a thread on your coat. And, as I recall, Grant was monitoring her thoughts and diverted the knife before it touched you. There was no threat on your life, Grayson, just a very human response to being bullied, which you, yourself, provoked."

"Then what do you propose, Gabriel? I'm sure you haven't been doing all this 'thinking' without some solution."

"I propose we recall the interns. I propose we go up there tomorrow morning and ask them what they would like to do. At this point, depending on how well he handled the situation this evening, she may be willing to go to Vancouver without him or not, but I think, given what you said about Grant's health, we should give her every reason to trust us—if it isn't too late. How many like her do we have?"

"But," Grayson said, looking at the knife.

"Grayson, that proves she takes her commitment to Grant very seriously and, through that, her commitment to our smallest brothers. You admitted to undermining her marriage, and regardless of Grant's feelings, that relationship is very real to her. Irrespective of your reasons, it was handled badly, but despite whatever disillusionment she felt, something or someone kept her here today when she could have so easily left. We should rejoice that she wants to be a part of our colony instead of seeking to, um, sever her relationship with the person she trusts the most."

At the word "sever," Gregory started to laugh, but Gordon kicked him under the table.

"Grayson, you were wrong. Gregory, you are despicable and weak."

He addressed his remaining brothers.

"Deliberate actions have been taken against members of the colony to the detriment of the colony's survival. I request sanctions against Grayson and Gregory Gates for their conspiracy to disrupt the harmony and continued survival of this colony."

Gordon and Garrett looked at each other anxiously. It was unusual in a colony for two members to have so much sway over the lives of their brothers. The minority rarely rules in such societies, and fear of retaliation can be mind-numbing. After a few moments' consultation, they decided Grayson had been, as Gabriel noted, justly held accountable for his part in the day's events and waived sanctions against him. This decision allowed Gordon to vote against sanctioning Gregory, which was overruled by a majority of two to one.

The other two proposals on the table—withdrawing the interns and allowing Grant and Carrie to choose if they wished to live together or apart—were approved. Grayson tilted his head and recalled all the interns to the tunnels so they could sleep.

After the meeting was adjourned, everyone looked at Gregory.

"Sure, sure, the serai. Well, you know, sleeping with those bones isn't as scary as you might think. Besides, I *was* getting a little bored with Gabriel's Grant and Carrie love fest anyway."

As they left the conference room, Carolina's knife still pierced the center of the table, its small blade invisible in the darkness.

Closing Time

Re–entering the dressing room, Grant secured the panel door and immediately crushed the sliding mechanism with a hammer. The apartment was too quiet. Surprised he could not hear Austin, he walked into the nursery and saw the empty crib. He had missed her then, but perhaps she took the babies first, then Suzanne. Their children would have been her first priority. That way, if she couldn't get back here, as long as she disposed of his access card, she could take the main elevator to the garage undetected.

He tested the bolts on the front door. He would not make it easy for them. Turning back into the apartment, he heard Grayson recall all the interns to the tunnels.

Ah, he thought, *we've been given a reprieve.*

Remembering the way Grayson lunged at Carolina that afternoon, he shook his head. *Too late, Grayson. Too late.*

Grant scanned the facility and found her. With time growing short, he couldn't believe she was helping them escape. *Humans were so predictable,* he sighed. Listening more closely, he realized that she believed she was helping *him* by getting them out of the building. Her kindness and care for him made his Carolina very predictable, too. *His Carolina.* Every part of him ached for her. *Soon,* he thought, *she will be back soon.*

Persephone's Children

Unlocking a cabinet in the children's examination room, he removed her laptop and, careful not to disconnect any of the wires or cables, opened it.

Yes. The camera angle was perfect. As patiently as his hatred would allow, Grant watched the screen and waited.

Escape – Part II

"This is it," said Travis.

"Is what?" asked Dan.

"What I was looking for, the extra space, and look," he said, pointing to the large rectangles of glass divided by a grid of steel girders, "The ant farm."

Following his gaze, I understood what he meant, but he was wrong. It was exactly the opposite of an ant farm. I tugged on his jacket. "We can't stop," I said. "Follow me."

As we descended the fourth level, the shaded hall lights brightened the exercise rooms one after another as the doors were opened and then closed. I pressed Tory against the wall.

"Damn, they're looking for you already. We need to hurry."

I urged them along, but it wasn't easy. The catwalk section of the building was unlit, and the humans could barely distinguish the black steel of the ladders from the platforms.

Following closely behind me, Travis asked, "How often have you used these stairs?"

"Twice."

"But it's so dark in here; how do you know where you are going?"

"I can see pretty well in the dark now."

"You know, Carrie, when we get out of here, I can help you rediscover your identity. Working together, we will decompress your mind, letting it expand slowly to include your family, your friends, and the life you had before GatesWay."

"The life I had before," I mused over those words for a moment. "I'm sure you mean well, Mr. Lau, but I didn't have a life before. Thank you, anyway."

"You don't understand. That's what you've been programmed to think. I can help you." He reached out his hand, but she had already gone ahead, and his words were lost in the shadows.

In The Tunnels – Part II

31 December: 11:50 p.m.

Despite his bravado, Gregory did not like sleeping in the serai. No one did. Sitting in the tunnel between it and the dormitory, he listened to his brothers' thoughts and waited for the jumble of dreaming to begin that would signal his chance to sneak into his own bed. He knew Gordon, the only brother who might hear him, wouldn't say anything.

His patience was beginning to pay off when Howard stumbled toward him.

"What happened to you?"

"Three people, two men and one woman, forced their way into the building this evening as I was closing up. I only saw the woman. I let her in because she said she left her gym bag in a locker, and then someone hit me on the back of my head. When I came to, I followed her scent and detected two male humans with her. I was conducting a section–by–section search for them when I heard the summons for everyone to return to the tunnels."

"What were you doing in the lobby? You were supposed to be watching Suzanne."

"Yes, I know, but I had to find her shoes."

"Her shoes were in the bag under the table."

"But Carrie looked and said they weren't there."

"What was Carrie doing in my office?"

Howard was troubled. He knew he shouldn't betray his mother but couldn't think clearly enough to lie.

"Apparently, Dr. Grant overheard our plans and told her. She said she refused to feed the babies unless he let her come up and say goodbye to Suzanne. She came through the adjoining panel while I was there, you know, bringing Suzanne her dinner and the sleeping tea. Carrie said she would stay while I went to find Suzanne's shoes. So, I left them alone."

Gregory's mind was a blur of possible scenarios. "Did you recognize any of the intruders?"

"Two. The woman was a former client of Grant's who met with him this morning, and one of the men was Carrie's human husband."

"You're sure?"

"Yes. It's impossible to mistake his scent."

Instinctively, Gregory knew that Suzanne was gone, that Grant and Carrie had somehow managed her escape, and that the people who broke in were mixed up in it as well. He smiled. *This was almost too easy.* He wanted to get everyone up and rush to their apartment, but that wouldn't be dramatic enough. He needed to set the stage—and make sure he was right—before calling in his audience.

Howard was confused as the smile grew wider on Gregory's face. "Shouldn't we get help and find them?"

"No, but you and I are going to pay Dr. and Mrs. Grant Gates, *and* Ms. Suzanne, a little midnight visit. Wait for me."

Like the action hero he had always imagined himself to be, Gregory ran into the conference room. With a sense of vigilante justice, he twisted the knife from the table and slipped it into his pocket.

"Let's go," he said to Howard.

The rumble and falling debris caught them off guard, and, as Gregory had learned from the films he loved, timing is everything.

Gregory had just enough time to wonder if he had not retrieved Carrie's knife to exact his revenge, whether he and Howard would have reached the catwalks before the explosion collapsed the tunnels, crushing them both.

Howard had no time at all.

Alone

At the stroke of midnight, the charges detonated, and the building rocked.

GRANT? The voices of his brothers rang together in his mind.

Yes.

You did this?

Yes.

WHY?

You may not have her.

Listening for a response, he heard nothing. For a moment, Grant thought he was deaf. As once before in the Sidereal chamber, the voices of the collective consciousness that had been with him all his life were silenced. This time, he knew there would not be a reprieve.

He was banished.

Aware he had betrayed nearly everything for which he had been created, and knowing he would soon be kneeling at her feet, Grant pressed his fists to his eyes and prayed, *Blessed Anya, mother of us all, please be merciful.*

Escape – Part III

Halfway down the scaffolding, the building shook and swayed. A deafening crack resonated in the darkness as the mirrored walls shattered from corner to corner. The perforated metal sheeting we were standing on slid sideways, and we had to press ourselves against the wall to avoid being struck by falling shards of glass. Then, to our horror, rivets began popping out of the wall one by one, detaching the railing. Swinging loosely, we held on as a torturously slow scraping sound echoed in the silence as the upper grating started to collapse. Moving from one foothold to the next, Tory slipped when the unbolted railing gave way, grabbing Travis's arm just before the stairs fell from beneath her.

"Happy New Year," I said softly.

Hand over hand, Travis pulled her up to the landing.

"What was that?" asked Tory, out of breath.

"The mall's New Year's fireworks display. Hang on, Tory, we're almost there."

I fueled their sense of panic as we hurried down the last few flights. Pushing and pulling them in the dark, I watched with satisfaction as they fell, tripping over each other as the catwalks slowly disintegrated. Trying not to slip on the glass, we finally arrived at the service exit. I looked out of the window and didn't see anyone in the parking lot.

Pushing past me, Dan pressed the bar lock and stumbled out of the door first, followed by Travis. Tory fell to her knees just inside the door and looked up at the broken stairs.

"Damn it, Travis!" she gasped. "We don't ... have the file. Thanks a lot, Dan! It's all ... over ... the floor in there."

"Don't worry about the file," I said smoothly. "I'll get it. I'm the only one who can get there and back in just a few minutes. You'll never find your way in the dark, and I'm sure they're still looking for you. If they are aliens, they probably won't hurt me, but they will kill you. I won't be able to stop them." *And I won't try, either.*

Tory stood up and limped over the threshold toward Travis. Dan turned around.

"What? Wait, Carrie! You aren't going back in there alone."

Moving faster than I expected, Dan grabbed my hand and pulled. I slipped over the threshold. The pneumatic door brace held for a moment, then began its slow arc toward the door frame.

Ten inches.

"No, Dan, no! Let go of me."

I pulled back in panic, but he only gripped my arm harder.

I looked back at the door. Eight inches.

A sense of calm came over me, and I stopped struggling. Instead of pulling away, I took a step toward him. Without my weight to balance his, inertia pushed him backward. Slipping on the ice and snow, he let go of my arm to break his fall.

Three inches.

I sprinted to the door and was able to stop it from closing with my fingers.

"Carrie!"

My only response was the sound of the door locking in place.

Fireworks

His muscles aching from running down the twisted and broken staircase, Travis walked slowly on the snowy asphalt toward Tory.

"At least our cars are still here," he said, helping Tory stand.

Dan did not take his eyes from the door as he pushed himself up from the ice. Ignoring the bang and crackle of the mall's millennium fireworks display, he began pacing rapidly back and forth in front of the entrance.

As kindly as he could, Travis said, "She's not coming out, Dan."

Trying to catch his breath, Dan replied, "Maybe she will. Maybe she just went back to get the file."

"You don't know anything about brainwashing techniques, do you?"

"Just what I've seen on TV."

"If you could have kept her from going back in, we might have had a chance. We would have isolated her and slowly brought her back to an awareness of her own identity, but she won't leave now, not voluntarily anyway."

Dan looked at Tory for her opinion.

"Sorry, Dan," she said.

"Don't you think there's some chance? Even a small one? If not tonight, then maybe tomorrow? I mean, after all you told her about how he used her? That she was a freakin' *lab experiment*?"

Travis shook his head. "You weren't watching her eyes; she already knew that. When you accused her of having 'drank the Kool-Aid,' you were only half right. She not only drank it, but I'm also pretty sure she helped make it, too. I don't know if he told her or if she figured it out, but she knew what he was doing and, apparently, cooperated. They aren't keeping her here against her will, Dan; she's keeping herself here. Twice today, she could have left with you, but she chose to stay. She doesn't see herself as your wife or Brendan's mother anymore. That doesn't mean she doesn't love you, but those feelings have been eclipsed. In the mental state she's in right now, she believes she belongs here."

"What about the police? Can't we call the cops?"

"To do what? It's not a crime, Dan, for a wife to choose to live somewhere else. However, breaking and entering an office building and assaulting an employee *are* crimes. Besides, all the evidence is still in there, and without it, we have no probable cause. We have no proof they are aliens or that they are breeding more aliens there. We have nothing but suspicion, conjecture, and a highly skeptical science fiction story. It's New Year's Eve; no one will believe us. Hell, I'm not sure I believe it, and I was there. Listen, today's Friday; no one will be back in their offices until Tuesday at the earliest. I'll contact some of my legal associates to see what it'll take to get a search warrant. Even if they aren't aliens, we may find enough evidence for a class action suit that will tie them up in court for years."

"How long for the search warrant?"

"At this time of the year, we should have it by the end of next week."

"And if it's true ..., if they are aliens?"

"Then they will be gone before we get back."

Still speaking calmly, Travis continued, "She's safe right now. They won't hurt her, Dan; she's one of them. But she's right about two things. If we don't get the hell out of here, they will kill us. And, if what we read is true—and if they ever find out we know—they will not only kill us, but they will also kill everyone we may have told, including Brendan. I'm sorry, Dan, but it's too dangerous to stay any longer."

Recalling the flashing eyes of the woman with the auburn hair, Dan realized she was as far removed from Carrie Taylor as if *she* were from another planet. He didn't want *her*, but wasn't his Carrie somewhere behind those eyes? Wasn't she worth waiting for?

"Thanks, Travis. I appreciate your help. I'll call you tomorrow about seeing Brendan. I'm not sure how to tell him his mom has been brainwashed by aliens."

"Then don't," Travis said as he helped Tory to their car. "He doesn't even have to know you were here tonight."

The reflection of the vivid colors of star shells and skyrockets danced across the snow-covered parking lot like a rainbow on fire. Momentarily defeated, Dan got into his car and turned the key.

Tory's last words to Travis, "She'll never come out of there alive," were lost in the roar of the explosion and carried away by the smoke.

In total silence, Grant gritted his teeth as he watched the humans leave the building. He saw Carolina leap inside and close the door.

She was coming back to him.

Staring at the screen and adjusting the trajectory arcs, his upper lip curled in utter contempt as he pressed the enter key. Smoke obscured the camera lens, and he felt, rather than heard, the explosions in the parking lot.

Not caring whether the humans lived or died—only that they, too, would be unable to follow her—he pulled the computer wires out of the wall. Within moments, he dismantled the laptop, removed the memory chips, and melted them over candle flame. After retrieving the hammer, he thoroughly flattened the rest of the computer and wrapped the pieces in the bloodied towel Carolina had left in the sink. Putting it all into the trash compacter, he pressed both buttons. The incinerator would take care of the rest.

After Midnight

I stood motionless under the flickering exit sign, listening and watching the broken glass above me for lights. There was no sound, no movement of bodies or shadows. Breathing a sigh of relief, I did not glance back through the window. Taken together, they were not worth one of my babies' lives or one hair on Grant's perfect head, but if I was found helping them, we would all die. Grayson would never believe it was just a coincidence that they were here. Not tonight.

Ignoring the reverberations from the celebration of cannons and rockets exploding outside, I made my way up the broken ladders as soundlessly and as quickly as possible. I knew Grant's brothers should be trapped in their underground rooms, but I couldn't be sure. I listened again for voices when I got to Gregory's office and, hearing nothing, moved the panel and slipped into the room. Unwilling to walk into another crowd, I tiptoed to the connecting door, listened again, and edged the door open. Grant's office was exactly as we'd left it.

It was important that no one believed that Grant's office was the intruders' objective. I quickly started putting everything away, saving the pieces of my file for last. I reviewed his notes, the printed report, and the drawings. It was all very clinical. Subject did this, subject did that, asked for ... reacted to stimuli ... vulnerability exploitation ... uses of affection as a means of domination ... behavior modification controls set in place ... subliminal techniques to leverage maternal relationship .... The level of detail was relentless. The report was a precise accounting of Grant's observations of my behavior and reactions to his "performance as a suitor" during my pregnancy and, after *Adam's* birth, how my behavior changed as additional offspring were introduced. He itemized my demands, housing and nutrition requirements, possible side effects of the V4 honey, and how I spent my free time (a very short list).

As I picked the papers from the floor, I found a sketch he'd drawn of me feeding Austin lying under the desk. It was beautiful. I put it in my pocket and slid the rest into the file. Taking it and all the papers in his desk into his examination room, I tossed them into the incinerator chute. I was sure Grant had entered the file's contents into the collective's archives, but now they would not become evidence in a police investigation.

Sitting in his chair, I looked through the mirrored partition into the nearly empty office. Grant's file had surprised me, but not the way Mr. Lau expected. I always knew Grant used the "experiment" as his reason for us to be together, but seeing our relationship described so clinically and the manner in which he objectified me was chilling. Perhaps he had always intended to seduce one of his prospective mothers as a personal challenge to increase the survival chances of the colony's offspring. That I was one of them was just a lucky accident for the collective. Vulnerable and susceptible to his affections, I was a likely target. Again, "*So easy, Carolina,*" echoed in my ears, and I could still see Tory and Travis's faces pitying my poor, brainwashed mind.

Their revelation didn't change anything. Brainwashed or not, nothing existed beyond this building that was more important than another five minutes alone with Grant. Walking toward the elevator, I saw an envelope in the corner that I'd missed. I picked it up from the floor to take to the incinerator chute—then stopped. On the outside, it read, *"For Caroline ... someday."*

Caroline?

I lifted the flap and removed about a dozen scraps of paper. I gazed at sketches of me wearing fantastical and beautiful clothes. My birthday dress was there, and my waterfall hair design, the dragonfly robe, my willow branch and orchid birthday kimono, the silver and gold butterfly caftan, and other designs I'd never seen. The women in the drawings were all me. I could not understand the words, but the dates were clear. The first was the twentieth of July. Feeling suddenly lightheaded, I sat back down.

That was almost a month before ... before Eric.

I could hardly breathe. *The rational reason and the real reason, Carolina.* He had loved me before he'd touched me, before Austin, and I was sure that even if I had not been pregnant, he would have found a way for us to be together.

I realized, with elation and terror, that my earlier suspicions were wrong. There would not have been anyone else in my place. I wasn't Grant's consolation prize or the easiest target. He had wanted me from the beginning. It was just a matter of time and patience. And I knew, because I'd wanted him, too, nothing would have changed. The honey, the pheromones, the physical and chemical attraction, everything would have happened exactly as it did.

I also knew Eric and Austin had saved Dan's life, maybe Brendan's, and possibly mine as well. *I am quite sure I would have killed you and died beside you before I would have let you go.* Yes, I knew who and what I had married. If, despite his love, he would have killed *me*—he would not have hesitated to kill Dan or Brendan or Eric or anyone else he perceived as a threat to that love—even his own brothers. I bowed my head and pressed my wedding pendant so hard the point of center diamond engraved itself on my chest.

In that one moment, all doubt fled from my heart and mind. The drawings in my hand blurred as I sensed a seismic shift in my soul as the last pin clicked into place. We *are* one. Irrevocably. Nothing could have altered our path, and it would still have all come down to today. When we make our final choices and live with them for the rest of our lives—however long, or short, those lives might be.

I stood to leave and hesitated. *Eventually someone would search the rooms looking for the intruders.*

His brothers were going to have to find something, or they would immediately suspect us, especially when they discovered Suzanne missing. One of Grant's fiercer smiles stole over my face as I went back into Gregory's office. Turning on his computer, I deleted all I could find regarding Suzanne in the GatesWay database. I located her file and threw it, her spa shoes, and my sketches into the incinerator. I took two random files and tossed the papers the way my file had been scattered in Grant's office. Taking the dagger from its sheath, I forced it into the access panel and broke the door open, leaving it ajar. I found Dan's cigarette and relit it. Dropping it on Gregory's carpet, I ground it out into the fibers. Exiting quickly through the connecting door, I closed it firmly and walked to the elevator. If there was anyone left alive to investigate, they would not be able to connect Grant to the break-in.

The elevator door opened. I pressed the down arrow. I knew I had been gone too long. Praying Grant would still be there, I sent gentle messages of love to him, asking him to wait for me—that I was coming home.

Stepping out of the elevator, I slowly drew the alcove curtain aside, but my shimmering bower was empty. A thin shadow outlined the nursery door, and I pushed it open. Sitting in his blue chair, head thrown back and eyes closed against the shaded candlelight, Grant waited in silence.

Farewell

She was taking too long. Grant knew exactly the amount of time it took to travel from the service entrance to his office and feared he might never see her again. He tried to scan the building for her thoughts, but his head began to ache, and he found he could not. To hold back the rising panic of dying alone, he walked through the apartment. Crashing dishes to the floor and upturning the chairs, he carefully set the scene he'd planned for his brothers' break-in. In addition to her bloodied handprints, he uncapped a vial of her blood and splattered the misty rainbow walls and scattered strands of hair taken from her hairbrush onto the carpet.

His jaw clenched against the pain and solitude, Grant ignored the disarray and saw it again as it was on their first night together. With every backward glance, a thousand memories returned of her laughter, her sweetness, her gentle touch; she had held their son here, read to him there, and loved them in every corner and curve of their underground sanctuary. Grateful, he bowed his head and, turning his back to the room, left the door slightly open. The boys' nursery and her bower would remain untouched because he could not bear to destroy them.

Hearing only the sound of his heartbeat, he opened a drawer under the bed and removed her dragonfly gown. Brushing the fabric gently with his fingertips, he brought it to his face and inhaled deeply. He folded it over the edge of the bassinet, and his hand lingered for a moment on the sash. The smile that the memories of her brought to his lips twisted into something ugly as lightning flashed behind his eyes. His hand became a claw and crushed the soft silk as he tried to breathe through the pulsating aches that followed. When they became manageable, he smoothed the wrinkles from the sash with curved fingers and walked slowly into the nursery.

Clutching the back of his chair for support, he sat down and eased his throbbing head against the cushion. His entire life had come down to a single desire: to keep breathing until she returned. There was one more thing he needed to give her before she left him.

His last gift.

He heard Carolina's thoughts before he heard the elevator. All for him. After everything she knew, and for every reason she had to hate him, all her thoughts were loving concern for him.

You will never have this, he transmitted to the brothers who believed he was writhing in agony because they had left him alone. Her love was his strength, and he sent them just enough of her mind so they would know that he was *not* alone.

The electric whisper of the elevator's closing door calmed him, and he tracked her soft footsteps through their darkened room, past the empty bassinet, the pristine bower, and into the nursery.

"My husband."

"Darling wife. Our sons?"

"All safe."

"Good."

"You?"

"Alone."

"I'm here."

"Thank you for coming back."

"You knew I would."

"I hoped, but I knew it would be difficult."

"Your brothers? The interns?"

"Trapped in the dormitories, I think. I cannot hear them anymore."

She rushed to the side of his chair. "Oh, Grant! I'm so sorry. I wish there'd been another way."

"As do I, but I left them little choice. It doesn't matter, love. It was a risk I was willing to take. I had to stop them before they could stop me. Or you. I'll finish the rest after you've gone."

"If the facility is destroyed, won't they be destroyed as well?"

"Yes."

"Can you do that?"

"For your escape? For our son and his brothers? For all their future generations? Of course. Survival, after all, is the foundation of our ... their ... our mandate."

He reached for my hand. He kissed the bandage on my palm and covered it with the syringe case he had shown me the week before.

"For the babies or for your brothers if they get out alive?"

"You choose," he said, "I cannot. Please do whatever is best for you, Carolina."

I nodded.

"But on whomever you wish to use them, whatever happens, save the last one for yourself. Do not let them catch you alive, Carolina, or all this would have been for nothing. They will make you hate me, and right now and forever, your love is the only thing I have left, the only thing I want to take with me."

"Do you want to take this?" I asked quietly, handing him the sketch of me holding Austin. All the questions I would not ask crowded behind my eyes.

"You promised."

"I know. When I saw your report referred to our son as Adam instead of Austin, I knew you were still protecting us, and I remembered I promised to forgive you ... for anything. I understand, Grant, how much you love me, love us. My darling, there is nothing to forgive."

"Thank you for that, Carolina. Because if you doubted me now, nothing I could say would ever convince you. Everything in the file is true, and everything in that file is a lie. I never told them why you reacted the way you did, why you came here to stay with me, why you loved Austin and accepted his brothers. They think they have a blueprint for subjugating the females of your species, but they don't because I omitted the most important information."

"That I loved you?"

"No, my dear wife, that we loved each other."

He brought my hands to his lips and kissed them. "Today. Tomorrow. Forever." Raising his eyes to my face, he whispered, "Remember?"

"Yes. Every day of my life."

My voice cracked with unshed tears as I knelt beside his chair. "Oh, please, Grant, don't make us leave you. Please find another way."

"Carolina, my own, there is no other way. I either stay here alone or leave with you. If I leave with you, they will spread out and find me, and when they find me, they will find you and our children. Consider how I would spend the last few weeks of my life. Ostracized from the collective consciousness, I would be powerless to prevent them from putting you in a glass box, watching you every moment of every day, analyzing everything you do, from how many times you comb your hair to the songs you sing while feeding our children. I would hear nothing but your silent pleas for help, and I would not be able to help you, Carolina. I would be forced to watch your brave attempts to adjust before you lost all sense of yourself, and it finally killed your mind. But before that happened, I would hear you learn to hate me, hate our son, hate *us*.

"Oh, my sweet love, you must leave me here. I don't fear the inevitability of death or even a silent life without you, but a living hell of relentless recrimination is something that terrifies me. Please, if you care for me at all," he said, looking into my eyes, "spare me that."

"Yes, Grant, I won't ask you again."

His hands slipped under my hair, and he pressed his lips to mine.

I closed my eyes as my fingers memorized the beauty of his face. *Thank you, Grant, my darling husband, for everything you are, for Austin, for loving me, and for giving me so much happiness. You are now, and until the end of time, the heart and soul of my life.*

Kissing her slowly, Grant sang the dearest words he knew in his most beautiful voice, *My wife.*

He knew he would never hold her again, and unwilling to let the moment pass, he fell into her mind.

You must remember this.

Tilting her head back, Grant implanted every memory of her since the moment she walked into his office: her first taste of honey, her face as she held his scarred hands, and all the times he touched her, watched her, and wanted her. Every cherished image, every tender thought, all his hopes for their son, every joy she had given him, the memories of their intimacy that had rocked them both, and every mental photograph he had taken of her and their children since the morning Austin was born. At the last, he added all the passion and love he felt for her. A kaleidoscope of fire flooded her mind, and honey dripped down her throat.

He pulled away from her lips.

"I will not allow those memories to be destroyed, Carolina."

Reeling from the images I had seen and unable to hold back my tears, I nodded.

"I understand, Grant, but how do I leave you? Oh, love, I don't … I don't know how to … to leave you."

He took my hands in his. Looking at me steadily, he shared the little strength he had left.

Tell me you love me, promise me you won't come back, and don't, he said, tapping the handle of the dagger, *let anyone stop you.*

I bowed my head over his hands and took a deep breath.

"I love you now, I'll love you forever. I will never come back here, and no one—human or Lyostian—will stop me from protecting our children."

He smiled slightly and nodded.

"But that isn't all. I must thank you, Grant, my heart, my husband, for saving my life and for giving me a life worth saving. I will never forget …" I looked up at him and lightly touched my throat, "anything."

He lifted me into his lap, and I kissed him for the last time. *I could die here with you, you know. Gladly.*

Yes, but I want you to live. Not only for our sons, but for yourself. I could not bear, Carolina, for your voice to be silenced.

His eyes moved longingly to my throat.

Do you want me to take that out before you leave?

"No, I'm not willing to let go of any part of you that I can keep. Maybe you will hear me somewhere, somehow."

As you wish. Thank you for being mine, Carolina.

I stood up and touched my forehead to his. *You will always be here.*

Yes. Take what you can of me with you and go. You can help our sons far more than you can help me.

Grant, I ….

I know, my sweet, soft wife. Struggling to speak, he whispered hoarsely, "I know."

Walking through the soft incandescence of the room I would never see again, I paused for a moment.

Grant?
Yes, Carolina.
Wait for me?
Say, please.
Please wait for me, Grant.
Yes, Carolina. Forever.

Those three words gave me the strength to step into the alcove alone. The curtain closed around me. Everything inside me screamed *No!* My fingers refused to press the arrows that would take me away from him. But I couldn't go back. I'd promised.

Grant's words echoed in my mind. "Take what you can of me and go." Knowing it would have been easier to thrust the dagger into my heart, I pressed the down button on the elevator.

I had to move toward the new life he had chosen for us. Wiping the tears from my face, I concentrated on putting one foot in front of the other and remembered a day—not so long ago—when I thought that raising Grant's son alone would be an adventure. Now, with four beautiful sons to love, I knew the adventure would never end.

Timaeus Tuzurias

Grant heard the elevator door close for the last time. *It was strange,* he thought, *how loud everything seemed when you only heard one sound at a time.*

He stood and pulled the door closed until there was just a thin line of light from her bower to illuminate the nursery. Before sitting down, he placed the sketch on her chair. His radiant wife, their perfect son, on the morning Austin was born, and they became a family.

As he looked at her picture and waited for her thoughts to fade completely from his mind, he knew two things. One, because he did not leave with her, he could spare the lives of his brothers, even if they no longer wanted him. They would dig out eventually, but not before she escaped. And two, if he died, his brothers would never hear her voice, never find her, and his beloved wife and sons would be safe.

Taking the sixth syringe from his pocket, he tested it and inserted the needle into his right arm. Slowly pressing the plunger down the barrel of the syringe, he allowed himself a congratulatory moment of success.

He'd accomplished everything he had set out to do that day; he'd kept both of his families alive.

Confident Carolina would keep her promise to love their children, Grant directed his thoughts to the child in the picture. *You must survive. Never let anything or anyone ever hurt your mother. Protect her as you protect your brothers. Remember, you are stronger than you know. Farewell, my son. I love you.*

The fierceness of the sudden wash of love he received from Austin made him clutch at his chest. It took the last of his strength to reflect it back. *Thank you, Austin, my own. Please share this with your brothers; I love you all.*

He reviewed his private scrapbook as poison gradually destroyed his heart. The final report she would never see revealed every calculated phrase, every flaw in her logic, every silken thread he cast upon Carrie Taylor to bind her to him, even to the point of surrendering control of her own mind. Her insights into what human women desire, which she unwittingly shared with him, gave the collective the key to the inevitable enslavement of her species. And, finally, the level of devotion it takes to win a woman's heart—and keep it. He'd documented every step of the slow seduction that brought her willingly to his observation habitat as his "wife," where she agreed to nurture her own offspring and half of the colony's orphans.

Gentle conquest of human females was vital to the survival not only of his species but of their adopted planet. He had archived his exceptionally successful report for the collective to draw upon as they needed mothers for future generations. When a teaching video was deemed imperative, he designed a tightly edited dream sequence, his finest work, for prospective mothers to experience during their pregnancy. It would be delivered on Wednesday to Vancouver. He smiled briefly. *The collective got what it wanted.*

As for his private journals, they were separate from the written file and were safe for a time; no one else need ever know the truth. Tonight, she understood everything. His son had always known, and that would be enough to keep him in their hearts.

"Oh, Carolina, my soft, sweet wife," he whispered to the image of the only dream he ever possessed. The joy on her face when she first held their son, and the look in Austin's blue-green eyes, knowing everything about him, accepting his choices, and *loving him*. The wonderful unexpectedness and personal validation he felt transcended his concern for the future of the collective. The unforgettable morning when, for the first time in ten earth years, he felt alive and *free*. Released forever from the unrelenting regret that it was his father's blood—and not his own—staining the sand next to the ravine where his mother died.

He never thanked Carolina for giving birth to more than just his son that golden morning. Never told her that they meant more to him than all the generations together and that losing them was worse than death; it was the endless echo of his voice calling their names. As he promised her, he had taken every precaution, neutralized every threat, and, dropping the syringe on the floor, done everything he could to protect them.

For the life he had taken from her, the pain and loss she had endured for his sake, for leaving her to face so much on her own, and, lastly, for the only promise he could not keep, Grant prayed, "Carolina, please ... forgive me."

A long shudder racked his body.

So, this is cold, he thought, and he accepted it as he accepted the crushing pain in his chest and the lightning flashes in his brain that he could not control.

He tried to smile at her picture. "So easy, Carolina," he whispered through clenched jaws, "you were so easy to love."

As blackness entered his mind, he sought the memories he'd saved for these last brief moments: his mother's face reflected next to his in the vanity mirror, and the sound of Carolina's voice, full of love and awe, her breath warm against his skin, sighing, "Timaeus ... Timaeus."

Her voice repeating his name resonated distantly in his ears, and Grant, struggling to open his eyes, stared at her face until it, too, faded into darkness.

Falling harmlessly from his curled fingers, the detonator for the second round of charges rolled next to the empty syringe beneath his blue chair.

Anya's Mercy

Poised at the outer edge of the oasis, he realized the labyrinth's path had not brought him to the dark oblivion he expected but returned him to the beginning. The sun shining through the palms above him did not hurt his eyes, and the cool breezes drifting over the lagoon brushed against the smooth skin of his hands. In the distance, two riders on a pale grey Arabian stallion leading another by the reins rode toward him. The tallest rider raised an arm in salute.

At the exact moment Grant's heart collapsed from the poison devouring it, a sudden feeling of recognition and joy filled Timaeus's chest, and he waved his arms.

Leaving his labyrinth of fire and pain to shimmer and dissolve in the desert air, Timaeus ran as a boy might—barefoot and unafraid—across the burning sand.

Requiem

It took nearly four days to reach the main corridor. Assigning the interns to clear out the secondary exits, Grant's remaining brothers, armed with axes and small amounts of C4, stormed the door to Carolina's apartment. Stunned by the wreckage in the front room and the odor of human blood, they moved cautiously toward the sliver of light shining beneath the nursery doorway. With his brothers close behind him, Gordon stepped forward and pushed open the door. Nothing they endured as they dug their way, inch by inch, through nearly forty feet of earth and rocks had prepared them for the sight of Grant sitting alone, his unseeing eyes staring at her chair where a sketch, propped up on two storybooks, and a toy bunny with its head quizzically tilted to one side, silently stared back.

Grayson picked up the syringe and detonator from the floor.

"Oh, Grant," he said, his voice heavy with guilt, "it didn't have to be like this."

Gabriel noticed a long shadow on the opposite wall and pushed against the panel. The bedroom door opened, and they all stared at Carolina's bower glowing softly in the darkness. None of them had ever seen anything like it—or imagined such a thing still existed—but they all knew instinctively what it was, what they had tried to take from him, and what he died to protect.

Persephone's Children

Grant's brothers lifted his body with a collective sigh. Singing Anya's lament, they placed him in the center of the bed and covered him with a dragonfly kimono they found folded over the edge of the bassinet. Each lost in his own thoughts, no one noticed Gabriel pick up the drawing and slide it into his pocket as they walked back through the nursery.

Grayson stood by the nursery door and surveyed the rooms that only a few days earlier had held their hope for the collective's retribution. Now, it was just another tomb.

"Report this to Vancouver while we reset the charges," he said to Garrett. "Ask them for permission to destroy the entire building today."

Garrett nodded absently. Something was just not right. Everything in the nursery was immaculate except for the large crib. He walked over to it and moved the rumpled blankets. He ran his hands along the edges and found four empty syringes tucked between the mattress and wall. With shaking hands, he wrapped them in a tissue and placed them carefully in his lab coat.

Although he had participated in Grant's requiem, Gordon, still bitter about Gregory's death, turned to Gabriel. "Where in the hell are they?"

Gabriel looked back at Grant's body and sighed.

"They are, dead or alive, wherever he wants them to be." Knowing he would never hold Monique's son in his arms again, Gabriel closed the bedroom door with a grieving heart.

The clanking sound of iron rods sliding into the steel door echoed throughout the apartment. Small pops, like firecrackers, shook the floor. Dust fell from the ceiling of the nursery, and the walls rocked while the brothers held on to each other to keep from falling.

The syringe and detonator fell from Grayson's hands as he shook himself loose from Garrett's grip and bolted for the front door. Gordon grabbed his jacket.

"You aren't going anywhere," he said.

The stench of burning electrical wires drifted into the room as smoke escaped around the edges of the doorway, darkly outlining the entrance Grant had tried so hard to conceal. When everything stopped shaking, they heard the metallic rasp of rods retracting into the wall and the soft click of a door lock no longer needed.

Gordon pushed Grayson toward Carolina's bower. "Open it," he said.

Looking for assistance from the other brothers in the room, Grayson watched as they lined up behind Gordon. Seeing no alternative and fully expecting to be instantly electrocuted, Grayson pushed the door inward and jumped back.

The ethereal tracery of Carolina's bower was destroyed. Strings of blackened lace draped the bed's iron skeleton like remnants from a nightmare. The metal rings supporting the nest that had been built with hope and care lay collapsed and bare. In the center of the once perfect oval, a silhouette of black ash was all that remained of Grant's brilliant mind and tortured heart.

Gordon brushed past Grayson. The room he walked into no longer resembled a love sonnet but a chamber in hell. The heat was nearly unbearable, and the adjacent rooms were open maws that led to more destruction. He did not enter them; he knew there was nothing left. Instead, he inspected the door mechanism, then examined the wall surrounding the charred and twisted metal scaffold of the bed. As he wiped his soot-covered hands on his slacks, the rest of the brothers approached the doorway.

Gordon looked at Garrett. "How did he know?"

"What do you mean?"

"This bed was deliberately connected to the incinerator. See? He set explosives to break through the firewall, turning this room into a vacuum furnace as soon as the door closed. Nothing, no one, would have survived." Tapping the blackened curtains, he stepped back as they disintegrated and fell away, exposing wavy blue bands on the steel layer of soundproofing that was still too hot to touch. Motioning Garret to help him, together they pushed the wreckage of the bed away from the wall.

"This relay system," Gordon said, pointing to the melted and fused switches, "was installed when the room was built. This was no accident."

Not wanting to find any other traps Grant may have devised, the brothers turned as one and stepped slowly toward the front room. Gabriel lingered in the nursery and was the last to leave. With a nearly overwhelming sense of loss, he gently closed the nursery door.

Gordon pivoted quickly. "No, don't!"

It was too late. The now familiar sound of sliding iron bars, muffled explosions, and the reek of smoke and melting electronics filled the room. When everything settled, the nursery door swung open on its own. They did not need to look to know that the nursery and examining room were now cinders and ruins.

Gordon broke the silence. "He wasn't taking any chances, but why destroy everything?" He turned to Grayson and demanded, "Who was he?"

"I ... I don't know. I was never told his birth name or," he swallowed, "his hierarchy."

The brothers stared at him. They had endured hardships and even a few life-threatening moments as they dug out of the collapsed tunnels, but nothing they had experienced then, or in their lives, filled them with the horror of Grayson's confession. The smell of fear permeated the room.

They were complicit—all of them—in the death of a Lyostian so important to the collective that it did not trust the details of his identity to the colony's leader. Even worse was the knowledge that their actions may have contributed to the deaths of a loving mother and four surviving infant brothers.

Gabriel was the first to sink to his knees, and one by one, they followed him in prayer. Their minds blurred with panic; only their voices, tinny and strained as they begged for forgiveness, betrayed their terror.

Lowering his hands from his eyes, Garrett looked past the nursery into the black caverns of the empty rooms.

He tilted his head.

Aftermath – Part 1

Timaeus Tuzurias was dead.

The news spread throughout the Lyostian governing hierarchy like wildfire. Although they rarely moved quickly—and then only after collecting all available data, deliberating every possible outcome, and discussing any and all issues until they all came to the same understanding and agreement—there was no hesitation in the elders' investigation into the death of the collective's last Fire Slayer.

Before Grayson had time to clean the soot from his hands, control of the colony had passed to the collective's demolition and sanitation experts, transports were arranged, and interrogation rooms were prepared.

Within four hours, the facility was wiped clean and evacuated.

Within eight hours, the facility lay in ruins. Shattered glass, twisted metal, and broken pieces of concrete and granite were all that remained of GatesWay Health Clinic and Spa.

Within twelve hours, the four surviving doctors, together with the five surviving interns, were in Vancouver facing the wrath of the elders of the collective. Their explanations and excuses quickly turned to screams and pleas for mercy that echoed throughout the tunnels and corridors of every colony across the globe, but their repentance did not help them.

PJ Braley

The brothers Grant sacrificed so much to save found little hope—and no forgiveness—as they stood naked and alone in the endless hell of the Sidereal Chamber.

Aftermath – Part 2

4 January: 6:00 p.m.

Watching the Channel 8 Evening News broadcast the grainy video of the accidentally imploded NAFTRAM building from his hospital bed, Dan called his son at home to tell him his mother had died, but no one answered the telephone. He made a mental note to contact Brendan's CO and let him know what had happened. The ROTC program had good counselors. That was important because, due to Travis's injuries, he wouldn't be able to see Brendan until spring break. The traction wheels groaned in protest as Dan hung up the phone and leaned back against the pillows.

"Lucky to be alive" is what the ER doctors said. The blast had knocked all three of them unconscious, but they were intact and still breathing when the ambulance arrived. The mall's pyrotechnic experts had yet to determine the malfunction that caused three aerial mortar shells to veer wildly off course and explode in GatesWay's parking lot. Dan tried to tell them, but they wouldn't listen and sedated him. Now, it was too late. Watching the news channel's rerun of the collapsing building—and not believing for one moment it was accidental—Dan hoped that someone had mercifully killed Carrie before the building fell and crushed her to death.

Suzanne, seeing the same program at her mother's house, put her head on Eric's shoulder, crying, "Oh, Caroline!"

Overwhelmed by his own memories, Eric held her as she wept. His mind went back to a rain-drenched afternoon, and with tears in his own eyes, he wondered for one moment and then never again, *What if I'd never let her go ....*

Brendan heard the phone ringing in the distance but couldn't move. Scanning the news channels for information about U.S. troop movements in the Middle East, his hand froze on the remote as he watched the NAFTRAM building fall again and again. The newscaster droned on about the potential loss of several residents when the building accidentally imploded nearly a week ahead of schedule. Rescue units requested cadaver dogs to assist in locating any human remains.

He picked up a printout of the email his mother sent him on New Year's Eve. His eyes lost focus as he re-read the last sentence where she wrote she loved him, that she was happy and not to worry, but it might be a while before he would see her again. He started to cover his eyes with his hand but brought it down hard, as a fist, on his knee.

Soldiers didn't cry.

Not even for their mothers.

Keeping Promises

It was only by forcing myself to put one foot in front of the other that I was able to walk away from the elevator. I opened the trunk to put the boys' suitcase away and stared at the number of suitcases and boxes already there. It was going to take a while, I thought, to go through all that Grant had packed for us, but then, I would have a lot of time. Checking on my children, only Austin was awake; the others were asleep, safe, and warm. I tried not to think about what was happening in our apartment and focused instead on Grant's instructions.

Drive east as fast as you can and, when you feel safe, pull over and look in the glove compartment.

Knowing Grant might implode the building at any moment, I didn't look back as I drove eastward, leaving GatesWay, the mall, Decker Court, and the university behind me. Once on the interstate, I remembered the TV cop shows I'd seen and tried every evasion technique I could think of: I slowed down, sped up, got off, did a U–turn, and immediately re–entered the highway. Although it was dark, I did not sense anyone tracking me.

Two hours later, I stopped here.

The all–night restaurant/roadhouse and hotel on the banks of the river looked safe enough. I just wanted to rest. The adrenaline propelling me for the previous twenty hours had drained away, leaving me weak, exhausted, and scared. I drove the car to the dock side of the main building, where it could not be seen from the road, and backed into a parking space between a delivery van and the embankment. I looked around and hoped that if I could not see anyone, they could not see me. Taking a deep breath, I put the car in park. A red light blinked on the console between the front seats. Worried I'd done something to the car, I looked at it closely. The word "swivel" was flashing. Not entirely sure what that meant, I pressed the button, and the passenger seat rotated 180 degrees.

Grant, I thought. I was pretty sure that such a convenience was not standard equipment, even on a Lexus. I took the little suitcase out of the trunk and opened the rear door. As before, only Austin was awake, watching me, his eyes serious and questioning. I needed to feed and change all of them, but I wanted a moment alone with my son. Unbuckling him from the car seat, I touched my forehead to his.

It's just us now, my darling boy, you, me, and your brothers. We are going to be very brave, aren't we, and do what your father asked us to do? He loves us very much, Austin, but he couldn't come with us. He ... he had to stay to protect us.

An overwhelming sense of love and sorrow emanated from him that, coupled with my own grief, destroyed all my attempts at bravery and gathering Austin to me, I cried for both of us. A few moments later, Austin patted the side of my face. I raised my head and saw Grant's "doctor" look in his eyes as if to say, "Enough."

I took his hand and kissed it. "Yes, you are right."

I balanced the suitcase on a small cooler tucked behind the driver's seat and removed some clean diapers, and the blue quilt Grant had packed for us. Using the suitcase as a changing table, I fed, changed, talked to, and loved my sons.

Investigating the cooler, I found cold tea, honey and crackers, slices of cheese, and a small container at the bottom. I held back the tears as I opened it to find strawberries in cream.

I smiled at the boys and, dipping my finger in the cream, touched each of their lips with just a dab of it. They smiled as they licked it away, and I told them that one day, they could eat as much of it as they liked. Austin stayed awake the longest, never taking his eyes from mine. One by one, they fell asleep until his eyes, too, fluttered and closed.

Lowering the windows for a few minutes to freshen the air, I tilted the swivel chair back and put my feet in the little space between their car seats. I brought the quilt to my face, and the honeyed scent that I associated with Grant and our life together filled my senses. Instead of being sad, however, I was strangely comforted as I tucked the soft blue fabric around the boys' car seats and pulled it up to my chin. With the quiet security of Grant's presence surrounding us, we slept.

It was still dark when I awoke to Alexi tapping my foot. Sitting up slowly, I saw they were all looking at me with sad eyes. I knew then that Austin had shared our sorrow with them. Taking their little hands in mine, I told them I loved them and that we were going to a new home where we would be safe. But I knew they understood something was different. So far from the colony, they couldn't hear anyone but each other in their minds, and without the colony members to link to, they were no longer connected to the comforting sounds of the collective consciousness.

"Your father would not want us to be afraid. I know it is very quiet right now without the voices of the colony, but you are not alone. I promise you will always have each other, and we will be strong together."

I watched them slightly tilt their heads. I smiled softly, missing Grant even more because he would have told me what they were saying. Just then, a warm, loving sense of trust flooded over me, and I looked at

Austin and returned their love and thought, *I love you, too.* They seemed to all sigh at once, and I brought them to me, each in turn, and fed them, cooing and kissing their little hands, all exactly the same.

We had lingered long enough; I needed a destination. I reached behind me and opened the glove compartment. Not knowing what to expect, I removed a large, thick envelope containing a file folder and several other envelopes. I knew the narrow, white envelope held a letter, and the other, a large, brown envelope, held documents. My hands reached for the letter first.

Inhaling the fragrance of the quilt from our bedroom until I could picture him there with us, I began to read.

My beloved wife –

If you are reading this letter, then I am not with you, so before reading any further, you must pull the car phone out of the console and destroy it. If it rang and you answered it—thinking it might be me—it could be traced, and you will be found. Pull the phone out now, Carolina. Please.

I turned toward the dashboard. Knowing I was destroying any hope of speaking to Grant again, I wrenched the car phone out of the console. It was like cutting my heart from my chest. Looking down at the raw ends of the wires, I wondered why they were not bleeding.

Determined not to cry, it was several moments before I could return to the letter.

Thank you. I know that was not easy, and I would have removed it myself when I put the cooler in the car ... when I still believed there was a chance I could go with you, but that is not to be. I am sorry, my darling, for leaving you to do so much on your own. That you will be wonderful, I have no doubt; I just would have liked to share it with you a little longer.

In the large envelope are the documents for you and the children. I cannot foretell the future, my love, but I have taken every precaution to ensure no one will find you. As you know, the boys will be called when they are twenty-five. Before then, they will only hear each other. If they ever hear anyone else, Austin will tell you, and you must be on your guard. Keep the syringes I gave you in a safe but accessible place in case of danger, but remember, save the last one for yourself.

I have packed a series of letters for Austin, one for each birthday until his twenty-fifth. Please read them to him until he is four. Do not read his letters after his fourth birthday or open the boxes addressed to him. If he wishes to share them with you, he will. It is important to me, Carolina, that I maintain a father's relationship with him throughout his young life and, through him, a father's relationship with his brothers. In the absence of the collective consciousness, they will look to him. He must know what to do and — more importantly — what not to do.

I have packed letters for you, too. One for every year to be read on the twenty-first of September in cherished remembrance of the first day I called you "wife," and you, my darling, called me "husband."

Remembering, I put my head back, closed my eyes, and tried not to cry. When I could, I raised my head and continued reading.

Nothing will change my love for you, Carolina. If, after all the danger you have been through this day, you decide you do not wish to keep your promise to raise our children, so be it. You will be doubly safe without them, for no one could find you alone. As always, I leave it to you to choose.

Thank you for being mine, Carolina. You have given me every joy I have known in my life. I will love you forever.

We are one, Grant.

Clutching the letter to my chest, I closed my eyes once again. When I opened them, Austin was looking at me.

Austin, your father says in his letter that he will love us forever. He says we are one.

He made kissing sounds with his mouth, and I thought he was hungry again. When I went to take him out of the car seat, he caught my hand and, pressing it to his face, kissed my palm. I stared at him for a long moment and heard the words *"are one"* in my mind.

Grant's last words were Austin's first words to me. My hand shook slightly as I moved it away from his face. I refolded the letter and returned it to the white envelope.

Feeling slightly dazed, I opened the file folder. On top were financial statements indicating that two million dollars had been deposited in the name of Carolina Grant, with interest being paid into a checking account. The number 1121 was written on the back of one of Grant's business cards and clipped to an ATM card.

My heart jumped in my throat at the sight of the second layer of papers. The very first one was a marriage license and certificate dated 21 September 1999 between Carolina Adams and Augustine Grant. A note attached to the marriage license read:

It is important to me that the human world knows you are mine.

Behind our marriage license were birth certificates for each of the boys born just minutes apart on November 21, 1999, first Austin, then Alexi, followed by Andre and Aslan Grant. A new social security card, driver's license, and birth certificate were tucked inside a passport with my name on the cover.

In addition to the boys' birth certificates were medical records designating a rare blood type, copies of their pediatric charts, and immunization records, all signed by Grant Gates, M.D. Leaving the dates blank, he even included high school physical examination records for athletics and team sports.

A second brown envelope was marked Real Estate Deed, and I heard keys rattling in it. Reaching in to get the keys, my hand brushed two small boxes. Each was wrapped in a scrap of white paper. On the outside of one was written *CT*, and on the other, *CG*. I removed the paper marked *CT* from the gray box.

Inside the box was Carrie Taylor's wedding ring. Looking at it, I felt nothing for the young bride who received it, all bright and shiny that day in June so many years ago, and no sense of loss for the years she tried to live up to her vows and her groom's expectations. Carrie Taylor's ring had no significance for Carolina Grant. I closed the box.

Barely breathing, I removed the paper marked *CG* from the red velvet box. On the unfolded sheet of vellum, Grant had written: *Today–Tomorrow–Forever.*

Holding it under the car's map light, I slowly opened the box. The ring seemed to catch fire. Rainbows danced around the interior of the car and reminded me of my bower the night I could *really* see it.

Austin waved his hands, and his eyes followed the pinpoints of color as I removed the wedding band from the box. Five diamonds, each competing with the other to see which had the bluest fire, were channel set in a pyramid-shaped filigree. The diamond in the center was large, with two slightly smaller diamonds on each side. Appearing to float between the two bands of gold, I was afraid if I turned the ring upside down, the diamonds would fall into my lap.

I examined the delicate filigree. On one side, the letters "G R A N T" were cast into the pyramid-shaped tracery, and on the other side, our wedding day, "0 9 ♥ 2 1." It was the most exquisite wedding band I had ever seen.

The difference in the intent of the two rings was striking. The purpose of the first was to signify my status within human society. Despite its elegant simplicity, however, Grant's purpose was to declare, in his own relentless way, that I was his. Now, more than ever before, he wanted a wall separating me from the rest of the world. It was not surprising that he would make this barricade as beautiful as he could imagine.

It was how he loved me.

A cold wind blew across the river, and I shivered slightly. To fight the growing chill, I folded the quilt over the boys and got out to start the car. Reaching into my pocket for the keys, I felt the packet of syringes Grant had placed there.

Was it just a few hours ago? Not even "yesterday" yet. Yes, I could still say it was this morning when he last kissed me.

Flipping open the syringe pack, I stared at the gap where the sixth syringe should be. That single empty space removed all doubt that Grant had died. Died loving me, trusting me, and *protecting* me.

Although he said I could choose how to use the remaining syringes, he knew I would not kill our children. Trusting me in their helplessness, they would not resist, smiling and loving me even as I poisoned and drowned them, one after the other. I could rationalize killing them based on the reason for their existence, but their deaths would not prevent the cataclysm their generation foretold. There were going to be thousands more. I did not believe the lives of these four perfect—actually ultra–perfect—boys would make a difference in the horrific times to come.

By The Rivers Dark

Standing alone on the strip of asphalt between the car and the wind-whipped river, I returned the syringe case to my pocket. Grant knew I would not betray their trust or his faith in our love. It would be far easier to kill myself. Only the hope of raising our sons and seeing Grant in Austin's face kept me from stepping too close to the slippery edge with my grieving heart.

Under the stars, where I hoped he could see me, I looked up into the lightly falling snow. Taking Carolina Grant's wedding band and directing the memory to Austin, I pictured Grant in my mind—not the way he looked when I last saw him, but on the night he asked me to marry him—confident, powerful, and breathtakingly handsome.

Snowflakes became liquid crystals as they touched my face, and although I knew the snow was falling from the sky, I felt I was rising up to meet it. With nothing between me and the limitless sky, I placed the ring on my finger and whispered, "I will."

The memory of Grant's singing voice saying *"my wife"* echoed in my mind, and the taste of bitter honey was in my mouth.

Sliding into the driver's seat, I wiped the melted snow from my eyes. Shaking house keys out of the envelope, I checked the address attached to the keyring and typed it into the navigation system in the car's console.

Hmm, Vienna Heights, Ohio.

Looking at my sons in the mirror, I smiled and said, "If we start now, my sweet boys, we'll be home for breakfast."

While the car warmed up, I walked to the end of the wooden dock.

I still had one promise to keep.

Alone beneath the lamplight, I tossed the car phone and the gray jewelry box over the railing. Saved for last, Carrie's wedding ring glittered in my hand.

Dawn, 1 January 2000

A flash of gold and Carrie Taylor is dead.

Her wedding ring glimmered briefly before disappearing beneath the river's icy darkness. Now, beyond the hope and help of those who loved her, I light a candle in my heart for each of them: candle one is for Dan, candle two for Eric, another is for Suzanne, and the fourth is for her darling Brendan.

Carrie's voice will never again echo in their ears; her name will never resound in mine. I do not mourn her passing, yet time collapses as I recall every day, every word and gesture that led to her inevitable demise.

Was it always inevitable?

Only the reflection staring from the dark water knows the truth. It is not my face rippling in the lamplight, nor is it hers. It is Grant—as fearless and strong as the first time Carrie watched him walk around the partition in his office, where she waited, nervous and excited, for her life to change.

Those are the best memories. Their warmth shelters me from the cold and empty space that remains. Shuddering in the winter wind, Carrie's candles flicker and fade compared to the others alight in my heart. The candles burning hottest and brightest, illuminating not only this night but every night to come, all belong to Grant.

PJ Braley

The cold air still carries the sounds of New Year's celebrations, but I cannot relate to their happy expectations for the future. Grant was so successful. I am not Lyostian, but I know I'm not truly human anymore. Watching the rising sun cast deep shadows into the night sky, I know he is with me, even as I stand at the beginning of my own journey.

Returning to the car, I realize that one by one, the wintry wind has extinguished Carrie's four flickering candles. I cannot grieve for them.

My heart is too full.

The End

Acknowledgments

There is something about writing an Acknowledgements note that always fills me with gratitude with the realization of how much goes into each author's work that is not always done by the author. So, it is with that gratitude that I would like to thank Liminal Books and Between the Lines Publishing and their team of wonderful, hardworking members, including Abby Macenka, Siân Hyleg, and their marketing and design experts. To Cherie Fox for her amazing covers. Thank you all for your faith, kindness, and guidance.

I want to thank Debra and Dale Fernandez, and Mary Lu Scholl for listening (without rolling their eyes even once) as I talked endlessly about revisions, character arcs, and research, and my wonderful readers and editors, Lindsey Hoefert, Ricki Huff, Emilee Valken, and Erica Orloff. I cannot thank you enough for your kind criticism, helpful comments, and patience.

And, as ever, thank you, Jim, for your wisdom and unfailing insight into my writing soul. *Je t'aimerai pour toujours.*

When PJ isn't writing about aliens negotiating the labyrinth of the human heart while trying to save the planet, you will find her sitting under the umbrella on the sundeck with her two rescue Aussies, Nymeria and Kaela.

Learn more about PJ and the legacy of The Fire Slayers at PJBraley.com or follow her on Blue Sky and X at @pjbraley.